ABOUT

Marianne Rosen is an emerging author of contemporary family sagas. She is a member of the Hay Writers' Circle, has performed at Hay Festival and is winner of the Richard Booth Prize for Non-fiction in 2018. *The Doors of Riverdell* is Marianne's debut novel and the first of the four-book Riverdell Saga.

For release updates: www.mariannerosen.com

THE DOORS OF RIVERDELL

MARIANNE ROSEN

ORIELbooks
www.orielbooks.com

THE DOORS OF RIVERDELL

ISBN 978-1-8380810-0-3

First published in Great Britain
in 2020 by Oriel Books
Copyright © 2020 by Marianne Rosen

Front cover design Amanda Hillier
Copyright © 2020 by Marianne Rosen
Incidental illustrations by Amanda Hillier
Copyright © 2020 by Amanda Hillier

For Alan and Ella

1

Of course, it all started with Kate.

She swung back a fist and planted it in Layna Carey's face while I choked on a gasp strangling a sob. Layna's nose crinkling like a sweet unwrapping. Her hand going to catch the flow of blood.

The class looked on in silent glee, hands to mouths to stem gasps of nervous delight at the fracas. It was the first time I'd ever seen a fight. A proper fight, not a squealing scuffle. Growing up with such an older brother I might as well have been an only child. Kate had grown up with five brothers, none of them more than a year apart. All I'd gathered from her stories was relief that only she'd been sent across the narrow Irish Sea to England and boarding school. And how glad of that I was. Kate had been a loyal friend even before my mother... well, before.

Layna's face screwed up behind her hand to make a noise. We all winced and sensed the thin walls of the mouldy huts. Privileged we might be, but the money paying for our education wasn't spent on the surroundings. At least the huts had low ceilings compared to the vaunted heights of the freezing rooms in the main house, though the wind could rattle their paper walls on a brisk day. Headteacher Porter was only two huts away and would hear her holler for sure.

'I wouldn't,' Kate told her, calm as a cucumber while I felt myself starting to shake. Flicking auburn wisps out of her eyes and flexing her fists. 'There's more where that came from if you ask for it. Deserved it for being so mean.'

'How dare you?' Layna choked.

'How dare you?' a voice drawled from behind us. The class pivoted their heads as one to look at the new girl. She was more beautiful than the rest of us put together, with a head of dark curling hair, a wide jaw beneath high cheek-bones covered in flawless olive skin and, now she'd spoken, we would have sold our bed quilts for a voice so rich. 'If you're going to pick on the kids with no mums you might want to do a headcount first.'

That first day of the new school year. Autumn term of '56. All of us old-timers waiting to see where the new kids would fall. The new girl, Rose – of course, it's so familiar now, but that was the first day we met – leaned against her desk in casual disinterest. Her brown eyes had a flash in them that could have cut a hole in Matron's steel locker.

Layna looked to her buddies for support. But whoever the new girl was, she was right about one thing. Whichever way you cut the cake there were factions to be found.

Rose stepped up to stand beside Kate, eyeing each other up. Height, weight, grin, guts. That was all it took.

'I'm Kate, this is Elsa,' Kate tossed a quick glance at my pale face.

'Rose, de Lavelle.' She added her surname with a shrug, like a cat's tail flicking. We all knew that name. The family de

Lavelle had owned the house many years before it became a school and were vaulted patrons. Rose knew exactly what sting it carried.

Mina Dewberry piped up in defence of Layna, 'Oh, so what, you're going to form an orphan's defence league or something?'

Layna, Mina and their three knuckle-wrapping, toe-tripping friends all laughed.

'Sounds good to me,' a soft voice added from behind.

Layna's cackle, reminiscent of a pheasant exploding into flight, died in her throat. The three of us, Kate, Rose and I, turned to watch another new girl stand up and walk forward to join us. She looked like she'd slip between the cracks in the wood panels with the first brisk wind that blew her way. Pale hair pulled back in a plait long enough to sit on, a pinched face outweighed by too large eyes. She couldn't intimidate a goldfish and no one had any doubts about my ability on that score either.

'I mean, if that's alright with you?' she asked with deference to us.

'More the merrier,' Kate said.

'I'm Beth,' the slight girl said. She was looking at Rose when she spoke, truth be told it was hard not to stare at Rose, but she glanced a sliver of a smile my way that warmed me to the quaking toes as she said to Layna, 'And both my parents are dead, so does that give me double entry?'

So, it started with Kate, but from that day on it was the four of us.

2

_____

I t's time to go.

His neck tingled with nerves, but Moth kept his head down. Trying to focus. Pulling back from the empty screen. Hearing the rising noise level. The café owner glanced his way, flicking the tea towel back over his shoulder. Clanking cups in encouragement. He'd dragged out a coffee for longer than was polite. Kate would have glared him out the door by now.

You're dawdling.

He was reluctant to leave. The café warm and full of life, reminding him of Kate's bistro. The comfort of being busy, having purpose.

He flicked his way through the pages of the small notebook, looking for the page that separated past from present, spreading it open. The pencil, shaved down to a needle's length, counting down the listed numbers. He halted on today. Day 257. 15th March 2013. His fifteenth birthday.

Big deal. Happy bloody birthday. This one doesn't count, remember?

His hand counted another nine lines down. Scribbling beside Day 266, 24th March 2013. Hotel Castello, Lovere. Kit. His writing clipped on the narrow lines.

You are not thinking about this.

The words stared back at him, isolated, vulnerable. A black mark adrift in the empty lines. He filled them in at night. Blank lines forward, etched-in names behind.

You don't put stuff in the future.

The future would begin exactly one year from this day. The future would begin when he turned sixteen. Until then, he counted the days.

He closed the cover. Ignored the stalking looks that came his way, customers checking out his intentions. Moth shut down the Skype screen, the web pages, accessed the settings, the browsing history, the cache. For all time.

If only it were that easy.

He selected the 'Last 24 Hours' option. One day at a time he could manage. He'd been there longer than the 'Last Hour'.

You did drag it out.

He wrapped his remaining pastry in the serviette. The vile coffee he'd managed three sips of left cold in the cup. He slid the notebook and pastry into the handlebar bag slung round his chest. Felt for his rucksack on the floor between his legs. The screen stared back where Kit's face had been, his own reflection blurred by the jaunty homepage of the café. A ship floating across an ethernet sea.

You shouldn't have called.

Nat's email had pulled him in. Not the whole email. Just that one line. That, and Ben's promise to cut off his account if he didn't get that 'wanker-arsehole-bastard' off his back. He could count the pressure Kit was putting on Ben in the increasing abuse inserted between the Kit and the de Lavelle parts of Kit's name. Moth needed that account.

You resisted the pressure for months, until that one line.

He grasped the rucksack, stood, and moved towards the door. Slipping into his coat, shifting the rucksack to his back. His coat did not catch on the chair. The chair did not scrape on the floor. His well-worn trainers were silent on the polished wood.

Moth paused at the door, engaging the halves of his coat, pulling the zip up. He checked the full view of the pavement through the wide windows. Reichenau, Austria.

A flat-arse, back-water, small town.

It was late afternoon, people were focused, intent on jobs and shops. Chins down on their chests against the keen spring wind. The sunshine more optimistic than warm. Moth opened the door. He pulled the thick grey and brown beanie hat out of his pocket, clamped it over his hair. It was ragged round the edges where the brim had fallen off and he'd stitched the unravelling threads in place. It made him feel less significant, reducing the combined impact of his height and hair. The apricot beacon tucked away from view.

Apricot? You're even thinking like him.

He shrugged his shoulders beneath the rucksack. It was heavy and bulging, boosted with the critical stuff from the panniers. Several streets away the church spire stood out, the bright sun highlighting the dirt on its western side. On a street north of that spire was his bike.

Moth moved into the flow of pedestrians. His outdoor gear blending in with the more casual tourists. His steady pace matching theirs. The locals, standing out by dress and purpose, wove between them. He followed the pace of a guy moving in his direction. He was big. Proud around the neck and shoulders. Powerful from intention and regular work-outs. It reminded him of Kit. The delight Kit took in his own perfect physicality, in the showcase of it. Sharp shoes tapping out a statement with fierce heels on the wide stone pavement.

Even sounds like him. Same smug satisfaction.

It irritated him. Kit somehow stepping beyond the phone call to here. Austria would suit Kit. It was proud without being flashy. Square and assured in its arrogance. Moth slowed down on his silent trainers, letting the space build between them. Well, it would suit him for a day anyway. Before he got bored.

An hour, more like. You're thinking about him. Again.

Kit wasn't the problem. That line in Nat's email, the throw away statement of a nine-year-old. Isabelle said to tell you Happy Birthday. The normality catching him unawares, punching hard with the desire to hear it. Two-hundred-and-fifty-seven days since he'd seen her. Since he'd left her at the station. And there was the evidence she thought about him. Isabelle speaking to Nat. About him. Remembering his birthday.

Yeah, big deal.

Inside the café it had been contained. Locked down in a line, the screen, the room. The hope that someone might care. Outside, it soared up into the sky. Lancing down the wide streets, curving round the crisp square corners. Peering down on him through the repeating windows and wide wooden doorways. The desire to hear more calling him back. Moth wanted to run, to run as fast as his long legs could take him, through the busy streets and away. Into the woods, back on the road.

Don't run, you'll call attention to yourself.

Turning the corner, he came out onto a long wide street,

heading towards the spire. People were thicker, the pace
slower. Pulling him towards the wide plaza of the church.

This is not a good place to be.

Too many people with time on their hands. Tourists
gawping, teenagers flirting, old men arguing in the sun. The
alien language heightened by happiness. It was a peaceful
place, full of people who belonged. Moth didn't. He needed
the empty quiet street down the far side of the church.

He moved towards it, tucking his chin down as he passed
through the open space. He heard the bells impinge on the
air, rattling the sky before sounding. Looked up at the high
spire as the hour struck. Long, unhurried chimes counting
out the afternoon. Lowered his gaze to the front door, seeing
it open. A woman stepping out. Blinded from the inner darkness as the sunlight hit her. Pausing, pulling her hand up to
shield her eyes. A young girl holding her father's hand, waiting, her high voice calling out. A small dog barking in excitement. Moth's stride shortening, failing, grinding to a halt on
the warm stone.

You shouldn't have called.

The clock chimes bounced off the tall houses and up into
the blue sky. The crackle of a foreign language faded. He
stared at the woman, emaciated by the deep light and
shadows of the afternoon sun. The girl all energy and enthusiasm. Moth ached. Numb with longing. Stranded in the
middle of the plaza as urgency crackled across his back.

You need to go.

He forced himself to hear the awkwardness of the
language. Let it blister him back into the immediate, far and
foreign moment. Watching the happy family reunion in front
of the church. How they reached out to one another. Smiling,

talking, touching. He knew there was a place he might call home. But that was not a choice open to him.

Not yet.

Back there, his choices were limited by others, and Moth was a free man. They might not think he was free to make his own choices, and they might not think he was a man. But he had a plan, get away, keep moving, stay invisible, until his age caught up with his life.

He turned away and strode for the side street. The church door swinging shut as he moved away. It was a narrow street between buildings, unfit for cars, full of back doors. He'd tied the bike up to railings towards the end, where the street ran out towards the valley fields.

Moth swung the rucksack off, pulled out the tent, the stove, rearranging them into place in the panniers. Soothing down the creases, tightening the tops. He unzipped his coat, took the handlebar bag from around his chest, strapped it in place. Unleashed the chain, wrapped it round the frame. It was cool in the darker street, the sun banished by the high walls and he began to feel it.

You'll warm up once you're moving.

In the end, packed and ready, he held the bike under his hand. It never got any easier. This moment. All those months, and he still found it hard. Swinging his leg over, pushing off.

It doesn't matter, easy or not. It's the plan that counts.

The plan was everything. Not how he felt, or what he thought, or what distracted him. Stick to the plan.

Get on the bike, keep moving forward. You know how.

He had a system. He counted off their names. Moving backwards, remembering faces. They were all there; Kit, Kate, James, Hester, Elsa. Isabelle. Nat. Nat's name stopped his thoughts.

You know what comes next.

He swung his leg over the frame, set the first foot, pushed the bike forwards. Nat stood between them. The family that came afterwards. The family before. His mother. Standing looking up at him from the bottom of the stairs. The memory that settled his other foot onto the pedal, let its motion catch him, rolling him out of the dark street, into sunshine. Warmth flooding over him.

Works every time.

It was on a similar spring day, one year earlier, when Isabelle came home.

She stepped onto the platform, lifting her head to catch the breeze as her hand trailed from the rough plastic handle, a newspaper clutched in her hand. 21st March 2012. Trying to adjust to the date. To the weather. To the country. She'd been away since November. Blue eyes searched the horizon, hair falling away from her face as she looked upwards. The church clock was not striking, the station was quiet, and even the air felt lazy as it brought the mid-week, mid-morning lull toward her. Nothing momentous stirred on its listless currents.

She hitched the bag onto her shoulder with its patched and stitched handles and pulled the trundling case onto the platform, its tired wheels grimacing and sticking. Glancing up at the church, tall and preening atop the hill. It was a long walk up to the house and she resented the religious smugness of the stone gargoyles leering down at her. She dumped the abandoned newspaper she'd rescued in the bin. It had been uncomfortable reading. War, politics, sport, abortion. That last was America, she reminded herself, where another clinic had been bombed. Finding a crumb of comfort from the detail.

Pushing open the door on the miniscule station house she tugged her case behind her up the ramp. The stationmaster was a stranger, replaced during the last four months of her absence, and bemused by her request to leave her case behind for collection later.

'It's not the usual,' he told her with such absence of tone in his voice that Isabelle wondered if he meant the abandonment or the case itself.

'That'll make a nice change then,' she suggested.

He made no response, looking from her to the case with a scowl. Covered in bright stickers and glued-on patches of fabric, shining beads and tassels, its original skin long buried, it was a case easily found at airports. She could see him reading the destinations, her name hidden amongst them, Isabelle Threlfall. Her thirty-two years of life effaced by the exotic roll call. The case far outshone her crumpled travel-worn layers of beige linen. Her weary face shaded out by the dull blonde mess of heavy chin length hair. She pushed it back, tried to be more convincing.

'I'm walking, and it's heavy,' she encouraged him. 'James Threlfall will collect it later.'

'Your husband, is it?'

Isabelle resisted the urge to embarrass the over curious and indifferent keeper of cases with a potted history of her and James' confusion about that point. To explain that for eighteen years they too had been trying to label their relationship. To claim, by being able to answer with a clear and understandable statement, some vibrant validity, and outshine the patchwork history of her case.

'No, my cousin.' She glanced at the door, longing to be gone.

'We shut at six.'

'It'll be before then.'

The guard smiled as she left, leaving an amiable sense of doubt in her.

Isabelle hitched the bag again and stretched her long stiff limbs amongst familiar streets, her India sandals cool on her feet, protesting their impracticality on the steep hill. She followed fiddling networks of alleyways, avoiding the main road with the grind of cars holding their clutches, and ducked through the backyard of the pub, climbing the stairs past houses buttressing the town walls, to emerge on the high plateau at the back of the church. She was looser and warmer. Adjusting the belt lassoing her hips, pulling the worn hems of her trousers from their communion with the ground. Dropping her bag onto a bench and perching on the low wall she squinted at the view. Hills wavering in a hazy tapestry of far and foreground, colour and texture overriding clear vision.

Mumbai had been tough, the job relentless. When she'd announced she had to go home the art director had abused her for a week in front of the cast and director to establish his lack of culpability and spent every evening sympathising over the grief of family demands. Her colleagues had been less voluble and more supportive, swallowing the work hiatus with supportive murmurs of understanding. The faux family understanding the needs of the real one. She'd done four months of the five contracted, forfeited her entire pay and owed a hefty favour to the replacement costume designer she'd dragged in to cover her departure. The English weather was a cool welcome by comparison to the storm she'd left behind. Mumbai felt a world away again. Receding into the background while she tried to adjust her mind to being home. In a few days it would feel as it always did, that her life existed in two parts. Here and there, never quite anywhere.

At the reaches of her flawed vision, the hills were shimmering, trees cavorting shadows across their flanks. She picked out land points, the compressed golf ball of the radar station shining on the Clee, the Mynd a long frown on the northern horizon, the grasses rippling across the meadow flanks of Climbing Jack and tumbling into the deep creases of the valleys. The breeze was firm, blowing across the long valley of the Teme, wafting the county up to her. The richness of the fields, the unctuous fumes of traffic, the dust from the development of the old petrol station, the teasing odours of bread, coffee, pie. She grabbed her bag, leaving the calm oasis and plunging into the town's belly, the tune of the vagrant piper following her through the streets.

It was a homecoming pleasure to pick out new degrees of the town's rolling mutation. The Warrens' latest garden ornament, the repainted mustard gate of the book café, the luminous fresh stone and baby yew trees of an ambitious knot garden. Outside the Briards' Georgian double frontage the vicious clearance of an overhanging dog rose bush that had snared pedestrians for decades brought her to a startled stop. It came with a fresh lick of plum paint on the front door and the starched angle of plump, freshly made curtains at the ground floor windows. It had new owner written all over it. She was astounded. The Briards had been there forever. She couldn't believe they'd up and gone in four swift months. It was inconceivable. She must remember to ask Kate about it. Later though, if Kate caught a glimpse of her, she'd not stand a chance of escape.

In the central square empty market stalls waited a busier day, she mingled with the lethargic weekday tourists. The vivid cerulean paint of the door to Kate's bistro preened on the northern side. Above it the hand-painted sign repeating its own importance, The Blue Door. Glinting back at her in the sunlight winking on its white outlined letters. Kate loved the peeling blue door when she bought the place and it had seemed a good enough name to work under the auspices of, adding her own to the sign, Proprietor: Kaitlin O'Hare, along with a fresh lick of paint to the door when the peeling finally turned to ribbons of detaching paint.

Elsa never failed to express her opinion that she should have gone with The Cerulean Café, but that was not Kate's style. It dictated that she was running a café and Kate did not appreciate anyone pigeon-holing her.

'Besides,' Kate protested, 'you're the only one who'll ever pronounce it right.'

Isabelle crossed to the opposite side of the square, pricked ears straining to hear Kate giving orders inside. Glancing back, she watched the staff buzzing round the tables that sat beneath the wide windows, nestled beside flowerpots assaulting the pavement, claiming their space. She hurried on.

The castle reared tall, implacable and decaying at the end of the square. She followed the bulging curves of its walls down the crowned hill towards the river. Its voluptuous curves flowing beneath the triptych of arches that carried the road across, beguiling her eyes so that she walked two steps past the sudden break in the mass of stone to her right. Isabelle smiled in delight, the near miss of the familiar gates, and savoured the river's view before turning away.

The ivy and wallowing yew spilling over the wall were cut

to fit the curve of the gate's arc. The name, Riverdell, italicised and gilded across the top of the two wrought-iron halves, was split across the open gates. To Isabelle it always seemed awkward, and she sympathised again with the blacksmith who must have gritted his teeth through five squat letters to one side and only four, with an excess of ascenders, to the other. No less than Elsa, who loathed it when guests called her home River Dell, as the split gates tended to pronounce it. Rivendell, with its Tolkien misappropriation, she could cope with.

'Oh, if only it was,' she'd murmur with a smile, her love of books allowing what her intolerance of poor grammar could not.

The empty gravel swept away from her across the large courtyard, braced on two sides by the house, on the third by the road wall and capped off by the hulking rise of the castle hill. Its edges graced by a stone path and softened by the multitude of bushes that tumbled out of the front borders. Moss did its best to creep towards the centre, thwarted by the pressure of tyres, where a grand old magnolia spread in smirking self-importance, its roots testing the low circular wall that bound it.

The stone path led to the nape of two mullion-windowed walls and a ponderous flat-roofed columned porch. Isabelle took the path, avoiding the biting gravel sneaking into her sandals. As she crossed the front of the house her reflection staggered from old pane to pane, until she disappeared beneath the porch, its wooden ceiling and double doors painted a dignified faded olive. Above them a sun ray window echoed the arch of the wall. The five-star AA rating gleamed beside it. It was one of her favourite times to come home, trains and planes allowing. A time for those running the house to run errands, for guests to be exploring. A time when the house might be empty. Isabelle grasped the worn iron handle, drew a breath and pushed.

She took three tentative steps forward on to the faded rug, it's corner rucked where someone had moved too fast for the fragile balance of polished floorboards and worn fibres, listening to the house. She advanced further, her hand reaching across the soft, rubbed velvet of the sofa back, feeling the life in the old nap, eyes drinking in the cushions with their fraying tassels. She breathed in the scent of cut flowers, dotted on windowsills, side tables, the grand piano nestling beside the stairwell. Rose, iris, clouds of gyp, stalks of grass, their stems drooping, losing potency. They would irritate Kit on first sight. He would want them fresher, firmer, sweeter. But Kit would not be there until the weekend.

The hall fire had been lit last night, the sofa cushions crumpled, inviting the sitters back. An illusion Kit engineered for the guests, to encourage a sense of intimacy to the enormous hallway that none of the family ever sat in. One touch amongst the hundreds he scattered over the house like fairy dust to help Elsa achieve those five stars. Post lay on the circular table poised like a roundabout in the middle of the hall, alongside a small bell and a polite notice to the guests.

She moved to check the envelopes, none for her. James' name splattered across many. It was lambing season and his daily visits were haphazard. He would be there later, after collecting her case, to collect his post. To see his mother, to see her. Somewhere between James being always there, and Kit being omnipresent, Isabelle knew she had decisions to make. She turned away from the table.

The high stained-glass windows on the landing were pristine, their soft colours muted as the light streamed down, seeking access but coming up against the closed doors. The long hallway of the east wing to her left was dim with closed doors. From its silence she knew the rooms were empty; the large family sitting room that commanded the view of the gardens, the dusty special-occasion dining room, the north-facing study with its heavy curtains and deep chairs, the morning room closest of all, light and airy with its single sash window that looked onto the courtyard. All empty.

To her right, commanding the west wing, the kitchen door stood closed, a subtle 'Private' notice attached at eye level. The fire door to the grandest room in the house, now the guest's sitting and dining room, was propped open by a heavy velvet doorstop she had made for the purpose, inviting access. The singular door left open was to the room none of the family used. Light from the huge windows within pushing back the coloured rays of the hall, its gilt, ruby and plum colour scheme framed with showcase precision by the doorframe. Nothing stirred there either.

Isabelle headed for the kitchen. Opening the door and feeling like space took flight into the cavernous room with its three sets of French windows looking onto the courtyard and the observatory sized window looking out over the river and gardens. The windows were all shut, evidence of the tempo-rary absence of all family as much as the fact that spring had not yet sprung sufficiently for Elsa. The simmering Aga vied for prime position beside an enormous oak dresser. She trailed her hand across its rippling polished top. Its wide shelves sagging with the weight of their vibrant majolica dinnerware display, an heirloom which they all loathed, but no one had the guts to get rid of. Here, where the guests were banned and the business rigour relaxed, the table was strewn with the domestic chaos of the family. Amidst the papers,

diaries, letters, cups, bowls of fruit with which Elsa compensated the bowls of chocolates and bonbons, Isabelle's eye was
caught by a sheet of paper filled with colourful scribbles,
pencils resting upon it with the haste of the departed.

She moved closer, looking at the shapes, lines and colour.
Full of energy but little visual purpose. Natalie's, she
presumed. They brought the first stab of reality to bear. Two
children in a house no longer used to children. She was home
early from location because of them and she'd arrived having
missed the funeral on February 29th by three weeks to the
day. She hadn't yet worked out how to greet relatives she'd
never met. It was hard enough greeting the ones she was intimate with. Looking at the drawings seemed rudeness itself
and she resisted a desire to cover them over. She left the room
and headed for the stairs, each tread an exhausting request,
her hand sliding along the smooth rail, holding tight at the
corners.

On the first-floor hallway the aligned portraits of former
family members stared at her. Squinting to see them, Isabelle
felt they were frowning back. Unhappy at their eviction from
the entrance hall, trying to decide if she belonged or not.
Riverdell had long since become a guesthouse to pay its way
and, all bar Elsa, the family had retreated to the top floor,
making seven en suite bedrooms available on the first. James
had the farm and Hester her own home and husband. David
was but a memory from her childhood, he'd been the eldest
and distant in his own life long before he'd fallen out with
Elsa. For years hers had been the sole occupied bedroom on
the second floor, until now. She walked past the closed doors
and wondered which rooms Elsa had given to the children.

At the end of the long corridor she pulled up outside her
own door, hand gripping the handle. Wondering if it was still

hers, dreading to find it emptied. She opened the door, the room revealing itself with constancy. Her photos tucked into the mirror, her clothes hung over chairs, accessories draped on bedposts, picture edges, chair backs. It was clean and fresh, the scents of starched linen and polish stirring to greet her. Elsa had placed fresh flowers by her bedside, water and fruit. Towels lay on the end of the bed and the corner of the duvet was turned back. The habits of home and business mingling in the space, leaving her unsure if she returned as guest or resident.

Isabelle dropped her bag on the floor and let the door swing shut behind her. She pulled the belt from her hips and, with each step, dredged a pocket, uncoiled a scarf, unwound a bracelet, and threw her extraneous dressings onto the end of the bed. She pulled the thick curtains together, blocking out the light, the view, the world, plunging herself into a dim intimacy with the room. Grasping the brass knob at the base of the bed as she rounded it.

Old and paint-chipped, its metal orbs dented, and frame bowed, the bed chronicled her slow induction into the family. Moving from guest bedroom, where she first remembered it as a young girl, to Hester's bedroom when their friendship had flowered – a combination of their same age, her loneliness and Hester's delight at having a female cousin when she'd only known brothers – to her own bedroom when the long summer holidays in India had ended and found her needing a permanent home, where she and James had explored the depths of their feelings and sunk into love. The bed a constant ship in the ever-changing sea of her relations.

Sitting on it made her ache with gladness and guilt and grief, held at bay behind its bars. She let herself slide into the comfort of feathers, aged mattress and linen, she and the bed

shaping themselves to each other. Long hours of travel
flushed out from her weary bones and into the deep she slid
towards.

KIT WAS in a prodigious good mood.

Despite crappy traffic on the motorway and the drudge of
the final haul across country roads broken from the wet
winter, he felt immense. It had been a long month. Splitting
the Italy job over three visits to accommodate the disaster
with David had more than trebled the challenge, and work at
home was backlogged from the incursions Elsa had made
into his schedule. Still, it was done. Italy, ticked, David,
ticked, the children, ticked, Elsa, never ticked but under
control, and Isabelle was back. Back three days and possibly
even back for good, and all was set for a glorious weekend at
Riverdell, where he, Kit de Lavelle, home and lifestyle guru to
the rich and never-to-be famous, might, at last, tick off a
fifteen-year itch.

The traffic slowed, he tapped the steering wheel with restless fingers, tweaked the music louder. The late morning sun
was warm on the windscreen, but the car stayed cool, the
flowers on the back seat pert. He didn't want them sweating
any more than himself. He crossed the bridge into town and
floored the Bentley Continental up the hill and through the
daunting narrow arch of the town wall. Past cars full of
tourists dithering over where to park, wondering whether to
follow his lead.

The market was in full swing and the seats outside The
Blue Door were filled with coffee stoppers braving the wind
whipping across the square. They were wrapped up in coats
and scarves, determined to enjoy the sunshine despite the

wind chill. Newspapers fluttering in mockery at their best efforts to control the pages. He smiled as he passed Kate's door, slowing and straining to catch a glimpse through the windows, the blue paint radiant in the vicious light. It warmed him, remembering the hours spent arguing over its shade, painting the wall of her flat in competing patches until they agreed, the result a perfect finale.

He cruised down the narrow road to Riverdell, cautious of witless pedestrians thinking the road was a footpath. The open gates let him swerve unhindered onto the gravel, savouring the satisfying crunch as he bedded the weight of the car in with the sharp brakes. Elsa opined that he ought to grow out of it, but knowing it irritated her fuelled the urge.

Kit stepped from the car grateful for the chance to stretch. Moist earth and stone and moss gleaming around him and the pebbles on the driveway glinting. The whole world seemed happy with him. The buds on the old magnolia looked fit to burst and he grinned in sympathy. He felt arousal in his sinews, his bones, his toes, and twisted his neck back and forth to loosen the muscles.

Straightening his car-rumpled shirt, enjoying its thinness over his chest muscles, the fine cotton emphasising his contours without being vulgar, he pulled his pressed trousers into line. He checked the smoothness of his chin, raked a hand through his hair, flicked the peaked strands into place, glanced in the blacked-out glass of the car and admired the careful highlights. His hairdresser was a skilful fucker, worth the extra it had cost him for an appointment at no notice. Grey flecks might be cool these days but they both agreed the sharper blond emphasised the odd combination of his brown eyes better. You had to count your genetic gifts after all. Six years ago, he'd hurdled the forty marker without a hiccup. He had to go a tad more often to touch up the encroaching grey, his shampoo now contained every version of ketoconazole legally available, and his daily work out had adapted to keep that extra definition whilst pandering to the threat of back pain. But, all in all, he was in peak form. The envy of many his friends battling baldness, greyness, flabbiness, and it felt good, real good, and today, it felt immense.

He grasped the bouquets in his arms and walked to the front door, pushing it open with his back to safeguard the flowers. The hallway was empty to his arrival. Kit took in the whole scene in casual, critical appraisal. The décor as effete as ever, the colours aged into aristocratic sludge, the furniture sagging and the abundant flowers limper than he would be leaving them for long. The impression was precise; a much descended, upper-class home made available to only the highest paying guests. He strode into the kitchen, likewise empty and, considering he'd been here a few weeks ago, less than spotless. The sink grimy with dirty crockery, the table with leftovers on plates, the work surface cluttered.

But he had other things to do beside housework.

He put the flowers down on the table and was turning around when his phone rang. He pulled it out his pocket and frowned, Henri. He swiped to accept.

'I thought I told you not to call today?'

'Yes, boss, you also told me to let you know if the D'Arbys called.'

'And they called today?' Kit fumed

'Of course they did.'

'We need to reconsider our available-all-hours policy, Henri,' Kit moved towards the sink. 'I'm fed up of kissing rich arse when they want it.'

'You won't get much argument from any of us with that, boss. Though, it has to be said, you do kiss rich arse so well.'

'They approved the budget?'

'They did.'

'What did they say to the lead time?'

'Less happy.'

'What excuse did you give them?' Kit piled dirty crocks on the draining board, ran the tap to lukewarm and filled the bowl. He pulled the wrappers off the flowers, plunged them into the water, his phone stuck between his ear and shoulder.

'Immense popularity and your refusal to delegate to your staff.'

'Excellent, and how am I getting on with the D'Arbys' project?'

'You are getting on with it fine, boss,' Henri said. 'It should be ready to begin by end of next month.'

'End of April! What are we waiting for?'

'The plasterers.'

'It's always those wankers.' He found fresh vases under the sink, scissors in the drawer.

'We've been through this before,' Henri reminded him.

'Well, listen again, I'm still irritated.' Kit snipped away at the flowers, stripping leaves from below the water line, peeling stems apart. 'Every time we have a project, they're impossible to get hold of.'

'Reynaud's get first dibs, and whilst you bought my loyalty, I can't buy theirs, and there's no one else as good. You tried it, remember.'

'I don't want to remember.' Kit exploded a rigid rolled package of gypsophila onto the discarded wrappings and trimmed it into shape. He coerced it between roses, behind alstroemeria, and kept it away from the tulips. 'It was a pig's guts.'

'Then stop huffing at me about it,' Henri suggested. 'You don't want anyone else re-plastering the D'Arbys' ballroom so quit whining.'

'I'm not huffing at you, I'm just huffing, and anyway, what's a huff? I'm not a cartoon wolf.'

'If you'd stop huffing, I was going to tell you, the D'Arbys accepted the timescale. It's only you who's huffing over it.'

Kit stood back from the sink, scanning the vases, resisting the urge to tweak. First and last, let it be done once or not at all.

'So, all is good?'

'All is good,' Henri agreed.

'How's my adorable Lou?'

'The tetchy bitch is fine.'

'You know you love her,' Kit teased.

'Grow up, boss, that's getting boring.'

'She is though, right, fine?'

'She's good, on top of it all. She even asked after my health this morning.'

'See, I told you she'd forgive you,' Kit said, tweaking a tulip into place, trailing a finger along its surging plum tongue. Damn floppy extravagant things, he loved them and hated them.

'You mean she's forgiven you,' Henri said. 'After nine months.'

Kit wasn't sure which had caused more offence, his hiring from their biggest competitor, or installing Henri over her. But Lou had a hairline stress fracture. She could cope with the toughest workload, the most impossible deadline, the Dickensian wanker of all workmen, but broke with the smallest squeal from a client. Henri, on the other hand, could eat the richest bitches for breakfast, spit them out for lunch, and they'd be creaming over his French accent by dinner.

'The boys on point?'

'As always,' Henri said. 'Ed's with Lou, Fred with Jamie. We're all fine, we can manage without you for one day.'

'You're a star, Henri,' Kit told him. 'Now, piss off, I've a fifteen-year itch with a head of steam behind it. I can't concentrate on work.'

'You don't say that often.'

'I don't often leave an itch for fifteen years.'

He hung up, looked at the kitchen, devoid of its culinary identity, bemused in the onslaught of the amateur florist. It was a mess. There was much that needed doing, but not more than the one thing he had come to do. He abandoned the vases, the trimmings, the detritus and the guilt, and stalked out of the kitchen.

3

Rose was our leader by bloody virtue.

We stood outside the infirmary and listened in admiration and shock as she swore the matron from one side of the room to the other for the privilege of informing her she would now be bleeding once a month for the next thirty years of her life. Understanding through her outrage what was going to befall us all.

'Jesus' fucking holy blood you are fucking joking me. Once a bloody month, this bollocks? I don't even want fucking children. Vile fanny-slacking cunts who rip your body apart and piss in the wind rather than show gratitude. It fucking hurts, you damn whore.'

She mixed her words with Gaelic curses she'd swapped Spanish profanities for with Kate. The effect was merciless, both unspeakable and graspable. I think this was her way of apologising. From the day Matron went white-lipped and shaking from the infirmary to the Head's office, Rose became our leader. She was the youngest of us all, her birthday the latest in our year. But, though Kate was the eldest, and I'd just turned thirteen, Rose was the first to adulthood in our eyes.

That was the day we moved into our dormitory in Raven House. It was a new building, purpose-built to house the increasing influx of children. According to my unimpressed father, the school had had to decide either to extend its client base or close. The decision to extend had brought Rose and Beth to Ludlow. Built on contributions from former students, whose children were then granted free boarding for the duration of their first three years. It was Rose who insisted she be allowed to stay in the new block her family had contributed to. It was Rose who insisted her nearest friends move with her. It was Rose who told Matron she could...

'...kiss my grandma's rich ass if you think I'm staying in that freezer of a dormitory with that evil hagwitch Layna Carey while my stomach's griping fit to birth a fucking whale. And if you think Mr Threlfall's going to thank you for taking his grieving daughter's best friends away from her you can think again. We'll all be moving and, Oh my fucking holy God screwing a pygmy, this pain!!!'

Kate's eyes widened with each curse she translated, as much as her grin.

'I love her so much,' she whispered to me and Beth. 'She's a genius and a filthy angel.'

Kate and I were speechless with joy and disbelief to pack our bags and leave the big old dorm and Layna and her cronies behind. The new dorm housed four students in each room. Rose walked into it clutching her belly and screaming loud enough to drain the blood from a hundred virgins. Matron couldn't shut the door quick enough.

We all looked at her writhing on the bed in concern. How were we supposed to deal with this? Would we be suffering like this? Even Beth, normally inseparable from Rose, was hanging back from the bed.

'Has she gone?' Rose whispered between screams. 'Check the corridor, Beth. Pretend you need to pee.'

Beth opened the door to go look for the bathroom, but it was clear. She shut the door and went over to the bed.

Rose jumped up in glee.

'So you're alright?' Kate asked.

'Of course,' Rose said. She went checking out the new room. We were the first students to move in. The walls were spotless, free of marks and scuffs and old Sellotape.

'It's not that bad?' I asked.

'Oh, it hurts alright' Rose reached into her bag and pulled out a box of pills. The name Panadol waved in front of our eyes. 'But Grandma prepped me at Christmas. She reckoned I was close. She says this is new, she gets it on prescription. I'm only to take them if it's real painful. She said I can share them with you girls, though.'

We all eyed the box, hypnotised as she waved it back and forth. Her grandma was legend. Lady de Lavelle had raised her. Rose's mother wasn't dead, like ours, just absent, but that was a long story apparently. All we needed to know was Rose had our back and Grandma had hers. And Grandma was fearless. And now Grandma gave out medicine and trusted her to use it. My father would have banned Rose from the county, let alone the house. And getting the girls to come stay me with at home that summer was the only goal I had in 1957.

'But no one needs to know that, right?' Kate asked.

'No one but us.' Rose agreed. 'Now, let's pick beds. Layna Carey can kiss our toasty heels while she freezes in that tombitory.'

We all looked at the beds, laid out in pairs. Two to each

side of the window, toe to toe, with a row of drawers separating the middle of the room, back to back.

I'd be going home each weekend, advantage of being the only one of us four who lived locally. While most weekends Kate could visit if she wanted, Rose and Beth had yet to stop over. My father was always slow to warm to people if he didn't know their parents.

'I think you should choose,' Kate said, looking for approval from the rest of us. 'You're the one that got us here.'

It was generous of her. I gripped her arm and nodded. Beth agreed. Rose looked round with a pursed full lip, eyes narrowing in contemplation and victory.

4

Moth cycled hard. Heading away from the valley floor on relentless uphill roads.

Afternoon merging into evening, a creeping dimness he ignored. Focusing on the swaying curves and mean switchbacks of the fading tarmac. His muscles protesting the return to the road. His head straggling back to the café and the email. The bike disjointed in his sweaty palms.

Small towns were his nemesis. Every problem he'd encountered was in or near a small town. Country was irrelevant. They were the same all over Europe. Too many people in too small a place with not enough to do. Sucking him in, reminding him of others. Making him long for the anonymity of a big city, where you could blend into the background. The sour taste of the call to Kit grew to a strong pressure of anxiety in his stomach.

Forget it, you made a mistake. No big deal.

He pushed himself into the chill and the dark, switching on the headlamp. Focusing on the diminishing world beyond the beam. It began to pay off. His muscles remembered themselves. The jarring effort of the bike beneath him became familiar. He would pay for it later, struggling to set up camp in the dark.

Keep going a bit further.

He settled into the saddle, building a steady rhythm. Forwards and away. The hum of wind broken by pockets of sound, cars roaring up from behind, sweeping onwards, leaving him in a vacuum. Hearing them approach, he swung to the side of the road. Slackening the pace. Switching off the light. Closing his eyes at the last moment of the bright lights passing, lessening the impact on his night vision. Listening for any change in engine pace. Wary of standing out. Of being noticed. Of strangers in cars at night on quiet roads.

The frequency of the cars diminished as he crawled on. Becoming more haphazard in their driving. He watched one swerve away from him, straighten, and sway to the wrong side of the road before righting itself.

Drunk bastard. Time to stop.

The road was passing through trees, his visibility non-existent. He was waiting for the river that ran along the tight valley to reappear. Its course straight while the road swerved up and down the hillside. Trying to hear its approach in the quiet interludes. That would be his cue to stop, his best chance to find a safe spot. He hoped he'd read the map right. He didn't want to cycle back to the last potential stop he'd seen. He was tired. Aching in his muscles. Quiet in his mind.

Back in charge.

It was the place he was heading to in life. When he'd counted down the last months of his childhood. He twisted his hands around the handlebars, reaching forward to that day. Feeling the breeze pushing against him, leaning into the resistance.

He heard the river over the low hum of the wind. The air changed, moistened. His legs slackened with the sound and he cruised to a stop on the bridge. Resting a hand on the stone span, his feet on the pedals. He switched the light off, his eyes adjusting to the dim shadows around him.

Woods stretched away from the road curving across the bridge, concealing both sides of the steep banks along the narrow, swollen river. The bank that he'd come from seemed more accessible. He cycled on, swinging off the bike as the bridge returned to the road. Walking along the fence that marked the woods leading upstream. There was no clear path. His hunch that this was the quieter side deepened. Moth swung the bike over the rails and leapt after it. He hefted the weight over his shoulder, balancing it over his head with his far arm and stepped through the woods with care. Fallen twigs and road tyres were no happy bedfellows. It was awkward. The loaded bike tough to manoeuvre. Low hanging branches, rough ground.

The river's too noisy, you won't hear anything else coming.

He veered right, further away from the masking sounds. It was dark beneath the canopy and he was moving on instinct. Sensing the space opening to allow a tent. Putting the bike down against a trunk, praying for his tyres, he paced the few precious metres between the trees to check for space. Three paces one way by two the other. Moth crouched down in the middle, twisted his shoulders to ease away the weight from the bike and listened, eyes closed, for long minutes. The birds returned to their trees. The silence was broken by the normal sounds of a wood at night. Snuffles, whips and cracks.

You're on your own.

Moving with the decreasing speed of exhaustion he clipped a light to his helmet. It pushed the shadows back to an intense blackness that hung around the small space, overwhelming in their unseen hugeness. Stretching up into the twitching branches.

This is shit ground for camping.

He looked down, kicked at the soil. Full of lumps and roots, packed with layers of mulch and rot. He set the bike on its stand, feeling the ground under the tyres with concerned fingers. Took the rucksack and handlebar bag off, pulled the tent from the left pannier, shaking it out over the frame of the bike. It was a quick process. A peg firmed in at either end, the arch of the tunnel pulled taut away from each tyre and pegged down. Three minutes of feeling the skin crawl over his back and he was inside with the zip shut down.

He pulled the sleeping bag from the right pannier and spread it out, chucked his trainers through the rhombus of the bike frame to the small storage area of the tent, slithering with experience into the tight space available and the warmth of the bag before he cooled down. He hung the helmet on the saddle, where the light swayed over him, and lay back. His head on the rucksack with its soft wad of clothes a pillowcase, his muscles tensing and resisting the charge to relax. Clenching his hands into fists. Feeling the rough blisters on his palms. Ignoring the sound of the branches creaking high above the fragile cover of the tent.

It's the same every night. Remember.

The relief of rest assaulted by fear of the dark outside. Heightened by sound. Unmitigated by walls and security. He'd seen Riverdell behind Kit, glimpses of the walls as he moved away. It had looked bigger, rearing over his head, the cliff of the castle swinging round for a brief second. Moth had forgotten its effect. Like an arm, reaching out to embrace you, the door nestling in the crook of the elbow. Kit hadn't said where he was. Moth knew why.

Kit didn't want you asking questions.

Kit liked to control the questions, not answer them. He wouldn't want Moth asking. If she was there, right there, near him, free to talk.

You're done with that.

Moth blinked, pushing away the memory. Riverdell. He hadn't expected that. In those months before the start of the notebook. When the plan he was developing had first gone adrift. When he'd been overwhelmed with the responsibility of Nat. His part in it all. When he'd had to wait, wait, wait. When Riverdell had first opened its door to him and Nat, and he'd wondered.

Wondered what?

Wondered if there was another option. That was what he'd thought, in those days and weeks. Perhaps life had heard him and sent them a chance. Offered up options.

Yeah, well it didn't. Think about your blisters.

He unzipped the handlebar bag on his chest, fingers probing past the solid lump of the pocket German dictionary. Finding the hard, slim metal container, pulling out the cigarette case. As he opened it the waft of lavender and alcohol intruded into the small space. He touched the dried sprig, crackling under pressure. Beside it, piercing the scrap of cloth, the chill of a slim needle. He pulled it free, a whisper of metal glinting in the weak light, the eye a nub he could feel, not see. He rested the case on his chest, using the needle to pierce the rising blisters on his hands, twisting his palms to find the swell of building pressure. It had a precise way of focusing him, the moment when the slim point pierced the skin, the pop of pain, the relief of pressure. Done, the dark pushed back, he replaced the needle, clipped the case shut with a firm clunk.

You need to stop thinking about him. About her. About them.

Moth looked at the rippling roof of the tent. Riverdell was gone. It hadn't been an option for him. He pulled out the notebook, the pencil tucked in the gap of its spine, rifled through the pages, eyes squinting to find the page, raising it closer to the torch. Day 257. 15th March 2013. Ratten.

Another thin line of victory.

He peered at the spaces between today and that glaring entry adrift in the white space ahead, closed the notebook with a frown. Tucking it away, zipping the bag, clutching it to his chest. The mulched padding of the woodland floor gave scarce comfort, but tiredness held the upper hand. Moth lay, blinking with the sounds outside the tent, until his fears gave up and let him sleep.

ISABELLE WAS aware of someone outside herself. Light stirring through her senses, the layers of mattress, bedding and familiarity. Trying to recall what day it was.

Same day. She'd come home. She'd slept.

A pungent whiff coaxed her eyes open. She stirred, turned, caught the antiseptic hint and pushed her hair from her eyes as she pulled herself up against the headboard, dazed eyes straggling round the edges of the room. A sliver of afternoon light poking through the thickness of the drawn curtains.

She found the chair in the corner, saw her case beside it.

Found the socks full of holes sucked adrift as they slipped from wellies, the legs clad in worn, ripped jeans, the hands stained and rough on the knees, the thick layers of checked insulated shirt. She followed the intimate form all the way to his rough three-day stubble and wrinkled, tired blue eyes and found James watching her back.

Four months, ten feet and a host of avoided issues separated them. A lifetime of loving hovered in the midst. It was an intangible mix. Texts, emails and phone calls mediated the distance but the first moment of reunion always foundered for words.

'Hey.' James coughed and cleared his throat round the word, his hand jumping to brush his amber hair forward over the battleground of age and indifference that sat between his thickening eyebrows and receding hair. Making him look as always older, more care worn, more exhausted than his thirty-four years should have claimed.

'Hey.'

This time it was impossible to negotiate. A silence she had no confidence to breach. She should have been in India, they'd planned to meet in April, a short break in London. They would have been able to talk through the difficulties, away from home, and where it left them, away from the family.

David's death had changed all that. The problems she'd gone to India to avoid hadn't waited for her to come home and resolve. They'd been brushed aside by more pressing matters. The pain between them was as raw as his voice

'It's good that you're home.' His voice softening as he moved past the first awful words. Kind, deeper than she was ever able to remember in the singsong world of India. 'Mother will be relieved. It's been a strain.'

Isabelle knew it had been a strain. She had spoken to Elsa often enough. James was calling in twice a day when the lambing allowed, evidence of his concern as much as his foundering capacity to help. Hester was visiting every two or three days and managing a little better, Kate was here daily, and Kit had been twice in the last month, attended the funeral, and was due back in a few days.

She knew the details of the car accident, the blood alcohol level, the double parental death. The orphaned children and the unfolding portraits of two grandchildren that Elsa had never met, her unexpected role as their guardian. Their lack of family, their homelessness, the threat of social service intervention.

Isabelle knew the painful consequences of it all, and the questions that hung between her and James had disappeared in the vortex. How they would drag it back out was beyond her. There was an unvoiced, selfish hope that perhaps it might stay ignored. Resolve itself without direct intervention.

'I guess I'd better make myself decent and meet the children.'

'I'll be stopping for dinner.' James stood and moved towards her, offering his hand and pulling her up from the bed.

She stood barefoot, level with his chin, her own height making his gangling door frame height of awkwardness disappear. James put his arms around her and pulled her tight for a hug. She felt the encasing warmth of his arms with a lump in her throat, wondering how it was possible to love someone so much, and yet not enough. A sickening sense that it might be the last time. That it might not be

'I've missed you, sweetheart,' he mumbled in her hair, kissing her head, and turned to leave. 'Don't rush.'

The words lingering in the sudden emptiness he made in the room.

Isabelle looked at the clock, looking for normality. It was mid-afternoon. She'd slept several hours away and felt no better for it, weak with tiredness and an aching desire to go back to bed.

She showered, indulging in the luxury of scorching hot water, in the exact position of bottles that she'd not picked up for months. The peculiar, precise impression the bathroom mirror gave back, the way it rounded her out, made her feel fuller. Its age spots mingling with her eyesight to give a mellow view. The hair cut close at the back, falling longer round her face. Her sharp features, fine nose, thin lips, bony chin. A delicate, feminine version of the hawkish Threlfall face. Blue eyes the echo of James' looking back.

The room righted itself as she dressed and unpacked in tandem, for each item she put on throwing two more into drawers or over chairs. Draping scarves around the bedposts, puddling beads onto the dressing table. She slipped on soft jeans, a light top, another over it. Found a belt, a gossamer scarf that snaked around her throat. She always felt strange getting dressed in England, struggling to change her dress habits to fit the place, to fit herself. She looked for her sandals, caught herself, grinned. It was the highlight of her dress disparity. She pulled the top drawer out, found socks, sheathed her toes, wriggled them at the strangeness, pulled them off. It was too soon to get used to socks, one more day of sandals and freedom.

Crossing the hallway, she picked up hints of activity. James' discarded, opened letters, indifferent to the prying eyes of guests. Muddy pawprints where Flynn had slipped through a closing door and gone looking for his master.

Creaks from the guest bedrooms upstairs. Voices from behind the closed kitchen door as she moved closer; Hester's, and the muted questions of a child. She paused a millisecond's worth of apprehension, turned the handle.

Three pairs of eyes met and turned from one to the other. Isabelle from the unknown girl to the known woman, Hester from her old friend to her newfound niece, the young girl from one silent woman to another.

'Hello,' she offered in the absence of any adult intervention.

'Hello,' Isabelle returned, smiling, wishing James was there.

'This is Isabelle,' Hester explained. 'Uncle James' girlfriend.'

Isabelle's smile lengthened in determination and she offered it to Hester, who looked straight at her and ignored the rebuke.

'This is Natalie,' she told Isabelle.

'It's nice to meet you, Natalie,' Isabelle said across the room, moving away from the door, letting it fall too behind her.

'You can call me Nat,' Isabelle watched her duck her head, back to the comfort of the drawings, glance back at her. 'If you like?'

Isabelle smiled and nodded.

'Hi, Hester.' Isabelle resisted the reflex of going to kiss her in welcome, a habit that wouldn't give up. 'You look well.'

Hester turned back to chopping vegetables by the sink, the sharp knife slicing hard against the board.

'We were talking about drawing. You should ask Isabelle to draw with you Nat, she's very good, much better than me. I'm afraid I've forgotten the habit. I'm so busy these days.'

Isabelle remained standing between the closed door and the strewn surface of the table, listening to Hester set up that steady polite stream of conversation with which she deflected the world. She and Nat looking from one another to the turned back, the voice addressing them over a shoulder. She moved to the chair next to Nat and pulled it out, a little removed for comfort, folding a leg beneath her as she sat down.

Closer now, Nat came into focus. Her sleek, dark hair drawn back in a ponytail with a purple velvet scrunchy, ending in a curl like a cat's tail. A neat, thick fringe across her forehead, echoing brown eyes peering out beneath. She was wearing a fluffy jumper, with silver embossed stars on it, and rainbow hued leggings that swung back and forth into view with her restless legs, toes whispering a soft scuff where they reached the floor. She was like a shiny new button sewn onto an old coat, bright and fearless and full of a strange vital energy against the faded fibre of the kitchen. Twirling the pencil in her right hand while she looked at Isabelle, her smile light and curious. She looked like Sandrine, a woman Isabelle had seen in photos, but never met. Isabelle felt a twinge of the deeper grief Elsa must be going through. She'd lost her eldest son twice, first through dispute and finally through death, and now had the evidence before her daily.

'Are you a good drawer?'

'Artist,' Hester corrected. 'Isabelle can draw and make all sorts of things.'

Isabelle shrugged at the girl in embarrassment.

'Elsa said that Isabelle could sew, and Hester could draw,' Nat told them. 'And you would both teach me how to be better.'

Hester didn't reply. Isabelle tried to be braver.

'Well, I can definitely sew.' She picked up a coloured pencil, her right hand feeling its weight, gauging the keenness of its point against the table. 'I sketch more than I draw but that's because I don't practise, like Hester.'

Hester turned away from the kitchen work surface and watched them. Isabelle glanced up. Even at a distance she could feel the lack of expression, the restriction of her mouth to a line not severe, yet not the deep, generous smile Isabelle had known as a girl. Hester watched her back, withdrawn, irritated, waiting for opportunity, restrained by Nat's presence.

'You have to practise to be really good.' Nat offered Isabelle a piece of paper. 'My teacher told us to draw something every day, no matter what.'

'It's good advice.'

'Why don't you draw any more, Hester?'

Isabelle noticed the polite nature of how Nat referred to the family by their first name, but with no prefix, no Aunt used. She wondered if that had been her choice or if Elsa had suggested it.

'I stopped practising.' Hester said.

Isabelle prayed that Nat would not ask why.

'But you can?'

'I could.' Hester turned back to the vegetables.

Isabelle looked from Hester's back to the paper in front of her and began to place lines on the page. Sharp, short and precise, all essential. There were advantages to her poor eyesight, it enabled her to see form, shape, colour, how lines made angles, to focus on details. Her work demanded attention to detail, she was both suited to it and had grown into the habit. If Nat had asked her to draw the room, she would have sketched the corner of the table, its jumbled contents. If asked to draw the house, she would have selected a window, marked out the panes. She could sense Nat's head glancing from Hester's figure to her hand against the page.

'What do you sketch?'

'Ideas,' Isabelle replied. 'Not proper drawings, ideas of things I want to make, so I won't forget them later.'

'What sort of things do you sew?'

'All sorts.' Isabelle placed line upon line, bringing the distant figure to the page. Hester, her slight frame, so unlike the rest of them, following her mother, the slim shoulders, the fine neck bent over her task, and her long hair like tea-stained linen, caught over her shoulder in an indifferent plait. It was Hester made jaunty, with exaggerated hip and shoulder, elongated back and legs, drawn in the style she used for costumes. She could feel Nat recognising the form, looking again from page to person and back. 'Mostly clothes, but also things for Elsa's house, curtains and cushions. Sometimes just silly things that make no sense.'

She finished her sketch, leaving it incomplete, open to interpretation. Her last stroke a long feather with a coil sticking from the top of Hester's head, a flicker of reflection from an imagined diamond quivering in the end of it. She pushed the page towards Nat. She would have liked to tell her that Hester was a brilliant artist, that she could draw the birds from the trees and paint the rain from the clouds, that she felt but a rough, right-handed craftswoman by comparison, and to encourage Hester to practise. But she had given up saying those things. Hester no longer cared to hear them, and least of all from her.

Nat took the piece of paper and straightened it in front of her, turning the page that Isabelle had offered askance until it was level with the table edge and smoothing its edges down as they threatened to curl. It made Isabelle smile, reminding her of Hester. How neat her habits, how exact her efforts. Silence settled into the room, falling hardest on Hester, for she broke it first.

'Have you met Timothy?'

'No, not yet.' Isabelle put the pencil down, rolling it across the table to re-join the others. 'I've just woken up.'

'Moth's in the garden,' Nat told her.

'Moth?'

'It's what he prefers to be called.'

Hester moved to find a saucepan, swept her chopped carrots into it. 'Tim-Moth-ee. Mother and I keep forgetting.'

'Moth, that's cool.'

'It's what Mum calls him.' Isabelle saw Hester freeze at the awkward tense, her hands holding flayed carrots in mid-stroke. 'And, anyway, he hates Timothy. Thinks it's a stupid name fit for a dog not a man.'

Nat's indignation brought an image of the disgusted Moth to Isabelle's mind, a bizarre composite dog-man-child. 'I'll make a point of calling him Moth then.'

'He'd like that,' Nat said. 'He likes peaches too, if you're going to look for him.'

Isabelle couldn't decide if she was being dismissed or encouraged. She took the suggestion, uncurling from her chair and reaching to pick a peach from a bowl.

'I think I'll go find Moth in the garden.'

Nat smiled at her and placed the sketch beneath a pile of her own, her legs swinging under the table. Hester carried on peeling as Isabelle left the kitchen for the boot room, her shoulders curled over the job.

As the door closed behind her Isabelle breathed out, took a deep fresh gulp in. Inhaling the mix of warmed coats and wax, of muddy boots and abandoned socks, of wet dog and vegetable peelings for the garden. She rummaged on pegs groaning with coats piled on coats and dug out one of hers, buried far back. She pulled it on, stiff and musty with disuse and shrugged her shoulders about to soften it, feeling odd inside its shell, scrunching it around her in discomfort. She placed the peach in one of the pockets. Moth might not want it, and she would feel daft holding a peach.

She walked through the far door into the rear hall where the back stairs rose to the floors above and fell to the basement. Ahead of her the garage door stood shut. She followed the curving stairwell down, pausing to look down the long corridor that ran away from her at the bottom. She resisted the temptation, pushed the lower garden door open and stood on top of the steps, looking out across the garden.

The high roadside wall with its wooden gate ran along her right side, the tall cliffs of the castle hill and its scraggy woodland slopes peering over the top of it. A car went unseen past the wall, its engine cautious on the narrow back lane that wound around the town perimeter. A fury of rhododendrons and ivy, crowned with scrawny birches, obscured her view of the weir. She followed the wall of the house, down steps to her left, out towards the main vista of the gardens. Savouring the reveal of the wooded hillside on the opposite bank. The river, released from the weir, curved around the grounds, opening out in the deft valley where Riverdell sat.

Elsa's garden was simple. Expanses of precision-mown lawn, old trees protecting worn benches and the river nibbling away at the grass, inviting guests to paddle in warmer weather. Elsa had no time for flowerbeds. The river flooded often enough to make it a disheartening endeavour, and the woods and the valley were ample visual effect. Kate called her a bone-idle gardener and they bickered over the potential of greater endeavour, but then Kate would have pulled the lawn up, planted every spare inch of soil, and dared the river to invade

Isabelle walked down the slope of the lawns aware of the house rising behind her, up and away, safe from the invading waters. Her stone steps, patios and balconies a precocious distance from danger. She resisted, failed, and turned back to look at its southern façade. At the large windows rippling light back at her. At the aged stone, moss and lichen, entwining rose vines and ashen slate roof. At the series of arched glass doors that faced the basement wall, glinting out from beneath the high verandah. Savouring another joy to come, for those were the windows to her workroom. The sole part of this house that most felt like hers. It would be morning before she had time to go there. To open the curtains that now showed their linings to her, let the light bring the room back to life. She remembered her mission, turned back to the river, and found Moth. Standing beneath a birch tree. Watching her watching the house.

Her weak eyes betrayed her. At that distance confusion reigned. It was James, it was her father, it was herself, even memories of David lingered there, until her faltering steps and squinting eyes took her close enough to meet the unknown, familiar, young man.

His height denying the child she had set out to find, the wide fledged shoulders of a man bracing the shallow chest of the boy. His slender hips seemed incapable of holding up his frame. The high cheekbones, the deep-set eyes beneath their wide brows, and the curved nose looking down on her, making her the child again, before her father. All tucked beneath a knitted beanie hat pulled low across his forehead, slivers of pale ginger hair sticking out the edges.

Moth Threlfall was no orphaned child, sat at the kitchen table and learning how to fit into a new world. He was a formidable young man who looked irritated by her disturbance of his garden.

She took a few more steps, stopped to catch her own confidence. He watched her the whole time, that quizzical frown upon his face that she recalled from her own father. The inherent menace of Threlfall height which James avoided in awkward, endearing apology for his immense physique by always sitting down. She felt disturbed by memories and pulled the coat a little closer around her, finding comfort in the pocket.

'I think you must be Moth.' She held the peach out towards him. 'Your sister suggested you might like a peach.'

Moth grinned, a light, crooked smile, soon snatched by the breeze. Her hand that held the peach out was shaking. He stepped forward, away from the tree, two steps that covered three of another man's and took the peach from her, avoiding contact.

'You must be Isabelle.'

She nodded. He hefted the peach into the air and caught it again in his left hand. Isabelle noted it, an artistic bent she had always envied, especially in Hester.

'Sis was right.'

'I'm glad.'

She smiled back at him, lifting her hand to pull her hair out of her eyes. She felt exposed in the garden. Her smile stretched thin on her face, the breeze chilling her toes.

He hefted the peach again, letting it soar before sinking

back into his hand. Careful to move his hand to soften the fall. 'Kit talks about you a lot.'

'Kit just talks a lot.'

'Yes, and all of it interesting.' Moth looked through the rising peach at her, catching it sightless. His eyes light blue, wide and fragile in the intense face as he looked for her response.

The hat, if it could be called such, had a brim, thin and trembling, curved down over the left eyebrow and towards the ear. She could see the rough knitting, the pulled surface of threads, the balance of iron and heath in the yarn, the clinging intimacy of it against his skull. Kit would be a good balance for this challenging young man, as light and frivolous as Moth was dark and brooding.

Elsa had called Timothy – Moth, she reminded herself – awkward, discomforted by how he kept his distance. She'd said that he talked to Kit a lot, and Kit to him, but neither of them to her about what they spoke about. Elsa hadn't said that Moth was a little frightening. Or maybe it was only her who felt it. Or because she was out here, with the river hard beside her and the woods bending over in the background and life, which always felt gentle and wild in the same breath at Riverdell, coalesced in the person before her. Rough energy and tension stitched up in a purled tea cosy.

'It's nice to meet you, Moth,' Isabelle steered away from talking about herself. 'Though I'm sorry for the circumstances.' She said it daring her own reticence, hating how people never mentioned the obvious.

'It does seem a harsh birthday gift,' he agreed. 'Lose your parents and gain a family.'

Isabelle had missed his birthday by a week. A birthday he'd refused to celebrate according to Elsa.

'I guess the only good thing about a crappy birthday is you get to hope for better next year,' she said.

She watched the river surging past behind Moth, who was watching her. She knew she should say more. It was a tough subject, and while she had her own ample experience of losing parents to dredge for the occasion, it was not a cure-all she would use to claim empathy with either of these children. Child being a word that did not fit the person she grimaced at with a sympathetic shrug.

'Kit said you think more than you talk.'

Isabelle laughed. 'I shall have to ask Kit what else he told you,' she said. 'Before I tell him to keep his opinion to himself.'

'So, what were you thinking about?'

'More than I wanted to talk about.'

'You'll tell me,' he returned. 'Eventually.'

The illusions of his maturity disappeared with that one statement. Isabelle restrained her retort. Pulled up by a resistance inside, something unnerved that made her natural walls of privacy close a little tighter.

'It would be nice to think so, with time.'

'Instead,' Moth took a gentle bite from the peach, a nibble she thought, as though aware he was in danger of consuming the whole thing in one fell swoop, or apology for the roughness of its flight path, 'let's talk about the family.'

'Where do you want to start?'

'With you,' he nibbled at the peach again. 'Of course.'

'Hmm,' she resisted.

'Kit told me,' he began, and she groaned, so that he laughed, and the whole moment lifted. The garden stretching away from them, light brightening the ground through the birch tree.

'I dread to think,' she pulled her coat around her again, regretting her sandals, missing socks and sensible shoes. 'But before you tell me what Kit Almouthy told you, how about we walk and talk? I have a need to see the weir.'

'Fine,' he gestured for her to lead the way, though he gestured, she noticed, in the right direction. 'Kit told me your father's the black sheep of the family.'

'He probably was.'

Moth's feet stumbled in his stride, taking in the tense. 'Oh, Kit missed that part out.'

'That's Kit,' she warned him. 'Maddeningly selective on crucial factors.'

'I'll take that up with him.'

'My father died fifteen years ago.' Isabelle found it hard to share, even invited. 'But, otherwise, Kit was right. He'd enraged his father and had himself disinherited by the time he was twenty-five.'

'Sounds like an interesting character.'

'Charming, impetuous, and forceful.' Isabelle had heard more about her father than she'd experienced. 'Quiet, reserved, considerate. Depending on who you speak to, idiotic, brave, selfish, kind to a fault.'

'He was Elsa's older brother?'

'Older half-brother,' Isabelle corrected. 'Their father was widowed and remarried Elsa's mother. I only just belong to the family.'

'Is that why he was disinherited?'

'I don't think so.' Her father had never spoken with her about it. 'More that he wouldn't do what his father thought he should. I'm not sure myself. Elsa would be able to tell you more, if you're curious.'

'Elsa.'

Isabelle flashed a sideways glimpse at the tone. Polite. Too polite. Brittle. It wasn't inviting.

'I remember your father a little,' she ventured instead.

Moth remained silent, and Isabelle continued walking, feeling the conversation stall. She focused on the garden and waited for a response.

The air was fine and light. The morning's volatile warmth gone, falling towards a damp dusk. The river was high but clear of winter mud and turmoil, and the garden seemed poised between budding warmth and laughter and the lingering harshness of shorter days and cold nights. It was harder to come home in the dour depths of a British winter from months in India. Now, the full length of summer awaited, and the days would grow brighter as the weeks progressed. The river rolled round the edge of the garden and they followed the stone path that led along the embankment as it tapered towards the toothy foundations of the mill building that had once sheltered there, shadows building in the gaps from the sinking afternoon sun. The millrace added a new rush to the watery sounds that filled their silence and the weir appeared out from thickets of birch to show its full length. She stopped to take its full sparkling curve in.

Moth came to her side, watched her taking it in as she turned to look past him at the house, the gardens.

'You like this place.'

'It's home.' She looked at him. 'I love coming back.'

'Even though it's not yours?' Moth frowned at her. 'After all, it should have been, through your father.'

'It makes no difference.' Isabelle could feel the nerve he was touching. A subject that was never discussed, the disputed ownership of Riverdell. The cause of the fall out with David. When she and Elsa talked about the past, they discussed Isabelle's mother, it was a more comfortable subject. 'I've grown up here, this is my family. It's where I belong, I hope. Kate always says you don't need to own something to love it, and I agree with that. I don't think love is dictated by possession.'

'That's not the sort of advice my father would have given.' Moth said. She could feel his contempt, though she wasn't sure if it was at her or at the thoughts. 'But that's why he fell out with Elsa, isn't it?'

She understood why Elsa thought Moth was awkward. He strung together his thoughts and convictions with a clarity that was hard to swallow. Elsa, who would be the first to admit that she liked life more palatable than honest, would find him awkward. Kit would find Moth easy. Kit never found it hard to say what he thought. Relished every and any chance to provoke. Deciding where she fitted in felt both important and immediate. Like his opinion of her would hang on this response. She was poised to keep walking but stopped, aware of all the loyalties and upsets that came with being part of the family. Knowing how hard it was to be honest with people you loved. She wondered where Moth would settle in, trying to make sense of a past he'd never known.

'Elsa never talked to me much about that,' Isabelle explained. 'And, if I'm honest, I never wanted to pry.' She could see him begin to draw breath to express disdain. 'I understand your father wanted more than she was ready to give, before it was his due.'

'But it was his due.'

'You should talk to her about it,' Isabelle said. 'Elsa avoids difficult subjects but, if you want to know, I believe she'd respect that. You may have heard another side from your father, but you seem capable of deciding for yourself. Now that you have the chance.'

Moth scowled the whole time she spoke, and she spoke with care. Hoping not to seem patronising, determined to defend a woman she knew better. The peach stone was in his hand, stripped of flesh, moist and ragged with residue, orbiting into space and plummeting back. His hands were large, wide in the palm and fine in the wrist. Emphasising the muscles as they flung and caught the gory kernel.

'Shall we walk the weir?' she asked.

'You serious?'

'Oh what, don't tell me you haven't already?'

Moth responded with an expression that made her shiver. He produced the Threlfall family scowl with such perfection that ghosts stomped across her back. It was James at work, it was her father in India, it was one of her earliest physical memories of barbed irritation: the head cocked sideways, the brows coming together, the mouth puckered.

'No, I haven't. Not all the way across, it's broken.'

'And that stopped you?'

She began to take off her sandals. Rolling her jeans up her calves, taking her time to feel the air fluttering around her ankles and grinning at his scowl.

'It's not going to be that warm, right?' Moth asked.

Isabelle felt that he might have preferred to do this on his own. That he had been happier exploring his new world, not being shown it.

'Right,' she tucked her sandals in her jean waist. 'Bloody freezing.'

Moth removed his trainers, heavier by far than her light-weight sandals and, tying the ends of the laces together, hung them round his neck. Isabelle turned away and took the few steps towards the fragile mesh bridge that crossed the mill-race. She swung down onto it, took three light steps across and pulled herself up on the other side. Moth followed, the mesh popping under his weight.

Isabelle walked across the first dry section of the weir, balancing on the tilted, water-worn rock, waiting for Moth to catch up with her. The sound of the river building, the mill-race deep and brooding at her side. The weir humped with moss and algae, stretching down to the well of the river in its wide bed. The stone was ragged in places as she moved to the point where water began to pour across the weir, and the aged crumbling stone with its dry pitted roughness gave way to dark, quivering, water-sluiced rock.

She glanced back past Moth to see Riverdell in the background, high-browed and proud on the vibrant grass embankments. Home was this place, this moment. The river running beneath her waiting feet, the meadows stretching away on the other side, the woods hovering above, the lawns like tempting velvet, the house watching it all. Every view was home. She saw Moth, head crooked, eyes crinkling, mouth curling, and offered her hand behind her. He took it, his broad hand strong and determined but reticent.

He glanced over her shoulder at the water ahead. 'It looks pretty full to me, what's the secret?'

'Confidence,' Isabelle looked back at the weir. 'And plenty of manpower.'

'Manpower?'

'More the merrier,' Isabelle confirmed. 'And we've all broken the odd bone as children on this old menace.'

Moth glanced back to the house, and she felt his motion passing through her hand. Flicking her hair away from her face she glanced too.

'What's up?'

'Nothing. Just checking Nat wasn't around.'

'Oh,' Isabelle felt a ruffle of guilt, 'it's safe enough as long as you're not alone.'

'I don't want her to see.'

She glanced away, unsure why. 'So, the secret is, stay close. Move your feet with my feet and that way we create a bigger anchor against the water.'

'That makes sense, kind of.'

Isabelle pulled Moth closer with her hand, hovering her foot with a slight wobble as she waited for him to respond. He moved closer, the warmth of his leg behind hers as his foot slipped forward, the sides of their feet glancing. She moved her foot down into the cool rush of water and planted it on the spongy, slippery moss, feeling it give and settle into the crooks of her feet. The water was icy, a brutal shock with a rush of sensation. Breath suspended in movement and reaction. She transferred her weight to the foot and pulled the other one up beside it. Moth moved closer, and they were standing feet together, his toes bracketing her heels. His body angling towards the weir, protective of the chance they might fall. Gasping with the chill.

They crabbed forward, the water deepening and creeping over their feet as they paced to the centre. Moving up their ankles, their rising feet grabbed, seeking a way back to the path before landing. Isabelle could feel Moth trying to hold his body close enough to keep up, far enough away not to be intrusive. It was a millimetre of difference, and in the unbalancing of the river the distance wavered. They were two-thirds across when she came to a stop.

The distance came to nothing and Moth bumped against

her back, muttering a swear, his arm grabbing hold round her shoulders.

'You could have warned me!'

Isabelle laughed, put her arm up to steady his. A comforting tap to relax him.

'How often do you do this?' he asked.

'Oh, most days that I'm home if I can.'

'Really?'

'Yes, but I must admit, not often in daylight,' she added. 'Otherwise Elsa yells at me.'

'Oh, totally ok for the family activity then. Not.'

'Well, we all do it,' she defended herself. 'Well, we all used to anyway. They're too serious now, and Elsa gets annoyed because I broke my leg once when I was about this old.' She held her hand out at waist level. 'She made me promise never to do it again.'

'It pisses her off that you break your promise?'

'Not as much as the fact that I hide it,' Isabelle looked down at the broken stone of the weir where she'd stopped. Tested the rushing waters with her toes, strong where the gap forced the high spring river. 'It gives her less chance to yell at me.'

'But this time you can blame me, right?'

'You're very bright,' she told him with a laugh.

'Yeah, great, thanks.'

'Come on, let's finish it. Now, this is the tricky part, because there's this piece missing, like you said.' She pointed down to the crooked wide gash, at the weighty course of flowing water a good two feet deep in the centre. 'When we were children we used to sit on our bums and wriggle across, then go home soaked. We'd sneak in and try to hide our clothes in the laundry room and run upstairs in our undies as fast as we could.'

'And now you're an adult?'

'We have longer legs,' she said, uncoiling his arm off her shoulders. 'Watch!'

She stepped away from him, toes curling over the gap, wobbled for a moment, leapt across and landed with her arms out to counter balance on the other side as she ran the final length of the weir. Staggering several times on the way and catching herself with wind-milling arms.

'Jesus!' Moth swore at her, unbalanced in the swift abandonment. 'No wonder Elsa yells at you!'

She reached the far side and turned back, waving at him to follow, pumped from the rush of it, grinning. 'Come on, Moth!'

He stood looking at the gap, frowning, and she was thrilled. Hoping he felt awkward now, wondering if he'd be brave enough to do it or go home in a huff at the challenge. He took a leap across the gap, landed with a wobble, his arms outstretched. Stepped across one reaching foot at a time, staggering in the deeper sections of the current. It was much easier if you ran. Scarier, but easier. Still, he'd done it. Awkward or not, as he crossed to her side, Isabelle decided she liked him. He had guts to go with the confidence.

She sat on a rock in the meadow to put her shoes back on, watching his brave pace, until he came to stop beside her. Pulling his hat off, throwing himself down in the grass and flattening his long limbs out. She pulled a leg up to her chest, crossing the other beneath her, perching atop the stone, and watched him close his eyes, take a deep breath and lie there, his fingers pulling and teasing the grasses beneath them. The beanie hat rising and falling on his chest.

'Now you're part of the family.'

'Was that a test?'

'An introduction.'

'Thank you. I think.'

'You're welcome.'

Isabelle sat in her crooked pose and let the dying warmth of the afternoon and the sounds of the town and the gentle hum of the fresh, keen meadow grass rise around them. Eager for the year ahead, unaware it would soon be tangled and burred with docks and nettles. Looking at Moth, seeing the softness of his skin, untouched by afternoon stubble. The sparkle of his hair unspoiled by age. Not dark enough to be ginger, not light enough to be blond. His skin winter pale at neck and wrist where it slipped beneath his sweatshirt. The tautness of his knuckles, the slenderness of joints, clothes resting loose upon wide bones lacking muscle.

It could have been her and James years ago, when they'd been young and firm and full of life. James as peaceful at her side, his hair untouched by the grey that had come too soon. When they'd been this relaxed with one another, before the years had taken them further. The meadow grasses bending inward over his crushing weight, and afternoon light settling in dust upon him.

The church clock struck five. Lying beneath the town in the hollow of the river, they felt the pressure of the first strike, reflected from the river and rebounding from the castle walls. Moth opened his eyes, looked up towards castle, town, unseen church. Somewhere deep in the warren of buildings a dog barked. A ragged response to the clock that floated and drifted out across the river, spinning in the sound waves along with the final chime. A voice called from the garden, high and excited, floating across the water.

'Moth!'

Neither of them responded.

'Moth!' came Nat's voice again. Alongside it the distant bark of the town dog.

Moth pulled himself up from the flattened grass to stand, shaking himself down. He offered a hand, she took it, unwound her legs and stood up. He turned away and walked towards the river.

'Nat!' he called across the river. 'We're over here.'

'Where are you?' her voice moving closer and clearer.

'Down towards the weir, far side.' He waited until she came to the bank and waved.

'Elsa's back,' she called. 'She wants to know where Isabelle is.'

'She's right here. I'll tell her.' He turned and started to walk away, looked back at her, 'Hey, Nat!'

She turned to look, he hefted the peach stone in his hand and hurled it straight and true across the river at her, calling 'catch'. Isabelle watched it rise and fall across the water as Nat reached to catch it.

'Great peach!'

Nat waved at him and walked away hefting the stone in her smaller hand, shadow of her brother.

'That was a good catch.'

'I taught her,' he replied. 'And it was a very good throw.'

Isabelle went to show him the way out of the meadow.

'Oh, no,' he complained. 'You may have impressed me with the weir-walking act, but I know this meadow!'

Isabelle followed his assured stride through the long grass towards the path that lay invisible ahead. He found it with ease, and they followed the well-trodden grass, walking left towards the bridge.

'I've got to know this place a little since we came.' He nodded up at the wooded banks above them. 'I know the woods and I've done both of those hills.' He pointed as he talked, and Isabelle looked to see that he had in fact gone some distance in his exploring.

'That's Climbing Jack Common, and High Vinnalls.' Pointing out the names of the two hills closest. 'What about the town?'

'A bit.' He focused back on the path. 'Nat's done more with Elsa, she seems to like it.'

Isabelle was glad to hear it, though wondered if it was a brave face. Aware that Moth and Nat had no option except to resettle here.

'She must miss home.'

'It's a lot to take in, but it's hard to miss anything in the face of all this.' He nodded to indicate the valley, the river, the town and house. 'My father was a selfish arse, keeping us away from all this, from our family. Just because he didn't get what he wanted.'

It shocked her, this anger against his father, even though it made sense. Because David had been selfish. Not just about Riverdell, but in other things too, and in that final moment most of all. She heard how Moth spoke with the same bitterness he'd used about Elsa's side in it. His anger cutting like the hidden path through the meadow grass that swayed round them. As soon hidden as revealed.

'I think she'll miss school more, but she'll make her own mind up, and she's got time.'

Isabelle knew the rough plan, the change to the local public school as a day pupil. It was the family tradition, but Nat was used to state schooling. Isabelle wasn't sure about a lot of it, even her own presence here. But Moth seemed confi-

dent in Nat, and she had faith in Elsa, so maybe it would all
come good in the end.

'She's quietly confident?'

'Only with strangers,' he replied. 'It's louder once you
know her.'

They reached the stile that took them to the road over the
bridge. Moth let her go first. When she stepped down on the
other side and looked back Moth stepped away from the stile.

'Not coming?'

'Not yet,' he looked at the sun curving round the hill, 'it'll
be dark soon. Tell Nat I'll be in for dinner if she asks.'

'Thanks for getting wet with me, Moth.'

'Nice to meet you, Isabelle.'

'You too.'

He turned and walked away from her. Isabelle watched
him stride across the meadow and break away from the path
towards the slopes of the wood. He crossed rough ground and
hitched onto another path you had to know was there. She
turned and walked over the bridge. Running her hand across
the warm, rough stone and glancing down at the river, full of
reflected trees and sky.

THE HOUSE FELT empty to him as Kit swept through the lower
floor, checking for life.

The market and the sun had taken all guests and residents out, no doubt many of them would be up at Kate's. Still,
he looked, to be sure. He climbed the stairs to the first floor,
checking Elsa's bedroom. Passed the grim old portraits with a
distasteful glance. Vile old buggers. Should have gone to the
sales, but they had their use awing the guests. Advanced to
the attic floor with a deepening sense of pleasure flooding

through him, sure of the emptiness of the house as he wanted it. Isabelle was crippled by jetlag and the chance of her being up and out any time before midday was slim. He placed his hand upon the door handle, turned it, and stepped into the darkened room.

The bed was a rumpled mass of feather and cotton. Nestled somewhere in the middle was an ill-defined lump of femininity that stirred at the disturbance. Kit kicked off his Oxfords. Unzipped his trousers, laying them over the back of the chair, watching the movements under the duvet as he pulled each button of his shirt apart. He'd showered with intent that morning and the aromas of gel and cream and soap rose to greet him, mingling with the scents of flowers on his skin, stirring him even more. He slipped the elastic of his pants down over his buttocks and drew them in to give power to the rising erection that jumped from the soft jersey as it slid down his legs.

The cool of the room sent a shiver across his flesh, pulling the skin tighter on his dick and making his balls tuck into his body. He played with them a moment, caressing and warming the soft skin. Stoking the hard on and encouraging it with thoughts he'd been savouring for fifteen long frustrating years as they explored the tempting permutations of intimacy but not that final commitment, whilst she wondered what to do about James. About how much she loved James. Or didn't. Wanted kids with him. Or didn't. Wanted to marry him. Or didn't. Wanted him. Or didn't.

Thinking about James, wondering how they'd last done it, made his erection more insistent. He recreated the image of them in the bed together. Isabelle's fragile waist and her long back. James behind her, swaying his great aristocratic dick into her. Like some prize stallion who couldn't quite hit the mark. James would be gentle of course, there wasn't any other way Kit could imagine it. All those generations of engrained reserve. Playing with his fretful dick, licking his thumb and passing its warm wetness over the straining opening, Kit let his fantasies play out as he imagined James trying to Saga cruise her to orgasm. He joined the party in his mind. Just there, right behind James. In and out they all swayed together, all warm and welcoming, all terribly restrained. The bed clanging a respectable chorus. The delicious thoughts mingled with the divine scents and he came upon his hand, straining back against his own muscles. Feeling the warmth in his palm and the scent of himself rising sharp in the air.

He sighed, feeling the tension ease. It was his second wank that day. He'd woken with nothing but thoughts of Isabelle to torment him. Despite his quietness he could sense her stirring. He moved to the bathroom, washed his hands, urinated with a struggle.

Kit returned to the bed, pulled the covers up and slipped into the cocoon of warmth and sweat. She muttered in the effort to wake up, relaxed and comfortable in the depths of that old bed. His hands ran across her back and over her shoulders, slipping down her arms, cupping her breasts. His thumb smoothing under the curve, avoiding her sensitive nipples.

'Kit.' Her woolly voice went through him like syrup, teasing his muscles with delight.

'Pretend I'm not here,' he murmured, moving down the line of her body.

He followed her ribs with his mouth. A fish feeding off her skin, teasing and tickling her flesh awake. He licked the line of her hip, followed the sharp bone of her pelvis, felt her legs part and straighten. Eased her hips round in the bed, pulling and kissing and flicking and licking until she woke up at last, twisting herself onto his tongue.

Steady now, he thought, hearing her groans rumbling under the thick layers. This was a moment he wanted to savour. They had hours, no need to blow the long-awaited moment in a hurry. He'd let off steam for a reason, not to rush her enjoyment. He pulled his tongue away, let his hands caress their way back up her body, his fingers kneading into her warm skin. He wanted to see her watching him as they rode each other to a magnificent crescendo. Not James, but his face, his eyes, his lips. Flushed from sucking her to a heart-stopping orgasm. Steady though, steady.

'Good morning.' He kissed her cheek.

She murmured blind agreement. He watched her twisting into her own body, eyes shut. He didn't disturb her, stroking himself again and taking in the physical pleasure she was lingering with. Her hair wrecked from the pillow. Her face streaked with crease marks from deep sleep. All those years, waiting for this moment, in between all the traumas of her relationship with James. Just a little longer. He waited for her to come back to him, caress and hold him. It might have been a long game, but Kit knew how to play this one. One tempting kiss at a...

Isabelle gasped, her eyes opening wide. Threw aside the covers and straddled him in one rushed, messy motion. Pinning his legs to the mattress before he could catch up.

'Whoa...'

She dropped her head and took his dick into her mouth with a demanding force that shook him from self-control. His surprise ended in a groan.

'I want you right now,' she mumbled round her mouthful.

'What?'

'Now,' she repeated, and pulled away from him, leaving him spinning in the sudden absence of her mouth.

She stretched towards the drawers at the side of the bed and dragged one open to find a condom. Her body arched over his, her thigh rubbing against his dick, her breasts tantalising his mouth. She rolled it on with her nimble fingers and slipped her mouth behind the motion, making him tense and gasp. Kit felt the moment slipping away from him, placed his hands round her slim waist to try and slow it down, groaning as she lowered herself onto him and with one long shuddering movement his long-awaited moment was gone.

Fifteen years' worth of desire, the thoughts he'd toyed with all that long morning, the glory of her naked body above him, her hip bones, her small breasts, her tiny buttocks, the weight of her body settling onto him, around him, all crashed in upon him at once. He hammered himself home. His legs twisting outwards against her thighs to push her open, to go deeper. It was over in seconds for him. The orgasm a poor, rushed third of the day. He lay gasping beneath her, holding her hips and watching her nipples move while his dick shrivelled inside her and she lost herself in a pleasure he had no part in. He was collapsed inglorious on the pillows, frowning, when she opened her eyes. She grinned at him, slipping herself out from the tangle of limbs, jumping from the bed and away to the bathroom while he pulled the collapsing condom off his dick.

'What time is it?' she called.

'Half-eleven,' Kit called back with an irritated guess.

He pulled a wad of tissues from the box on the bedside table, cleaned himself and tried to rearrange his mood as she walked back to the bathroom doorway and stood, naked, looking at him on the bed.

Kit made no effort to conceal himself. Spreading his legs a little wider to wipe himself, the muscles in his thighs rippling with the motion. Puffing out his chest, proud of the ridges across his stomach. He was a sublime product of natural engineering and precision maintenance. He was not about to burrow back under the covers or dash for his clothes, as James would. Isabelle needed to know this was but the start.

'I'm sorry,' she said. 'I rushed you.'

She walked over to the bed, crawled up against him and ran her hands over his body, cupping his balls and tracing the ridges of his muscles.

'A little,' he grumbled, cupping an arm around her as she came to rest beside him.

'Just had to have you.'

'I'm guessing it wasn't all about me though?'

'All about me.'

'You did it then?'

'We did,' she agreed.

'Free at last?'

'Indeed.'

But she wasn't looking at him and Kit noticed she pulled the blankets back up around them.

KIT GAVE up the pretence that they could spend all day in bed with the first hunger pang.

He dragged Isabelle into the bath, turned on the shower and went down on his knees for one final indulgence. Sluiced under the water until he came back up for air, his hair clinging to his skull. Sliding himself between her thighs from behind, hot water streaming between them, as he took one last desperate, Oxford style attempt to snare the morning's long promise. But her thighs were too thin, and he too spent. He sat on the hard ridge of the bath lip, probing with his tongue, sucking the water from her skin and caressing her with his fingers until she shuddered against the cold wet wall, her arms curved across her bullet-hard nipples. The bathroom was a sodden mess behind the ineffective shower curtain clinging to his back, his overhanging arse dripping water onto the floor.

'I am starving,' he told her, kissing her neck and stepping out of the bath. 'It must be lunchtime.'

He left her in the steaming bathroom and dressed. Flinging the bed covers back to air, fluffing out the trashed pillows, throwing the used condoms in the bin and raking his fingers through his towel-dried hair. He looked fresh from the nest and grinned at his own reflection, straightening his collar in the mirror. He was counting on James being there for lunch.

He rattled down the stairs, cutting the corners with a leap from the second step and breezed into the kitchen on full sail. It was full of family and flowers. Elsa stood in bemused uncertainty trying to decide which part of the mess to fix first, Hester unpacking shopping with nowhere to put it, Nat holding cutlery and unsure where to lay it without guidance from the flustered women, James sat down doing nothing to help as usual, mooning over the gloom that was the *Telegraph*.

'Morning cupcakes!

'Kit, where have you been?' Elsa gasped in relief. 'What am I supposed to do with lunch when the table is full of flowers?'

'Move lunch?' he suggested. 'I've been waking Isabelle up.' He glanced at James, who stiffened in gratifying response. Kate walked through the door with two vases of old flowers and heard the tail end of it.

'How heroic of you.' She thrust a vase at him, her look more withering than the flowers.

He hadn't been expecting her, but Kate always surprised him. As defiant of age as Elsa was accepting, pushing aside their mutual sixty-eight years with disdain to fashion and decorum, while Elsa pulled the tweed and cashmere closer with delight. Kate had a blue silk scarf tied at her throat, emphasising the choppy cut of her hair, a windswept mix of grey and blonde. She always looked as though she'd fallen out of a plane and landed sunny side up, dusting down her elegant, wide-legged, low-slung trousers, slipping back into her mules and looking for the next rush. He smiled at her across the drooping daffodils, but she moved past him, her eyes rolling.

'It's a tough job.' Kit looked back at James whose eyes hovered over the paper. 'But someone's got to do it else she'd miss lunch again.'

'And we wouldn't want that,' James muttered as he looked down at the paper again.

'That's not a bad idea.' Elsa grasped the idea and went to move, frowned and asked, 'Hester, what do you think?'

Hester looked round from the food she was trying to put away with an irritated, sweeping expression. 'About what, Mother?' She stared hard at Kit who grinned back at her. James crackled the paper and Kate sighed.

'Lunch, dear,' Elsa explained as though she were being obtuse. 'Why don't we move lunch rather than all the flowers? We could eat in the garden, it's warm enough.'

Hester turned back to the plates. Kate put down the vases in a clatter.

'Elsa, it's warm enough outside for coffee if you're a tourist, not lunch. The wind is strong enough to freeze us within half an hour. If it's fresh air you want, let's open the window in the dining room instead.' She grabbed another vase of fresh flowers, kicked Kit with her foot as she walked past. 'Grab some plates, Superman. And you, Moth, don't just stand there, help your sister.'

Kit hadn't noticed Moth. He was leaning against the window onto the driveway, concealed by curtains, watching the scene with interest. He crossed the room towards Nat and took some cutlery.

'Hey, Moth,' Kit said.

'Hey.'

The kitchen door pushed open as Kate got to it and Isabelle stood there. Bemused and sleepy, wet from her shower, assaulted by the noise and activity, which stilled to their collective acute awareness of her. Of Hester turning away from her entrance, of James looking up and seeming to lose all sense of anything else, of Elsa frowning in worry and Kate in vexation, of Moth watching her, knives held aloft and poised, of Nat looking from Moth to Isabelle to Elsa and back to the forks in her hand.

Kit took it all in, aware of a new shade in the discordant scheme of the family dynamics, but unsure what it was. Kit didn't like being unable to pinpoint a colour. It was a point of professional pride. There was a shade for every situation, every room, every emotion. Shades he'd spent hours chasing down, cataloguing, defining, matching, and right now he was struggling to name it. He followed Isabelle's gaze to Moth, saw her awkward smile and the fleeting grin Moth returned, followed by a longer sullen face as Moth's eyes came back to him, Kit. Elsa stood in the middle, worrying what a mess lunch was turning into. Hester thrashing the freshly cooked sausage rolls onto a plate, ruining their flaky pastry. James's ears warming behind the paper. Some grim sepia tone underlined with rouge. Not a combination he would ever advocate. Kit wondering through the drooping daffodils what was wrong with the whole damn situation. Because it wasn't lunch, or the flowers, or the crumbling sausage rolls, or him.

'Hi,' Isabelle said to the room in general.

James went back to his newspaper, Moth turned to Nat, the moment of Isabelle's arrival ended, and Kit watched as Kate pushed her straight back out the door, the hems of her trousers flicking with the movement. Kit could hear their lining swishing against her skin in the strained silence.

'Come open the door into the dining room for me.' She swept Isabelle along with her. 'Is this the earliest you could make it out of bed? You probably stayed up 'til dawn, didn't you? You won't cure your jetlag like this.'

Behind her nagging irritation the others followed, trailing toward the dining room. James stood up, folded his paper and turned to look at Kit.

'You never did waste much time.'

'Nature abhors a vacuum.' Kit moved towards the sink, put the vase down beside it, and turned to face him. James was nearly a foot taller than him. A challenge he needed to step back from rather than kink his neck looking up at. 'Better me than some other man?'

'Not really.'

'Don't be sour old puss.'

'Don't be callous, you old queen,' James retorted. 'I mean it, you be kind.'

'I've never been anything but kind to Isabelle,' Kit

defended himself. 'I've waited long enough while you two pissed about going nowhere.'

James opened his mouth and drew breath for a retort that stuck in his throat. Kate breezed in to gather more plates, ignored their silence with a cheerful harrumph of derision and left again. The fire-hinged door closing like slow-sucked vacuum pack on their indifference, compressing it into dislike.

'Perhaps.' James tightened his paper into crushed quarters, tucking it under his arm. Kit watched him brush a hand across his large forehead in frustration, a habit that was not helping his encroaching years, and suppressed the urge to fluff up his own thick waves. James was a decade younger than him but looked worse for wear by far, though it had to be said that the grey creeping up from behind was doing him a favour in taking the edge off the carrot shade. 'But I say again, be kind. And I don't just mean to Isabelle.' He walked towards the door.

'What's that cryptic statement supposed to mean?'

'Work it out yourself, bright spark,' James told him, pushing open the door.

'Well at least take a bloody plate with you,' Kit retorted. 'Still expecting to be waited on, I see.'

James came back and picked up a plate, stood staring at him over the pungent waft of ripe cheeses and walked out, holding the door for Elsa to come back in.

'Bread please, Kit. Could you slice it up, dear?'

'Of course.'

'And serviettes.'

'Right here.'

'Oh, we should have moved the flowers. Not that I want to

sound ungrateful, they are beautiful, you are kind, really. I just feel a bit rushed.'

'I'll help you put them all out after lunch,' Kit said, soothing her feathers down, feeling his own might need a bit of a brush too.

5

My father was slow to warm, deep to love, long to grudge. As with Kate, he came to love Rose and Beth and, by the summer of '58, it was set in the immovable rock of Father's heart that we girls would spend a month together at Riverdell.

Kate's father had been as indifferent to her going home as she was herself. A wallowing farm of 2000 acres, five brothers to compete with and a house with no wife meant her trips home were taken up by housework, man feeding and loneliness. She used to say the only times she thought of her mother were when she was home being castigated by her paternal grandmother and the odd occasion she needed to open her Crying Box.

The May my mother died, in 1956, the year that we met Rose and Beth, Kate emptied the contents of her Crying Box into a paper bag and gave it to me. I was tucked up in bed with Father hovering restlessly over me. Both of us trying to figure out the depths of our pain. Father had moved out of their bedroom into the furthest room on the first floor and I'd refused to get out of bed since the funeral. My brother, Ted, home from India for the calamity, was stood by the window watching.

'Here, this is for you.' Kate pushed it into my hands.

'But this is...' I tried to push it away.

'I know, but you need it more.' She put it firmly back into my hands. 'You remember the rule?'

I nodded my head.

'What's the rule?' Ted asked us.

'Every time you feel like crying,' Kate told us all, looking only at me, 'you open the box, take everything out and have a damn good cry. Then you put everything back in the box and put it away. Until the next time.'

'Is that it?'

'Yes, but it's best to share it with someone.'

'I don't want a Crying Box,' I cried.

'I know, neither did I.' She had been seven when her mother died, sent off to England and boarding school two months later. 'But you can either cry and be miserable, or cry and cheer up. Memory is the closest thing you have to bringing them back.'

'What did you put in the box?' Ted took a few steps closer to the bed. My father, who had now buried two wives, took two steps closer to the door.

'Everything I could steal from my father and brothers,' Kate said. 'If she'd touched it, I took it. Photos, books, letters, her favourite hanky, the top from the last bottle of milk she opened. The soil from the garden she had.'

Ted sat down on the bed and reached out to open the box.

'I think we can find some stuff to put in this together,' he said with a determined smile at me.

It was Kate and her Crying Box that got me out of bed.

From that moment on Father took her for one of us. Her visits home truncated to a week in summer and a week at Christmas and otherwise Kate moved in with us.

And in the long sweet summer of '59, after Beth and Rose had gone home, and Kate and I lingered on with the wonderful weather, Ted finally came home to visit again. It was the last week of August and the summer seemed eternal. We were fifteen and full of the joy of sunshine chased out by swimming in the shallow river, afternoons spent lying on the hallowed bed in my parents' old bedroom dreaming of our futures, evenings spent reading in the drawing room with my father. Ted's arrival was the icing on the cake and he brought a gift for Kate.

It was a box. A stunning thing of warm red wood banded with dark gleaming wood, inlaid with silver, mother-of-pearl and ivory. The lid was curved and rose on tiny hidden hinges. Lined inside with a vivid peacock coloured silk. We were both of us speechless with admiration, touching the fine design and soft warm fabric.

'One good deed deserves another,' Ted told her. 'Though I know it can never replace the original, I hope it's a good effort. I spent a lot of time looking for one I thought you'd like. It's a Vizagapatam Box.'

And Kate wept over her new Crying Box. Ted patted her hand and made her laugh through her tears, and in his high-backed chair I saw Father wipe away a tear.

He was jarred into the new day by sound. Thoughts rushing at him. Confusion trying to pinpoint the noise. But it was gone, his eyes blinking in the thin light. Trying to recall what had woken him.

He reached out a hand and pulled the zipper up a ragged foot. Felt the cool rush of the morning air, retreated and tried to remember where he was. When today was.

Yesterday had tossed him round the tent all night long. Yesterday woke him with an accusation of stupidity. Yesterday presented him with clear evidence he was a massive dick.

He shouldn't have stopped. Should have picked a different day to check his emails.

You should never have made that bloody call.

Moth felt the rush of fear and sickness mix with the hard on and rose to his knees. Hating his birthday. The stupidity, the weakness, the longing to know that someone cared. He crabbed his way out of the bag and the tent to escape yesterday.

Today, think about today.

Standing amongst the uprising trees, until the hard on gave up.

South, you're going south.

It didn't matter about the date in the diary. He didn't need to see Kit. He'd made the call. Ben would be happy. Kit could go hang himself if he thought he was going to change the plan just like that. Turn up for coffee and a chat, like they were still friends.

Like you were ever friends.

He'd liked Kit. The easy way he made friends. Didn't bullshit.

Kit's only a friend to himself.

Moth looked round, pushing Kit away. The clearing he'd found last night was a dent between trees in daylight, the tent defying its edges. He pulled the sleeping bag out and threw it over a nearby branch to air. Grabbed the handlebar bag and his rucksack, heading down to the river. It was slow going. The ground rough, the bank steep, and the water fast when he got there. He found a small swirling pool hiding behind a rock that jutted out into the current. When he lowered himself into the stick and leaf strewn edge the shock pushed all thoughts away. The spine snapping freeze retreating to biting power. The river pulling at his legs, trying to drag him into the current. This was no gentle Teme swirling past the lawns at Riverdell. He held onto a stout branch, washing with one hand, teeth braced.

He soon backed out. Shivering on the bank, drying with the dishcloth towel, wringing it out. Struggling to get his wet body back into dirty clothes. He was due a campsite, and a proper wash. He packed, ears twitching at every odd sound. The tasks familiar and quick. Focusing on the day ahead.

Yesterday's gone, don't waste time over what you can't change.

He followed the traffic sounds back to the road. Lurking in the shadows of the last trees he consulted the map. Its pages curled and creased with use, the covers falling apart through a secondary coating of Sellotape.

He was heading south towards the border, looking for a good quiet road to cross from Austria into Slovenia. Checking and rechecking the border between the two countries, irritated when his eyes glanced west towards Italy. It was even closer than he'd thought. He ate a final handful of nuts, took a long swig of water before slotting the bottle back into its holder on the bike frame.

South. In as straight a line as he could manage and then west, down to Bleiburg and the border. He had that long to consider Kit's news.

Before you rub out the date.

To stick with the plan. Heading further into Europe, down towards the Greek peninsula. South and east for the winter. He traced the line, his finger hovering further west, a line straight down to the Lakes. Iseo, he'd never even known there was a Lake Iseo. He pulled his eyes away from Italy on the map.

It's too far in nine days.

It was beyond a stretch. It would take him longer than that. And how long would Kit be there for? He could call him sure, but that would be too satisfying. Kit would know he'd tempted him.

Stuff Kit. Forget it.

He folded the map back into place, the day's route set in his head. He set his feet upon the pedals and pushed off, gathering speed, stretching further away from Vienna towards the southern border of Austria.

His day passed in snippets of other lives. Sound passing over him. The varying tones of fields and villages. Of sudden industrial buildings and plants. Long stretches of rushing traffic. Soft bubbles of people talking, a child crying, doors shutting. He watched the interplay between two strangers as he sipped from his bottle. The hands waving commiseration, irritation. The smiles putting all right at the end. A repeat performance of humanity for his solitary audience. The long morning ride took him across one box of the map on minor roads, towards the larger arterial routes of the borderlands. He stopped when his energy ran out.

It had taken him months to work out the riding. Achieving the maximum output for the longest period without giving in to days of burnout. It didn't always work. The road got too hard or too fast. Wariness intervened, the need to camp and hide until the anxiety left him. There were curve balls.

You could call them that.

But on an ideal day he rode hard all morning on light food and much water, traversing a box on the map, and in the afternoon found a place to eat and rest for several hours. Pushing on until twilight for another box worth before finding somewhere to camp. Somewhere hidden. Vulnerable but free. Or somewhere paid. Safer but visible. Neither perfect.

It was the afternoon stop he cared most about. Fresh food and a long rest. It was the harder choice of the day. He could look at the map for hours and guess his best options, but he would never know until he got there. There was a way around this. The internet, a mobile. He saw other travellers using them all the time. But that would make getting in touch too easy. Too tempting. It was hard enough having to check the emails from Nat.

You don't need easier options. Look at yesterday.

Even a watch presented its lure. He'd started with a watch but ended up counting the hours, not just the days. He'd left the watch behind with Beau.

When he pulled the bike up on the outskirts of Gleisdorf he knew only that it was what he was most wary of, a small town. The empty windows of shops and houses like eyes on his back. He cruised around the streets looking for busy shops, buying the cheapest food he could find, and not leaving the bike for more than a few minutes at a time until he had all that he needed, heading back out the way he'd come. To known territory.

He hitched the bike, pulled out his map, and spread his main meal of the day out. A loaf of yesterday's bread, meat and cheese, and three sparkling jam encrusted pastries that had been put ready for the bin. He ate with relentless determination, feeling the sugar content hit his tired system. All washed down with a pint of milk. A full belly more potent than fear.

He needed that feeling to stop depression and despair from entering through a crack and swinging shut the door behind it. A dark room where he lost days, weeks.

That won't happen again.

After Ventoux. Cycling too hard and losing weight. A great yearning emptiness that he tried to out pedal. Until true misery settled upon him and taught him that the earlier emptiness had been hunger and exhaustion. Taught it hard. On the cusp of his first winter. South of Biarritz. On his way to nowhere. He'd lost nearly a stone since leaving England, was battling through the miles, was exhausted from the moment he woke up and wept himself to sleep at night. He'd looked into the savage Atlantic Ocean and wanted to end the whole miserable realm of his existence.

Yeah, that was a crap day.

The horizon full of storm clouds and ill intent. Crushing him, folding his knees until he was crumpled on the ground, sobbing. His pathetic effort to reinvent himself breeding a desperate, engulfing pit of self-loathing that could only be drowned by the waves. Hating the weakness that made him turn away from the waters and walk into the nearby town of Guéthary, the bike limp beneath his hand. Hating Nat for that one moment, because thinking of her made him unable to do it.

Thinking of her kept you going.

He caught the attention of an old woman clearing tables outside a tired looking café. She called him over, her French furious and fast beyond his understanding. Pulled him inside, sat him down, fed him. Simple plain food. Served with a drop of life in a red-rimmed glass.

Moth reached into the rucksack and pulled out the creased plastic bag of postcards. He flipped through them, found the one of Beau Jeanu's restaurant and lay back, looking up into the bright afternoon sky. It had taken him two long months to leave Guéthary. Beau had taught him the importance of fullness. He must eat, and eat well, in order to ride well. His meals might be stale, or dull, or cold, but he ate well. Once a week he slackened the pace and made a point of eating hot food.

He placed a protective hand upon the bike beside him and slid into a sugary doze. When he woke, the bike was sun warmed beneath his hand. He tucked the precious postcards away, packed and left.

The traffic increased with the afternoon. Everyone wanting to be somewhere else. He had to focus to stay safe. A spark swept along in the great current of homecoming.

He passed through Kirchbach, into darkness on the other side of the lights. Found a quiet road that lay beside trees, pulled off the tarmac, into a dusky field and settled down for the night. He opened the small notebook. Day 258. 16th March 2013. Kirchbach.

One line closer to that smug bitch of a date.

He poised the eraser end of the pencil over it. He didn't need to scrub it out. He could look it in the eye and ignore it.

Ride right over the top of it in eight days' time.

Rubbing it out now was too easy. Moth closed the book, tucked it beneath his head and shut his eyes.

He spent the next day trying not to think about that date. Traffic was in his favour, demanding his attention as he crossed the two main arterial roads south from Graz. Shuddering in relief as he cycled away from the clamour. Riding into the early evening the houses were full and glowing, family vignettes behind the windows. He ignored them all, pedalling hard to gain the final few kilometres of the day. He found a campsite on the far side of Wies. Fresh-painted and viciously trimmed from its winter renovation.

He pitched up and dragged himself into a long shower, the luxury of the water hypnotising him. Watching the dirt run in gritty swirls that gurgled down the drain in a froth of stolen soap. There was always a forgotten bottle of something in campsite shower rooms. The echoing room wasn't full enough to be warm and the mirrors failed to steam up as he shaved in front of them. His pores raised by the chill and complaining about the process of dragging a six-month-old razor across them. The hairs sprouting on his upper lip and on the corners of his chin were pale, insignificant things. Lighter than his hair, hopeful at best. But the act of shaving made him feel older. It gave power to his right to be there.

A man, wielding a razor, riding a bike, travelling alone.

He looked at himself in the small mirror, trying to reconcile the outward reflection with all that rattled inside him.

You look shiny.

His shaggy hair slicked back from his head and falling onto his neck where it dripped down his bare back and clean shorts. His face staring back, oversized in the small mirror.

Kit would see you in a different light now.

He raked his fingers through his hair. Used the damp cloth to rough-dry it. Dragged the comb through its tangled lengths. He still looked odd in the mirror. Moth pulled the beanie hat on. Glancing back at the mirror from the doorway he looked more himself.

The evening was gone, light reduced to discreet footpath guides. He put his second set of clothes in the washing machine, left them to run and headed back to his tent.

He hadn't stopped at a site for weeks. It always jarred. Going to sleep without fear of the creaks and whispers outside the tent offset by the overwhelming closeness of others. He kept his eyes down as he moved past the other campers engaging in socials. Indulging in the space, setting up a few patches apart and yet unable to resist company. Vans outnumbering the few tents. In the morning he would have the usual jobs to do of being on pitch, checking the bike and all his kit, finishing his laundry, repacking and getting a decent breakfast.

Tomorrow is three-hot-meals-easy-ride day.

He sat cross-legged in front of the gas burner, mixed milk and oats, stirring it to stop the mix from catching on the bottom. He scattered the sugar from one precious sachet over it, failed to resist temptation, opened another and added that. He crawled into his tent and bag, cradling the full pot of porridge. Head resting on the rucksack he ate the warm, sugary comfort. Scraping the sides clean, licking the spoon to a shine.

Writing in the book. Day 259. 17th March 2013. Wies.

Listening to the camp bedding down around him.

Leafing through the small dictionary and repeating German.

Lulling himself to sleep with the syllabic effort.

ISABELLE CAME through the front door as the last light of day was following Moth into the wooded hills. Casting itself through the coloured lead lights and ricocheting off the ceiling of the hallway.

In the kitchen she could hear Hester and Nat's muted voices. The steady patter of paws across the stone floor told her James was there. His sheepdog, Flynn, diverging from one person to another in incessant nervous attention. Upstairs the floors creaked, guests readying themselves for an evening's feasting upon the town. A lingering trace of lavender furniture polish tickled her nose and she held her breath and squinted her eyes to avoid sneezing. In the intensity of the scented moment she caught a waft of Earl Grey tea in the air and moved toward the study. Elsa had retreated to her own space for an hour's peace before dinner.

She padded down the corridor of the eastern wing, found the furthest door on the northern side, tapped twice and turned the handle. Inside, she found Elsa. Pouring tea into two cups, the fire glowing to keep back the evening chill. Isabelle stood in the doorway, taking in the room. Its ancient maps, its tall glass-fronted bookcases, the puddles of comfy chairs and small tables, arching lights reaching over them. It was the private shield of Elsa's public house and it wrapped itself around the tidy woman in her upright wing chair, all lights pointing towards her ailing eyes and the large pile of books waiting to be read.

'Darling, I'm so glad you're home.' Elsa's voice was as mellow, precise and presented as the house itself. She rose from her chair, slipping a bookmark between the pages and sliding her book into the gap between cushion and arm with the ease of one used to being disturbed. She moved to embrace Isabelle with delight until, pulling away and holding her at arm's length with the habit of a lifetime, scrutinising her face and form, she ended the enquiry with a long, 'Hmm.'

Isabelle knew what that meant. It meant she was thinner than when she'd left, whiter than four months in India would warrant from being locked in the vaults of the costume department and shrouded in too many layers of clothes and scarves.

'It's good to be back,' Isabelle effused. The door clicked closed behind her.

'Come, sit, we've a while before dinner. Enjoy the quiet, tell me everything.' Elsa moved to the table, picked up the teapot. 'How was India? Did you get out of the contract all right? Have you met the children? Have you seen James? And Hester?' Elsa passed her a cup of tea, sat and lifted her own cup in front of her chest, its steaming rim on a level with her chin, a smiling gap between cup and saucer.

'In any particular order?' Isabelle took her seat opposite

Elsa, stretching her feet out to the warmth of the fire. Feeling the inadequacy of her choices as she looked at the damp rims of her sandals.

Elsa's feet were clad in sensible tights and supported with low court shoes. Her knees concealed beneath a chocolate corduroy skirt. It was a simple A-line style and Isabelle had made hundreds of them for her, in varying earthy, lichen, berry and rustic tones, the hip width widening over the years whilst the length had never wavered up or down a single inch. They made the most of her short legs, the least of her plump bottom and complemented the immense collection of cashmere twin sets that constituted her all season wardrobe. Her face wore an undercoat of protective moisturiser, a casual scatter of powder, a flick of peach lipstick, making the best of what age was stealing away. Her grey hair was set in soft waves, held up with the gold spray can of starlets. Isabelle's hair fell across her face as she looked into the milky depths of her own tea.

'Your choice, but don't forget anything.'

'I've seen Hester,' Isabelle started with what she felt was closest to Elsa's heart. 'She was... more distant.'

'Hmm.' Elsa frowned into her teacup.

'I don't blame James,' Isabelle willed her voice to be calm, felt it wobbling like the flickering fire. 'I don't. They've always been close. It can't be easy for her, not with, well...'

'James talks to his sister more than is useful,' Elsa interjected, twirling her teacup round as she put it back on the hovering saucer, aligning the handle with perpendicular care. 'Some things should stay between two people.'

'He meant no harm by it,' Isabelle defended him, 'it's just his way.'

Elsa did not respond, her blues eyes blinking over the rim

of her cup. It was not Isabelle's place to tell Elsa about her own son. Isabelle glanced back at her own cup, a slight shimmer across the surface where her hand was less steady than she'd like.

'What chance is there for Hester?' Hester would not talk to her, and James and Elsa were careful to keep her confidence. Isabelle knew that what irked Elsa most was that James did not return the respect for privacy to Isabelle.

'No more or less than there has always been. She persists, so she must have hope.'

'It's a hard thing to give up hoping for.'

Elsa resisted being pulled into the conversation. 'And James?' The conversation moved on, 'What of you and James?'

Isabelle looked back at her, the question like sour milk in an old jug between them. The shimmer deepened to a ripple.

'No hope there at all, I think,' Isabelle told her, strangled for adequate words. Finding only quiet, useless ones, weighted with dread.

Elsa creased the skin between her eyes a little and turned the cup on its saucer a fraction further into inscrutable place.

'I'm not surprised, darling.' Elsa gave a small smile of support. 'You've been trying to tell him for a long time now.'

'He's not an easy man to tell.' Isabelle placed the cup and saucer on the table beside her, before it could give her away with a rattle. 'Though I should have been firmer, it should never have come to this. Again.' Her hands gripped the curving arms of the Victorian chair she sat in, her legs longing to curl up beneath her.

They sat in silence, Elsa sipping tea out of her delicate china, moving on fragile moment by moment.

'If you ever want me to leave, Elsa,' Isabelle started, her

voice not as strong as she'd hoped it might be. She gulped, tried to strengthen it and continue.

'Oh, tush,' Elsa interrupted her. 'Don't start that nonsense.'

'I have to,' Isabelle insisted. 'It's the least I can, please, I mean it... if there's ever a time, if you need me to leave, I would understand, I would.'

Elsa let her finish, the words trailing off inadequate to the task, raising her eyebrows. 'How long have you been practising that?

Isabelle grimaced, went to curl her leg up to her chest, resisted, and ended up crossing her legs into an awkward pose.

'Silly girl. It's not my place to tell my children how they should live their lives, or when they should go and stay.' Elsa shrugged her shoulders at the room around her. 'Riverdell has always been your home, even more than any of your cousins. And now you are needed, as well as wanted, and not just by me.' She savoured her words, choosing with the same care and precision she dressed with. 'What happens next between you and James is between you. James has the farm to think about and I don't wish to hear this nonsense about you leaving ever again.'

Isabelle wanted to persist yet knew she couldn't. True persistence would be to pack her bags and leave. But she didn't have the courage to do it. Any more than she'd had the courage to leave James in all the years gone by, the years between the first and this most recent crisis. She could only sit and wait to see what evolved, grieving over the mistakes they'd made along the way. On good days, in India, she told herself it was patience, humility. The kind that let life reveal itself. On bad days, here, she saw herself through Hester's eyes.

'So,' Isabelle drew a long breath. 'The children.'

'Indeed.' Elsa emphasised with a strong smile.

'What's next?'

'Such a difficult question.' Elsa poured a fresh cup of tea into her cup, held the teapot aloft for Isabelle, barely waiting for the shake of her head. 'I'm nervous of going wrong. I don't know these children, let alone how to make the right decisions for their future.'

'There's not much of the child left in Moth.' Isabelle focused on the fabric of her armchair, on the curve of its arm as it rolled over the front. The compulsion to speak and the urge not to rolling together like the paisley design of the fabric. 'I find it hard to think that anyone will make any decisions for him.'

'But decisions must be made. For the moment they're both on compassionate leave from school. Moth is expected back after Easter, though he refuses to talk about it. Natalie will join our old faithful as soon as she's ready.'

'And their home?'

'Being sold, we have yet to find out what will be left to them or not. The solicitors are being obtuse. I suspect David was living beyond his means, there may not be much left for them.'

Isabelle watched Elsa retreat behind her cup and saucer again. Cross her ankles over. Guarding the depths of that old pain.

'But you have legal guardianship?' Isabelle asked.

'I'm the only living grandparent, and there's no appointed guardian.' Elsa tapped one foot, observed it, stilled it. 'Though, for myself, I'm glad. Even under these circumstances, it's a wonderful thing to suddenly find grandchildren in my life.'

Isabelle looked at her, wondering how life could get so complicated. Elsa seemed to sense the fullness of what she'd said, its repercussions settling between them.

'And now, my niece home too.' The well-polished court shoe tapped against the carpet again. 'I meant what we talked about Isabelle. I need your help. I know you and James have some sorting to do, and sort it at last you must, but I need to know you're here to stay. Moth is, well, Moth is withdrawn. Hester is wrapped up in her own problems, so lost in them, in fact, I daren't ask anything of her. James believes the sun rises and sets behind his farm gates, and so you, I must ask. There is so much here I need your help with. Tell me you are home to stay?'

Isabelle sat immobile. Aware any movement of hers would be interpreted as a wriggle by someone who believed deportment spoke louder than words. An intense itch in her palm was not helping. Home to stay. Such a simple thought. Home. Staying there. Such impossible doubts that surged in her hands. Made them restless. The clock ticked in the silence, indecent in its confidence. She focused on the paisley swirls under her fingers. They had to go one way over the inside of the arm, and the other way on the outside. Joining at the invisible seam to maintain the illusion of harmony.

'Isabelle?'

'I'm here, yes, to stay.'

'Was the contract terribly hard to break?'

'It cost me,' Isabelle admitted. 'Rather a lot of favours and a substantial portion of my pay, but it's done.'

'It's well done, darling,' Elsa told her. 'And you have enough work piled up downstairs to ease the annoyance of it.'

'I can imagine.'

'Kate's joining us for dinner tonight,' Elsa told her. 'And Kit is expected in a few days, which will help no end with Moth.'

'Wise help?'

'I prefer not to think about that.' Elsa rolled her eyes. 'Moth talks to him, which is a start. How did you find Moth?'

'Guarded.' Isabelle crossed her legs over, folding her hands to rest on top.

'You did well to find him.' Elsa drained her teacup, put it upon the saucer. 'He keeps to himself.' She placed the cup and saucer on the tea tray. A firm clink in the act suggesting a whole range of necessities, beginning with the urgent need to move on from what she was doing.

Isabelle stood up, put her unfinished cup down on the tray, planted a light kiss on Elsa's cheek. 'See you at dinner.' Elsa was reaching for her book even as she left.

In the hallway, colours strangled one another as they crawled over the polished veneer of the piano. She checked the clock, fifteen minutes until dinner, moved to the piano and sat in the middle of the long stool. She lifted the lid and slid her fingers across the keys. Unable to play, but loving the cool feel of them, the clarity of their inky black and luminous white. Her eyes found the photo that always sat there.

Four young women sat upon the same stool. Looking toward the photographer, away from the music they were playing and frowning at the disturbance. It was an honest, unchoreographed shot. Elsa had an upturned book in front of her on the piano, a disturbed irritation on her face trying to make itself sociable, her hair an echo of Hester's in its mousy tail across her shoulder. Kate had a robe thrown over her swimming costume, her wet pale hair slicked back and darkened from the river, her throat exposed in the deep V-neck of the robe. A frown of concentration on her face as she stared at the keys. Rose, the stunning one, was sat at the far end. Flamboyant dark curls tossed high upon her head and cascading over her shoulder, a simple cream jumper emphasising the effect. Her forehead creased with a scowl of irritation, her tanned, olive skin the only feature that she shared with her son, Kit. Beth was tucked between Rose and Kate in the middle of the stool, the heavy golden hair falling across her face and streaming over her wrists. The barest shaving of a cheekbone and whisper of her lips to show she was looking up. The fleeting curve of the singular smile in the photo.

Isabelle lifted her own fringe away from her face, the identical hair but hacked shorter. It was her mother's smile that hooked her to the photo, the smile at the photographer, her father. The barest connection of a relationship that developed there and led all the way to her, where the connection lay broken. She laid the top back over the keys. It had sat silent for many years. The four friends parted by marriage, oceans, death.

She walked to the front door, longing for a last gasp of evening air before braving the kitchen. Staring across the drive she saw emptiness before she grasped the absence of Hester's car. Isabelle had not heard it leave and the solitary presence of James' battered Land Rover confused her, she had been sure of her tense presence at dinner. The night was less full of ghosts and she felt the remote stirring of hunger. Crisp steps upon the gravel caught her straying thoughts.

'Well, I wouldn't give even a penny for those!' Kate told her, crossing the courtyard at a sharp pace and pulling Isabelle into a mighty hug.

'Ever the wise investor,' Isabelle muttered in her ear, hanging on hard with delight.

'The solace of the single woman,' Kate retorted. 'How's the delightful family reunion going?'

Isabelle rolled her eyes. Kate walked straight past her and tossed her jacket from around her shoulders onto the nearest chair, where it began to slide off. She'd already moved past it to the centre of the hallway, where she could see all ways with equal clarity, fingers tapping on the round table. Isabelle picked up the coat and straightened it out on a hook, watched Kate flicking her hands through her hair to ruffle it up. Light bouncing off the array of silver blonde flicks, a large blue-lacquered ring shining from her index finger, staring down the eastern hallway with confidence as her wide trouser hems stilled around her ankles, settling back over the heels of her mules. It always amazed her how Kate could command casual slip-ons at the breakneck pace she lived at.

'Queenie!' Kate called into the gloom. 'Do get out of that damn tomb and come feed me!'

Isabelle smiled at the nickname. It infuriated Elsa as much as it amused everyone else, for Elsa did seem to model herself on the Queen once it was pointed out to you, deny it as much as she did.

'I'm starved, I tell you, I do hope she has a decent supper ready. I've been flat out all day, idiot tourists nonstop, all wanting to talk to me. Talk about what? I have no idea. Quee-nie!' Kate directed her tirade at Isabelle in Elsa's tardiness. 'Like I don't know it's a wonderful bloody town, like I don't know how the river curves around the whole bloody town, or the church sits right at the bloody top of it, like they aren't talking to me about what I bloody wrote about that brought them here in the first bloody place.'

'Really, Kate,' Elsa admonished, bouncing down the hallway on her courts, gathering up her friend by the elbow and herding her towards the kitchen. 'Like you don't know half those sanguineous tourists are paying my housekeeping as you curse them in the hallway.'

'It's so diminishing when you use those big words.' Kate grinned over her shoulder at Isabelle.

'That's the intended effect.' Elsa pushed her through the kitchen door.

Isabelle followed them, moved to the fridge, found ice, located glasses. Listening to the sweet bickering as she loaded glasses with sourness, a deft pour of gin, a long squeeze of lemon. Edging into the comfortable background. She laid the table with those few things that Hester deemed unworthy. The small dishes and spoons, the tea lights, the linen serviettes. James sat with Flynn tucked to his side and Moth and Nat came in together from the hallway as the hour struck. Kate drew her last deep breath of the evening and began talking. Where had they all been? What had they all done? Who had they all seen? Full of admiration for Nat's drawings, inspired as she told Moth the history of a new pathway he'd discovered.

Isabelle sat in her habitual spot, second from the end of five chairs on the back wall, looking out over the garden through the sink window with the driveway windows behind her. As they took their places, Elsa at the head of the table with Kate at her right hand, Isabelle was intrigued to watch Nat take the middle chair beside her, where she'd first found her sketching, and Moth the chair next to Kate, opposite her. It left James adrift, alone at the far end of the table.

'James, I'm too tired to shout down the table all evening,'

Kate chided him. 'I want to hear about the planting. Move up here.'

Isabelle focused on the table. Saw from the corner of her eye as he pulled out the chair next to Moth and sat down. Felt the stinging absence of the empty chair between her and Elsa. It felt like some weird game of musical chairs. Too many chairs and not enough players. The family trying to adjust around the two children who had entered the game late.

'Isabelle, you must come up and meet the new managers.'

Isabelle tried to concentrate. 'New managers?'

'Do at least try and pretend you're listening,' Kate stabbed her fork in Isabelle's direction. 'It does flatter me.'

'Sorry, Kate.' Isabelle saw James duck a smile at the table. 'I'll come up in the morning, I promise, and you can tell me all about it again. And I'll be a bit more focused.' Moth and James both smirked at her.

Isabelle made more of an effort to listen, but it sounded like waves to her. Crossing her thoughts, not penetrating them, rebounding off the jetlag barrier. Dinner passed in such controlled banter and afterwards they dispersed, Isabelle finding herself alone with Kate in the sitting-room.

They talked about the bistro, staff, customers, India, the cancelled contract, the flight home. Kate more relaxed by the time they were joined by James and Elsa, her mules discarded, painted toes tucked between the sofa cushions. The sky an indigo backdrop outside the undrawn curtains. The only curtains Elsa ever drew were in her study and her bedroom. Isabelle would have drawn every pair in the house for the pleasure of feeling the fabric in her hands.

'Where's Moth and Nat?' she asked Elsa.

'I have no idea about Moth,' Elsa replied, smoothing her skirt over her knees. 'We rarely see him after Natalie's in bed.'

'Something about our family dinners seems to put him in a bad mood,' James added, opening conversation. 'He needs a dose of fresh air afterwards.'

Isabelle didn't ask further. James had never absorbed his mother's disapproval of gossiping, and Isabelle loathed the idea of talking about the children as children, to be picked over by the adults in privacy. As she often prayed she was not discussed. She wondered where he was, glancing at the dark windows. Wondering if he were looking in even as they were looking out.

The solitary thoughts became luxuries and soon the room emptied to a stillness that demanded her attention. Kate and Elsa had left, and all that remained were James and the deep, unresolved silence. He sat in the chair opposite her, plucking at the frayed fabric of its tatty arm. The tarnished primrose threads unravelling from the pattern as he tormented them. It was another job that needed her attention.

'It's mild out,' he said. 'Would you like to walk?'

'Hmm, sounds good.'

The windows to the sitting room opened onto a long, high verandah, raised over the sloping garden by curving iron supports. James loosened the stiff wooden sash and she grabbed one of the many small throws that lay around the room. They stepped out and walked along the old wood, winter slipperiness in the green glaze underfoot. James whistled a sharp splinter into the night. There was the distant sound of gravel lurching and moments later Flynn came crashing through the shrubs that barriered the space between the house and the high walls of the entrance. Slipping ahead of them on the path.

The evening was laying a damp hand across the surface of

the grass and slipping her arm into James' seemed as natural as taking a cautious pace across the ground. Before it settled in the crook of his elbow, she felt a surge of dread. That she should not have done it, that she might never do it again, that she could not undo it.

They walked in silence across the lawns and to the river, turning to walk downstream along its bank. James slipped from her grasp to collect small pebbles along the way, tucking them into his pockets. She chose a few for herself. They passed beneath the road bridge and into the gated field that lay on the other side, walking until they found the fishing platform.

'You've repaired it.'

'Had to.' He walked onto the platform and stamped its new rigour. 'The number of kids who kept coming down here was making it dangerous.'

Isabelle stood beside him amidst the patches of new and old wood, shiny nails and rusted, James pooling his stone collection on the edge overlooking the water. She added hers beside them. His were superior, flat and round, grasped with an intentional eye. Hers chosen for their unusual shape, none sculpted for a task she had never been able to master. He threw his first few, warming up to the task. Flynn alert at his feet but soon forsaking the river to snuffle his way down the bank.

'Will you stay for a while then?'

'Of course.' She threw a stone, watched it sink without a single skip, feeling the words as wretched, ill-chosen things that plummeted to the bottom of the river.

He skipped several more, catching the feel for the evening, the river, the stones. She wondered how often he came here to do this when she was away, or if he did at all, if he found the time.

'You won't be stopping with me at the farm, will you?'

Here it was. A moment dreaded, avoided and not to be denied. A moment that seemed to demand more of her than she felt capable of saying, or of trying to explain. Inside, words twisted and jumped and tried to make a sentence. Words she had tried out many times in her head. A sentence that would make sense of this moment, make it profound and beautiful.

'No.'

His stones stretched further and further into the night, aching to reach the far bank.

'I remember the time I asked you,' skip, skip, 'if I could reach the far bank,' skip, skip, skip, 'would you marry me?'

'I remember.'

'You told me I would never reach the far bank.'

'I did.'

'I never stopped trying.' They both watched the last stone fall far short of its destination. Isabelle thought of the lighter peach stone that Moth had hurled straight and true across the river. She turned away from the rippling surface, sat down on the edge of the platform where it met the dampening ground.

James followed, sat down cross-legged in front of her, struggling with the pose but inching forward until their knees touched, and taking her hands in his he looked at her sad eyes and grim mouth.

'There's a girl who works in the agents' office,' he told her. 'I see her when I go to deal with the farm business, just for a few minutes, and she's always friendly.'

Isabelle felt tears come to her eyes and she looked at him in mute horror, her throat a swollen lump.

'She's from Poland.' He rubbed his rough thumbs over her palms, both of them focusing on the touch, easing the words. 'She's been working there almost two years now. I look forward to seeing her. I'm disappointed if she's out. Her name's Asha.'

The shape of what was happening took the form of this name, this other woman. Isabelle wondered how many times he'd looked forward to seeing her, and how many times he'd not done anything more. Thinking of them, hoping for them instead. She tried to swallow the lump, released the tears instead and closed her eyes against them.

'I think she's lovely, and I'm going to make a complete arse out of myself and ask her out for a date.' His voice was coarse, trembling, drawing shallow breaths. 'I want to ask you if that's ok?'

James would never do more than this. He would never ask her why, as was his due. Why she stopped overnight at the farm but never moved in? Why she worked away for months at a time? Why she wouldn't marry him? Why she couldn't bear the thought of having his children? Why she loved him so much, but not enough? He would just do this. Suggest a way forward, offer an option, see if it worked.

'I'd like that.' With her one free hand she wiped away the tears and looked up at him, took in his face with a freedom she knew would not be hers to use again. The blue eyes, the gentle mouth, the kindness so deep it etched lines in his skin. She raised her hand to feel his rough cheek, to push through his thinning hair. 'I'd like you to do that.'

He let out a huge slow breath. Looking down at her hands he leaned forwards and kissed her on the lips. A chaste kiss, a removal from what they'd known and touched with salt. Lay two fingers to her cheekbone and let them trail down to follow the line of her jaw, leaving her face chilled when he stood up, looking across the river.

'I think as you get older, you learn when to stop trying the impossible.'

He held a hand out for her but she shook her head and stayed cross-legged on the wooden platform, hunching into the blanket.

'Don't get cold, Mother will blame me.' He turned to leave her. 'I'll see you tomorrow, same as always. Goodnight, Isabelle.'

She listened to him walking away. Confident feet crossing the field towards the guests' car park, past the old barn, back to the house. A quick whistle, a dark shape fleeting to his side, staying tight to his legs. Leaving her listening to the silence he left. Through empty thoughts and glimpses of sadness, feeling the tightness of her throat begin to lessen and the grip around her stomach loosen. Weight lifted from her with each cooling breath and she wondered if James felt the same, step-by-step lightened of the sadness that had crept upon them.

Tiredness washed across her with a huge yawn. Hours of travelling, hours of anticipation, years of confusion, all ending in a few kind words. She shifted and lay down on the wood, hearing the water swirling beneath her, pulling the throw around her shoulders.

She let her eyes close against the bone-crushing weariness of it all. Stifled another yawn.

.   .   .

SHE WOKE STIFF AND COLD, as James had warned her not to. Shivered and pushed her cold aching body up from the wooden platform. Turning to find Moth's eyes upon her, resting on his haunches above her on the slope. She should have jumped or cursed him in shock, but neither reaction came to her.

'I didn't mean to wake you.' He shifted on his feet. 'It didn't feel right to leave you out here asleep by yourself.'

'Don't worry, I should be glad you woke me.'

'Seems a kinda odd place to sleep.'

'I wasn't sleeping, just resting a moment.'

'It's long gone midnight.'

'Hmm, and now I'm hungry.'

'Ok.'

She led the way home, through the basement door and up into the silent kitchen. Humming as she found a saucepan, milk, oats. Grabbing a biscuit as she began to stir the mix on the Aga, feeling herself warm through. Moth leaning against the window watching her. Both of them mediating the strangeness by pretending it was normal to be here in the middle of the night, aware of the whole house sleeping above them.

She found two earthenware bowls, filled them with the steaming porridge, poured maple syrup over the top and put them on the table, tempting him to join her. Sitting, she pulled her knees up to her chest, wrapping herself in the throw and settling into a blissful cocoon of sun-bleached old wool and steaming porridge.

'You don't seem surprised to see me.' Moth took his seat, pulling the bowl towards him.

'Should I be?'

'Elsa or Hester would have a fit if they knew I was out alone at this time of night.'

'Probably true,' she licked around the edges of her spoon. 'But I don't tell them everything I do either.'

'What's the matter with Hester?'

Isabelle looked at him and blinked, spoon frozen on its way back to the bowl.

'You don't take any prisoners, do you?'

He shrugged, refusing to be evaded. She tried again.

'What did Kit tell you?'

'That she can't have babies.'

'Then why are you asking me?'

'He told me to.'

She frowned into her bowl, wondering what else Kit had said.

'Nothing's wrong with Hester,' Isabelle dipped the melting syrup into the lumpy putty waves. 'But she feels there should be. As though, if she could find the problem, she could cure it, and so the problem has become not having a problem.'

'Right.' Moth looked at her over his bowl, spoon poised in disbelief. 'Well that's clearer, thanks.'

'Hester wants something in her life that people take for granted.' Isabelle knew she was being obtuse. 'Something she's always wanted and assumed would happen, but it won't. Not for any good reason that can be put right, but because it seems it can't happen.' Isabelle tried to explain it, looked across the table and, remembering Kate's favourite trick, turned it back on him. 'How would you feel if that were you?'

'I'd make it happen.'

Isabelle looked at him, heard his confidence, and felt a flutter of jealousy. Not because she could remember how it felt to have that sort of conviction but because he made her realise that she'd either never had it or not even noticed it slipping away.

'I suppose you think that sounds dumb, or childish?'

'No.' Isabelle listened to the high ceiling echoing back his defiance. 'I can't even begin to tell you how much I envy you that confidence.'

'What?'

'I don't think I've ever felt that sure of myself.' Her voice didn't echo. It sat without making a stir in the air between their two bowls, rising no higher than the steam and trailing away.

'Why does Hester have a grudge against you?'

'Oooh,' Isabelle tried to lighten the question. 'Not sure I even want to know what Kit told you there.'

'I didn't realise Kit had anything to tell me,' Moth pointed out. 'I never knew there was a problem between you and Hester until Nat said how weird you were with each other. Plus, she disappears after cooking dinner, just as you get here. She's always stayed before, if she's cooked. But I will ask him, when he gets here.'

She leaned back in her chair and pulled the wrap around her. Left the last of the porridge to cool in a lump in the bottom of her bowl, pushed aside by the spoon. She must remember how much children saw and shared with one another.

'Of course,' Moth was scraping his final spoonful out, 'you could tell me yourself.'

Isabelle thought about it. An intense, turgid thought; the uncomfortable shape of a detailed discussion about her relationship with Hester. Rising behind that solid block of painful thought an idea was hiding. That, perhaps, one of the few advantages to having ended her relationship with James might be, possibly, that such a conversation need never again happen. A hope that struggled against her desire not to dismiss Moth.

'I'll offer you a deal.' She stroked the handle of the spoon, feeling its warmth begin to wane. 'For each question you ask, you have to answer one of mine too.'

Moth scowled at her, surprising her all over again with its familiarity. She felt the age between them appear in a gulf, where she was on the far side of a world of adults he didn't trust, and close again as his frown became speculative, to a gap she might yet manage to cross.

'Do I get to know your question before you answer mine?'

'Only if you're prepared to wait for my answer until I've thought of it.' Isabelle spoke slowly, trying not to confuse herself.

'And you mustn't discuss any of this with anyone else.'

'And you must most definitely not discuss any of this with anyone else.'

They stared at each other across the cold porridge bowls.

'Ok, deal,' he said.

Isabelle leaned forwards in her chair, stretching her hand out across the table but, as Moth went to take it, he scrunched his face up and kept his hand outside her reach.

'What level of evasion are we allowed here?'

'I'm not sure,' she admitted. 'I guess if one of us isn't happy we'll call it.'

'Evasion about the evasion, and you call this a deal?'

'It's the best I've got.' She kept her hand held out.

He looked unconvinced but took her hand and they shook and grinned at each other.

'You might decide not to like me after you find out more,' Isabelle told him as she settled back in her chair.

'I was thinking the same myself.'

It was on the tip of her tongue to ask him what secrets he could have accrued in such a short life but the habit of her silence, and with it the considerable amount of thought that mired her words, saved her and the moment. Moth rushed on over her habits.

'So, in response to my question, "What's the matter with you and Hester", what will you ask me? And please tell me I won't have to wait a week for you to think of something?'

'No, you're in luck. I want to know why you're determined to dislike Elsa.'

'Oh. That.' Moth scowled at her. She smiled back but he wiped it off her face by saying, 'But I asked first, so you go first.'

Isabelle let out a long sigh, so much for leaving this conversation in the dying embers of her relationship with James.

'Hester wants something she can't have, and I've chosen not to have what she can't get.'

'Crystal clear, great,' Moth complained. 'That's not helping me understand anything.'

'Think it through.'

'She wants kids and, for whatever reason, can't have them.'

'Yep.'

'And you can, but don't want them?'

'Indeed.'

'That's it?'

Isabelle wrapped the throw tighter, nodded at him.

'Because you won't do what she can't?'

Isabelle resisted, wrapped in a tight moment that felt huge. Wanting to let it go and feeling the sense of deceit in leaving it there, the cowardice.

'Not won't do,' she added. 'Have chosen, adamantly chosen, to not do. To not have babies. Her brother's babies.'

'She's mad at you because she can't have kids and you won't have her brother's?' he offered. 'Is it just me who thinks that sounds pretty unreasonable? Not to mention sort of... I don't know... incestuous?'

Isabelle grimaced at the word. Here she was, trying to tell a person she had only met this day, a person wrapped up in both youth and his own problems, something that she had refused to talk about to anyone bar Kate. What idiocy had started this? She remained in miserable silence, waiting to see how he would twist the conversation to an even worse place from which she stood no chance of recovering it. Moth surprised her.

'I'm sorry. I lack manners.'

'How so?'

'I don't always think things through before I speak.' He sat back in his chair, so she had to squint to see him. 'How long have you and James been together?'

'Always. From when we were young.'

'As young as me?'

'A little older perhaps.'

'And all that time you knew you didn't want kids?'

'Pretty much.'

'How do you know something like that?'

'How do you know anything?' She ran her fingers along the edge of the table, feeling its well-worn grain. 'How do you know you don't want to settle, or to marry, or to run a farm.

How do you know the many things in life you aren't comfortable with?'

'I suppose you have to have some experience of them to know if you don't like them.'

Isabelle smiled a wide-eyed stare back at him, she'd said as much as it was in her to say. How to explain the overwhelming horror that pregnancy had brought on her? The sense of panic that becoming a parent made her feel. The sense of complete inadequacy. She couldn't face it herself, or explain it to James, or Elsa. Only Kate had ever understood. She wasn't about to peel off that plaster, even for the chance of earning his trust. The rest he would have to get out of someone else or figure out for himself.

'How about my question?' she asked.

'Evasion.'

'Absolutely.'

They looked at one another, assessing the moment and, with some relief, she realised he was prepared, at least for now, to let her off the hook. Perhaps if they came back to it, he might know her more. Judge her a little less.

'So?' she prompted again. 'You, and Elsa?'

'She reminds me of my father.'

'Ah.' She hadn't expected that. 'And it's not a nice recollection?'

'My father was an arse.'

Isabelle was shocked by the strength in the statement. Blinking in the lights trying to digest it and said, 'I sympathise. Genetic habits like that can be very unnerving.'

'You're not kidding.'

'Do you realise how like my father, or James, you are?' she asked.

'A little, perhaps. Not that much.' He shrugged it away.

'To you, maybe. We see ourselves in 2D. In a mirror or photo. It's hard to grasp how much similarity lies in the actions of a person.'

'So?'

'So.' Isabelle felt as though someone had dropped eggshells amongst the cold porridge. 'A person can seem familiar to us, who feels different to themselves.'

'What?'

'I mean, how like James do you feel?'

'Not. Like, at all.'

'Well good, because you're not.' In all their years together, James had never had a conversation with her like this. 'But you have some similar habits to him.'

'Like what?'

'You have the same way of standing up.'

'Standing up?'

'Yes,' she said. 'I noticed it at dinner. You both pull the chair up with your hands when you rise, to avoid it scraping on the floor.'

'No way.'

'Yes, and you both leave your left hand on the edge of the table.' Which had surprised her more because James wasn't left-handed like his sister, or Moth.

'Really?' he seemed stunned. 'What else?'

'I don't know yet, I've just met you after all.'

'I'm nothing like him!' Moth protested, adding to soften it, 'Not that I don't like him.'

'I'm sure, but that doesn't mean you want to be judged as the same from a few external similarities or habits.'

Moth went to speak but closed his mouth. Looked at his left hand sitting on the table and removed it.

'I get your point,' he said with all the irritation of youth proved wrong. 'Still, I might have good reason for not wanting Elsa to be like my father.'

'In any particular way?'

He didn't answer her. Straightening up in the chair, hiding his hands on his lap below the table.

'Maybe I want to know what made my father the person he was.'

Isabelle did not respond. Whatever David had been to his son, she knew the chance to work it out was gone. In her own experience of losing parents she had come to realise that death was a closed door. Beyond it you could never know anything, whilst the desire to know never abated. She couldn't stop wanting to know more about her mother, she couldn't stop wondering if she could have been closer to her father. Questions she couldn't answer which mutated into a thousand other queries themselves, most of them focused on what part of her was like them.

'I think,' she tiptoed around the eggshells, 'what worries you might be less to do with Elsa, and more about yourself.'

Moth refused to look at her. It wasn't unpleasant. It was a private silence, not angry or brewing and she enjoyed it. The kitchen soothed by the popping metallic sounds of the Aga, the house brooding over them.

'I think,' Moth echoed her, looking up at last, 'what worries Hester is a lot more to do with her, and less about you.'

To which response she had none. Not even sure if he was being genuine or mocking her. They sat a few more moments in silence and Moth stood to leave. He was halfway up from the table when he realised that he'd grasped the chair and lifted it in the way she had described. He frowned and she tried to hide the smile it caused and failed.

'Perhaps you could keep any more observations like that to yourself?'

She shrugged back, amused and unrepentant. Watched him gather his bowl and take it to the sink, ever polite.

'Night, Isabelle.'

'Goodnight, Moth.'

KIT's good mood of the day was being tested.

Lunch had been a talkative affair, with Elsa and Kate doing most of the talking. His efforts to mention the meteoric shift in their lives had been drowned in talk about silverware, guest bookings, or some irrelevant rural gossip, which distracted him with more effect than he wanted to admit. News about the Briards' retirement defection to France, and the daughter-in-law's spending on the refurbishment niggled him with a failed opportunity he couldn't help but tot up.

Isabelle pushed her food round her plate and ghosted herself out of the room at some point that no one even noticed. As Moth and Nat left the dining room with James to go to the farm, Hester took up the gauntlet.

'Of course, I suppose you approve of all this.' She swiped a crumb off the table onto the floor. 'You've been waiting for Isabelle and James to fall flat on their faces for years.'

'Of course I approve of it.' He stretched back in his chair. At last. Someone prepared to have a fun chat. 'I'm delighted about it. I'm surprised you're not.'

'Why on earth would I be happy about it?' Hester asked him, tense and upright on the far side of the table from him.

Kit noticed Kate and Elsa weigh up the atmosphere. Elsa blinked, Kate grimaced, and he could see he was about to be abandoned before they even got to their feet and started to collect the empty plates.

'You've been disappointed in Isabelle being James' girl-friend for as long as I have.' Kit laced his fingers and stretched them behind his head, watching as Elsa scurried for the door and Kate shook her head in amusement and took another plate before leaving. 'I'm confused that you aren't celebrating the event. You know, bit of a bachelor party, invite all your divorced friends to meet him, perhaps get him online dating.'

'I'm glad you're amused by all this,' Hester told him. 'I'm devastated for James. How could you think otherwise?'

'But not for Isabelle though?'

'James has put his whole life into that relationship, he's tried everything to make her happy, and now she throws it all in his face and leaves him. He's being very stoic about it, but I think it's despicable of her.'

'Yes, James has always been pretty stoic, I'd say that.'

'What does that mean?'

It was a strange dose of misery, Kit thought, the one that affected Hester. She was so caught up in herself she'd lost all scope of reasonable thought. There weren't many people Hester could talk to, they couldn't cope with the bitterness that drenched every word she spoke. In her own way she was becoming as quiet as Isabelle. The two of them prancing around each other, holding their thoughts in and dashing for the nearest exit while any bystanders ducked their heads and changed the subject or the scene as quickly as possible.

'Oh Hester, come on, don't be so blind!' Kit complained. 'James hasn't been stoic, he's been idiotic. He's known all along what the score was but didn't want to accept it.'

'You mean she's kept him dangling and now dumped him just as he's starting to get a bit less of a catch!'

'Well, I know he's going bald,' Kit agreed, running a smug hand through his hair. 'But I think that's a bit harsh overall.'

'James is a wonderful man. Any woman would be thrilled to have him.' She scrunched her napkin into a ball, released it, and watched as it loosened out upon the table. Snatched it up, folded it into rigid lines, and tucked it under her plate to pinion it. 'Any other woman would have married him and had those babies. She's so selfish I can't bear it.'

'Any other man would have accepted she doesn't want to get married, or have babies, and moved on.' Kit thought she would have chewed on the tablecloth if she could get it to her mouth without bending her back. 'Damn selfish of him if you ask me, I've been waiting long enough for him to get the bloody hint.'

'Well you'd be the one to know about selfishness.'

'Because I think people should give me what I want?' Kit asked, smiling at her. 'Even when they don't want to?'

'Exactly.'

'And how is the latest round of IVF going, sweetie?'

Hester gasped. Looking like she would slap him if she could gather breath to do so. Kit sipped from his wine glass and smiled over the tilted rim. Her husband was refusing to engage in a fifth attempt at IVF, insisting they learn to be happy with their life as it was. Elsa would have gasped too if she knew he'd imparted that bit of knowledge she'd armed him with. But Hester should have known not to get into this conversation with him.

'I wouldn't expect you to understand.' Hester told him. 'How like you to try and confuse my life with Isabelle's. I suppose, for someone like you, it must seem somehow connected.'

'Someone like me?' Kit was beginning to enjoy himself. In the way it is only possible to enjoy arguing with someone you have known most of your life and never liked or disliked. Sometimes, when they were drunk, he and Hester would have long close conversations about life and its mysteries, other times they would end up loathing each other. He had a sense of where it was going today.

'Um, you know, someone without any true sense of purpose in life.'

Kit laughed. 'You mean someone whose sense of purpose in life is so different to your own that it's unfathomable to you?'

'I'm sure in your head you think you have some purpose, and morals.'

'Hester, honestly, it's such a shame.' Kit took another sip of the wine, watching as her fingers tapped on the napkin, its softness padding the sound of her irritation. Hester had beautiful hands, fine long fingers and fragile wrists. Hands that belied the frigid plainness she displayed everywhere else. Hands that should have been wrapped round a paint-brush, or a baby, or a lover, or anything other than her own emptiness. 'Someone as intelligent as you are, incapable of thinking there are other life choices than your own.'

'I'm quite capable of seeing other life choices.'

'Oh, I'm sure in your head you think you can.'

'You are being deliberately provoking.'

'You are being deliberately stupid.'

'Look, I'm not here to play this game with you, Kit.' Hester thrust backwards in her chair, wrapping her arms across her chest. 'I think you should know how disappointed we all are with Isabelle. She's got a real nerve coming back here, dumping James and expecting us all to get on with life as normal.'

'I think you should stop trying to convince yourself that other people agree with you,' Kit told her. 'I know it would be comforting to think that your mother, and your brother, and all the rest of your family and friends feel the same way you do about Isabelle, but I think I have a moral duty to point out that's a complete load of self-satisfying bullshit.'

'I don't know why I'm surprised that you're backing her up!' Hester threw her hands up, letting them fall onto the table with a loud slap. 'You're as bad as she is.'

'Thank goodness for that, I'd hate to be as good as you are.'

'I don't think you have to worry about that.' She pushed her chair away from the table with a savage dig into the old carpet that he had to resist the urge to wince over, and stood up. 'I should have known not to expect any kindness from you, let alone reason. But you can tell Isabelle from me, she's not welcome here any longer. She should have the decency to leave.'

'That's fine, I'll just run that by Elsa first, shall I?' Kit asked her, smiling again. 'Though of course you could try telling her yourself? After all, I'll probably mess up the message.'

Hester looked hard at him again. They both knew it was false bravado.

'If she were decent, she would have left,' Hester spat out at him. 'But I suppose, if she were decent, she would have had those babies.'

'Because of course it would be so much more decent for her to be a miserable mother than a happy woman.'

'I don't know how she can live with herself.'

'Happily, if you'd give her a chance,' Kit told her. 'It's you who can't live with her. Perhaps you should stop deluding yourself that it's anything other than your own jealousy and bitterness you see when you look at her.'

'And I wonder what it is you see, Kit?' Hester shoved her chair under the table, stood with her hands on the curving back. 'I suppose happiness for you is no further than the end of your prick and where it reaches to. Good luck finding happiness in that quarter, you're going to need it.'

Hester left the room in as mighty a huff as any he had ever seen, a grey cloud storming through the house. Not that he thought for one minute it would last beyond the end of the corridor. He felt flattened. His best effort at being a sounding board to her misery leaving him stung. She was like Lou, both nursing old wounds like rotten eggs. Though even Lou couldn't hold a grudge for as long as Hester. He hoped James would pull his finger out and get laid by someone else quick enough to disperse Hester's resentment. He hoped that she would be plump and stupid, and full of good will towards all women, and get herself knocked up so quickly and so repeatedly that Hester might at last understand there was no relief from her own misery.

He gathered a few stray plates and headed for the kitchen. There were flowers to deal with, and a few details of his own that needed sorting before he tracked Isabelle down. Hester's stinging tirade had at least reminded him of that.

KIT FOUND her sat at her garden table. Surrounded by potted plants and the strewn remnants of the paper she'd been attacking.

The wind had caught the irrelevant sections of life and tossed them among the tangled gaps of the flowerpots where they struggled to escape. There was a faint odour of horse manure emanating from the terraces which stretched over three levels and around the corners of the hodgepodge of roof lines that constituted the garden. Kit's nose wrinkled as he approached, the present he'd brought tucked in his pocket. She had her ancient samovar on the low wall beside her, chipped cups arranged in disorderly piles beside it, looking like an old despot sitting on an egg waiting for it to hatch.

'Lunch was fun,' Kate told him, refusing to look up from the papers.

'Yes, I thought so,' he agreed. 'Though everyone else seemed a bit wound up if you ask me.'

'I should make a point of kicking your arse.'

'Yes, but you know you enjoyed it too.'

'You're a big bastard pebble.' She looked up at him with an evil grin. 'I do love watching your ripples spread.'

'The waters are so stormy round here I feel redundant.'

He pulled out an old wrought-iron chair and sat down with a wobble while Kate poured him a chipped cup's worth of warm tea. He dropped a sugar lump in its depths and stirred in a desultory slump.

'Oh, don't be maudlin. I'm sure there's plenty of mayhem you can cause, even with Hester on a self-destruct course that doesn't need you.'

'The misery of that girl is beyond reasonable.'

'Selfish pig,' Kate laughed at him.

He changed the subject. The word selfish was getting a little too worn for one day. 'And what of you anyway?'

'Me?' she asked. 'What about me? Here I am as usual, shoulder to all, lover to none!'

'You dumped him?'

'Oh Kit, he was sooo boring!' Kate wriggled in her chair, crossing her legs, flashing her eyes like a teenager caught in parental crossfire.

'No. He was charming, intelligent, motivated. He was lovely!'

'Well, exactly, I mean what do you expect? Lovely has never been my type.'

'I went to a lot of trouble on that one.'

'Kit, for Christ's sake, he was into microbrewing!'

'You run a bloody pub,' he told her, putting the spoon on the table. 'How was that not a bonus?'

'It's a bistro, thank you,' she corrected. 'And people come here to drink beer and relax, not to listen to my erstwhile boyfriend bore them about how he makes it.'

'Bore them, or bore you?'

'Look I know how hard you tried, and it was really sweet of you, but...'

'... but nothing, I spent hours, days, going through internet sites to find him and you were ungrateful...'

'... if you would just listen for a moment...'

'... just because you had to get off your arse and travel to see him...'

'To bloody Dorset!' Kate burst into his head of steam. 'Three sodding connections by train. Though that's not the point.'

'Well what is?'

'He was useless in bed!'

'You're just saying that.' Kit sipped his tea, refusing to meet her eyes.

'No, I mean it,' she grinned at him, knowing she had the upper hand. 'He hated having the lights on, he never took his socks off, and he thought I'd lost my glasses when I tried to give him a blowjob.'

'You're making that up,' Kit mumbled into his tea.

'He had a dick the size of a thimble.'

'You have too large expectations.'

'And a wart on the chin.'

'Total bollocks,' Kit told her, but he was grinning back at her.

'It's not my fault anyway.'

'Oh, of course it isn't.'

'You set a standard that's hard to follow.'

'Obviously,' Kit agreed. 'But you did promise to try.'

'Yes, but only because you got me drunk,' Kate pointed out. 'And I can't even remember what your reasons for dumping me were.'

'I feel the need to offer loyalty to Isabelle.'

Kate roared with laughter. 'You do talk some crap.'

'You talk it right back.'

'You can't dump me now I'm old you know, it's most ungentlemanly of you.'

'It's a constant complaint I get.'

Kate pursed her lips into a tighter line, let out a breath and looked unblinkingly at him for a long moment. He found himself staring into the unconvincing depths of the tea to escape her thoughts. Wishing he hadn't put the spoon down.

'You think Isabelle splitting up with James is going to change this thing you have with her?'

'I do.'

'Kit, come on. Isabelle? You? Commitment?' Kate reached

a leg out towards him, nudged his shoe. 'That's not a great bet.'

'You can't know that for sure.'

'Can't I?'

Kit bit back his response. She knew where to sting him.

'Not totally.'

'It wasn't James. It won't be you. She doesn't know what she wants herself to know who she wants to be with.' Kate's forehead was creased with concern, the wind ruffling her hair, stirring the lost papers.

'You sound like Hester.'

'In a different way, but yes, I suppose.' Kate softened her voice, genuine affection filling her face with lines and thoughtfulness. 'She needs time, not a new relationship. And you're no one man band yourself.'

'I have a proven track record when it comes to commitment.'

'Yes, but hardly a soloist.'

Kit avoided responding. The tea tasted bitter after the wine at lunch.

'Anyway, that's your realm to explore.' Kate drew a line under the conversation, sidling her toe up the outside of his calf. 'What about me? I'm lonely Kit, are you going to abandon me? It's not easy fishing when you get older you know.'

Kit looked at her shoes, abandoned on the stone, her bare feet reaching out for him. Feet she looked after, pampered. Their age sheathed in moisturiser, touched with a pearled polish. Blush. A colour he used whenever he could. It was the inner lining of the lips, the moist invite of a tongue, the sole of Kate's pedicured foot. It was his secret colour, the one he slipped in to as many designs as he could, a quiet shade that added warmth to many frigid rooms. He reached his hand out, caressed the inner sensitive curve of her foot, pulled it towards him. Lowered his mouth, kissed her ankle.

What mattered was that he'd tried. He felt free to pursue Isabelle having tried his best for Kate. Kate knew now, she knew where his intentions lay. All the years of their secret relationship deserved that much honesty between them.

'What would my mother say?' he teased her.

'Not much, she's dead.'

Kate never had been one for nostalgia. He got up from his chair, reached into his pocket to take out the small gift, and knelt to offer it to her. She beamed at him and unwrapped it to turn a small box over in her hands.

'A vibrating bullet?'

'Trust me, you're going to love it.'

'I do hope so.' She leaned forward and kissed him on the lips. 'I can't tell you how dull it's been without you.'

He pushed his hand to caress her breast, feeling the nipple harden through her clothes.

'How long before you need to go to work?'

'I arranged extra cover for the start of the evening,' she told him between kisses.

'I think Isabelle is pretty much locked up in the work-room.' He pulled her up out of the metal chair and wrapped her in a comforting, familiar cuddle, his dick straining its way towards her.

Kate tucked her feet into her shoes, holding onto him while she righted their abandoned soles, then walking away towards the flat entrance. A pep in her step and a swing to her rump that swished through to her trousers, making his dick leap forward after her.

After all, it was only polite, to say farewell properly.

7

CLIMBING JACK COMMON, LUDLOW. OCTOBER 1960

I 'm pretty sure I could blame Rose or Kate for everything that went right in my life.

In the case of Richard it was definitely Rose's fault. She was the one that left the gate open. Townies. Honestly.

We were on our way up to the bird tower one Sunday morning, in late October. To celebrate Kate's birthday. Father had given us a special meal at Riverdell the night before. He'd gifted her a stunning necklace, from his first wife's jewellery collection. Sixteen was a milestone in Father's eyes and he'd made sure we knew it. How proud we were, sat round the dining room table, drinking wine, eating cake. We all of us knew we'd get as good a birthday celebration in the coming year; Kate's had set the standard. On the way up to the tower, on the twenty-third, her actual birthday, we were all a lot less pretty. Rose and Kate both had tempers to match their hangovers and Beth was white with lack of sleep and stomach cramps. Beth's periods had started last and hit hardest, they used to wipe her out for half the month. Whatever painkillers we could all find by then were hers to have, but they hadn't mixed well with the celebration champagne.

But I was determined we needed the fresh air and the compulsory birthday visit to our gang hang out. So I charged on ahead, far enough that I could justify not hearing their complaints. I reached the base of the final climb through heather and gorse, across the open common, and had time to catch my breath. It was wet. Everything was wet that year. If the summer before would stick in my memory as one of the finest of our youth, that autumn all I can remember is the filth half way up my trousers legs and turning round to see Kate throwing up in the gorse. Her sick looking like out of season flowers on the spiky bushes.

Which is when I saw the cattle. Nosing their way through the gate we'd come through and idling up the path behind Rose and Beth, who were walking arm in arm and dawdling their way behind Kate. I threw down the basket in despair and hollered at them.

'You left the gate open, you idiots.'

For two intelligent girls they looked between me and the happily chomping cattle making their way up the path with total apathy. Idiot townies, didn't they realise that once they reached the common we were stuffed? Kate, who was closer, and had sense enough to act, was speaking only to the bushes.

I took off at a run. And I could run, back then. Cross-country captain. I got to the cattle as they were nearing Beth and Rose and yelled at them. Grabbed a stick from the nearest hedge and thrashed the air. Even Rose looked impressed. Cattle are big close up, easily intimidating. But Father had taken me often enough to the home farm. I'd watched Albert handling the herd. We're bigger to them than they are to us, he'd always said. If I could keep them on the path and herd them back through the gate, we'd be saved. If they bolted past me, well, we'd be out here 'til Christmas rounding them up and Heaven knows Father would make me to do it too.

I never saw Richard until I'd hollered the last one through the gate and shut it with relief. Sagging on the gate watching the cattle mooch their way back down the field.

'You know you shouldn't use this gate to access the track?' he told me, taking off his cap and screwing it up in his hand.

He was splattered in mud and looked as out of puff as me. His trousers sticking to his thighs with mud, a great splodge of it on his waxed waistcoat, a streak up his left chin where he'd taken his hat off. Floppy brown hair falling over his blue eyes. Both of us gasping for the air to start an argument.

Later, I'd found out he'd been late out of bed to move the herd and panicked when he realised they'd found the gate unlatched. The ground, sodden from all the rain that year, and poached to the stone, had been slick and treacherous and tipped him over as he tried to cross the field.

I could have pulled rank. He was a tenant on Father's land after all, Albert's eldest son and barely a year older than me. But he spoke the truth. We'd only come this way because the girls wanted to go the shortest route and I'd have been the first to tell off a member of the public for leaving a gate open.

'Why don't you come over here and tell me again,' I suggested. I wasn't usually so bold, but I'd singlehandedly averted a bovine disaster and was pumped with exhilaration like I'd run the Junior Nationals. 'I'll cake the other side of your face in mud while you're at it.'

Then I turned and strode off back up the hill, trying to ignore the stitch threatening my side.

He threw a perfect shaped ball of mud over the gate and right at my retreating backside. I squealed when it struck and turned round in fury, ready to let loose all my superiority. But he was already walking away, grinning back at me and waving his cap in salute as he sauntered off. By the time I got to Rose and Beth I was livid. And they just grinned some stupid more.

'Oh, stop it, you useless townies,' I shouted. 'It's all your fault in the first place.'

'You're welcome,' Rose told me as I huffed past them. 'Get the tea ready, Queenie.'

I stopped to drag Kate off her knees.

'Why do you smell of cowpat?' Kate asked, clutching her stomach again.

'Cowpat?' I demanded. I tried to look at my back, and the stench rose from there. Fresh moist cow dung. All over the seat of my pants.

'Why are you smiling?' Kate asked, gagging. 'You stink.'

8

Moth woke late. Full of contentment and simmering pleasure. The tent warming in the sun.

He resisted moving on the hard ground. Waking further, remembering. It was the smooth, bump-free ground of a well-managed campsite. He stretched into his good feeling.

Outside the glow of his canvas existence he could hear people stirring. Campervan doors opening, voices calling, children laughing. The smell of breakfast stirring his appetite. Security flooding him with desire. Sensations that surged straight to his dick and brought his hand to comfort it. He came with convulsions. A bursting need for someone, anyone, to hold. Stunned in the aftermath. Breathing through clenched teeth.

That was better than normal.

Not one thought had interrupted him. No memory. No anger. A pure flood of desire. For that ragged moment he considered what it might be like to share that with someone. There, around him and upon him. Hands touching him.

You touching them.

For that split, aching moment, he remembered her, and his own desire, and the freezing water. Then the moment collapsed in a pickled stench. Into the looming pit of other thoughts. He twisted in the bag, pulled himself up.

He crawled out, stretched and took stock. He'd pitched furthest from all the amenities, in the far corner of a field.

You might as well have hung a 'fuck off' sign on the bushes.

It gave him a good view of all the others. He scanned with intent. He knew what he wanted. Not a family. People with kids were wary of male strangers. Not another single person. Somewhere between wary, competitive and flirtatious, single travellers asked too many questions. He found it.

English plates, older van, not too shiny. Perfect.

The quiet retired couple. Touring the continent in winter and heading home for the summer. He grabbed his porridge pot, slung the sleeping bag over his shoulder and headed for the wash facilities. They'd parked two pitches away from it. He could see the door open and steam escaping. The old man fussing at details only he could see. The woman wandering between the cooker and the doorway, spatula in demonstrative hand. Talking, knowing he wasn't listening.

The sleeping bag went in the wash as he pulled his wet clothes from the night before out and put them to dry. He had a quick brush up in the shower room, washing off the smell of spunk and the fog of a deep night's sleep. He sauntered past the van, hands full, dropping the clean porridge pan on the gravel outside their patch. Two heads turned to face him.

'Damn.' He grabbed it back up, looking around. 'Sorry!' he called. 'Didn't mean to disturb your peace!'

'Not at all,' the man called out. 'Val makes enough noise to wake the entire camp anyway!'

'Ken,' she said. 'Do be quiet before I burn your toast.'

'Wouldn't be the first time!' Ken told him with a wink.

'I wouldn't mind a woman burning some toast for me,' Moth returned.

'I wouldn't mind burning the toast for someone a bit more appreciative,' Val chirped back.

It was enough, accents claiming them as kinsmen. They started to talk, moving those few hesitant steps towards one another.

'I'm Tom,' Moth introduced himself.

They invited him for breakfast and, though the toast was a bit burnt and the egg a bit soft, it was a plate full of free food. It tasted wonderful and he ate the lot. Accepting extra toast and drinking three mugs of tea. He could feel himself swell to the size of a real person again.

First hot meal of the day done.

He shared road talk with Ken while Val cleaned up and went to put her own washing on, she even put his sleeping bag to dry while she was gone. It was what they needed, a brief break from their own company and some shared enthusiasm in the life.

Fair price for the food. Don't linger too long.

He told them he was heading home from working in Greece, looking up friends on the way. They commended him for cycling the long journey, admiring his youth and energy, and bemoaning the loss of their own. It was gone 10 am by the time he took his dry washing back to the tent and began to take it down. He left the campsite with a wave at Ken and Val. Glad for the campervans of the world, and the opportunities they carried.

Gladder to leave them behind.

The morning ride was easy. The sun warm, the wind cooling and the traffic kind. Sixty km to Bleiburg for lunch, heading for Eberndorf by the end of the day. He was skirting below the south eastern curve of the Alps. Away to his right he could see the mountains rearing up. He wouldn't make it that far. At Eberndorf he would turn south and head into Slovenia. He wanted to ride along the Adriatic, before turning inland and heading across the top of Greece. Thoughts of Kit were gone. Disturbing thoughts of home and what lay behind.

Your biggest challenge today is lunch.

The smaller foothills stretched away from the road as it wound through the valley. Taunting him. He'd ridden the Alps before, on the northern side.

Mountains suck.

It had been a battle. Still recovering his riding stride after his winter stop with Beau, he'd had to admit defeat, retreating to longer, lower roads. It had left him frustrated, with a sense of failure. He'd given up. Beaten by a stronger opponent. Thoughts of Kit stirred through the irritation. Something he needed to put right, man up to. He pushed the thoughts down into the pedals.

Not yet, another time. When you're stronger. Older.

The mountains shadowed him all the way to a late lunch on the outskirts of Bleiburg. The sense of failure pulling out the maps on the scratched plastic of the table in the roadside café. Perhaps he could fit in one last attempt at the mountains before he headed away from them. He had no pressing urgency. His time was his own.

The mountains are north. You're going south.

He wouldn't go north. His curious fingers read the dark

ridges of height on the map, found the region south of Sillian,
lacing through the heart of the Dolomites. Small roads with
high passes and weather restriction warnings. Arrows and
mountains spattered across the page. They were almost
south. Only a little west.

You don't have anything to prove. Not to him, not to
anyone.

He sat in the busy café on the road that snaked its way
along the border with Slovenia, lingering over the options.
He'd eaten cheap hot food and plenty of it. Potatoes with
steaming vegetables and thick sauce, a floundering hunk of
meat he'd struggled to identify. Enough salt in the sauce to
overwhelm any doubts. Alternating between the map and the
pudding menu, trying to decipher both. Focused on the
options to the point that the purpose was drowning. The
mountains an itch he tried to ease into the plan.

An itch? You sound like Kit. Get real.

He settled on the plum pudding and looked up to catch
the waitress's eye. To find her watching him, eyes flickering,
chin tight under her pursed lips. A ripple went down his
back. He looked round to check the scene.

The café was still busy but hushed. Lost in the maps he'd
missed two sets of road police arriving. They were busy
ordering from the other waitress. Sat at a table between him
and the doorway. His mouth went dry, and he moved to put
the map away. A folding process that could never be rushed,
the steady cross and re-cross of paper into a shrinking pile.
The rustling louder in his anxiety.

You shouldn't have got them out in the first place.

He shuffled closer to the window, the booth obscuring
him, pulling the hat further down around his hair. Out in the
parking lot their two cars were parked central outside the

doorway. From under his hat he watched one, then another, glancing round.

Well-trained observant eyes.

He could feel the other customers retreating into themselves. Feeling guilty, most with no reason.

Unlike you.

He regretted the too long focus on the map. He should have seen them pulling in, been long gone before they were heading for the doorway. The corridor to the toilets was behind him. A possible way out.

They're going to notice if you disappear in the bloody toilets.

A probable route for the officers stuck in their cars all morning. They'd want a piss as soon as they'd ordered.

They're going to walk right past you.

The girl who'd served him stopped at his table on the way back from another customer.

'Dessert?'

She asked him in English. Moth winced. It was his fault. The morning with Ken and Val had made him slip, ordering in English without thinking.

You dick.

'No thanks,' he murmured, forcing a smile. 'The bill, please?'

'You don't like?' She spoke in a monotone voice at a low level. She had taken his order without a murmur. Now she seemed to linger, angling her hip against the table edge, blocking his view of the police.

'No,' he said. 'Just full up, thanks.'

'I not mean the food,' she said, putting her pad away and tucking the pen back into the top of her head where it stuck out from her ponytail.

Moth looked up at her. She flicked her eyes over to the tables behind her, never moving her head a fraction. Her body stiff where it had been indifferent, shoulders creeping up around her ears.

She's nervous too. You know all about that.

She was younger than he'd first noticed, perhaps not much more than his own age.

Young and pretty, not that you noticed. Looking at bloody maps.

She was sucking the upper corner of her lip in, waiting for him to respond, uncomfortable with policemen in her café. Her hands tucked in her apron pocket. She might be able to help.

You don't know her. Be careful.

'I don't like,' he told her, and flicked a finger to the map he'd folded away, and out through the window to the bike tied against a rail, hidden from the road in a corner of the lot behind bushes.

'Ah.' She glanced at the corridor leading to the toilets, back to him and scowled an unmoving negative at him.

Moth tried not to grit his teeth. Better they think he was flirting with the waitress.

'You have dessert,' she said. 'Wait ten minute, bus come, you go quick to get it.'

'I can't leave my bike,' he told her.

'I look after bike, you come in one hour. They will be gone.'

Moth squirmed on the sticky vinyl seat of the booth. Leave his bike here. With all his stuff.

It's not a great option.

But otherwise he had to get up, walk out past them and let them watch as he got on the bike.

That's not great either.

'Plum pudding for you,' she told him and went off to get it.

Too slow dick, now you're stuck.

Moth forced a smile on his face. Forced himself to look after her as she walked towards the kitchen. Feigning interest. Sliding the maps off the table and onto the seat beside him.

She came back with a fresh mug of tea as well, and the bill for all his food. He handed the money over in silence. He felt so much the tourist he thought it must be screaming from his temples.

You look nothing like a tourist. Stop freaking out.

He was glad for the excruciating packing choices he'd made all those months ago. His clothes second-hand and worn, colourless, identity-drained. The cycling shorts hidden under plain combats. The trainers over clip shoes. The helmet left tucked on the bike. He ate the pudding, not sure which part of it was plum. Trying to look like he was enjoying it. Watching for a bus pulling up at the stop outside. There were people waiting and he saw them stir, gather bags, rise and hustle forwards. He gathered his rucksack, shuffled towards the edge of the booth, feeling the pudding heavy in his stomach.

At the other end of the cafe the kitchen door snapped open and both waitresses came out together, their arms piled high with plates. Behind their busyness he slipped past, out of the door, and ran across the tarmac to catch the bus as the last person boarded.

He paid for one stop and stood at the front, hoping it would be a swift one. In the end it was a ten-minute bus journey along the road to the next village.

You look a right idiot stood here. The whole bus staring at you.

Moth flung himself off in a sweat and stared back down the road as the bus pulled away, multiple passengers eyeing him up as it left. It was further than he could walk back within an hour. Moth hugged the bus stop on the opposite side of the road. Willing a bus to come along every dragging second. No bus came for almost an hour, leaving him hating the dreary and empty place.

Dull and meaningless on the way to fucking nowhere.

He was clenching his knuckles in tension when he boarded. Sat down on a nearside seat at the front. Approaching the cafe, he could see the police cars had gone. The car park quiet, the lunchtime rush over. The bike tucked away from sight of the road. He sprinted over the tarmac, rounded the bushes to see his bike. Still intact, still tied up.

Still there. You lucky bastard. That was too risky.

He breathed a deep sigh of relief, felt the sickness that was rising in his stomach give way to intense pain. His legs going weak, the true cost of loss even worse now the fear had gone.

Get over it, you need to be gone.

He straightened up, stowed his bag on the front rack, packed the rucksack on top of the panniers, released it and relocked the chain round the frame. He was about to hitch up when he heard a whistle from the café. The young waitress was walking towards him, devoid of her apron, pulling a coat out of a bag slung over her shoulder.

Oh shit.

'You go without thank you,' she accused him, pushing her arms into the coat.

He threw himself onto the saddle, pushed off and

wheeled over to her. He reached over and balanced on her shoulder, his weight steadying her and keeping her immobile, spinning the pedals backwards. She was pouting at him.

'You in trouble with police?'

'No.'

'You in trouble with someone else?'

Her persistence reminded him of Nat.

'I'm in trouble with you.'

She shrugged at him. Pretending it wasn't true. Admitting her hurt. Moth wanted to go, the afternoon was wasted, and he'd struggle to get to Eberndorf. But she was young. Pretty in a way that was confusing. And he was grateful. Like he'd been that morning with Ken and Val.

This sociable crap is wearing off on you.

'You have family here?' he asked. 'I could walk home with you?'

'No, no family,' she said. 'I live on bus, next village.' She nodded in the direction he'd just come from.

Moth considered the grim place he'd kicked the bus shelter walls in. It hadn't been much of a village. Her shoulder beneath his hand was thin. Seeping warmth. Devoid of the apron she looked younger and older at the same time. Her café uniform sagging on her hips, crumpled round the middle, tight across her breasts. She looked too fragile to be living between this café and that home. Her hair, loosed from its ponytail, framing her face. Falling over one shoulder, dark brown and curling at the ends, split with poor condition.

You don't owe her anything more than a thank you.

'I could see you home. You catch the bus. I'll see you at the next stop.'

'You will not be there.'

'I will.' He owed her that much.

Nothing more. She's not your problem.

He let go of her shoulder, rode round her twice in a tight circle until she smiled at him. It took him back to the morning again, that moment of campsite happiness. Her irritation gone he took off, wondering how much of a head start he had on her and the bus. Wondering what difference it would make if he kept going. One more drop of disappointment in a rolling ocean.

You'd never have to find out.

He knew how that worked out. The not knowing leading to endless wondering. A door in his mind he couldn't shut.

He pulled up at the bus stop. Sat on the saddle, leaning against a lamppost, watching the weather worsening and knowing his plans for the afternoon were eroding when the bus pulled in. The first drops of rain were hitting the pavement when she got off. She looked brighter, smiling at him, scowling at the weather. Easing the weight inside him.

'We're going to get wet,' Moth told her.

'I live not far, you wait there until rain is over?'

Moth looked at the sky. Looked away from her. The suggestion making him nervous. More delays. He needed to be riding through the stinging rain, not taking cover from it in her house.

You should have kept riding.

It was worse, to leave her again. Having waited in the first place. She turned and walked away from him, beckoning. He jumped off the bike and pulled it round to follow, caught up with her shorter stride in two steps.

'You go everywhere with her?' she asked, eyeing the bike.

'Everywhere.'

'Your girlfriend?'

'My best friend.'

'Where you going?'

'You ask a lot of questions.'

'You don't ask none.'

Moth knew it was true. Questions invited confidences. Confidences raised hopes. He'd stopped asking questions after Isabelle.

'I'm Milena,' she told his silence.

'Nice to meet you, Milena.' He tried out her name, rolling his tongue around it.

She laughed at him, repeated her name and made him try it again, and once more.

'Try Mila,' she suggested.

'Mila, Mila,' he tried again.

She shrugged so, so at his last effort. The rain began in earnest and she pulled her coat closer and stepped up the pace, rounding the corner from the bus stop. A three-storey house with a narrow side alley that smelled of piss. A small back door and a tight stairwell beyond it that made his shoulders itch. She pointed out a lean-to against a dilapidated wooden fence, where several bikes were tied up. He added his to the mix, clocking the holes in the roof and the near useless sides of the building, pulling out his bike cloak, throwing it over the bike.

She waited, sheltering in the entrance. Arms crossed over her chest, peering into the rain and glancing down the side alley. Inside the doorway he was conscious of his height towering over her. They went up the stairs, grim with age and dirt and haunted by the smell of frying.

Oh, this is nice, real nice.

Moth wishing he'd kept cycling, holding the rucksack between them, stifled by the stairwell. Outside her front door she scrabbled to find a key in her bag, looking near tears and he didn't know if she was more scared of him or he of her. Squashed together on the narrow landing. The wretched paint peeling off the damp walls.

'Hey, I can go,' he touched her shoulder. 'Now you're home, I can go. Thank you for helping me.'

'No,' she told him, grabbing his wrist as he retreated. 'Please, have coffee with me.'

'Why?' Moth looked at the door, resisting the urge to snatch his wrist free.

This place is not good. She is not good. You are a dumb dick.

'Just for be nice,' she said. 'I have no friends here.'

She dropped his wrist, looked up at him.

'No family, no friends,' she went back to trying to find her keys. 'I miss to talk to people, nice talk.'

He didn't respond. Taking another step towards the stairs.

'Ok,' she said, finding her key, putting it in the lock and opening the door. 'It's ok. You go if want, I am good.'

Light streamed through the opening door and the hallway expanded. Mila went through and shrugged her coat off, left the door open. Moth stepped closer, peering round the doorframe. It was a one-room bedsit, the sort filled with unhappiness across Europe. It was anything but ok.

It's a shithole.

But she'd made it a nest, and it was palatial after the bike tent. He put one foot over the threshold. Checking that it was empty, looking back down the corridor and the stairwell.

You're going to end up stabbed for a body part.

Mila put her bag down on the small table and went to fill the kettle from the sink. Her pride in her tiny home giving her confidence. Moth followed her change of mood through the door, turning to shut it behind him.

'I'll have coffee, then I must go.'

'Yes, one coffee, then you go,' she told him, back in control. Wanting her nice moment, wanting it over.

Moth looked at the two chairs by the small table, squashed against the wall between the kitchenette and the doorway. Or there was the bed, opposite the door, covered with a blanket and cushions, doubling as a sofa. A doorway beside it was closed, and the only light came from the single large window that stretched to the ceiling behind the sink. Suggesting the room it might once have lit, before mean necessity cut it into rented accommodation. It was a faint reminder of Riverdell.

'Can I use your bathroom?' Moth asked, gesturing to the closed doorway.

Mila looked, nodded. They were both nervous. Moth walked over to the door, opened it. A chipped corner sink, a stained old shower tray with a haphazard curtain. The door banging against the toilet. He squeezed into the space. It was pathetic and spotless.

And empty.

He took time pretending, flushing the unused toilet, washing his hands, looking at his own strangeness in yet another mirror before leaving.

She'd put cups out on the table, milk, sugar and a plate of continental biscuits. They filled the surface. He pulled a chair out and sat down at a slight distance from the table, it looked rickety enough to be toppled by an ill-placed leg. She came over with a large pot of coffee. Pouring for him, retreating, wiping down the square of work surface by the sink.

'Thank you,' he told her, adding sugar, milk, choosing a

biscuit. Looking around the room, which was filled with photos. Smiling people, happy and connected. 'Your family?'

Mila looked at them, nodded. She picked up one from by the bed and brought it over to him. There were eight women in the photo, all varying ages of the same face.

'My grandmother, my mother,' she pointed them out. 'My aunt, my sisters, my nieces, me.'

She was the youngest of her sisters from what he could see, both with small children clinging to them, one pregnant again.

'Why are you here?' Moth asked, reluctant with questions.

'To work,' she said. 'There is not much work at home. I come from Mitrovica, in Serbia, in south.'

'There's not much work here either.'

'I not always be here,' she told him. 'I work, make money, move on.'

'Where to?'

'Somewhere better. It not matter where.'

'You go home much?' he asked her.

'No,' she said, and looked at the photo with a longing stare.

Moth didn't say anything. He didn't want to ask why. He sipped at the coffee, added more milk, it was strong, and cheap.

'You go home?' she asked him.

'No.'

'You have no family?'

'No.'

'You have no one?'

'Just my bike,' he smiled, making it a joke.

She grimaced at him. Not convinced by the lightness.

'It is not good to be so alone.'

She edged her way along the kitchen cupboard and sat down at the table. Picked up a biscuit and began to nibble the edges of it. Moth was on his third. Watching her reticence he realised how poor she must be, supporting herself alone on the wages from the restaurant. He felt bad for eating too much of her food.

'Are you working again, later, at the restaurant?'

'No,' she pointed at a pile of bags in the corner of the room. 'I not work late, not safe at night. I press for other women. Work breakfast and lunch at café.'

They sat in quietness, drinking the powerful coffee. Moth ate another biscuit. Trying to be polite. To share her hospitality.

How long does a coffee take? You don't even like coffee.

Trying to ignore the urge to leave. Aware of his size towering over the small table, his legs consuming the space around it, her slim frame tucked in the other chair. She reminded him of Nat.

She's nothing like Nat.

Of what Nat might become. A girl-woman, in a world full of men.

You're not responsible for all of them.

'Why did you bring me here?' he asked.

'I never bring anyone before,' she told him, pulling back from the table. 'I don't know why.'

'I could be anyone. It's not safe, to bring men to your room.'

'I miss my family. Here I am stranger. No one talks to me, unless they want something. People are not kind.'

'No,' he agreed, 'they're not.'

'Why you don't like police?'

Moth stared at her. Her insistence, armed with bad

English rather than sisterly bluntness, reminded him again of Nat. Would Nat ever do this? Be alone and invite men she didn't know back to her room, when she was older? He shouldn't be here, he should be there, looking after her. Like a proper older brother.

You had no choice. And Nat's safe enough for now.

But was she? How would he know? He pointed to the picture she'd put back by her bed.

'You have a father? Brothers? You sister's husbands?'

'No, no father, he die in war. An uncle, my aunt's husband. He is mean man. He make my older sister marry his son. My other sister, no husband. My uncle make marriage for her. Bad marriage.' She looked at the photo too, tucked her hair behind her ear, crossing her arms tight over her chest, making him twist inside.

One more bastard in the world. Big deal. Add it to the list.

Moth hated the man on principle and felt sick with the thoughts, wondering what she was running away from.

Don't ask. Just don't ask. Don't. Bloody. Ask.

He curled the coffee cup in his hands, looking into the reducing depths.

'Where are you going to?' she asked.

'West,' he told her, and she pouted at him again. 'Ok, I'm going to Italy.'

No, you're not.

He might be going to Italy. It wasn't a full lie. Better than telling her the truth.

'Why?'

'To meet someone.'

Telling her about Kit would make it easier to go south.

'A girlfriend?'

'No, a boyfriend.'

She raised her eyebrows.

'Not like that, not a boyfriend, just a friend. A boy-friend,' he said.

That's the second time she's asked about a girlfriend.

Moth could tell she was so lonely she would have welcomed the first chance of company. She was pretty in a way that would cause her enough trouble.

She's causing you enough.

It overwhelmed him. The image of her ending up here, in a dead-end house with a dead-end boyfriend. Pregnant like her sister. Not moving on at all. He couldn't see a computer, wondered if she had access to a world bigger than this room.

'You have a boyfriend?

'No.' She glared at him. 'And don't want either. Boyfriends want too much, give nothing back.'

Perhaps she does have some sense after all.

Moth finished his coffee and put the cup down, leaving the soiled dregs in the bottom. Their understanding dispelled the awkwardness, with the end of the coffee came a desire not to end the visit. The rain that had been tapping against the window came stronger in gusts. She rose and went to the window. Looking at her against the light he saw how thin she was, and how hopeful she was despite it.

If you don't leave now, it's going to get harder.

He took out his notebook, pulled the pencil out from the spine and opened it at the back, to an empty page.

'Write your name here,' he pointed to the place, 'and your address.'

'Why?'

'So I can write you.'

He left the pad turned towards her on the table, his finger holding the page open until she stepped across, took the pencil and wrote out the details. Her writing was European, tilting and falling in a foreign way to him. He took the pencil from her and wrote it out again, to make sure of it in his own hand and showed it her for approval.

Great, so you can be sure to not write to the wrong address.

He tore off another piece of paper and wrote his email address out, the one Nat used, put it on the table.

'This is my email address. I have to go.'

'You're going to get very wet.'

'I know, it's alright. I'm used to it.'

'I don't have computer,' she told him, looking at the piece of paper.

'Me neither,' he said. 'But I use a café, check my email. You can do that, write to me. Tell me when you move on.'

'Like friends?'

'Like friends.'

'Why don't you like questions from police?' she asked again, picking up the paper, scrutinising it.

Moth sighed at her persistence. Nat all over. Girls in general.

Rubbish. Kit was always the nosiest one.

'There are people trying to find me,' he told her. 'Not because I did anything bad, but because I am young, like you.'

'But you give me this?' she waved the piece of paper at him.

'Yes.'

'To find you?'

You utter dick.

'To be a friend,' he told her.

She smiled at him, folding the paper up and putting it in her pocket.

'Then that is thank you,' she told him. 'Why you take my address?'

'So I can write to you.'

He zipped up his bag and hitched it on his shoulder, opening the door and checking the corridor. He turned to say goodbye to her.

'You never told me your name,' she accused him from the sink.

Moth hated this moment. It never got any easier. Giving away this piece of himself to strangers. Doubting them all.

It's time to go.

He needed to be gone. Wondered what name to use, real or false. A variation of any.

False. Tom was good. How about Bill? You've not been Bill yet.

'It's Moth.'

His name making the gift real.

That's not what you're doing.

Perhaps he was trying too hard, but he had amends to make. If life was giving him another chance, who was he to question it.

'Goodbye, Moth.'

'Goodbye, Mila.'

He pulled the door too and left. She watched him from the window while he pulled his bike out, pulling the cloak over him and the frame. The backyard grit turning to mud. He looked up at her figure and she waved. He threw a hand up in response, wobbled his way down the narrow side passage. It was late afternoon, and the day was a mess, but he had enough tension in his chest to give him energy.

He flew past Eberndorf in a few easy hours, not even pausing to think about stopping, eating again. Images and ideas hurled around in his head and he pushed it all into the pedals. Trying to find his way back.

Forwards. You, the ride, the plan. That's all you can do.

Helmet lights bright, furrowing through water, until he came out the far side of Klagenfurt, following the shores of a wide river. His legs heavy, his arms and hands weary from the tension of gripping the bike.

He crossed a bridge and slowed. Ahead of him a bank of trees, outlined against the paler night sky. Tall old conifers, scraggy and streaked through with starlight, laced with occasional traffic beams from the road. He pulled the bike off the road and set up camp, hidden from the road. The train track and the lake north of him, the river below him to the south. Overhead, airplanes took up the emptiness of the night sky and droned at him.

He wrote in the notebook, Day 260. 18th March 2013. Worthen See. Looked at her address on the back page, closed the book around it.

At least you're not looking at Italy.

Moth lay in the dark, eyes blinking against weariness, mind full of the day and all its events. Nat hovering in the background behind Mila. Guilt gripping him for both of them.

Look after yourself first.

He remembered what that felt like. Making a choice that put himself first. The guilt deepened.

It's not your battle.

It was a battle that lurched into sleep.

. . .

IT WAS FRIDAY AFTERNOON, two full days after coming home, by the time Isabelle escaped to her workroom.

Elsa had swept her on from the reality of her split from James and into the rush of Riverdell's concerns. The details about the funeral, about David's chaotic estate, about Elsa's worries and fears for the children, about the state of the third guest-bedroom bed linen, about Kit's plans for redecorating two bathrooms, about Kate's excessive workload, about life in general, in a rush of speech that ended in a weary sigh which embraced the fact that Isabelle was home and no figment of her imagination. Elsa, relieved, left Isabelle with the same brain freeze that coming home always gave her. The onslaught of everyone, everything, and all its vital significance pummelling her after the blissful anonymity of the movie backstage.

Today had passed in a similar blur. She'd spent time with Kate and met the new managers at The Blue Door, had an hour drawing with Natalie before Hester intervened, and tried and failed to find Moth. Elsa had snagged her after lunch and kept her busy until she finally turned her attention to dinner and, before she could draw breath and start talking again, Isabelle requested to be excused from the event. Hester and her husband, Rob, were attending, as was James. Elsa's unrelenting need of her and the rawness of her break with James could not endure an evening of Hester's brittle conversation. She claimed the need to see to her workroom before Kit arrived for the weekend.

'Well, I suppose if you exhaust yourself today you might get back into a sensible sleep pattern,' Elsa said, voicing the lie which Isabelle knew she would present to the family.

She fetched her notebook from her bedroom, gathered supplies in a basket, murmured a grateful 'thank you' to Elsa, kissing her on the cheek and leaving the kitchen through the boot room.

She fled down the back stairs to the basement. Padding in soft leather boots down the corridor, alongside the boiler room and the storerooms, ignoring the glass windows to the garden room that graced the corridor with light, turning left to the wooden door that opened into her workroom with full hands and a light heart. It was one of the few in the house not coerced into behaviour with the fire closing hinges. It had that satisfying click that came with being shut at a normal pace. Being shut by someone. By her, shutting the rest of the house out.

Ignoring the light switch by her side she teased out the contents of the dim room. The heaped shelves and piles of baskets, the tables and chests of drawers, the boxes stacked in haphazard piles only she understood. A precarious, determined arrangement that reminded her of the Mumbai slums, work connecting the points of her life. She felt her way forwards, passing the near end of the long high workbench, feeling the dusty plastic that covered the taut calico surface and the curving wooden seat of the bench that rested beside it. She placed the basket and her notebook on top of it and moved onwards, towards the windows.

She found the heavy folds of the curtains. Feeling the napped softness of the faded velvet in her fingers, grasping the immense weight of their many layers and laying her face against their musty comfort before pulling with a mighty swing to the high pole overhead so that they swept aside in a storm of afternoon light upon her senses. The fabric in her hands came to life, shimmering as its weight settled to the far side of the pole with a ponderous stirring of dust. She moved to the next window, repeated the process, this time with a loose-woven, heavy, linen fabric. Then, at the far window, the dainty, disintegrating silk. Full of tiny embroidered flowers and trailing vines, threads expiring as her hands gripped them. These were the oldest of the three pairs, made from fabric brought in India by her father, crumbling apart in a slow rot, and they were the pair she most needed to replace but couldn't bear the thought of taking down, or know what to replace them with that would give her as much pleasure.

Silk was the fibre she most adored, the fibre that connected her to what made sense. To India, to memories of her mother, to her delight in sewing, to her work in Bollywood. All fabrics spoke, but silk could sing through the body as well as the eyes, its inner life warming her skin. She let them trail out of her fingers and turned back to the huge room.

To the towering walls, the vaulted ceiling and the pathways between her collections, where the sprung parquet floor peeped between boxes. Mirrors were propped with a diffident hand around the room, reflecting the light deeper. To her right, a dresser, and a makeshift sink that James had plumbed in, agricultural style. On the wall next to them a huge old map, painted on silk, faded and sagging, with all the original names for India hand-scripted across territories that no longer existed, a pre-colonial glimpse of the country she loved. Her eyes could not see the looping cobwebs, the layer of dust, the grime on the mirrors and glass.

She zigzagged her way to the fire on the far side of the room, wood stacked high to the side. Higher than she had ever seen James stack it and it hurt to think of his doing so. Perhaps for the last time he'd thought, or decided even, as he laid it ready for her. Stacking and stacking as he came to terms with that long-evaded truth. She took the matches from the mantel and struck one, watching the huge draw suck the fledgling flames up the blackened mass of the chimney. Piling ever larger pieces of wood upon the grate until she could feel the warmth from the iron back plate reflect back at her.

She moved back to the table, caught the huge sheet of plastic and threw it back over itself, rolling it into a loose swirl of dead flies, dust and age-dulled creases. Isabelle eased herself onto the stool and unsnapped the strap holding the notebook together, splaying open the pages, letting the contents loose. A needle lay tucked into the padded surface of the table. She picked it up, pulled it between her fingers to check for any damp roughness, threaded it through her jumper and felt complete.

Spilling from between the sketch-filled pages were many small squares of fabric. She laid them out, reaching across the surface of the table, to fill a semicircle of colour against the creamy calico. Pulling first one piece of fabric to her hands, then another, feeling the weight and the fibre and letting the memories come to her. Huge markets and tiny shops, and bolt after bolt of fabric. People she'd met, talked to, shared time with, worked with. Friends, strangers, colleagues. She'd convinced them all to give her a patch of their own garments, or a throw, or a blanket. A three-inch chunk cut out and the gap re-stitched by her. She came home with her notebook filled with scraps of life.

Arranged and pinned upon pre-cut calico squares, she found thread and began to stitch. Large, loose, running stitches that held them together. Later, as her confidence in them increased, they would progress to the sewing machine. Later still, they would make their way to the large baskets that held the finished items, stacked beneath the table, on the floor, piled on the shelves. One day, when she decided how to piece the squares together, they would make something. Something she could use, a fabric created from a thousand other pieces of fabric. Something with purpose.

Arranging, remembering, stitching, Isabelle reached a point where she had reconnected to her place in the world. Perched on the stool, negotiating the distance between India and England, her toes snug in old soft boots, she pulled a packet of biscuits from the basket and turned to her real work.

She had a pile of repairs, alterations, and remakes all placed in her workroom by Elsa. Projects from around the house, commissions from people in town, orders from old trade customers. There were requests, scrawled on the house paper by Elsa, contact such and such, looking for this, can you do it by such and such a date, will this fabric suit. She made a list on a large piece of plain paper and pinned it to the wall beside the sewing machine, stacked all the jobs to one side and began by tackling the easiest.

Between work, stoking the fire, moving the travel scraps and munching on biscuits, her awareness of life outside the workroom disappeared. It confused her to see the large door opening at the edge of her sight, made her wobble on the stool. She glanced up, mouth full of pin heads, poised to stitch, blinking.

'Hey,' Moth stuck his head through the door, looking around the huge room to find her. 'Sorry, I did knock, you didn't answer.'

'Oh,' she mumbled, raising her free hand to remove the pins from her mouth. 'I didn't hear you, come in.'

He came in with a large tray balanced on his hand and nudged the door shut behind him with his back.

'I brought you some dinner, Elsa suggested you might be hungry.'

Isabelle squinted at the clock on the far wall. It was gone nine, she'd been down here for over five hours. She put down the work she was on and stretched.

'I didn't realise it was so late,' she admitted. 'How did dinner go?'

'Oh yeah, real fun event,' Moth rolled his eyes at her. 'They're teaching Nat how to play bridge. I offered to bring this. Hope you don't mind?'

'Not at all, thank you,' Isabelle went to take the tray off him. 'You're welcome anytime, as long as you don't mind me being boring.'

'This is some workspace you have down here,' Moth told her, glancing around.

He was doing a good impression of having not seen it before, but the tone of his voice was too familiar. Isabelle had a feeling there were few places in the house he'd not explored, and she knew for a fact that she had the most wonderful room of them all. She would have found it hard to resist too, and it was her choice not to lock the door.

'I'm very lucky,' she agreed, taking the tray over to the pouffe between the fire and the sofa. 'This used to be a damp hole full of old crap and mice before I cleaned it out.'

'Elsa let you have this?'

'Yeah, years ago, when I finished school. Mind I worked my guts out at clearing it out.' Isabelle poked at the embers, threw another log on. 'I think she was happy I was paying to sort the damp problem out and using the space to make money too. You got time to sit with me a bit?' she asked. 'Or are you needed back up topside?'

'I'm done.'

'Grab us some glasses,' she pointed over to the dresser. 'There's a bottle of wine, or some beers if you prefer.'

She sank onto the sofa, feeling stiff from work and glad to stop. She could hear him clinking, opening cupboards, finding bits. He came back with hands loaded. Isabelle watched him pour her a glass, retreat empty-handed to stand by the fire, looking at the options of where to sit. She wriggled out of her boots, reached forward and took the plate from the tray, sat cross-legged in a corner of the sofa and balanced it on her lap, wine glass in one hand, fork in the other.

'How's your day gone?'

'Good. I've been helping James. He kept me pretty busy.'

'I can imagine.' James was relentless at work. Demanding on his staff, leading by exhausting example.

'I like it,' Moth stayed in front of the fire, scuffing the dusty hearth with his feet. 'It's nice to be busy, not that I would want to do it for a living, but it beats school.'

'What do you want to do for a living?'

'Not sure yet,' he admitted. 'But not farming.'

'Knowing what you don't want to do is a sure step towards finding out what you do want to do.' Isabelle focused on the plate of fish pie. Home cooked by Elsa, it was one of her favourite dishes to make, the layers crafted with care and pride. Compared to the food she was used to, it seemed bland and tasteless. It would be a while before her palate adjusted.

'What about all this?' he shrugged to suggest the contents of the room around them. 'Did you always know this is what you wanted to do?'

'In a roundabout way.'

'Why roundabout?'

'I suppose it took me longer than most to realise that I

was supposed to do something in life. By the time that sank in I'd sort of fallen into this and realised I enjoyed it enough to keep doing it.'

'Perhaps, the reason you don't talk much is because when you do you don't make much sense.'

'Possibly,' Isabelle conceded.

'Or maybe you need more practice.'

Isabelle dallied with the fish and peas, covered in coagulating sauce. Drinking more often from the glass of wine, enjoying the end of day feel and the relax into the sofa.

'I suppose, if you're accusing me of being obtuse, I was drifting my way through life when I realised all my friends had found their path and were carving away at some immense career rock face. Everyone kept asking me what I was going to do, that's how I realised I was supposed to make a conscious choice in the process.'

Moth hovered on the brink of the hearth, deciding what to do with himself, moved to the far side of the sofa and sat down, his face turned away from her, staring at the fire. His hair darkened in its glow.

'My father was always asking what I was going to do,' Moth told her. 'I hate the idea.'

His voice was harsh, vindictive. Full of teenage conviction that no adult could understand what he was thinking or feeling. She felt the rawness in it. Grief masquerading as anger she thought. It would take time though, to let go of the anger that must wrap itself round what had happened. Both parents dead, him and his sister homeless. All because of his father's drinking. Her glass recriminated her with its indulgence.

'My father wanted me to be a lawyer,' she told him,

remembering the feeling well, putting the food down on the tray. 'I can't tell you how much we argued over it.'

'How did you convince him?'

'I didn't. He died while we were still arguing. I guess you could say I won, after all, I didn't become a lawyer.'

'It's not a great way to win an argument,' Moth said.

'No, but maybe it was the only way.' Isabelle twirled the wine in her glass. 'I know that makes me sound horrible, but otherwise, I don't think we'd have ever stopped disagreeing. He was determined I become something significant, contribute to the world, make a difference. But all I enjoyed doing was making stuff.'

They sat a while longer, staring at the fire.

'That's a lot of wood,' he told her, nodding at the pile.

'It's a big fire.'

'James asked me to keep an eye on it for you.'

'Did he?'

He nodded his head, flashed a quick smile at her.

'You don't have to work for us, Moth.'

'I like being helpful,' he told her. 'It's an annoying habit.'

'Well, I guess I can't argue over that. I'm always trying to help Elsa. But anyway, not me, you don't have to help me out.'

'Even if I want to?'

'Only if you want to, not because someone else asks you to.'

'Why not?'

'Because someone else might ask you not to help me,' Isabelle told him. 'And I'd rather think you were doing what you wanted to, not what other people asked of you.'

He didn't respond and Isabelle wondered what people had been asking of him. Silence settled into the space that yawned between them on the sofa. Moth staring into the fizzing fire, lost in thought while she sat curled in her corner, watching him through her wine glass. Absorbing the profile of his face, his eyebrows, the hooked angle of his nose, the protruding lips, and sharp chin. The way his hand plucked at the knee of his trousers. The gentle tap, tap of his right foot, tap, tap, pause, tap, tap, pause. Upstairs she could hear the distant sound of laughter. Outside the cars rumbling on the road bridge hummed a sporadic note through the closed windows, sounding like lost bees.

'I have another question for you.' He startled her into awareness.

She groaned in exaggeration.

'I spent some time with James today.'

'You said.' She rearranged her feet, tucking them closer, grateful for the socks she'd succumbed to.

'I asked him about Hester, about the kids thing.'

'Uh huh.' She curled her spare hand around the crux of her crossed legs.

'He's a lot more communicative than you,' Moth looked at her, turned his body, pulling his right leg up onto the sofa. Settling into the opposite corner and engaging her attention. Isabelle hid behind her wine glass. 'I thought men were crap at talking, but round here, with Kit and James, I'm finding it's the blokes you need to ask if you want to know anything.'

'You counting yourself in the garrulous crowd?'

'No,' he grinned at her. 'The curious crowd.'

'We're a puzzle you want to work out,' Isabelle told him. 'I wonder where you'll end up putting us all.'

'I wonder too, but without working it out, I won't know.'

'You can't take us at face value?' she offered. 'Someone is nice to you, they like you. Someone is mean to you, they don't like you.'

'No.' He barked contempt at her. 'That's bollocks. Someone's nice to you, they want something. Someone's mean to you, they want something.'

She was surprised by his bad language, the odd tone she'd noticed before deepened by the words. 'I don't agree with that.'

'Because you don't want to, not because it's not true,' he said, looking back at the fire, excluding her from his thoughts.

She could feel him inching away from her.

'I think I'd feel the same as you, if I stayed here all the time,' she reached forward to top the glass up from the bottle on the tray. 'That's why I go away a lot. I can't cope with being permanently westernised. I'd end up feeling like you, that everyone wants something. Hiding it under something else.'

She waited for him to stop ignoring her, to look back at her, respond. Thankful when his shoulders lowered and he said, with his eyes flicking her way, 'I'm going to travel.'

'Do it,' she told him. 'Don't lose track of that. Make sure you go, and travel.'

'I will, but not until I've worked you lot out.'

'Why?'

'Because I need to know if I can trust you,' he said. 'You and Elsa, Kit, James, all of you.'

'We are your family.'

'I should trust you because of that?' He stared at her, sullen, irritated by her presumption. 'Really?'

Moth looked back at the fire, pulled his knee off the sofa, retreating further. He was the epitome of a teenager, engaging one minute, derisive the next. She expected him to walk out, felt frustrated and confused. How Elsa thought she was suitable to this task was beyond her.

'Why do you want to trust us?' she asked, trying to find a side door to bypass his annoyance. 'It seems important enough that you want to work it out. Why does it matter?'

'Because I need to know I can trust you with Nat,' he told her. 'I have to know she'll be safe, when I go... back to school.'

'Oh,' Isabelle said, surprised. 'I thought, I mean, oh, ok.'

'You thought I was worried for myself?'

'I suppose.'

'I'm not.'

They looked at each other, across the divide of the squishy cushions. He grinned, shrugged a sort of apology.

'It's no different to James asking me to do the wood for you,' he said. 'It's a brother thing. You wouldn't understand.'

'Oh,' she said, admonished.

He stood up, swamping her with confusion. The moment had healed and was fine, and she, thinking he meant to go, felt deflated. He put another piece of wood on the fire while she withered and, when he straightened up, the burst of flames warped his height, reducing her more, shrinking into the sofa and feeling its softness in the brittle bones of her uselessness.

'As I was saying, I asked James about Hester and you.'

'Oh, yes,' Isabelle recalled the conversation had started somewhere different. 'He was much more helpful than me.'

'Yes, he was,' Moth agreed. 'He told me all about Hester for a start, he was a lot less reserved than you.'

'Or a lot more trusting?' she mocked him, trying to turn it back on him.

'And he told me pretty much all about you.' Moth batted the effort away.

'And now you want me to confirm it?' she sounded defensive even to herself.

'No,' he said, 'I'm pretty confident I got the gist of it.'

'Great.' Isabelle was damned if she was going to help him. She sipped at her wine glass, annoyed by its near emptiness again.

'Which leads me to a few conclusions.'

Isabelle looked at him in silence. It was shocking how tense she felt. It made her feel ill, waiting to hear what he'd say.

'Ok, so, never tell James anything in confidence,' Moth said. 'Like, really, nothing.'

She smiled at the painful truth. There wasn't even a whisper of capacity for secrecy in James. He never did anything wrong that he could see the need for secrets.

'Also, never do the opposite of what Hester wants.'

He was being evasive, making her wait for a kick of ever impending magnitude.

'And, never ever do the opposite of what Hester wants, twice.'

Her smile this time was soured with bitterness.

'And never ask you a question that wants a straight answer.'

'That seems a bit harsh,' she defended herself on the smallest aspect.

'Maybe,' he agreed, looking behind her. 'This is my question. What are they?'

He gestured his head behind them, and she peered up over the sofa to see what he was looking at, grimacing. He was looking at the overflowing baskets of scrap squares, which even to her now looked haphazard and chaotic, left where she'd pulled them adrift. When she looked back, he was grinning, challenging her to be straight.

'They are a work in progress.'

'Towards?'

'I don't know yet, that is what a work in progress implies, unsure destination.'

'How did they start?'

'They sort of evolved, from something that I wasn't sure what to do with but had a compulsion to collect.'

'And how long have they been evolving?'

'A while,' she admitted through a sip of wine.

'Hmm, something you weren't sure of, becoming something you don't know, for a period of time you can't specify,' Moth summarised, counting off the points on his fingers, the fire behind him turning them into flaming digits of inquisition.

'Is this a character assassination?' she asked. 'I'm still trying to work out how they fit together!' Illuminated by the words she defended herself with, pointing out, 'Like you are, with all of us.'

'Perhaps your ideas about how they should fit are wrong.'

'How's that?' Isabelle asked.

'Maybe they don't fit together at all.'

'Maybe my idea of what fits is different to yours.'

'Is that your way of telling me off?' Moth asked.

'No,' she said, surprised at the idea, the quick offence he took. 'It's just what I was thinking.'

'Well, I still feel a bit of a shit.'

She laughed and leaned into the sofa. She knew how that felt. Hester could spin her words into any meaning she chose and weigh them down with history. She and Moth had no history.

'Well, no need, it wasn't intended,' she said. 'Though you could put some more wood on the fire if you feel a real shit.'

Moth did as she asked, returned to sit on the pouffe,

nearer to her than the end of the sofa. She watched him place his chin on the heel of his hand and lean on his foot as he crossed it over the other knee. The fire was behind him and he took the immediate warmth with him.

'What's your question?'

Isabelle looked at him, confused.

'A question for a question, remember?'

'Oh, that,' she said. 'I did want to ask you something, but perhaps next time. I should concentrate more on keeping up with you, or drink less perhaps. You're like Kit, he runs rings around me sometimes. I can imagine you two get on great!'

'He doesn't talk like anyone else I know.'

'You mean he says what no one else would dare?'

'Yeah, as though someone forgot to give him the script the rest of the world is talking from.'

'That's perfect,' she said. 'You've nailed Kit.'

'It makes a change.'

'I know,' Isabelle agreed. 'Though it can be exhausting too. Sometimes, I think he says stuff just to be provoking.'

'But, what was your question?'

Isabelle remained quiet.

'You think I won't like it?' Moth asked, and she swayed her head. 'Or I won't answer it?'

'I don't mind that.'

'But?'

'But... I don't want to upset you, by asking.'

'Why don't you build it up some more?'

'Ok.' She drew a breath. 'I wanted to ask about your mother. You haven't spoken about her.'

He remained silent, eyes looking straight at her from the guard of his chin-cupping hand. She left the question hanging in the air between them. The darkness and huge scope of the room flickering around his glowing shoulders.

'I miss her,' he said. 'It's not something I've worked out yet. Her... being... gone. I don't know what to say.'

'But your father's different?'

'I don't miss him.'

'Not at all?'

'His being gone is a relief.'

'That might change, with time?' Isabelle suggested.

He stared at her, not blinking, not speaking. Daring her to tread further. She felt like the sofa was sinking into the ground.

'Tell me one good memory about her.' She moved away from that sore, looking down at her glass, back up at Moth with a sad smile. 'I remember the smell of my mother's hair. It was sharp and sweet, like a gin and tonic.'

'Perhaps you just remember gin and tonic?'

'It's a memory, connected to her,' Isabelle said. 'One I never forget.'

'Lavender,' he mumbled around his hand.

'Lavender?' Isabelle repeated, unsure she'd heard him right.

He raised his chin off his hand and said, 'Yes, lavender. She was half-French, or maybe a quarter. She always wanted to go and visit the lavender fields. Kept lavender in the house all the time. Sachets in the drawers. Plants in pots on the kitchen window.' He sat upright, put his leg down and looked at his own hands, curled them into fists. 'It had a distinctive smell.'

'That's a good memory,' she said. 'Strong.'

'I hadn't thought about it before.'

'You should,' she said. 'It helps, to remember the little things.'

'I suppose,' he said. 'I was trying not to think about it much at all.'

'Optimistic, if unrealistic,' Isabelle said. 'Memories aren't that easy to control.'

'Some things seem to end up more complicated than they should be,' he said.

'Most things in fact, I find,' Isabelle agreed.

KIT STOOD IN THE HALLWAY, taut and uncertain, hand tapping the surface of the round table, checking for dust, his phone against his ear, dialling and not being answered.

Where was she?

Sunday afternoon, he had a few hours left and had to hit the road. Henri had read the riot act about being back in Bristol to prepare for meetings tomorrow. His clients were getting narky. He hung up.

Where the hell was Isabelle?

He'd spent all day on the house with Elsa and not seen a sight of her. He'd been down to the workroom twice; empty. Well, hardly empty. Filled to the gunnels with a load of old rubbish, and dust, and spider webs. He hadn't seen her since he left her in bed that morning, gone for a coffee to perk himself up and been dragged into work by Elsa. Standing in the kitchen in her nightdress and robe, worrying about the milk supplies for the guests' breakfast. Something about Elsa in her nightdress always undid his resolve. By the time he made it back upstairs Isabelle had gone.

He twisted the watch on his wrist. Listening to the empty

house. Wishing the polish didn't overwhelm every other scent. He'd told the cleaners numerous times not to overdo it but they used polish with the enthusiasm of a sixteen year-old getting his first tube of lube. All the guests had left that morning, Hester had stayed away since their argument, and Kate had been wrapped up in work all day. Moth hadn't been anywhere in sight, working with James no doubt. He hoped to high hell Moth didn't get that farming bug, get into tractors. Kit rolled his eyes. Tractors. Why did they send people round here crazy? He couldn't hear a thing. Her phone cut to answer message.

Where the hell was she?

He walked through to the kitchen, paced straight on into the boot room. He tried not to look at it, it was a source of endless irritation, and sprang down the steps two at a time. He tried, again, not to notice the neglect as he swept down the corridor and was already wondering where to try next, when he heard her laughing in her workroom. He twitched in response. Great, now all he had to do was get her back upstairs. He opened the door wondering why she was laughing. Isabelle wasn't the laughing-to-herself type.

But she wasn't. Laughing to herself.

'I've been looking for you everywhere,' he announced in a voice loud enough to fill the enormous space and silence the laughter.

'Me?' they asked in perfect unison, and both laughed.

'Christ, you two are in a good mood,' he told them and walked across to the sofa where they were sat.

Well, where Isabelle was lying. Moth was sat on the pouffe, right next to her. Looking all roughed up and fresh faced, with a streak of mud across his right cheek. It had dried to a shade of glowing amber, which was ridiculous, looking like a warrior paint daub, not a splash of dirt. Anyone would think he'd drawn it right under his cheekbone on purpose.

'What's so bloody funny anyway?' He threw himself down on the sofa, picking Isabelle's legs up to drape on his lap.

'You're in a sore mood,' Isabelle said, pulling her feet off him and sitting up at the far end of the sofa, tucking her legs under herself. 'Long day?'

'It would have been shorter with a bit better company,' Kit told them. 'Where have you been, I haven't seen hide nor hair of either of you.'

'We went for a walk,' Isabelle told him. 'Called in on Kate for a coffee and stopped for lunch.'

'You miserable buggers, and none of you invited me?'

'We thought you were busy,' Moth said.

'Doesn't seem you thought much at all,' Kit said.

Isabelle kicked him with a foot, frowned and smiled at him, leaving him wondering which one he was supposed to react to.

'Well, it's over now, why don't you have a drink and chill out.'

Kit thought hard about it. He needed to head back. Henri would freak out if he didn't sort the final details for the Millers before he met them. He couldn't afford to spend another night here. He watched as Moth grinned at Isabelle and she grinned back.

'What a good idea,' he said. 'Moth, how about you go sneak us a drink from the kitchen?'

'No need,' Isabelle said. 'I'm fully stacked.' She stood up and went over to the dresser, found herself a biscuit while she unscrewed a bottle of wine and grabbed two glasses. 'Moth?'

'No, I'm good thanks,' he said.

Kit watched Moth watching Isabelle. 'Where did you go

walking?' he asked, demanding Moth's attention. 'Looks like you fell off a cliff.'

'Out of a tree,' he said.

'A tree?'

'Yeah, we had a dare to see who could go the highest, and I won by far.'

'And slipped getting down,' Isabelle said, coming back to the sofa and passing him a glass of wine. 'Scared me to death.'

'Why would you climb a tree in the first place?' Kit asked. 'Surely you outgrow those things?'

Isabelle sat down with a thump, looked at him and said, 'Are you telling me to grow up?'

'No, I'm jealous,' he said. 'Off climbing trees with kids while I have to do renovation budgets for bathrooms all morning.'

He dropped the snide dig between them, felt its sourness spread across their faces. He was being a right arse, and he couldn't help it. Moth's fresh ruffled look irritated him. Combined with the fact that he wanted to be alone with Isabelle and get her prone again.

'I guess you're either into climbing trees or you're not,' Isabelle said.

Moth looked down at his hands and pretended not to care. But he'd taken the dig to heart and Kit couldn't decide if he felt glad or bad about it.

'City boy at heart,' Kit tried for contrite, managed a bit less grumpy, 'always preferred a pub myself.' Isabelle sat in the sullen corner and refused to comment. It riled him all over again. 'And here's me worrying you were getting hooked on tractors up at the farm.'

Moth looked up again, that had irritated him even more.

Isabelle glared at him from the end of the sofa and Moth went back to looking at his hands. How much of a hint did he need to give to get some space?

'Well, what do you think of Isabelle's dust nest?' Kit asked instead, enjoying the pull of the wine on his irritation, glancing round the room. 'Has she told you what she uses all this stuff for, I've never been able to work it out.'

'Work in progress,' Moth offered.

'Oh please.' Kit sighed. He knew that excuse all too well. 'I reckon half these boxes haven't been opened in decades, filling time and space, more like.'

'It's not space being used for anything else,' Isabelle said, smoothing down the arm of the sofa.

'Yes, but it could be, if you cleared all this stuff out.'

'The whole world doesn't need to be as organised as you,' Isabelle told him. 'It would be a huge empty space with nothing in it, and just my worktable. I feel more comfortable with all this round me.'

'It drives me mad,' Kit said, glancing round. 'Makes me feel I need to do something. I never can relax in here.'

'It's a good job it's not your workroom,' Moth said.

'Exactly,' Isabelle agreed. 'Not that I'm saying I couldn't tidy it up a bit.'

'That'll be the day,' Kit said.

'You are so grouchy,' she snapped back at him.

'You know I can't cope with a mess,' he retorted.

'It's not a mess to me,' Isabelle said. 'Most of other people's tidiness makes no sense to me, why shouldn't I have a space that's how I want it to be.'

Her voice had risen with the complaint and ended on a high accusatory note that made him laugh outright.

'Oh, shut up,' she told him. 'Bringing your bad mood

down here and throwing it at us. We were having a good day, and you're jealous because you were too busy to join us.'

Too busy? Not fucking invited more like. He held back a final retort between clenched teeth. It was making him sound petulant. If she wanted to run about with Moth and make him feel more at home, why should he care? It was work well done and they had time enough. He would leave later and get work straight before he went to bed. Right now, all he needed was for Moth to get the hint and piss off. Moth stood up from the pouffe.

'I'll head off,' he said.

'You don't need to go,' Isabelle told him. 'Don't let his bad mood upset you.'

'I need to go see Nat,' Moth said and headed towards the door.

'I'll see you in a few weeks, when I'm up at Easter,' Kit said to him.

'Look forward to it,' Moth told him in a flat tone. 'Bye, Isabelle,' he said in a warmer one that made Kit grit his teeth.

'See you later,' Isabelle replied.

Kit didn't mention that Nat wasn't even in the house, she'd left with Elsa ten minutes earlier. It was a minor detail. He watched the door shut behind him, grinned and turned back to Isabelle.

'I thought he'd never leave,' he complained.

'He didn't want to,' she said. 'You were vile.'

'I've been lovely all weekend, to fucking everyone. I'm all out of loveliness,' he said, putting his glass down on the floor and throwing himself across the sofa at her.

'Kit, mind my wine!'

'Put that glass down and give me some attention or I'll hurl it at the wall,' he growled.

'Now who's acting like a child,' she protested as he took her glass away and pulled her down on the sofa.

'Nothing childish about this,' he told her and put her hand on his hard on.

'You're insatiable.'

'I'm going to be away for two weeks,' he told her between kisses. 'Will you miss me?'

'No,' she said, but it came out round a smile. 'I'll enjoy the peace.'

'Moth should keep you busy enough,' Kit said. He struggled to find his way beneath her many layers. 'How many bloody clothes do you have on?'

Kit felt her pull away from his hands. Struggle out from under him, back into her corner.

'Kit, not now.' She held her hand up as he advanced. 'Moth could come back in, or anyone.'

'What were you laughing at anyway?' He pulled back, looking at her. Her evasive air was driving him crazy.

'Laughing?'

'You were laughing, when I came in.'

'Was I?' Isabelle picked her wine glass back up and sipped again. 'I have no idea, you chased it out of my mind with your bad mood.'

'I wasn't in a bad mood until I heard you laughing with him.'

'What?' Isabelle said. 'Why would you be bad tempered about my laughing, with anyone, let alone Moth?'

'Because you weren't laughing with me.'

'Aren't I allowed to laugh with anyone else now?'

'Well, not within my hearing, anyway,' he retorted.

'You're being ridiculous.'

'You're being evasive.'

They looked at each other in surprise. The snap of the fire crackling in the background. Kit laughed, picked his glass up and took a swig.

'You're right, I'm being an arse,' he admitted. 'I wanted to spend time with you, and I've ended up spending it with everyone else instead, all weekend. And you've ignored me.'

She looked guilty. 'It's not the quietest of houses,' she said. 'I'm not as demonstrative as you.'

'Is that why you've been hiding?'

'I was not hiding,' she denied. 'Just because I don't want to throw myself headlong into PDA's with you does not mean I was hiding.'

Kit looked into his wine glass, resisting the urge to drink. He should have told her he needed to head back. He should have been more reserved. Kate's comments needled him, her long commanding finger jabbing him in the small of the back. He'd not drunk enough to be an issue yet. They could spend some time chatting. He went to put the glass down, to be reserved. Positively fucking decorous.

'Besides, I was trying to spend some time with Moth, get to know him,' she added. 'Elsa asked me to.'

Kit could have hurled the glass in the fire. He covered the moment, took a slow sip of wine. 'Fine,' he said. 'You were being good, and I was grumpy. Now, how about we forget all of them, and think about ourselves for the rest of the day?'

'There's not much of the rest of the day left,' she said, upset.

'There's enough, I have all evening to make it up to you. Come on, what's it to be? Shall we run naked through the garden?'

'Don't be ridiculous.'

'How about we go for a swim?'

'The river is freezing, Kit.'

'How about I strip naked and dance round your work-room until you can't resist me?'

She frowned at him. She was beyond precious about her space down here.

'How about we make a nest up in your bedroom?' he pleaded. 'We'll watch an old movie and make out. I'll tell Elsa we're not coming down to supper and we can eat biscuits in your bed.'

'The crumbs drive you mad,' she said, but she held out her fingers to him along the spine of the sofa.

He took the tips of them, held them between his. Finally.

9

RIVERDELL HOUSE, LUDLOW. AUGUST 1962

We were all restless that summer before we went to university.

The future seemed held together only by the fact that we were all going to Swansea. Everywhere else it seemed to be falling apart. We were all anxious. Well, all of us except Rose. Rose never had an anxious feeling in her life. She would have looked at anxiety like a bug that needed removing from the room. And, actually, I don't recall Kate being much of a namby-pamby either. She'd taken to having lengthy discussions with my father about politics and class. Kate was all up for the activism welling up in the outside world. And Beth? Well, Beth was happy to go wherever the rest of us went. She valued the days she wasn't suffering by then. Beth always seemed able to grasp the essence of life. When Marilyn died and we were all stunned with grief, Beth spent a day rewatching her every film on the television Father had had installed in the morning room. He'd said it was only for us, but he'd spent most of the summer in there muttering at the news. Bloody MacMillan had become his favourite epithet of the summer. It meant nothing to us, he might as well have been screaming Bloody Wallace for all we cared about politics. Well, perhaps for all I cared for politics.

I suppose, really, it was only me who was anxious.

I felt stuck on the cliff face of a big world I wasn't ready to enter.

Richard and I courted for two years before we went to university. I took to cutting through the fields every Saturday morning on a solitary walk to the tower while Kate slept in, and found him always leaning against the gate. For almost two years we'd hardly missed a weekend walk together. And if, for any reason, I couldn't make it, I would fret for the next seven days with no way to contact him. If it hadn't been for the girls' determination we were all going together, I think I would have given up the dream of a degree and stayed home to marry him. Well, that, and I hadn't the courage to even intimate to Father that I was having doubts about getting a degree. Or that I had fallen in love. Let alone with the son of his tenant farmer.

Would Richard wait three years for me? Would any man? Rose didn't think so.

That last summer weighed me down with worry.

Richard knew of course. We talked about everything other than the impending separation. We talked about Father, the girls, the new music he loved, Marilyn, cows, silage levels, books. We even talked about the birds we watched from the tower. It was something else we had in common, not a clue about which bird was which, bar a robin known from Christmas cards and a crow because they were the bane of a farmer's life. And, by the time we were laughing about our ignorance over birds, we'd have talked ourselves back into each other's arms. And kisses. And all over again I didn't want to leave.

It was my decision. That summer morning towards the end of August when we met at the gate. I'd left all the girls asleep in the house, weary from an evening of planning our future living arrangements.

I was walking up the hill towards him and the morning sun was full on his face. His eyes closed to drink in every drop of the warmth. When he opened them I was about four paces from him and the smile he gave me, well, it felt like a ray of joy and warmth between us. It jumped between our eyes, right down through my heart and landed with a thump in my nether regions. I decided then, right in that moment. I can remember it even now, like yesterday. I'd never felt so certain about anything.

'Richard,' I was breathless with love when I reached him, fell into his embrace. 'I want us to be together. Before I go away.'

He held me even tighter. The chill of the wind blowing through the cool morning lost in the glowing exertion of my climb, the heat radiating out from him. He looked down at me.

'You're sure?' he asked, tucking stray hairs away from my face. 'It will break my heart if we do and then you fall in love with some bright lad at university and never come back?'

'I want to leave myself here with you,' I told him. Oh, how full of Heathcliff and Catherine I was then, I was such a fanciful thing. 'To convince you not to fall in love with some farming wench while I'm away.'

'You know you don't have to prove anything to me?' he said. 'I love you, Elsa. I'll wait until the ground freezes six feet down before I'll look at another girl.'

'Don't you want to do it?' I asked, burying my head in his chest. Any moments of courage with me were always brief but huge bursts, following months of anguish and doubt. Like a sore that festered then burst, leaving me soon depleted.

He whispered in my ear. Oh, what he whispered. And the kiss that followed those words. I could have thrown myself on the grass to stop that kiss from ending. But we didn't, we ran, hand-in-hand, to the tower. I think, somehow, we always knew it would happen for the first time at the tower. We'd squirrelled away a cushion here, a blanket there, a book, a torch. Anything to feather our nest. Never setting an intention, but letting intention grow in us.

We were so wrapped up in ourselves we burst through the door kissing each other, hands already reaching for clothes.

'Whoa!'

Startled voices and rustling greeted us.

I squealed. Richard swore and pushed me behind him.

'What are you two up to?'

I knew that voice.

'Rose?' I asked, peeping behind Richard's shoulder into the gloomy interior. Rose's head popped up from the pile of blankets and cushions we'd made against the back wall.

'Elsa?' Rose demanded. 'Jesus, Mother Mary, you gave me a shock.' She let out a huge breath, slumped back against the wall, letting her outstretched arm lower to pull a blanket around her bare breasts. Richard wasn't the only one being defensive. 'What on earth are you doing here?'

'What am I doing here?' I demanded, as high and mighty as guilt could get you. 'What are you doing here?'

Which is when our eyes adjusted enough to see who she'd reared up to protect.

10

Moth woke to dampness. Hanging in the air. Telling in his muscles. Aroused, full of sensation, numb with sleep. A moment that withered. Pushed aside by the sound of planes, traffic, birds. Thick raindrops plopping on canvas. Moisture smothering him.

By the time he crawled out, got the tent down and the bike stowed, he was soaked through and sweating with the battle. The ground mossy and treacherous. The image of Mila stuck in his head. That dark staircase, the grim backyard.

That was yesterday. Forget it.

He'd hoped to wake up and have forgotten about her. Instead his dreams had lurched from one level of grimness to another. Filling him with remorse and guilt until he stood beneath the dripping trees, beside the road, pulling on his cycling gloves. Needing every thin layer of resolve.

This is a fine start.

The morning was brittle with traffic building in the thin light. He was too tired and wet to care about being seen. The road south was calling, the plan screaming. But the voice was strangled, knotted up with his thoughts. He clenched the gloved hands into fists. Villach was about ten km northwest.

You don't need to go north. You're going south.

If he didn't go and sort the knot, it would drag at him all the way south. His legs were stiff and aching, his back rigid from the neck to the hard, brutal seat and his damp shorts. He stood on the edge of the road, looking south. He couldn't do it again.

It's different this time.

Moth got on and headed north, curling his fingers round the handlebars. It would be different this time, he'd make it different.

HE RODE into the outskirts of Villach in the middle of rush hour. It was wet and overcast, stinging his breath, like spring had slipped back into winter. He bought a greasy bread breakfast from a mangy café, found the bus station, echoing in the eerie stillness after the morning rush. Crammed himself and the bike into the disabled toilet. He pushed the handle of the bike against the on button on the drier. Steaming, stinking, eating the vile food, he warmed up.

You're going to need more money.

Extra money that would mess up his monthly budget. Enough money to buy a train ticket, and he couldn't afford to get it wrong by skimping.

Which means calling Ben.

He'd have to purchase the ticket himself. Which would make him visible. He was nervous, and watchful, but warmer now. Soothed by food in his belly.

You're sticking your neck out.

It was a little unexpected work, an irritating expense, and he could move on. Unburdened by thoughts of what he could have done.

He unloaded the bike, hitched it up in one of the crammed bike racks. Devoid of its pannier bags it disappeared into obscurity. Stowing everything bar the handlebar bag in the station lockers he caught a bus to the nearest public swimming baths.

He had a short swim, took a long watchful shower. Used the changing rooms to smarten up. By the time he left he'd acquired a messenger bag and found a white shirt that fitted him. With his one pair of grey trousers, his dusted-off trainers and his rain jacket he felt neat for the first time in weeks. Not just clean, but trim, and sharp. He put the beanie hat away in his new bag, his hair still wet from the shower, slicked back.

You look like an office worker, or a business student.

That was what she'd said. The day they parted. Not a schoolboy.

The weather as he came out of the baths seemed to be aspiring with him. The wind taut, the clouds rolling back. The steel sharp light glinting at their edges loaded with the promise of sunshine. Moth headed into town.

His first stop was a pharmacy, he bought a tin of spray hair colourant and some gel. In yet another disabled toilet he stripped off his new shirt, streaked the spray through his hair. Watched as he went from damp rusty to chestnut streaks, finishing off the sharp look with the gel and chucking the tins in the bin. At the newsagents he bought a pack of large padded envelopes and a newspaper. Wrote her address on the envelope, slipped his notebook, some money, and the cigarette case inside. Had it weighed and stamped at the post office. They were heavy enough to cover the stamp of the true contents he'd put in later. The spare envelopes and the unread paper he threw in the bin. By midday he'd found another internet café. By the time he plotted out the train and bus route Mila would need to take, his teeth were aching with the Diet Cokes he was binge drinking.

Next stop, the bank.

He found a public telephone and punched in the memorised numbers. Ben picked up on the second ring.

'Hey, Ben.'

'Moth! Is that you, you little runt?'

'Yeah, how you doing?'

'Did you ring that arsehole yet?'

'Kit?' Moth said. 'Yeah, I rang him.'

'About bloody time, I swear I was going to tell you to stick it when you rang. He is a major ball-busting full-time wank...'

'Yeah, he's a princess, I agree,' Moth interrupted. 'But hopefully he's off your back now.'

Ben grumbled but took his word. 'So, where are you?' he asked. 'I'm missing you.'

'I doubt it. How's business?'

'Stellar,' he said. 'Come home and I'll tell you all about it.'

'Tell me now, maybe I'll come home.'

'Hah,' Ben laughed at him. 'Somehow, I don't believe you.'

'Wiser than ever.' Moth looked round him at the street, conscious of his accent, keeping his voice low. People were hurrying past, nervous of the changeable weather.

'Is that what you're ringing for?'

'No,' Moth said. 'I need an extra transfer. £1200.'

'What for this time?' Ben asked. 'Bike falling apart again?'

'I need a ticket,' Moth said, thinking over past lies, thinking about this one.

'A ticket home?'

'Perhaps, but not for me.'

'You ever going to trust me?'

'You're the one who said not to trust anyone,' Moth told him. 'But I like you, so you should be flattered.'

'Yeah I know, I heard it before,' Ben told him. 'Who's the ticket for?'

'A girl, in a bad place.'

'There's always a girl in a bad place, you know that.'

Yes, you do. If only Ben knew.

Moth didn't think Ben would care if he did know. Ben was more likely to be causing trouble than rescuing people from it. He wasn't the friend Moth would have chosen, all things considered.

You didn't have many options.

'I'm not asking for a favour, Ben. I just need the transfer.'

'When?'

'Now, I'm outside the bank.' Moth looked across at the cashpoint. They were all covered with cameras these days. He never liked withdrawing money.

'I have a life you know, meetings, clients.'

'Yeah, I know, all of them dodgy too,' Moth said. 'I know it's short notice. I'll pay you double.'

'Triple.'

'You robbing bastard,' Moth told him, fuming at the lost money.

When he needed money, he rang Ben. Ben transferred money from the funds Moth had given him to a bank account no one knew about and took a ten percent cut. The mutual bank account in Ben's name held money for about five minutes, between the call that Moth made and withdrawing it. The shallow boundaries of their friendship and the ten percent cut was all that held the agreement together. Moth thought about the funds he'd put aside before leaving. He'd spent more than half, and this was an extra chunk not allowed for. Each pound lost was a decision he couldn't pull back.

A choice that might matter.

He thought about Mila, and the image pulled others closer.

'Ok, done.'

'Wow,' Ben exclaimed. 'I didn't expect you to agree, she better have fucked your brains out for this one.'

'She makes amazing coffee,' Moth lied.

'Christ, you rescuing a waitress, or what?'

'Or what.'

'Ok, twelve, in your account, I'm sending it now. It's good to hear from you, don't stay quiet for so long.'

'No promises.'

'Not much longer left though,' Ben told him. 'You could start thinking about coming home.'

'Home?' Moth repeated. 'Where the hell is that anyway?'

'I guess it's wherever your sad little heart thinks it is.'

'I'll be sure and ask, next time it speaks to me,' Moth said.

Ben laughed at him. There was another silence neither of them wanted to end.

'I'll see you, mate,' Ben said.

Moth hung up.

IT WASN'T FAR off five o'clock when he got to the station. The crowds pushing through the gates thick enough to give him confidence.

He pushed his hand through his hair, it was stiff with gel, damp with perspiration, leaving a slight stain on his palm. He checked the collar of his shirt in a window but couldn't see. He looked for the gents. Decided against it. Another chance to be seen. The perspiration gathered into a sweat.

This is a bad idea. You should leave.

Not yet, he'd get this ticket first, then get gone. The bike was waiting, and he would cycle out with the evening rush hour and be gone south by the end of the day. He adjusted the strange bag across his hip and headed for the ticket counter.

The noise was aggressive. Rushing feet and phone conversations. People ignoring people, pushing past each other, irritated by the sheer numbers. All of them looking at him, seeing right through him, past the strange clothes and the slicked back hair. His hand went to pull his beanie hat down further and fisted in panic with its own habit. Smoothed across his hair to justify the movement. Queues at so many counters it was hard to make sense of anything. All of it alien, and him most of all. Language, fast and foreign, hurling at him. Moth found the ticket counters, moved to join the shortest queue. To find the one two down was going faster.

He had the piece of paper in his hand, each link written down in neat capitals. His German was adequate, and most people's English was better, but silence was better still. He waited. Shallow breathing, feet tapping, skin crawling. Shuffling from foot to foot, feigning boredom mixed with irritation. Watching people pass the time on their phones.

They have their uses. You can hide behind a mobile. Everyone does it.

He scanned the crowds instead, keeping his head down. Aware he was the only one looking round. Wondering if he could steal a phone for moments like this.

There's a lot of policemen here.

He counted them, by stairs, by walls. All stood, walking or talking, in pairs. He preferred them in pairs. He didn't believe two heads were better than one. Each head trusted the other one to do the job for them. He moved two steps closer to the counter, one customer away from the cashier. There was nothing to fear.

You look no different to anyone else here. You're nobody.

The person in front of him moved forward. He rubbed the piece of paper in his hand, looked up and around one last time.

Followed the thick shoulders of a uniformed double act walk past him, towards the entrance. Taking up a stance by the doors, hands on their radios. Moth looked to the next set of doors, more police.

They're at all the doors.

Moth watched his exits being covered. His breath a freezing ball of panic stuck in his chest. Sweat swamping his hair and forehead. His fingers rigid on the surface of the soft paper. The urge to run coiling in his muscles. But the policemen were by the door, by every door. So many.

How did you not notice?

If he stepped out of line now it would be like banging a bell.

See it through, you've got no choice.

He turned back to the counter, battling the bile, watched the counter clear. He made his legs work, pumping the blood through the wobbling muscles, moving forward. Paper pushed over the counter. He got a grunt in response. The piece of paper did what he wanted.

Stay calm, get the ticket.

Moth looked away, back to the doors. The policemen were paired up at each set of doors, but they weren't giving anything away. They weren't checking people or bags, but they were waiting, and they were watching. He could see other people failing to notice them. It wasn't obvious what was happening, no wonder he'd walked in without seeing them.

And you're going to walk straight back out past them.

He turned back to the cashier, the sickness spread from his throat to his stomach, clenching, rumbling. He saw the cashier grin at him. Moth grinned back. One man to another. He handed over the wad of cash.

He drummed his fingers on the top of the counter. The tickets were printing now, an interconnected string of stops, each a step for Mila. A place in the map that he could see, a road out of the dump she was in, ending in a place he could leave her.

Forget her.

With Beau. In a restaurant she couldn't manage and wouldn't leave. In a small kind village overlooking the wild sea. Mila would fit in there. Beau would see her safe.

Safer than you are getting her there.

It was done, tickets in hand. He had to turn and face the crowds and the doors. His stomach churned again and got a smile of approval from the cashier.

'Hungry?' he asked in English.

'Hungern,' Moth agreed in German.

'Dieser Ort ist gut,' the guy pointed behind him.

Moth turned to look at a food stall. A short queue, customers walking away, their faces down in a serviette full of steam. 'Ja, gut?'

'Ha,' the cashier patted his belly, leaning back in the chair to show his girth. 'Jeden tag!'

'Danke,' Moth said.

'Bitte, bitte,' he waved him off, out of the way, calling the next customer to the desk.

It was the only idea he had. He got himself a serviette full of food, ducked over it and walked for the exit. Bag over his shoulder, head down to lessen his height, he walked with the concentration of the hungry to the door.

The stairs to the platforms swelled with an offloading of passengers and they swarmed into the foyer. Shouts broke out. He turned and looked, fighting an urge to run so strong he needed to piss. He couldn't see anything. People crowding closer.

You're part of the crowd, invisible in the middle.

His skin was crawling. Body parts pressing in like a landslide. The sharp fermented warmth of the sauerkraut sticking in his nostrils.

Policemen came running past him, heading toward the commotion. Those at the doors stayed put. Peering over the crowds to the platform stairwells, hanging onto their radios in concentration. The crowd's eagerness to get out pushing him towards them. Moth unable to resist, desperate to get away. White knuckled as he passed under their noses and scanning eyes.

Don't look at them.

The doors opened and he was through, into the damp fresh gusts of dusk. The blaring fury of waiting taxis and traffic rushing up into the sky. He chucked his sauerkraut mix in the nearest bin, ran towards the bus waiting at the stop.

That was too close. Stupid bloody idea.

Moth sat on the bus, swaying and jerking with the stop start crawl back to the station. His moist hands struggling to get the tickets into the envelope. The serrated edges catching the soft bubble wrap inside. Their insignificance berating him. It had been too big a risk. For what seemed so little.

What will she do with it anyway?

She had enough sense to distrust him. She'd put all his effort and money straight in the bin. Moth curled his shaking fingers into fists. Unclenched them, willing them to be calmer.

You think she's going to pack up and go on a whim?

He pulled his handlebar bag out, found the postcards in their plastic wallet. Guéthary at the top of the pile. The front of Beau's restaurant with its flowering baskets and check-clothed tables. He turned it over, read the scrawl on the back, the three shaky kisses of her old hands.

That's all you have of her.

He tucked it inside, sealed the bag and hugged it to his chest. He posted it outside the bus station, wondering if it would be enough. Hand reluctant to let go. It wasn't about Mila. Whether she did something with it or not. It was about knowing he'd done something.

He changed back into himself in the disabled toilet, pulled the beanie hat down with relief. Tweaked the hat into position in the cheap tin mirror. It showed the signs of his life, ragged round the edges, battered from the trail. Perhaps he couldn't stitch himself up like he had the hat. But he could make adjustments.

You can't make amends.

He couldn't change the past. But he could try to do better than the past. And what was a postcard worth compared to peace of mind?

Moth hailed out of Villach as fast as exhaustion could take him on roads swollen with the evening rush. The first road out of the traffic went west, chasing the final hues of blue in the sky. Pulling him onto a good, quiet road heading further northwest. He hurtled along it.

Time to look at the map later.

The night turned dry in a wind that was keen and cold. Biting into his exposed skin. Cycled out and hunting for somewhere to stop, in the last minutes of the day, he found a cheap hotel mainstaying a ragged band of motel lodge rooms. Lights illuminating the all-night petrol station. The extra cash left from Ben persuaded him. He bought a straining plastic bag full of food, took a lodge room, locking the door and pushing a chair under the handle. Set the bike against the chair. The room as tired and dingy as he was. The bed stained around the base, with ill made sheets. The furniture slick with use. The paint chipped and flaking. Mould pacman-ing its way round the bathroom tiles. He despised it.

He ran a bath and lay in it for an hour, letting the hair dye drain into the water. Wrapped himself up, naked and wet, in the single clean sheet that was folded in the wardrobe and let it warm and dry him. Spread his maps out beneath the heater, focusing what was left of his energy on them, eating the cheap food as he traced the road he'd followed.

You need to work out where you are.

He was on the Austrian border with Italy, heading towards Mauthen. He could head back the way he'd come, through Villach and onto the road south, cutting across Slovenia and into Croatia.

That means going back on yourself.

Or he turned straight south, cut across the northeast corner of Italy and round the bulk of Triglav, meeting up with the southern road in Slovenia by Trieste. He hadn't meant to come this far west. His finger followed the road he was on even further west. Eyes seeking out options, trailing until they found Iseo.

It's on the same page of your map.

Moth counted the distance with his fingers. His rough judgement allowed two boxes a day. It wasn't a set goal, but two boxes a day was his norm. A swift way to lay out his day. Iseo was in the seventh box. Kit was supposed to be there in five days. He was closer than he'd realised.

It's a long loop back east if you go.

There was no point in going. He was on the border, about to head out of central Europe, down towards Greece, and away. Where the plan took him.

And what if you do go? What for?

He looked at the boxes between him and Iseo. Fingers hopscotching across the triangles. The Dolomites. A last chance to ride the mountains before he left Europe.

Are you sure this is about the mountains?

It wasn't about Kit. Sod Kit. He'd curve west, through the mountains, and head south later. He'd follow the route east, to Venice. Catch a boat to Greece even. Make up the change of route.

Moth soaked up the details. The distances, the heights, the passes, distance versus diversion. How many miles each road would mean, how many days. Toying with options, trying to focus on the plan. Letting the plan stay solid, moving the route to get there.

It's your plan. You can change it, as long as you stick to it.

He gave up trying to make sense of it, pulled out the post-cards and spread them across the floor in front of him. Each one a memory. Taking him away from doubt and uncertainty.

You did all this. By yourself.

Criccieth. Dublin. Ventoux. Guéthary, absent, a hole he

left in the spread on the grim stained carpet. Vienna. Venice would look good in the pile. He wrote Day 261, 19th March 2013. Methuen in the notebook. Stared at his scrawl on Day 266, Hotel Castello. Five days away. Refusing to rub it out. Wondering where he might be instead when the day came to fill it in. Wondering how long Kit would be there. He fell asleep, wrapped in the sheets, curled up on the floor beneath the blasting heater.

ISABELLE SAT AT HER TABLE, guiding the needle through the crumbling dusty fabric and pulling the edges together stitch by stitch.

The smell of something old and rotten puffed out with each pass of the needle. She persisted, determined to exert control over the bolster's attempt to offload itself over her table. She pulled the last inch of the hole together and secured the stitches. Snipping the thread and stabbing the needle in the pincushion. The bolster was finished, but she still felt frayed at the edges. Isabelle packed the repairs up in a tube of plastic, squashing the air out of the package, tightening it with sticky tape.

She stretched away from the table, glancing at the pile of finished work. It had been a productive morning. Kit's attentions over the weekend had cured her jetlag. She'd woken early, relieved to be in the bed alone, jumping out with determination and rattling downstairs to her workroom through the peace of a Monday morning. Elsa enjoying the absence of guests, reading the paper in the kitchen and as reluctant to engage as she was. Isabelle squinted at the clock, 11.25 am. She would take the repairs back and have her breakfast up on the common. Grabbing a tote bag, shoving the invoice

inside and grasping the large sausage shaped package, she
left.

The client, Mrs Staines, lived in a double-fronted Georgian house with a crumbling pebbledash finish revealing
stonework in need of repointing. It had belonged to her
family for several generations until Elsa's father bought it for
the Riverdell estate. One day, Mrs Staines would die, and the
house might stand a chance of getting a facelift. For now, she
resisted any effort by Elsa to improve it, repairing the soft
innards one agonising choice at a time, while the house
succumbed to a slow creeping damp and the garden to a swift
growing ivy that waged war with the hydrangeas and rhododendrons.

Isabelle knocked on the door and waited in the damp
morning, hefting the slippery package. Three minutes later
she knocked again. After the third knock the door opened, to
Mrs Staines' housekeeper, Marge.

'Oooh, Isabelle, how lovely.' Marge addressed the carpet
from a spine bowed with arthritis. 'She'll be thrilled, do
come in.'

Isabelle stood on the mat, refusing to let Marge shut the
door, knowing she'd be pinned down inside for an hour or
more. She should have waited until Easter and sent Kit. Mrs
Staines and Kit would talk the sun down and he'd have
cleaned the kitchen by the time it was done. As Marge shuffled down the hallway in her curving slippers, Isabelle shifted
on the coir mat.

'I'll wait here, Marge.'

'No, no, do come, do,' Marge said.

Isabelle stayed where she was, waiting. She glanced at the
pictures that covered the walls, drowning out the faded flock
wallpaper. At the ceiling there was evidence of damp teasing

the paper off the plaster. It would end up like the dining room, where the paper had peeled downwards and hung off the topmost pictures, halted in its descent and crisping over. Neither Mrs Staines nor Marge could any longer look up that far, and visitors were too polite or too embarrassed to mention it. Marge soon came back, trailing behind Mrs Staines, who swept down the hallway in a long plaid skirt and an ugly cable-knit cardigan, a smart silk scarf attempting to liven up the outfit, tied at the side of her neck. On Kate it looked suave, sexy. On Mrs Staines it looked girlish and incongruent.

'Isabelle, darling, how wonderful,' Mrs Staines boomed, wafting her face to either side of Isabelle's in precise and elegant greeting.

'I told her you'd be thrilled,' Marge said.

'And you've done the work, you angel.' Mrs Staines took the package off Isabelle and handed it backwards to Marge.

Marge attacked the wide sticky tape, unpeeling an end and, with the sausage trapped upright between her stocking-rumpled knees, started pulling the work out, exclaiming in happy little puffs of enthusiasm, 'Ooh, look, marvellous, ooh, how clever, oh Isabelle, how perfect.'

'Come in, come in, you simply must see...' Mrs Staines started, but Isabelle was ready for her.

'I wish I could, I'm running errands for Elsa. I can't stay this morning, she'll be furious with me.'

'How selfish of her,' Mrs Staines declared. 'Marge, did you hear that? Elsa is keeping Isabelle all to herself.'

'Well, the children, I suppose,' Marge replied, holding the bolster up and peering to find the repairing stitches. 'Marvellous work, can't see a thing, you're a wonderful seamstress, Isabelle.'

'Thanks, Marge.'

'Oh, of course, the children, I forgot. Poor darlings, just terrible.' Mrs Staines gripped Isabelle's elbow in a show of sympathy. 'Poor James, how awful for Elsa, losing her son like that.'

Isabelle froze in shock.

'David, it was David that died,' Marge told her, plumping a cushion to her sagging bosom as though it could hold up her curving back. 'Not James.'

'Oh, silly me, of course not.' Mrs Staines waved the mistake away. 'James doesn't have children does he, well not yet anyway, eh my dear?'

Isabelle squirmed inside and edged backwards, reclaiming her elbow.

'Have you seen these cushions?' Marge asked, taking the brunt of Mrs Staines' interest off Isabelle. 'They're as good as new. I think we should upgrade them to the snug, what do you think?'

Mrs Staines turned to look at the cushions.

'Marge, put them where you wish, but we must pay Isabelle. Do fetch my purse, will you.'

'I don't know where you've put it,' she told Mrs Staines, handing the invoice to her employer. 'I cannot fetch what I cannot find.'

'Oh dear, not again.' Mrs Staines went blustering down the hallway. 'My memory's not what it used to be.'

'Now, when's Kit coming down next?' Marge asked her. 'Mrs Jones at the Copse told me he was just in town and he never came to see us. I think a mouse has moved into the drawing room over winter. Nests of feather and fabric everywhere.'

'He's coming for Easter, Marge. I'll make sure and tell him to come see you.'

'You make sure and tell him I'll have his ear if he ignores us this time.' Marge listened as, in the depths of the house, they heard a tinkling smash. Mrs Staines looking for her purse.

'What have you broken now?' Marge asked as she came back to the hall.

'The teapot lid,' Mrs Staines replied.

'Well what had you put the purse in there for?'

Mrs Staines ignored Marge and counted out the money to Isabelle. The missing of Mrs Staines' purse was legendary, but all the tradesmen in town knew the two women played this game to conceal where they hid their money. Isabelle thanked them and backed out of the house, spewing false promises to return soon.

Freed of her large burden she climbed the steep narrow lane of Upper Linney and wove her way through the back streets round the church once more. She got a coffee take out from Costa, queued for the sandwich bar to open and took a box of salad and egg. At the bakers she grabbed fresh soft rolls and pastries. She walked down Broad Street, passing under the arch of the old walls. Smiling at the optical illusion of the clipped oval yew tree. At least some things in Ludlow stayed the same. Crossing the bridge with a happy glance to the horseshoe weir she passed the Charlton and turned along the gravel riverside path. Rather than descending to the river she took the higher path to climb up over the town and out onto the common, puffing with exertion at the hill.

Sitting on a bench she could see over the rooftops, to the hills on the far side of the valley. The church tower aspiring to compete with the taller hills that circled it. The crumbling castle squatting on the steep eastern bluff and, at its base, Riverdell. The green skirt of lawn lapping against the river edge. Rising above the dull air that sat over the town, bold behind the tall hills, the sky was bluer and the clouds fanciful wisps. Unsure of what they were or where they were going.

Between sips of coffee and cloud gazing she managed to ignore her thoughts. No longer the Isabelle that lived at Riverdell, or had finished with James, or needed to manage Kit, or had to help Elsa. Not the Isabelle who cringed in front of Hester. Not even the Isabelle that worked away and lived a different life. Herself, free of all expectations, and trying to grasp the freshness of her life.

'Mind if I join you?'

Isabelle jumped out of her liberated skin and spilt coffee over her hand. Moth came forward from behind the back of the bench and grinned at her.

'Sorry,' he offered. 'Didn't mean to scare you.'

'I never heard you coming.'

'Did you burn yourself?' he nodded at the coffee she was wiping off her hand.

'No, not at all.'

'So, may I?'

'Oh, of course, yes,' she shuffled away from the centre of the bench, 'please, do.'

He sat down, the faded green runners of the bench stretching between them. Isabelle felt her peaceful moment take flight and run for the distant hills with their sunny tops.

'I'm sorry about Kit, yesterday,' she said. 'He was such a grouch.'

'That's ok, I can take a hint.' He stared out over the hills, stretching his legs out and crossing his feet at the ankles. Shoving his hands deep into his pockets.

She wrapped her fingers round the warm coffee cup, wishing for the close woods they'd walked through yesterday, not this long vista with the haughty shoulder of the Clee turned against them. The conversations she thought to start withering in her head. She sipped her coffee instead.

'I can't decide if Hester and Kit get on or not.' Moth spoke to the view, without turning to look at her.

'I think it depends on the day,' Isabelle said. 'And their mood.'

Isabelle listened to the cars passing behind them on the narrow back road. Watched dogs snuffling in front of them across the common, small birds diving across the rough clumps of grass and tufts of gorse. Moth's long legs sticking away from the bench. His feet in their plain, well-used trainers. His shoulder nearest to her. He had the beanie hat on and a large puffa jacket that made him seem even bigger than normal. He didn't respond to her.

'Do you mind if I eat?' she asked.

'Course not.'

She pulled her bag open and reached inside to pull the food out, offering him a bread roll. Moth looked at it, then pulled his hand out of his pocket and took it, tearing small pieces off. Each crumb seeming to erase the diffidence, so that he pulled his legs up to the bench, sat up from his slouch and put more attention into the warm fluffy roll.

'I saw you heading into town earlier,' he said. 'Looked like a big package.'

Isabelle could hear the curiosity in his voice. She delved into her salad box, pulling leaves and pepper slices from the mix with her fingers. She wondered how he had found her here. Had he followed her the whole morning?

'Some work I had to deliver,' she explained. 'Elsa stockpiles it while I'm away. I like to try and get through it as soon as possible.'

'I would have carried it for you, if you'd asked.'

'I told you, Moth, you don't need to work for me.'

'I know, but it's nice to have something to do,' Moth told her. 'It gives me a chance to meet people too.'

'Trust me,' she said, waving a limp stick of tenderstem broccoli at him. 'You wouldn't have thanked me for introducing you to Mrs Staines and Marge.'

'I like meeting people.'

'I'll take you next time.'

'How do you know them?'

'It's a small town,' she said, munching down the length of the stem. 'Everyone knows everyone. I can't even remember when I first met them, they were old when Elsa was young.'

'Who's Marge to Mrs Staines?' Moth asked, watching her root through her salad box, the roll reducing by chunks.

'Well, that's a question we'd all like to know the answer to,' she said. 'Marge has been her live-in housekeeper for as long as anyone can recall, but I reckon it's more than that. Mrs Staines was widowed, when she was quite young, I think. But don't quote me on that.'

'When did Marge turn up?' He broke the final lump into two pieces, rolling them into doughy balls between his fingers.

'Again, way before I was old enough to register it. But she's been there ever since, watching over Mrs Staines and all her reputed wealth.'

'Sounds more like a guard dog than a housekeeper.'

Isabelle laughed. 'That's not a bad analogy. They're nice enough, just old, and odd. Keep their money stashed all over the house in china pots. She broke a teapot this morning to pay me.'

'They sound worth a visit.'

'You should go with Kit when he comes at Easter. He loves them to bits, spends hours there winding them up.'

'That sounds like Kit,' Moth said and put one of the doughy pieces into his mouth.

Isabelle rolled her eyes in agreement and chased the final salad leaves into a corner of the box, wrapping them into a ball and fishing them out. The boiled egg was left wobbling in a corner. She pulled it out, shut the box and put it aside, took out the other bread roll from its bag.

'Bit of an odd breakfast, isn't it?' Moth asked.

'I'm an erratic eater. I like eating at odd times, and odd things at those times.'

'Like porridge at midnight?'

'Or salad for brunch, or curry for afternoon tea.' She tore open the roll, put the egg inside and squashed it down together, feeling its softness split inside.

'Is there anything you like doing the same as anyone else?'

Isabelle thought about it. Work, relationships, family, kids, homes. She seemed to feel differently about all those. She looked at the egg sandwich. Eating was one of her worst quirks. As was drinking. Something she preferred to do alone, not a social habit. All that came to mind was sex, and she blushed. She wasn't sure how she felt about sex after the weekend, but she was confident she didn't want to talk about that with Moth.

'Sleeping?' She suggested. He grinned at her, and she blushed even more. She looked back at the unchallenging view. 'I guess I like doing my own thing when I want to do it, how I want to do it. What about you?'

'Are we talking about eating?' he asked. 'Or sleeping?'

Isabelle tried not to squirm on the seat. He was testing her, or punishing her, for spending too much time with Kit.

'Whatever you want to talk about,' she told him, determined to be open.

He looked at her again, leaning forward on his leg, cupping his chin on his hand once more. Looking back at the bread held like a jewel between his finger and thumb, holding it up to the light.

'I'm still figuring it out,' he told her. 'What I like and what I don't like.'

Isabelle felt the crisp air of the high common stir her hair, whirring the threads of their conversation. Moth threw his final crumb out over the common, towards the birds, and they dove and squabbled over it, the hard-rolled nugget giving fair sport.

'You'll make a good traveller then,' she said. 'Curiosity is the best of qualities for a traveller.'

'I can't decide if you're a traveller or not.' Moth sat back against the bench, stuck his legs out once again.

'Oh?' Isabelle finished off her roll, chucking her final crumbs to the birds, but they were light wispy things and didn't reach as far as his rolled nugget of dough. 'What makes you say that?'

'Kit said you never stay home longer than six months, and you only go away to work in Mumbai. I'm not sure that counts as travelling, so much as living in two places.'

'That's not entirely true,' she protested, folding up the empty paper bag. 'I do spend a lot of time in Mumbai, but I go to other places when I'm there.'

'Mostly in and around India then?' Moth asked.

'I guess I tend to go there for work, and take a break during work, and then come home.'

'Nowhere else you want to go?'

'Oh, loads of places!' she said. 'Loads.'

'So how come you don't go?'

She tucked the empty paper bag inside the box, put the box away in her bag, took out the final paper bag, and thought about it.

'Honestly?' she asked, and he raised his eyebrows at her. 'I think I get stuck between home and work. I feel I don't spend enough time in either place so can't justify doing all the other travelling I'd like to.'

'Because of money?'

'Because of willpower, more like.' She set the paper bag on her faded denim knees. 'I'm not extravagantly paid for my work, but it's enough to do what I want, and I'm very lucky. My father left me some property in India so I have a small income on top of that.'

Moth continued to watch her, one eyebrow raised in a manner that looked as pitiful as it did curious.

'I don't have any debts and don't spend all that I earn, anyway, so I could afford to do more.'

'So why don't you?'

'I get stuck,' Isabelle said, looking out over the view. Finding his gaze unnerving, his tone belittling.

'Lots of people do that.'

'Yes, they do.'

'I'm going to be different.'

'How so?'

'It's all about having a plan,' he told her.

As though it were the simplest thing in the world to cure,

this life of hers that seemed to waver between choices and achieve so little. Isabelle wanted to both laugh at his youth and conviction, and cry at the reality that would overtake him. That had overtaken her.

'Life is what happens while you're busy making plans,' she told him instead.

'Life is what happens while you're busy making excuses,' he retorted.

Then she did laugh.

'What?' he asked, his face puckering in irritation.

'You and Kit, between you, me and my useless willpower are going to take a hammering!' She ripped the paper bag on her lap open and revealed two pastries, gleaming with sugar, offering him the choice.

'Now you're talking,' Moth said and reached over to take one.

ISABELLE SETTLED INTO A ROUTINE. Working from early in the mornings, taking the completed orders out to customers in the afternoons, settling back into work in the late afternoons.

Around mealtimes, and between entering and leaving her workroom, she helped Elsa tackle decisions about the house and the children. Child. Because Moth didn't fit that category and, no matter how much Elsa spoke about Nat and her brother in the same breath or with the same concerns, Isabelle was troubled by the idea that anyone could negotiate Moth's future other than Moth himself.

He helped Elsa with Nat, encouraging and suggesting, but when Elsa tried to talk to him about his own arrangements, returning to school, or changing school, he remained impassive. Isabelle held her silence, unwilling to negotiate. Making suggestions over what she could; the house, the guests, visits or outings for Nat.

Hester turned up regularly, voicing her own thoughts, which Elsa seemed to end up agreeing with. Making it clear to Isabelle that the future care of Nat was something she had little influence in. Nat enjoyed Hester's company and, when the three women went out to tackle their latest enterprise, Isabelle retreated with relief to the familiarity of her workroom. Her first week at home passed by, the weekend flurry of guests came and went, and she made it into the second week before realising she had found her place in the house again.

Moth would find her at some point in the day. Fiddling with some scrap or other abandoned on the table, asking her about the family, about Elsa, about James. It was during the silence following one such question, on the quiet Monday afternoon a week after Kit had left, while she was working at the machine and most distracted, that Moth moved away and wandered deeper into the room.

'Do you even know what's in these boxes?' he asked.

Isabelle looked up at his head amongst the towering stacks.

'I hope so,' she said. 'I've put it all in here, so I ought to.'

'You reckon you'll use it all at some point?'

'Hmm, that could be stretching it.' Isabelle focused back on the cushion pinned by the needle. Raising the foot with the knee pad to turn the fabrics at the corner, pulling the thick layers into shape to continue down the next side. 'Repairs are all about using what you have to patch up the damage. It's hard to do that if you don't have anything in reserve.'

'Mind if I have a look round?'

'Go ahead, bore yourself senseless.'

She carried on sewing. It was the last of three cushions she was making as a break to the tedious job laid out on the table. A pair of interlined curtains that had a rotting silk border on three sides. Snipping away the worst of the hanging silk threads, tucking in what could be left, wrapping the new border around the thick edge by grafting it onto the interlining beneath. It was finger-numbingly painful and slow. A job she'd started two days ago and had to keep taking a break from.

'How do you not end up with mice?'

'Determined pest control,' she said. 'I had a few bad experiences when I first moved down here and after that I got good at loading bait boxes on a regular basis.'

'That's a bit barbaric.'

'Yes,' she agreed, holding the cushion layers in place as she sewed to the next corner. 'But I worked hard to claim this space, I wasn't happy when they decided to share it without asking.'

He went quiet and moved on. She turned the last corner, sewed back to the start.

'Are these yours?'

She peered across the room, unable to see what he was up to. She finished off with a backward stitch, took the cushion out from under the foot and put it with the others. Flipped the steady hum of the machine off and walked over to where he was stood. Looking at a set of canvases stacked up against one another.

'Ah, yes, some of them are.' She crossed her arms over her waist. 'Some of them are Hester's.'

He looked at her, eyebrows rising.

'We used to paint together,' she told him, pulling a couple of the frames forward. 'This is one of mine, this is one of hers.'

'They both look pretty good to me, not that I know much about art.'

'We worked together at the end of school, for our final project,' she explained. 'Then, when we left school, we took a year out before going to uni and did a load of exhibitions together. Elsa gave us the old drawing room to work in, the one the guests use now.'

'You two used to be close, huh?'

'I guess, yes. We were all close. James, Hester, and I. We had a lot of fun together. A lot of arguments too.'

'But not my Dad?'

'He wasn't around much.' Isabelle stopped moving the pictures, thinking, frowning. 'Do you know, I forgot about this. Look, this is about you.'

'Me?' Moth asked, looking at the picture.

It was a strange medley of images. Acorns, hands, sweeping currents of watery impressions. It was one of the more abstract pieces, confusing and puzzling.

'Hester did it.' Isabelle explained in slow recollection of the dim events. 'You were born that year, the year we left school. The year after my father died. Your father had lived away for years by then. He fell out with Elsa before you were born, when his own father died.'

'Seems a complete mess,' Moth said.

'The picture or the past?' Isabelle asked.

'Both.'

'Fair comment.'

'What happened to your art partnership?'

'Ah, well,' Isabelle sighed at the thoughts. 'It ended.'

'Evasion,' Moth told her.

'They weren't the best of years,' Isabelle said, stepping

away from the paintings, wanting to go back to her cushions.

'I'd like to know,' Moth said. 'I thought you were helping me understand?'

Isabelle couldn't think how her own personal history would help him understand anything, but she knew her own resistance would fuel his.

'Ok, I'll tell you. But only in return for an answer myself.'

'Go on then, what's your question?' Moth asked, confident she didn't have one.

'I want to know what you're going to do about school.'

Moth scowled at her. 'You want to know, or Elsa does?'

'I want to know, because I think you're evading the question,' Isabelle said.

'And then you'll tell her.'

'No, then I'll tell you to tell her, and feel I've been fair to you both.'

'Really?'

'I'm not a very good go between Moth,' Isabelle said. 'Elsa's asking me to ask you because you won't tell her. Sooner or later she'll get fed up with my failures and ask Kate to talk to you. You might find Kate rather more forceful.'

He remained silent, tight-lipped beside her.

'Your choice. I'll tell you what you asked, if you tell me what I asked. That was the deal we made, right?'

'Fine, I'll tell you,' Moth said. 'Now, you first.'

He let the pictures fall back into place against one another and looked at her. She had to think back to that time, it was a strange blur of unhappiness with pinpricks of clear memory that mattered.

'So, Hester and I were always going to go to university, to do art degrees, but we didn't want to leave James when it came to it. He was trying to manage the farm, and he'd never had the chance to do what he wanted to. We felt bad about following our dreams, so we took a gap year to focus on our work instead. So, we were all here, living and working together, and you were born. Hester was devastated that David never came to see us, she tried to negotiate between him and Elsa about getting over their fallout. She went to see you a few times I think, but I don't think it went well. David wouldn't let Elsa visit.'

Moth frowned at the pictures, stuck his hands in his trousers. Isabelle wondered how painful it might be to hear about his father, rushed on to finish. The rest of it was her story, it wouldn't make much difference to him.

'Anyway, the year soon went, and we were getting ready to go and do our degrees. We'd both been accepted at University College. Then I found out I was pregnant. James wanted me to stay and have the baby, and I wanted to do my degree. In the end I chose not to have the baby, and Hester never forgave me. The way she saw it, there was you, the grandchild no one got to see, and I wouldn't have a grandchild everyone could love.'

'You were what, eighteen, nineteen?' Moth asked.

'I was nineteen.'

'And James?'

'He was twenty-three, and he'd always wanted kids, so it was horrible for him too.' Isabelle wrapped her arms around her waist, keeling inwards over the memory. Hurting James had been horrible.

'What happened then?'

'Well, Hester refused to talk to me. She went off to university and I didn't feel I could go.' Isabelle moved away from the paintings. She hadn't looked at them in years.

'What did you do instead?' Moth followed her towards the table.

'My father had left me property in India, and I needed to go and see what to do with it, but Elsa hadn't wanted me to go, when he died. So, I figured it was a good time to go.'

'By yourself?'

'No, Kate went with me,' Isabelle said. She glanced back at Moth, his voice had been quick with excitement, not disbelief. 'She and Elsa didn't want me going alone.'

'How long were you away?'

'Kate stopped a few weeks, but I stayed about a year in the end. I got some work in the film industry in Mumbai, been there ever since.'

'So you never went to Uni?'

'Not in the end, no.'

'Because of Hester?'

'No, not at all,' Isabelle told him, scooping the cushions up from the small table, laying them out on the calico top of the big one. 'I went past it. I was busy working and I liked it.'

'Then you came back after that?' Moth asked. 'Got back with James?'

'I came home, and Hester was still at Uni. I guess it gave us the chance to be alone for a change. It was a lot different, happier.' Isabelle could feel his question drifting into others.

Moth looked around the room.

'Is that when you started all this?'

'Pretty much. I had to do something, and besides, Elsa had turned our art studio into a guest dining room by then, so I had to find somewhere else.'

'What was James' dream, the one he didn't get to do?'

'Oh no, that's another question altogether. You have to

answer me first,' she protested, picking up a cushion and tussling with it.

'But you'll tell me, afterwards?'

'If you make dinner while I finish these curtains, then yes, I'll tell you about that too,' she said, flipping the inside out to judge the finished effect. 'But, first, the answer to my question. What are you planning to do about school?'

'I'm fourteen, right, so I guess I don't have much choice.' He picked at the roughened calico edge of the worktable. 'I have to go back at some point, but I want to stay around Nat as long as possible before I do.'

'Is that what you want, to go back to your old school?'

'No, I fucking hate the place.'

She stood with her finger poking the innards of the cushion, shocked at his language again. She lay the cushion back down, smoothed its outer face.

'You could move school, somewhere nearer.'

'What's the difference,' Moth told her. 'I don't want to go to school, but it's not my choice. The law says sixteen. Two more years before I can do what I want, not what I'm told.'

Isabelle winced at the anger in his voice. She hadn't expected to provoke a tirade. Moth hid it well behind indifference.

'Sixteen? I thought they'd changed it to eighteen?'

'It's not gone through yet, but even if it does, I can choose, at sixteen, as long as I'm working.'

'It seems kind of a shame if you can't enjoy it somehow.'

'It's what my father wanted, that school, uni, work, all that stuff. To be like him.'

They looked at each other. Isabelle was pulling another cushion right side out, digging her fingers into the bulky reluctant corners to push them through. Moth had his hands dug into his pockets, staring back at her. The cushions were resisting, they had too many layers inside and didn't want to be pushed into place.

'But that's not you, right?'

'I want to get on with my life. I'm sick of sitting in lessons knowing I'm never going to use the knowledge. I want to do something, anything, other than school.' He reached a hand out, trailing it along the table. 'I've wondered about seeing if Elsa can get me compassionate leave for a few years.'

'You could try asking her about home schooling?' Isabelle suggested.

Moth looked at her in surprise.

'She has spoken about it as an option,' Isabelle told him. She enjoyed the reaction, a blink of surprise followed by a scowl of confusion that fell into a glare at the calico table.

'I might talk to her about it.' He looked back up. 'What do you think?'

Isabelle turned the front face of the final cushion out, wondering what it would be like if he stayed around. Who'd get the most out of that. Moth or Nat? Elsa? And what about her?

'I think you should consider all the options,' she told him, laying the cushion on top of the others, smoothing the upper-most layer of fabric and glancing over at the fire. 'I know it feels like you don't have many choices, so, it's got to be what you think. Not anyone else.'

Moth moved towards the fire and put a log on it, looked back at her and said, 'Right, dinner, then you tell me about James.'

He left the room before she could prod him about school again. She packed away the cushions and returned to the laborious task of the border. She'd finished the curtains and was dressing them into neat vertical folds on the table when she heard the fumbling door handle. Moth came into the room balancing a tray on one hand.

'They're not back yet,' he told her. 'I had the kitchen to myself.'

'I love that,' Isabelle said. 'A rare occurrence.'

'Where do you want it, there or by the fire?'

'Over by the fire, please.'

She finished tucking the reluctant new border into shape where it stiffened and protested under her hands. It would work better when gravity was pulling it into place. She left them stretched out on the table to pack afterwards and went over to the large pouffe. He'd brought a bottle of wine and was over by the dresser opening it. She looked over dinner, hungered by the fact she didn't have to make it, and laughed.

'What?'

'That's got to be the most interesting dinner I ever saw,' she told him. 'You're going to need to work on your culinary skills if you want to be self-sufficient in the world!'

'You like eccentric,' he said, coming back over to look at it. 'Pick and mix, right?'

'Salad leaves, chopped apple, cheese on toast, as in cheese, on toast, crisps, chocolate biscuits, carrots, as in whole carrots, pickled onions, where did you even find those? Peaches, boiled eggs, more cheese and cheese biscuits.'

Moth handed her a glass of wine, 'Well, at least I brought wine, right?'

'Oh yes, that's fine then, all culinary skills excused in that light.' Isabelle said, sipping it. 'Not unlike James, again,' she added. 'He never has learned how to cook. Food is something that appears before him. Or a microwave dinner.'

'I'm not like him,' Moth protested. Isabelle cocked an eye

at him. 'I'm not going to be like he is, anyway, I just need more practice.'

'Well, that's something anyway. Perhaps ask Kate, she could teach you,' Isabelle suggested, sitting down and starting her dinner. 'Pick and mix, I like it.'

Moth sat down on the other end of the sofa.

'Surely this isn't all for me?'

'I sort of ate a lot while I was doing it,' he told her.

'I guess I should be impressed you can boil an egg,' Isabelle told him. 'You're one up on James there, he destroyed a saucepan and almost set the kitchen on fire trying to prove Kate wrong.'

'I bet she loved that,' Moth said.

'She might have mentioned it once or twice.'

'Why did he want to prove he could cook an egg?'

'She claimed he'd never survive past the county border, he couldn't even cook an egg, so he decided to try, and something happened on the farm...'

'... as it does...'

'... and he went to see to it...'

'... as he would...'

'... and came back an hour later to exploded egg on the ceiling and a burning saucepan on a gas hob,' Isabelle said, grinning as Moth shook his head.

'Where was he going?'

'Around the world, a bit like you, but I won't mention that similarity,' Isabelle said, peeling an egg apart, warm on her palm. 'That was his dream.'

'I thought James always wanted to farm?'

'He did, but he wanted to travel first.' Isabelle looked over her shoulder into the depths of the room, memory stirring in the darkness. 'Hmm, I think it's still in here somewhere.'

'What?'

'The tent we made.'

'You made a tent?'

'A prototype bike tent. He was a keen cyclist when he was younger, used to go off for days at a time. We made a tent that fitted over the bike. He was going to get it patented but I think that got abandoned too,' Isabelle said. 'Anyway, he decided he was going to cycle round the world, see how far he could get. He had it all planned out. Except of course he couldn't cook.'

'That's hardly the biggest issue,' Moth pointed out.

'Yes, I'm pretty sure that's what he thought too.'

'But he never went?'

'His father died, a few months before he was due to go. He had to take on the farm or lose it. He gave up the travelling, never had a chance to go back to it.'

'And the tent is here?' Moth asked, standing up and looking out into the room.

'Somewhere, I think. Hang on, let me finish this delicious dinner, and I'll look for it.'

'What about the bike?'

'I think James might have it up at the farm, you'd have to ask him.' Isabelle looked at him, caught up with the impact of her idle ramblings, concentrated on the flush in his cheeks, his eyes staring out into the room with sweeping interest. 'Not that I think you should go cycling round the world, Moth. That's not what I'm suggesting, right?'

'No, I know,' he said. 'But it's a pretty cool idea, you must admit.'

'No, I must not admit,' Isabelle countered. 'Why would you want to cycle your way round the world, do you realise how big the world is Moth? That's why we have cars, and trains and planes. I never got the idea myself. Wales for a weekend maybe, even Scotland, but beyond that it seemed a very, you know, blokeish thing to want to do.'

'Well, seeing as how you think I'm so like James, maybe that's why I think it's a cool idea,' Moth suggested.

Isabelle sipped from her wine again. Nibbled at dinner. Moth even reached over in the silence and took a cheese-laden piece of cold toast, eating it. A flush of anxiety crept over her. She needed to think about what she said more with Moth, a thought that made her feel manipulative.

She rose to get away from the mess she was sitting in, wandered into the room full of boxes, and started looking. Things were piled in a rough chronological order, but it wasn't what you could call organised. The tent for the bike was in a thin box, crumpled beneath the weight of others. She couldn't even remember why it was with her, not James. Moth trailed along in her shadow.

'Here it is,' she said. 'Help me get it out.'

Moth took the boxes she was unstacking, piling them around him as she tugged the package from beneath a larger box.

'Do you ever think about having a clear out in here?' Moth asked.

'Yes, that's usually when I decide to go away and work for a few months,' Isabelle told him.

'How long since you last had this out?' he asked, carrying the tent back to the open space in front of the fire.

'Not since it was first packed away,' she told him. 'James never wanted it again.'

'It's very small,' Moth said, looking at the narrow tube of dark green fabric.

'That was the idea.' Isabelle retreated to the sofa with her wine glass. 'It had to be light, and pack away into a small space. Look, these are the few pegs it needs, one for each end, and each side of the frame. And those,' she pointed at the dark blue fabric left in the bottom of the box, 'those are the pannier bags. We made those too, to fit the tent.'

'How does it stand up?' Moth asked, pulling at the fabric and trying to make sense of it. 'Where are the rods?'

'You need the bike,' Isabelle explained. 'The bike supports the tent. There are no rods.'

'And you made this?'

'We made it together. This was the last one, there were a few before we settled on this design,' Isabelle looked at the stitches. 'It's a bit rough, I've got a lot better at sewing since then, but it worked. James took it off on several trips away before he gave up cycling.'

'Would it be possible for me to have this?' Moth asked. 'If you don't think you're ever going to use it?'

Isabelle looked at him, picking over the remnants of the old tent, its musty smell warming in front of the fire. He reminded her of James, sat watching her piece the tent together, excited at what they were doing. It had been the first thing they'd ever done together, Hester having no time for sewing. It had marked out the beginning of their closeness, when she was only fourteen, a bond strengthened by the death of his father, and then hers.

'You should talk to James, I'm sure he won't mind, and I don't,' Isabelle said. 'I'm not sure what happened to the bike, the tent might not fit a different bike. One condition though.'

Moth looked up at her, full of his own ideas and glowing with excitement, cocking an eyebrow in query.

'Please talk to Elsa about this,' Isabelle asked. 'Don't disappear without asking her first. I don't want her giving me grief for telling you about this.'

He didn't respond, pulling at pieces of the tent, desperate to see how it worked, frustrated by the lack of a bike.

'Will you talk to her, for me, please?' Isabelle asked. 'About the tent and the bike, if you get anywhere with James.'

'If I get anywhere with James, of course I will.'

TWO DAYS later Isabelle was sat at the overlocking machine, covered in hessian dust and sneezing. Working through an order for 450 sacks and finishing off number 232. She was looking forward to number 250, when she'd promised herself a pause. There was a knock at her door. It wouldn't be Moth, he no longer knocked.

'Come in,' she called, unwilling to get up and disturb the dust, craning her head to see who it was.

James came in, holding the door in front of him. 'Hi, you got a minute?'

'Yes, of course. You don't have to knock!' Isabelle told him. 'Honestly, don't start that.'

He shrugged and she had the feeling he'd been outside the door debating the choice. She heaved the pile of hessian cloth off and rose from under the piles surrounding her chair, sneezing in the process.

'You're not still doing that awful job, are you?' James asked.

'Yes, of course I am,' Isabelle said, dusting off her clothes. 'How do I get out of it, without offending one of your mother's oldest friends? Got time for a cuppa?'

'Ehm.' He looked at the kettle, back to the door. 'No, sorry. I wanted to ask about this business with Moth, and the bike.'

'Oh, he talked to you about it?' Isabelle went to put the kettle on. Number 233 could wait.

'Yes, yes he did,' James said. 'I told him he could have the bike, as long as he paid for it.'

'Oh,' said Isabelle, looking at him in surprise. 'Is that necessary?'

'I know,' James said, taking awkward steps forwards into the space. 'It seems a bit mean, that's what I wanted to check with you.'

'Shouldn't you ask your mother?'

'Well, I'm not sure,' he said, leaning against the edge of the big table, unwilling to go further. Isabelle was at the far end of the room by the dresser, looking for a clean cup. The space seemed to stretch out between them, James hazy in the distance. 'He said you gave him the tent.'

'Was that wrong?'

'No, not at all,' he said. 'And it's not about the money, for the bike. I thought it would mean more if he earned it. I didn't want him feeling like a charity case I suppose.'

Isabelle leant against the dresser while the kettle boiled, realising how observant James had been, wishing she'd thought of it herself. Immediately hating the idea of asking Moth to earn anything and realising she could not have done what James had.

'I told him he could work for me to earn the money. He seems to like working at the farm. But, now, I'm a bit worried. I mean do you think that's alright?'

'That was astute, James,' she said. 'And kind. I wish I'd thought of it.'

'Really?'

She wondered when he would find someone else to ask approval of. Reluctant to worry his mother over any details he could avoid, missing her confidence. They hadn't been alone together since they'd separated. She'd seen more of

Moth than James. If Moth reminded her of James then, right now, James reminded her of Moth, and she realised she preferred the time she spent with Moth. The box-stacked space that stretched between them seemed full of history. She hadn't missed it, and the pang of that hit her, how she only now thought of it. Whilst perhaps he had. Missed her, and the ways in which he pulled her into his life, asking for approval, or opinion. She turned back to the clarity of the dresser.

'Did you ask that agent out yet?' she asked, looking at the water pouring into the cup, hissing and steaming round the teabag. The aniseed taint rising into her deep breath. She let it brew, turned back to see James blushing. Heat spreading through his face, up above the line of his unshaven face and towards his eyes, which blinked rapidly. She could see the shade of his discomfort in his rising shoulders.

'Yes,' he said. 'We went out twice. For coffee, and a meal.'

'Twice is good,' Isabelle said. 'You must have enjoyed it.'

'I think she did,' James said. 'I mean, I did, and I hope she did.'

'Are you going to see her again?' Isabelle turned to stab the teabag to life, squeezing the heart of it, dredging it out to chill on the side.

'It's her birthday tomorrow, I'm taking her out for the day.'

'On Good Friday, that's great. Any nice plans?'

'I thought possibly... Hay-on-Wye for the day. Maybe canoeing on the river.' James said.

'And lunch afterwards?' Isabelle asked. 'At the Cross?' She turned back to face him, the scalding cup nestled between her jiggling hands, raising it up to her lips to blow on it. 'Sure you don't want tea?'

'No, thanks, really, I can't stop.'

'She'll love it.' Isabelle was shocked at the absence of jealousy or anger inside. It had been one of their favourite trips, and there was nothing inside that smarted at the idea of him doing it with someone else. Perhaps it had always been one of his favourite things to do. 'Plus, if she doesn't, you've shown her who you are, so you'll know it's no good anyway.'

He shrugged in silence. She could have shaken him. Except it was no longer her job.

'Have a great day,' Isabelle said. 'Kit's coming up tomorrow, he's taking Moth out for the day. He reckons we're smothering him with provincial boredom.'

'Well, he won't get that tomorrow.'

Isabelle grinned at the scowl in his voice, leaning against the dresser, her skin adjusting to the heat of the cup.

'Isabelle,' he started.

'Yes?'

'This thing, you know, you and Kit?'

'Yes?'

'Is it, I mean, you will, you know.' He stopped, crumbling with the effort, running a hand through his rough hair in frustration.

'I think you did the right thing about the bike.' She changed the subject before he tried again. 'It will mean more to Moth that he earned it.'

'It's pretty rusted up,' James said. 'It's been in a leaky barn for too long.'

Isabelle looked straight at him. 'Nothing a bit of TLC and patience won't put right.'

James' shoulders sagged, hanging his head and reducing his height beside the table. Even from that hazy distance she could recall the bashful detail of it, and she felt her stomach flip. Well, at least she could still feel something. She had always adored how humble he was. She smiled back, sipping from her mug, steam rising into her eyes.

'Thanks,' he said. 'I'll let you get back to your sacks.'

'Oh great.' She watched him turn to go, open the door, and was about to walk through when she thought of something.

'James,' she called. He paused, holding the handle. 'Make sure you order the sharing platter at the Cross, it's the best thing on the menu. And, James, don't tell her that we used to go there. You don't need to be that honest.'

He turned his head over his shoulder, not seeing, listening, and pulled the door too behind him without responding.

Isabelle looked out at the sun lingering over the gardens. The day had been gorgeous, and Kit would be back tomorrow. The weeks since he'd left had flown by, distracted by work, and Elsa, and Moth. The weekend would be manic, the family were coming for Sunday lunch, and she longed to walk by the river before it began. She looked back at the sacks. They wouldn't get done any sooner. She sat back down at the overlocker and began feeding two pieces of fabric together through the charging needles. It was a simple enough job, but she had to concentrate, the machine was clumsy and the loose, raw hessian had a habit of pulling in different directions. She'd try and get out tonight, before the weekend, and Kit, and the family. Moth hadn't been to see her all day. Now she knew why, working the bike off. She was glad for him, but it would have been nice to see him. Before Kit came back.

KIT FOUND her on the Friday morning in her basement workroom.

He'd arrived at seven, swept through the house and into her empty bedroom, taken in the open curtains and the bedclothes drawn back to air. On the way back downstairs, he'd bumped into two house guests, Nat and, to add to the delay, Elsa. Amazed at the hour, commenting on the quick trip he'd had, how early he must have been up. It was gone eight before he made it down the dusty back stairs and shoved the heavy wooden door aside.

The fire was going strong and the air was musty and warm. A lingering scent of dust and confusion that needed tackling stirred in the draught he made. He sniffed in disagreement. Searching through the visual chaos he found her at the machines.

'At last, there you are!'

'Meaning, here you are!' she retorted.

She put the fabric away from the machine, turned it off and rose. Moving past the big table to him, a happy smile on her face. He felt a tug in his pants. Somehow, he didn't think she was going to be happy enough for that. He'd done the right thing coming up the night before. Last time he'd swamped her. He opened his arms and glimpsed weariness in her eyes before she disappeared beside his neck, her skin warming him through. He wanted to tell her how much he'd missed her. How hard it had been to stay away. How many times he'd wanted to ring. Over the times he had rung.

'You've been working too much,' he told her, tilting her face up, brushing her hair away from her face. 'Have you tackled the backlog yet?'

'Not quite,' she admitted, looking away from him into the room. 'But I've made a dent in it.'

'So, am I going to see you this weekend then?' he asked.

'Or do I need to come and sit at your feet and beg for the crumbs of your attention?'

'No,' she said, cuddling back into him. 'I can spare you more than a few crumbs.'

Kit held her tight, his chest swelling with delight. Breathing in the scent of her hair. She smelled of old fabrics, mildewed and mothy. That smell reminded him of his great grandmother, of growing up, of things he couldn't pinpoint, but knew. She had no business smelling like that. He liked her fresh from the shower, when he could smell her skin, her hair damp with the coconut conditioner she used. He pulled her chin up and kissed her.

'You have to go and see Mrs Staines and Marge,' she told him.

'One kiss from me and you think of two old women?'

'Yes,' she said. 'Because you'll make me forget I need to tell you and then I'll feel bad.'

He kissed her again, holding himself back. Sweet soft kisses that closed her eyes, followed her cheekbone, lingered on her lips. Feeling their warmth, their firmness.

'Have you seen Moth yet?'

'No, not yet.' He intensified his kisses. Running his tongue along the fault line of her taut lips, pulling her upper lip between his, wrapping his arms tighter round her thin shoulders. She responded for a few moments, warming up, her arms snaking around his neck. Kit began to melt inside. Isabelle stiffened up, resisted his kisses. God, it was hard not to grab her. He gritted his teeth as she pulled away, stretching backwards against his arms.

'Are you sure you don't want to come with us?' he asked. 'A day amongst the art galleries?'

'It sounds bliss,' she said, her voice wistful, then glanced at the table. 'But no, I've too much to do, and it'll be more fun without me.'

'Not for me,' he said.

'Well, for Moth, at least.' Isabelle pushed him away. 'You're the one who said he needed a break from us all molly-coddling him.'

'That's not what I said.'

'Near as dammit.'

'Perhaps,' he conceded. He tried to pull her back in for another cuddle.

'No.' Isabelle waved him away. 'Go on, go find Moth, go have your day together.'

'Oh, come on, one more minute before I go, please.'

'No,' she said, backing away. 'You'll be late, go on.'

THEY PULLED out of town less than ten minutes later. Kit unlocked his phone and threw it to Moth in the passenger seat.

'Check out Birmingham,' he said. 'I haven't been there for ages, let's see what's going on today.'

'What do you fancy?' Moth flicked through screens.

'Best place to shop, lunch, art galleries, modern art mind, not some crusty old affair, exhibitions, plus hot clubs.'

'How long we going for?'

'As long as it takes to get this rural taint out of your hair,' Kit told him. 'And I want you to come stay with me in Bristol after Easter. I'll talk to Elsa, sort it with her.'

'Do I want to come to Bristol?'

Kit heard an edge of obnoxious irritation in his voice.

'Don't you want to?' he countered with wounded shock.

'I don't know,' Moth said. 'But it would be nice to have a choice.'

'Moth, would you like to come and visit me in Bristol?'

'I'll tell you at the end of the day, if that's alright,' Moth returned.

'How sensible.'

Moth swirled his fingers around on the phone some more, concentrating, murmuring reluctant approval, 'Birmingham looks quite cool.'

'Ever been there?' Kit asked. He thrashed the Bentley up the Angel Bank of the Clee as it reared away from the town, feeling like he was taking off from the silt of its rural drudge. 'I love this hill, look, all sheep, coarse bracken and amazing view. Imagine how much shagging goes on here.'

'Nope,' Moth said glancing out of the window at the barren common land and stunted looking sheep. 'It looks a bit bleak if you ask me.'

'Yes, but look, the long view, all the way to the city and freedom.'

'You prefer city life?' Moth asked, head back down and flicking.

'Any day,' Kit said. 'It's nice to visit and all, but I lived here long enough, I couldn't wait to get away.'

'You wouldn't come and live here then?'

'Couldn't, not wouldn't,' Kit said. 'I'd die from boredom.'

'Isabelle seems to like it here.'

'She likes both, she could cope wherever she lived.'

'She seems settled on staying for the moment,' Moth said. 'Lunch looks good around the St Peter's district, lots of positive reviews for somewhere called The Carpe Diem, d'you know it?'

'Never heard of it, like the name though.' The car felt alive under his hands. The twisting country roads were made for her engine and grounding, weight holding her into the turns. He floored it round three switching bends and roared uphill on the straight.

'Sharp car,' Moth said.

'Love this little bitch.'

'Had it long?'

'Thirteen months,' Kit said. 'Due for a change but our affair's lingering.'

'You always change your cars so often?'

'Every March, it's nice to freshen things up for spring.'

It took them an hour to drive to Birmingham, the pace slowing as the roads got busier. Small villages coalescing into towns and sprawling into the suburbia of a greater city. In that hour Kit convinced Moth that Riverdell, Elsa, Nat, and Isabelle in particular, were topics best left on the other side of the hill to focus on the current agenda.

'This seems pretty ambitious,' Moth said.

'That's because you've been countrified,' Kit said. 'We need to get your blood moving a bit, you'll be going backwards if you stay much longer.'

'I guess I better not stay much longer.'

'One last thing; find me a privileged parking spot,' Kit told him. 'Did you get the postcode right, I haven't got a clue where I am, oooh, look at that, did you get that in on our trip?'

Moth looked up but they'd passed it, 'What's a privileged parking space?'

'Oh, check my apps. You don't park a car like this in any old car park, bastards scratch the shit out of it.'

Moth got back onto the phone. He punched another code into the satnav and it flashed in consideration before highlighting a new route. Kit followed it and pulled up in a private, attended car park. Moth stretched himself out of the car with gratitude, grinning in the sunshine and looking round with interest.

At last, Moth had relaxed. Kit had been right, about getting him away from Riverdell and all those women fussing over him. Kit grabbed his jacket from the back seat and locked the car up.

'How much dosh did Elsa give you for today?'

'I earned some money off James, I brought that.'

'I told her to give you spending money.'

'Yeah, I know, she did. I gave it to Nat,' Moth told him.

'Your choice,' Kit said. They walked out of the car park, Kit gleaning a few more gems of advice from the attendant. 'Now, I need to shop, so come on, you can be my buying bitch for a morning.'

'Buying bitch?'

'Yeah, you know, buddy you go buying with?'

'Never done that.'

'What, never skipped school and gone to town on Saturday morning instead of service?' Kit asked.

'Nope, skipped sport and spent the morning surfing the web,' Moth told him. 'Guess it's a long time since you were at school, huh?'

'Oh, piss off,' Kit told him. 'It's not nice to mention a guy's age you know.'

'No, it's not.'

'Ha, touché,' Kit said. 'But, come on, there must be something you want? What, what, come on? The whole of Birmingham, what do you fancy?'

Moth scuffed his feet on the pavement. Kit could read desire in any form.

'You might as well spill, I'll get it out of you one way or another.'

'You're going to laugh.'

'Try me,' Kit nudged his shoulder as they strode along the pavement, heading for the steps of a subway.

'I could do with a cycle helmet.'

'What the fuck for?'

'I'm getting a bike off James.' Moth shrugged in embarrassment, looking down at the steps. 'I'd rather not take chances, that's all.'

He was dead serious about it, Kit roared with laughter. 'Jesus, you've been spending too much time with James, never mind Elsa!'

'I was trying to be safe,' Moth said. 'I knew you'd laugh.'

'Buddy, I never laugh about safety. Never.' Kit twirled round and walked backwards through the subway, laughing at Moth's scowl, the sound bouncing off the low ceiling. 'Bike helmet, I'm on it. But let's get me a nice shirt first, yeah?'

THEY STOOD BEFORE THE PAINTING, heads twisted to one side.

'What on earth?' Moth asked.

'Hmm,' Kit said. 'I know, you need to see it upside down.' He turned his back to the painting and bent over double, looking at it from beneath his legs. 'Nope,' he said. 'Still not a clue.'

'Perhaps from the side?' Moth asked. 'You know, like a fly-by?'

'What?'

'Like speeding by in a car and you know you missed something,' Moth said.

They glanced around the gallery. It was arranged with lots

of strange twists and turns, abrupt arrivals in front of the
confusing pictures. For the moment they were alone. They
nodded at each other, walked over to the far side of the small
dead end and picked up speed, sliding past the picture with
their shoes skidding across the polished concrete floor and
thudding into the wall at the opposite side.

'Get anything?' Kit asked.

'A mild concussion.'

They both laughed then hushed each other as they heard
feet approaching from behind a screen. They stood tall in
front of the picture as one of the gallery attendants joined
them.

'Wonderful resonance, hasn't it?' he asked from behind.

Kit turned to face him, Moth's shoulders heaving at his
side, his face stayed looking at the painting.

'It's certainly got something,' Kit enthused.

'Are you looking to increase your collection?'

'Hell no,' Kit said. 'If I buy anything else this month my
wife will leave me, but it's always interesting to find new
artists.'

'This is a Beyoni.' The combination of amusement and
embarrassment in his voice was something Kit wanted to
punch him for and decided to practice on his next new client
in the same second. 'Have you not come across him before?'

'Obviously not,' Kit said, moving forward to stand closer
and saying in a voice that reached over partitions and round
corners. 'Any more Beyonis?' Kit waved a dismissive hand to
indicate the whole gallery. 'I'm not sure if I can face any more
of this bollocks.'

The man laughed, a high-pitched, fading attempt at
amusement, and stepped back from the intimidating
closeness.

'No, no, a mixed display today. All on the contemporary theme of course, we honour the striking and diverse here.'

'But not the ignorant?'

The man laughed his uncomfortable laugh again and backed away. 'Let me know if I can be of any assistance.'

'Any assistance?' Kit asked, his voice low and lewd with suggestion.

The man scurried away.

'Wife?' Moth asked as he left, holding his stomach from laughter.

'Never hurts to have one,' Kit told him. 'Come on, I'm bored with this place, let's look at another.'

'You have the attention span of a gnat,' Moth told him.

'I'm hyper-focused. I see stuff a lot quicker than most people.' Kit took Moth's elbow, steering him towards the door where the sales assistant sat at a magnificent plastic desk, her legs crossed and visible underneath them. 'Terribly uninspiring,' he told her.

Outside Kit scanned the street, checking his phone. Moth stood looking at the canal basin in the refurbished artsy area they were in, the helmet they'd found tucked under a possessive arm, the other stuffed in his jeans pocket. He looked young, and out of place, and Kit wondered what they looked like together, stood outside the art gallery.

'Three-thirty, should be a few bars starting to liven up. Come on, let's see what Birmingham has to offer on a Good Friday afternoon,' he said to Moth, setting off down the street.

'Didn't you have a few glasses of wine at lunch?' Moth asked. 'What about getting home?'

Kit drew breath to tell him off for nagging. The look on his face stopped him dead. Kit held up his phone at him.

'Don't worry, Moth. I get the drink driving thing,' he said. 'I'm looking for a driver to get us home.'

'That's a job?'

'Of course it's a job,' Kit told him. 'Not always this last minute a job, but don't worry, I'm on it. If we can't get a driver, we'll stop the night at a hotel.'

'I'm sorry.' Moth gripped his helmet tighter. It looked like he was carrying a head under there. Kit had begged him to choose one of the neon bright options. The sort of colour he couldn't use in interiors and wouldn't be seen dead in but could never not be attracted to. Moth had gone for as plain as possible. 'I don't want to be a killjoy.'

'Moth,' Kit said, taking him by the elbow again and steering him down the street. 'In your whole life, no matter what the circumstances, you will never, ever, need to apologise, to anyone, for being aware of the consequences of drink driving. That's a ticket you have fully paid, my friend.'

'Great.'

'But don't let it stop you from enjoying life either.' Kit pulled Moth up, so that they were blocking the pavement, gripping his elbow to get Moth's attention. He was doing his best to look anywhere else. 'Experience is like interest. You have to decide if you're going to put your money in the bank or on the credit card.'

'What if someone else already put it on the credit card for you?' Moth asked, looking into the dark, sleek waters of the canal.

'There is no debt you cannot clear.' Kit released his elbow, moved aside to let a young couple pass, and leant against the railing that edged the canal. 'If you're focused enough on getting into credit.'

'You believe that?'

'Hell, yes.' Kit began to walk again, and Moth caught him up. 'The only thing that keeps you where you are is the belief that you can't change it. Look at me. I started out cleaning toilets.'

'You clean toilets?'

'Oh, heavens no, I have staff that do that now. But I used to.'

Moth laughed at him and said, 'No way, I do not believe it.'

'Well, you've misjudged me,' Kit told him. 'I cleaned my first toilets at not much older than you and I never looked back. Thanks to Mrs Staines and Kate I found my calling in life, and it began realising I was not going to spend the rest of it cleaning toilets, but that toilet cleaning is one of the great and tedious necessities of life.'

'Seriously?'

'Indeed.' Kit warmed to the topic, he liked having a stage to speak from. He'd once considered life coaching as a career diversion, but Lou had stared at him with horror. In truth, patience wasn't his strongest point. 'I was out of school more than I was in it when I came to live with Elsa, then I got thrown out at oh, well, you know, about your age. So she sort of gave up, and Kate took over, told me I had to work. She gave me the worst job she could think of and made me do it for months on end. Turd unblocking and toilet cleaning. Not just hers either, she hired me out as a cleaner to Mrs Staines. Old lady turds. I think she thought it would get me back to school.'

'I'll make sure and refuse to clean toilets if she asks me.'

'Yes, good luck with that,' Kit told him, thinking about all the evenings in Kate's bed which had really kept him on the straight and narrow. 'But for me it was a revelation, all these houses that need caring for, and every owner of a big house will tell you that the hardest thing to get is good staff. It was my lightbulb moment.'

'So, you clean houses?'

'I clean lives, dear boy, lives,' Kit said, stretching his shoulders out. 'A house is an expression of its owner. Or, more to the point, the expression that owner wishes others to perceive. And every detail has a cost, and costs must be managed, which means budgets, financing, goals, discussions... the list is endless.'

'So, a house cleaner and an accountant?'

'Who needs a job title?' Kit asked. 'It's so limiting. I am what I need to be and what someone else is prepared to pay me.'

'Isn't that prostitution?'

'Screw you,' Kit told him. 'Sex is never free anyway, there's always a cost to pay somewhere. Ooh look, what do you think?'

They looked through the windows at the opulent bar, lights blazing, colours clashing, mirrors reflecting the room away from itself.

'Looks perfect for you,' Moth told him.

'Shall we?'

'Ok, let's do it.' Moth agreed. 'But no driving home.'

Kit waved his phone at him. 'Ten more minutes, I'll either have us a driver or a hotel booked. After you.'

THE THIRD BAR was their favourite. It had an air somewhere between them. Not too full, which made Moth wriggle. Not too quiet, which made him yawn. They had their backs to the bar, people-watching.

'So, what's your poison?' Kit asked.

'I'm good,' Moth said, raising his glass. He had agreed to his first lager and was avoiding drinking it.

'No, not drink. What's your preference?' Kit asked, gesturing outwards with the dregs of his own frothy tall glass to the people they were watching. 'You know, what's floating your boat?'

'Oh.' Moth looked out over the room, his eyes roving.

Kit wondered where they'd settle. The group of middle-aged mums in out-of-date eveningwear they kept smoothing down around their hips, trying to forget their cares and remember what make up and high heels felt like. The five younger girls at the table next to them, positioned to heighten their discomfort, all short skirts and high boobs. Beyond them, a group of well-dressed lads, eyeing up the younger girls. All tasty enough that they'd catch Moth's eye if that was the way he looked. Dotted about were couples of all ages, some intimate, some ignoring each other. It would be a different scene on Sunday night, when the weekend had worked it's magic and they remembered they liked each other after all.

'Well?' Kit asked again. 'Anything catch your fancy?'

'No, not much.'

'Already attached?'

'No, just not looking I guess.'

'Everyone's looking,' Kit told him.

'Not everyone is.' Moth turned away from the room and toyed with his lager again, sipping the frothy top without taking any of the liquid in.

'Ha,' Kit countered. 'There's your first mistake. We're all looking, all the time. Can't help it, even if we don't want it. It's built in.'

'Cynic.'

'Realist. Sort out a game plan buddy, else you'll waste a lot of time fucking frogs.'

'It's weird,' said Moth. 'You seem like a person who doesn't like rules, yet most of the day you've been telling me to get a plan together.'

'I don't like other people's rules,' Kit said, draining his glass. 'Doesn't mean I don't like my own.'

'How many of these rules do you have?'

'Twenty-one, so far.'

'So far?'

'They expand as experience dictates.'

'I think this beer is making me feel weird,' Moth said.

'I'm not surprised, you've done nothing but suck the bubbles off it.' Kit turned back to the bar. He raised his hand to the waiter and ordered two Diet Cokes. Moth pushed his beer glass back with relief. 'Now, come on, back to this game. Who would you choose to go out with, if you had any choice before you, in this room?'

'None of them.'

'Why not?'

'I don't know,' Moth said. 'What about you?'

'I'm stuck,' Kit said. 'Between the cute quiet guy who's trying to act straight but fancies one of his mates, the long-haired blonde mum who looks like she can't remember what interaction is, and the bright girl with the plait who's being bored senseless by her yob of a date.'

'So that would make you bisexual, or plain confused?' Moth asked. His voice was careful, making light of the conversation. Hiding something if ever Kit had heard it.

'Labels again, what's with you and labels?' Kit said, turning his back on the room to look at Moth in the mirrors behind the bar. 'Labels are an expression of other people's discomfort, not my experience. Many people seem attractive to me, and that gives me the opportunity to be many things myself. I'm open-minded. Which I can afford to be because I have clear rules.'

'Name me one.'

'Never talk about your past relationships.'

'Why?' Moth was looking into his glass, twirling the ice with the cocktail stirrer.

'It's inappropriate to your current one, and it's disrespectful to your past ones.' Kit told him. 'And most people who ask don't give a shit, they're looking for a hold on you.'

'I'll remember that.'

'Yes, but it's not easy,' Kit told him. 'People need to know. They always ask about your past lovers, so you have to be careful not to reveal without seeming secretive.'

'You talk a lot of drunken bollocks.'

'Good, let's go try another bar.' Kit knocked back his drink.

'Do you ever stay still for longer than one drink?'

'You know, that's another good guideline, I might consider that one.' Kit told him. 'Come on, one more bar and I'm done. We'll go and have tea at Kate's, we've missed it at home.'

'Home?'

'Riverdell.'

'Is that home?' Moth asked.

'It's one,' Kit said, pushing away his Coke. 'Let's go see if I can find out what catches your eye.'

Moth groaned at him, 'It's like spending time with Jeremy Kyle!'

'How dare you,' Kit complained, gathering his keys as

Moth picked up his helmet. 'Have you seen the man's dress taste?'

THE DRIVER ARRIVED as they were arguing over the choice available in the next bar. Moth was trying to convince Kit that he wasn't interested in anyone and Kit was having none of it. The driver sauntered up to the bar and asked the barkeeper for Kit by name, then turned to where the barkeeper had pointed them out. Kit watched him walk over to them.

'Moth, if you can't make your mind up, you could do a lot worse than this,' Kit told him.

The driver was dressed in a smart grey suit, with an open-necked white shirt showing off his matt skin underneath, dark trainers silent on the floor and a head full of dreadlocks pulled back in a long ponytail. He was taut, with sharp shoulders under the suit and a broad smile that welcomed the room but still felt sharp. Kit felt, as he always did round Ed and Fred, pasty, whiter than white, like a skinned fish. The guy didn't walk towards them, he danced, reminding Kit of his friend, Jay. He was the epitome of cool, looking like he'd arrived straight from a modelling gig, and Kit enjoyed the blush on Moth's skin as he turned to see. Against that ginger hair it looked hideous. No, not ginger. Apricot, that was it.

'Do you realise you have apricot hair?'

'What?' Moth asked in a gruff voice as the driver reached them.

'Kit Lavelle?' the guy asked, his voice like a kiss in the air.

'De Lavelle, don't forget the 'de', it's very important,' Kit told him, holding a hand out to shake.

The guy's grin widened, and he shook hands with Kit, dancing on his toes with amusement. Nodding his head as

Kit's handshake impressed him with its firmness. The guy had a handgrip like a vice. Kit thought the evening was getting better by the minute.

'Yeah, no problem, de it is,' he said, his voice slow and soothing. 'You guys been having a good time?'

'Immensely,' Kit said. 'Out from the rural sticks for the day and enjoying the break.'

'Ready to head off yet or do you want a bit longer?' he asked. 'Your day, your choice. I'm in no hurry.'

'I think we're already overdue,' Kit said. 'This is Moth, my wingman for the day.'

The guy offered his smile and his hand to Moth, who shook it. Kit leered at him, mouthing the words 'fit as fuck' over the driver's shoulder. Moth never batted an eyelid, but his skin stayed pink. Blush and apricot. What a terrible combination.

'Good to meet you,' Moth said.

'You too Moth, I'm Bern,' the driver said. 'Nice bar man, you guys have good choice.'

'Moth chose this one,' Kit said. 'I must admit I wasn't sure about it, but it's been good. Do you want to go get the car while we finish up?'

'Yeah, sure deal,' Bern said. He pulled his wallet out of his pocket and took out his driving licence, showing it to Kit, then offered him a contract to sign. Kit read it, then signed. 'Fee as agreed, Mr De Lavelle, paid into my account before we start, please.'

'Bank details?' Kit asked.

Moth watched them negotiate the deal, his skin returning to a normal colour. It was the first time Kit had pitied him the ginger tinge to his hair. He'd thought Moth managed it well. Outdoors enough to keep his skin tanned, blond enough to not be painful, without that vile shade James had suffered before the grey improved it. But he couldn't blush. It ruined the cool look he was working on, and blush was a shade that Kit was possessive about. He pushed aside the thoughts, it was time to get home.

'Check that's gone through, Bern,' Kit said. 'We could be selling drugs for all anyone knows,' he added holding up his phone at Moth. 'No one takes any notice these days, this stuff has changed life forever!'

'Now you really sound middle-aged,' Moth told him.

'All good, Mr de Lavelle,' Bern told him.

Kit handed the keys over and gave him the address and the code for the parking lot. He left them to finish their drinks.

'Apricot?' Moth asked.

'Yeah, apricot.' Kit looked around the room. 'Well, for what it's worth I think you swing left of centre,' he said. 'But I don't think you've settled it yet.'

'Are you going to drink up or what?'

'I'm thinking about telling that guy over there you're checking him out,' Kit teased.

'That has to be the worst chat up line ever,' Moth told him. 'If you want to get his attention tell him how cute his haircut is.'

'He does have a good cut,' Kit agreed, looking at the man they were discussing, wondering if it would work on him.

'Come on,' Moth said, finishing off his drink. 'Kate will be waiting.'

'Kate?' Kit asked, blinking at him. 'Why will Kate be waiting?'

'Because you said we'd be having tea at hers,' Moth looked at him in confusion. 'I assumed you'd prearranged it?'

'Oh, of course,' Kit said, knocking his drink back. 'I forgot. Yes, Kate, come on. I'm going to be starving by the time we get back.' He grabbed the unfinished bottle of wine as he stood up.

Outside, the city was bright with lights, noise echoing off hulking structures that towered above them. Cars were thick and slow on the busy street, the air full of damp excitement.

'Easter always feels so different to Christmas,' Kit said, pulling his collar up around his neck against the chill. 'A bit lost and unsure of itself but somehow full of potential.'

'How poetic.'

'It's a bit like you,' Kit told him. 'In fact, it is you! Moth, you are the Easter fucking bunny.'

'Hilarious.'

'I'm serious!' Kit protested. 'All that moist growth burgeoning up from the ground, all that potential, all that hope, so little identity yet. Ooh, it gives me goosebumps. I can't wait to see you blossom. Sprout that little cherry and fucking lose it.'

'What makes you think I haven't?'

'What makes you think I think you haven't?'

'What?'

'Keep up,' Kit mocked him.

'Why are you so obsessed with this?'

His voice was relaxed, indifferent. Too indifferent, Kit thought. A lad his age should be shaking with testosterone, raging with desire. He could feel a tightening of his own thinking about it.

'Curious, not obsessed,' Kit corrected him. 'So, have you?'

'Have I what?'

'Lost your cherry?'

Moth sighed. Kit grinned, it had the tonal quality of a

victim worn down and about to divulge some information at last.

'Look, I'm no fresh-faced choirboy, alright?'

'But not sure about what you fancy either,' Kit said. 'Sooo... I'm guessing whatever experience you've had has been less than satisfactory.'

'Yeah, something like that.' Moth refused to look at him, looking up and down the road for the Bentley instead.

Kit studied the hunched shoulders, the fists in the pockets.

'First time's always the worst,' he said. 'Doesn't mean you should judge the entire event by the opening ceremony.'

Moth huffed in the darkness.

'So, were you the injured or the injuring party?' Kit asked.

Moth turned around. 'What?'

'You heard me fine.' Kit told him, swigging from the bottle. He knew he was pushing it, hoping that Moth would think he was drunk and not get touchy. 'Nothing personal, I'm not judging you. But it's a mistake to assume who's the victim.'

'I didn't hurt anyone. And I'm no fucking victim either.'

Kit heard the edge on that swear word, the way it was ground out between close-knit enamel. He was heating up a little, almost, but on the edge of getting somewhere he could see Moth pull back. Kit kept staring. Break, you stubborn bastard, he thought. He took another swig from the bottle. Moth studied the pavement, the road, the towering buildings opposite.

'Never talk about your past relationships,' Moth said, looking up at him in victory. 'That's what you said.'

'Wow,' Kit said, tucking the bottle against his chest, admiring him. 'You do listen to me.'

'I listen to everyone,' Moth said. 'I don't often do what they say.'

'Handy.'

'Yes, I think so.'

'Right, well as you won't tell me I'm forced to guess,' Kit told him. 'I reckon you got hooked up with a housemaster, or an older prefect. Sounds like private school nastiness to me, never could stand the fucking place. I'll bet there's many a healthy homoerotic desire that's been waylaid by a private school dorm and turned sour.'

Kit counted himself blessed. His own cherry had been lost behind the tennis courts of his old school, where he and another desperate schoolboy had satisfied their shared lusting after the new PE teacher. Several years before he quit school and found his way to Kate's bed. It had been a mutually happy, never spoken of, spur of the moment liberation. Not everyone was as lucky, he knew. Humiliation, pain and guilt accompanied far too much sexual awakening, and he'd had his mother to thank for his own happy experiences.

Moth never said a word, never dropped his glance. Kit swigged from the bottle, watching him back.

'Are you done yet? Because the car's here, and I don't want to discuss this any further in front of the driver,' Moth said.

'Really?'

'Yeah, really, and I'm not getting in the car unless you promise to shut up.'

'You killjoy,' Kit complained. 'I thought we were bonding.'

'Promise, or I'm out of here,' Moth told him as the Bentley pulled up beside the kerb.

'Ok, I promise, Scout's pigging honour.'

Moth climbed into the back and pulled the forward seat back in place behind him. He tried to heave himself into a sitting position and found there was no space for his long legs. Kit got in and stretched all over the front seat. It was going to be a fun trip back.

BERN DROPPED them off at Kate's fifty minutes later, having thrashed the Bentley all the way from Birmingham. In that time Kit had found out all about the guy. His family in Oxford and Stroud. His upcoming thesis for a Master of Engineering degree. The money he earned driving in addition to his job as a race circuit mechanic. The deposit he was saving toward a house in Bournville. His preference for wine over beer. A wish to travel to Japan. Kit liked life stories. They were always revealing. Finding out a life story was like undressing a new lover. Forever surprising.

Bern parked at the back of Kate's bistro like he was stroking a woman to climax, crooning her into the tight spot, and loosed them out. Kit was still laughing as Moth managed to get out of the back, looking an intriguing shade of nauseous under the streetlight, leaning against the nearest wall and giving Kit the finger. Bern locked the car up and handed the keys over to Kit.

'Come and have a coffee before you head off?'

'Thanks, but I'm going to leg it down to the station,' Bern said. 'There's time to catch the last train back if I leave now.'

'Of course, head straight down this street, hang a left at the end, down the hill and then right at the traffic lights,' Kit told him.

'Good to meet you both,' Bern said. 'You look after yourselves now.'

Kit watched as he turned and started a swift, easy run down the street away from them.

'Come on, lil' hulk.' He grabbed Moth's arm and hauled him toward the back door.

It was ten past ten and the bistro was heaving and loud as they pushed in and walked towards the front of the house. The large building was split into small sections, tables hidden behind wooden benches and rustic wooden panelling. Cyanic shades abounded in a riot held together by the strong nutty tones of the wood. It was exuberant and cool in the same glance, and Kate pulled it off by tossing a hundred different patterns of fabric across any surface that would take it. Upholstery fabric, blinds, cushions, voluminous lamp-shades which pulled the high ceiling down, all united with the cerulean shade of the front door. Stoneware pottery in shades of aqua and blue lined the wall behind the service area and hand glazed tiles bounced the light back behind the bar. Moth pulled his arm away, Kit left him his dignity and tracked down Kate. She was sat at a table with Elsa, James and a woman he'd never met.

'Whoa, what's this?' Kit announced as he pulled up, his voice loud enough to make heads turn all the way from the bar. 'A family party and we're not invited!'

He watched the table register his presence. James wincing at his voice, Elsa glaring, the unknown woman smiling in uncertain welcome and Kate struggling between a frown and a grin.

'Moth, do you see this too? Are my eyes deceiving me? Is this shameless or what?'

Kit watched them all looking from him to Moth and back at him as Moth waved a feeble hand and said 'Hi.'

'Why don't you join us, boys?' Elsa said in acidic invitation of the inevitable.

'I'll fetch seats,' Kate said. 'And coffee.' She stopped to

look at Moth as she stood up, grasping his chin. 'And some food.' She grasped the empty bottle from Kit's hand as she left. 'Heathen, you drank this from the bottle?'

'And who is this?' Kit asked of the unknown woman, grinning at her. She was smart, dark-haired and making the most of plain looks. Makeup sparkling on her doughy skin, brown eyes dressed with a fleck of gold shadow, and unremarkable lips made fuller with a shade of plum gloss that added tantalising depth to her face. 'Please, introduce us, James.'

'Asha' James said, offering his companion's name. 'Please meet my nephew, Timothy, and...'

'... Moth, he much prefers Moth,' Kit interrupted, 'and I'm Kit, de Lavelle, his nemesis.' He gave a pointed sideways roll of the eyes at James.

'A rather drunk Kit de Lavelle,' Elsa added.

'Nephew and nemesis?' Asha asked with a grin. 'What an interesting pair you make.'

'Oh, you have no idea,' Kit told her. 'This partnership rocks, let me tell you, we have had a great day.'

'I'm not sure I want to know all the details,' Elsa interjected.

Kate came back with a member of staff carrying chairs, a tray of coffee in her one hand and a platter of bread and oil in the other which she slid onto the table.

'You, sit,' she told Kit, pushing him towards a chair away from Asha and James. 'You, sit and eat,' she told Moth, nudging him onto a chair next to Elsa. 'Be nice, Kit. The family is trying to make a good impression on this lovely lady, don't spoil it after all James' hard work today.'

'Ooh, tell me all,' Kit said. 'What has he been doing to you?'

'We have been rowing on the river,' Asha said, smiling at

James and back at Kit, 'and all round a town full of such sweet shops, all selling books. And had lunch, and then more book shops, and a walk in the hills too.'

'Ah, Hay-on-Wye, eh?' Kit asked.

The table stilled to a hush. Moth was the only one who didn't raise his eyes with a pointed glare.

'Yes, that's it,' Asha said. 'Have you been there?'

'Oh, back some time,' Kit breezed, dipping a chunk of warm bread in the oil and sucking the drips off. 'Did he take you to the Cross? They always did amazing food there. Yes? Oh, good choice, James.'

The others remained silent. Kit was sure if Kate had been in foot-reaching distance she would have kicked him, and James looked like he was about to swallow his own eyebrows.

'So, where have you been?' Asha asked, looking at Moth.

Kit let Moth answer. It was to his advantage to see James move on as fast as possible, and she seemed a decent option. Bright enough to be interesting, not pretty enough to be distracting. Holding her own in a daunting situation, no tension in her hands, no fiddling with her hair or the simple silver rings on her fingers. No looking to James before engaging with the others. She was sipping from a small glass of wine and displaying no irritating habits. Perhaps Kate was right, perhaps she was delightful, in that dull way that lovely gets repeated. She would suit him well, and he must like her, he'd even made the effort to polish himself up, with a shirt that wasn't swamped in so many insulative layers you could see his well-formed chest and broad shoulders. The collar was a bit worn around the seam, rubbed to the thread, like James himself. The only advantage Kit could see to being a farmer was that you didn't need to work out, the life gave it you as compensation. Kit hated the gym, it was a necessary evil of life, but he'd rather be bored for an hour a day than bored for life. Which was what he'd be if he farmed. Which is what she'd end up being if she married a farmer. But that was not his problem, he'd saved Isabelle from that fate, Asha would have to take her chances.

'So, Asha, how did you meet James?' Kit asked when a lull in the questioning gave Moth a chance to return to the bread.

'We've known each other for a few years,' Asha told him. 'I work for Moldicotts, as an agent.'

'Great, so you have farming in common too?' Kit asked, his estimation falling.

'Oh, no, though I do know quite a bit about the agricultural side of the business from being round the office, I'm in the property department. I deal with houses and estates in marketing and sales.'

Kit perked up. Now this was something he could relate to. 'I bet you get to see some amazing places doing that?'

'Yes, I do, it's a great job. I am very happy to do it.'

She meant it too, Kit could tell, her eyes lighting up with enthusiasm. The slightest slip of her words creeping in, like a bum note in an otherwise flawless rendition. He wondered how long she'd been in the country. She was about as naturalised as it was possible to get. Living life in another language and making it look easy.

'I work with houses too, in management,' Kit told her. 'I love how nothing is ever the same. It keeps it fresh.'

'Yes, Kit likes a change,' James added. 'Never one to let himself get bored.'

'I like that too about work,' Asha said, looking from one to the other.

'I agree,' Kit said. 'I couldn't imagine doing the same thing from one year to the next, I'd die of boredom. What about you, Moth, what do you fancy doing in life? Endless repetition or constant variety?'

Moth looked at him with a silent 'Get lost, you are not dragging me into your shit' grimace and shrugged his shoulders.

'Spoken like a true teenager,' Kate said. 'I tell you Moth, if you don't know what you want to do yet, you could do worse than getting a bar job. You won't go far wrong in life if you can open a bottle of wine, make a decent coffee and serve food professionally.'

'What a brilliant idea,' Kit exclaimed. Moth sighed at him.

'You're stuffed mate,' James told Moth with a grin. 'There isn't one of us who haven't served time behind this bar and woe betide you if you don't learn fast, she's a demanding boss.'

'I'm a delightful boss,' Kate said. 'High standards do not make me an ogre.'

'Ogress,' Elsa countered.

'Perhaps I was using it in a non-gendered way?'

'Were you?'

'Really, now?' Kate asked Elsa.

'I'm sorry,' Elsa said. 'It's a habit I can't get rid of.'

'An irritating one,' Kate told her. 'Asha, my advice to you, if Elsa starts trying to correct your language in any way at all, tell her off, right from the start. I made the mistake of asking her advice, oh way back, and I've never been relieved from the misery of it since.'

Kit couldn't decide if Kate was being tactless suggesting Asha might need some language correction or open about the fact that English was not her first language. He twirled a spoon in his coffee, mixing in the froth, trying to decide if this counted as provincial backwaterism or outright racism. It was the kind of statement Jay would have shot him for and Kit would have defended with vigour.

'You're a famous author, Kate,' Elsa told her. 'Your English should be impeccable.'

'I'd love that sort of feedback,' Asha interjected. 'I love all languages and learning them. You can correct my English any day you want.'

'Excellent, there you go Elsa, a new student for you to pester,' Kate told her.

'You might want to reconsider that,' James murmured into Asha's ear.

'Your English is so natural, why torture it into an upper-class abomination?' Kit said across the table, taking another chunk of bread.

'What other languages do you speak?' Moth asked, picking his bread into pieces and soaking them in a pot of oil and balsamic.

Asha laughed at them speaking over one another and answered Moth. 'English, German, Russian, Spanish and some Mandarin, as well as my mother-tongue, which is Polish.'

'Holy shit, James, you're so out of your depth here.' Kit drawled, oil dripping back into the pot as he confided in Asha. 'He only speaks Salopian.'

'I like to learn the language of every country I live in. In Poland when I was growing up, we had to learn Russian, it was still communist bloc then. Then, when we were liberated, we had to learn English. I've lived in Spain and Germany and I studied Mandarin for part of my business degree. Which languages do you study?'

'Eh, French, German, Latin,' Moth said. 'Not out of choice.'

'But you enjoy it?'

'Not really, maybe,' Moth said. 'It all seems a bit pointless.'

'You need to learn a language in its country. Then it's worth it,' Asha said. 'For me, language is like a gift. You're just a visitor until you know the language, then, when you can hear the people, and speak to them, laugh with them, you are part of the place. It is magic.'

'Magical,' Elsa suggested.

The rest of the table groaned.

'It is magical,' Asha said. That she said it without an ounce of self-consciousness was impressive, Kit thought.

'Anyway, back to you Moth,' Kate said. 'How about it then?'

'How about what?'

'Coming to work for me?'

'Ehm...'

'It's not a question,' Kit stage whispered at him.

'... ok, I think.'

'Excellent, come on then,' Kate said standing up.

'What, now?'

'Yes, now,' Kate said. 'We need some more drinks. You can come and help me get them.'

'He is underage,' Elsa pointed out to her.

'I'm sorry, are you telling me my business?'

'No, but he is mine.'

'He's old enough to make coffee,' Kate dismissed her and went off with a firm hand on the back of Moth's upper arm.

Elsa sighed.

'Give over, Mother,' James said. 'It will do him good, he needs to work.'

'Something we agree on at last,' Kit said.

'Heavens,' Elsa said.

'Yes,' Kit pointed his oil-soaked piece of bread at James. 'James is spot on. He needs work, and lots of it. And stop going on about school, which is the last place he needs to be.'

'Which you've realised in one day together?' James asked.

'Which I've concluded after this particular day together,' Kit retorted.

'Well, that didn't last long,' Elsa said under her breath. 'I was merely pointing out to Kate that he's underage to serve behind the bar.'

James and Kit looked at each other. It wasn't going to be them who told her that Kate had had them all at the bar well before the law allowed.

'Is she really a famous writer?' Asha interjected.

'Yes,' Elsa said. 'She pretty much single-handedly put the town back on the map of Britain. Back when she opened this place Kate got herself a column in the *Telegraph* and started writing about food production, and cooking, and the history of the town. She began a series of chefs-in-residence, profiled food industry malpractice, championed farmers markets, organic production, all sorts of things. Eventually she put it all into a book. These days she tries to stay out of the spotlight, but she's quite famous for what she started.'

'That's fascinating,' Asha said. 'And she lives here too?'

'Yes,' Elsa said. 'Though she does keep threatening to retire and move somewhere she can have a garden.'

Kate and Moth came back with a tray of drinks. Behind them another staff member brought a tray full of food plates. Tapas-style snacks steaming out of small clay dishes. The scents brought them all leaning inward and sharing the pleasure of seeing what each bowl contained. Moth sat down at the table, but Kate was straight back off.

'You set me up,' Moth told Kit.

'Of course I did,' Kit said, 'but you'll thank me for it later.'

'It would have made no difference,' James said. 'She'd have nabbed you sooner or later anyway, Moth.'

'I'm afraid he's right,' Elsa said. 'Kate's always seemed to think my children lacked a decent work ethic and set herself the task of instilling it in them.'

'It seems to have worked,' Moth said.

'Yes,' James said. 'A summer of working with Kate convinced us all to get a decent job.'

'Will it be for the whole summer?' Moth asked.

Elsa shrugged, refusing to be drawn in. Kit was almost tempted to push it a bit further but one look at her face made the chorizo-drenched tuna look sweet.

'James told me you run a hotel,' Asha said in the silence that three men and food produced.

'Bed and breakfast,' Elsa corrected her. 'We let the rooms, do breakfast and then encourage them to come and eat in the town. It was another of Kate's good ideas, mutually beneficial.'

'That's a lot of hard work.'

'Oh, not really. Kit organises the staff and they're generally a nice bunch of guests. I've grown so used to it I hardly notice they're with us.'

'This is your house management?' Asha asked Kit.

'Exactly,' Kit said, around his food, pointing a fork at Moth and back at Asha. 'See, she gets it.'

Moth rolled his eyes at him and kept eating.

'Besides,' Elsa said, 'it's a large house and this way we manage to keep it looking respectable.'

'It sounds beautiful,' Asha said.

'Well, I'm not sure about that, I've lived there my whole life, so it's just home to me.'

'It is beautiful,' Kit countered. 'In that prissy old-English kind of way. Needs a bit of a refresh if you ask me, but the guests love it.'

'You must come and decide for yourself,' Elsa told her. 'In fact, why don't you, on Sunday? We're lucky enough to have the whole family together for Easter so please do join us, if you're free?'

Asha looked startled, James stopped eating, mouth hanging open, blinking at his mother, and Moth looked across at him with wide eyes. Kit felt his toes curl in excitement.

'That's very kind of you,' Asha said. 'But I'm not sure what I'm doing on Sunday.'

'Well, it's up to you, I shall quite understand if you can't make it,' Elsa said. 'But the offer is genuine, it would be lovely to see you at Riverdell. If not this Sunday, come another time.'

'Oh, do come,' Kit enthused. 'It will be such fun to have someone new there.'

Kate walked back and caught the tail end of the conversation, her hand leaning on the back of Kit's chair and poking a finger into his neck.

'That's a great idea,' Kate said. 'You might as well meet the whole family before you decide if you like him or not. James is adorable on his own, but a family gathering can show a man in a whole new light!'

'Thanks, Kate,' James said.

Kit opened his mouth and got no further when the finger at his neck stuck a sharp nail in the skin just above his collar. He wriggled away from it and picked up the final piece of chicken. Just wait until Isabelle heard about this. But maybe he didn't need to be the one to tell her.

'Kate, this has been lovely, thank you so much.' Elsa wiped her fingers on the napkin and drained the last mouthful of her wine. 'I ought to be getting back now. Will you all excuse me?'

'Yes, I must head home too,' Asha said. 'It's been so nice to meet you all.'

'Moth, are you free to walk home with me?' Elsa asked him.

Moth looked at Kate, then Kit. 'I think so?'

'Fine by me,' Kate said.

'I'll be right behind you.' Kit raised his half-full glass to explain.

Elsa and Moth stood up from one side of the table, Asha and James from the other. Kit rose to give them room to leave. He kissed Asha on each cheek and said goodbye in as many made up languages as he could think of. She laughed at him and said goodbye in English. She thanked Kate again for the food and drinks, asking if she could pay for it. Kate refused but thanked her for asking. She didn't put a foot wrong, Kit thought. She could do with about three more stone on her hips and a couple of babies and she would suit James a treat.

'That should make for an interesting Sunday lunch,' Moth said at his side while the others were being polite.

'Bloody fireworks and brimstone I'd say.'

'Do you think she'll come?'

'I'd say there's a strong chance.'

'Someone might want to mention it to Isabelle?'

'Someone might,' Kit agreed. 'Now, be sensible, don't tell Elsa too much about our day.'

'Duh, only look stupid.' Moth said. He walked away with

Elsa, James and Asha following them. By the time they reached the door they were holding hands. Kate must have seen it too.

'I don't suppose there's any chance she might be busy and not come Sunday?' she said beside him.

'I fear not.'

'Fear not, my arse. That would suit you down to the bloody ground.'

'It was nothing to do with me.' Kit sat back down. 'Elsa sprung that from nowhere, I thought James was going to choke on his chorizo.'

'I'm not sure she thought it through.'

'Oh, come on, when do either of you ever do anything by accident?'

'Only when it suits us.' She sat in the chair beside him. 'I suppose you're off now too?'

Kit looked at her. He reached a hand out, lacing his fingers through hers. 'Is that ok?'

'Not really.'

'I've parked the car at the back, can I pick it up tomorrow?'

'It will cost you.'

'I do hope so.'

He could sense the bistro emptying around them, tables being cleared away by staff, noise diminishing. He moved to kiss her, she stood up, breaking the contact.

'Cheat,' she told him.

'Wimp,' he said back.

She brushed a hand across his shoulder as she left. He toyed with the last drops in his glass. If he took his time walking down to Riverdell, Moth should have managed to find Isabelle before him.

11

It took me until the second year of university to enjoy it.

Swansea changed our little gang. Not changed as in, changed beyond all recognition, but changed as in shifted. Rose and Kate blossomed. Like two flowers kept in the wrong conditions for too long they developed a beauty, a grace, a joy in life that made them glow. Not that Rose hadn't always been bright, but the school had seemed almost scared of her. In the boredom of being able to get away with most anything she'd become indifferent to everything. Now she had a whole university of men and boys telling her to find her place, get a degree and marry up a notch with it. Modern debutantism they jibed us. Rose took that growth opportunity like horse muck on roses. She and Kate were a formidable duo. They did everything. Every society, every club, every sport, every spare class. My God, they were frightening. And they bonded more than they ever had before in the challenge. Beth found happiness in her own quiet way, hiding behind Rose, hiding behind books and rock samples.

I spent the whole year trying not to make eye contact with

any boys, wishing Kate was still my closest friend yet not
wanting to admit I was homesick to her, worrying if I
wouldn't get my degree, worrying what I was going to do if I
did. Then there was the worry of our having to find lodgings
for the second year. Would we find somewhere together?
And, if not, who would go with whom? Plus, I had a complete
dress crisis. Trousers too inflammatory, shorts too skirt,
colours too modern. Trying to find my own sense of style
while Kate and Rose sank into the 60s fashion pit like they'd
concocted it themselves. God, that year, I worried that up was
down and down was up. Mostly, I just worried that I'd get
home and find Richard had abandoned me.

It took a summer full of kisses and a whispered proposal,
on his knees in the hay piled high in his father's barn, to put
me straight.

Oh, the memory of that summer makes my breath catch
even now. He'd spent a year waiting for me, stockpiling
condoms, learning how to please me, dreaming of ways to
hold me. Working hard to distract himself and growing into a
strong man. The muscles I found on his back. In his bottom
and thighs. He stripped away any idea of shame I ever had
and turned us both into a pair of horny frogs. When he asked
me to marry him he was stark naked, hard as rock and his
mouth dewy from, well, you know. But, yes, that summer, he
took my anxiety away. We'd survived a year apart. My father
still didn't know about us. Richard had learnt everything
there was to know about arousing a woman, which he
promised he'd only done theory in and I was to be his practice and masters, and I knew exactly what I was doing after
my degree was done. And I was going to do it as often as I
possibly could.

I returned to Swansea in the autumn of 1963 with a new

confidence in my step. Father had sold a huge tract of land on the outskirts of Wolverhampton, it was to become a new town. MacMillan, no longer Bloody MacMillan, but Ballsy Bugger MacMillan, had decreed the new town of Dawley would solve the Midlands housing crisis. And Father had somehow wrangled the location to include a thousand acres of an old package of outlying agricultural land he'd bought on a whim twenty years earlier. Normally I would never have known about these details, but this affected all of us girls. Father had used some of the money to reinvest, and he purchased Miss Shorrock's house in Swansea and kept us together when we thought we might finally have to separate.

Miss Shorrock accommodated the change by giving Rose and Beth the unused attic, Kate and I the smallest room on the upper floor, and managed to lift her eyes to notice us. She was very much warmer to us all. More encouraging of our studies. Pushing Rose and Kate to consider their Masters. Checking on our research, keeping in touch with Father directly about how we were doing. Sometimes, in the light of my own newly found intimate knowledge, I wondered if they were doing more than keeping in touch. But I wasn't about to raise that question with Father in case it came back at me; I kept my suspicions to myself and enjoyed the renewed confidence in my life.

I told the girls, of course. Showed them the ring Richard had given me, which I kept on a chain tucked inside my bra so it wouldn't accidentally swing free.

'Well, I'm not surprised,' Kate said. 'You've been grinning like an idiot every time his name is mentioned from the day he covered you in fresh cow muck.'

'But, marriage?' Rose asked. 'You're sure you want it, this soon?'

'Face it, Rosie,' Beth told her with a nudge, 'not everyone wants to conquer the world like you. Some of us just want a happy life and a warm bed, with sweet arms to hold us.'

'I've nothing against that part of it,' Rose said and Beth grinned at her with a raised eyebrow. 'But marriage, it's all a bit traditional, isn't it?'

We were sat in the kitchen, all cosied up one night with hot cocoa, trying to keep quiet so as not to wake anyone else in the house. Beth with her knees tucked up to her chin. Rose with her feet up on an empty chair. Kate slicing up a loaf of bara brith she'd made.

'I think it's the sweet arms that have swayed her brain,' Kate said with a grin. 'Did you see the muscles on Richard this summer? He looks like he could lasso a wild horse and make it sit. No wonder she can't wait to get back home and hitched.'

I protested it was more than that. We were in love. They laughed. The more they laughed the more I protested. The more I protested the more they all talked about sex. In the end I went to bed in a huff. But the talk had set me thinking and it wasn't long before my fingers brought my memories to a happy conclusion. Wherever Richard had been learning his tricks, he'd been learning them well.

12

The images were lies. Comforting lies. He knew because of the flowers.

Around him the lavender fields stretched toward the Mont. He was washed through with their colour, hypnotised by the swaying lines. The flower heads were dancing in a warm wind, the scent curling around his body in a calming fog.

It's a dream. You should wake up.

But it was a good dream, this one. Filling him with warmth. He clung to the details.

The light brilliant. Birds whirling in the air. Insects frosting the crops. Distant in the ribs of the violet field, she was moving away from him. Beyond her the road glinted between the plants. Above her the vast whiteness of the mountain, glowing as it absorbed the light. She stopped and turned to watch him watching her. He could see every detail of her face. The brown hair and eyes like Nat's, the fine shoulders and petite height that had been swamped by her husband. By her growing son. She was being swallowed by the brightness of the sun.

He heard his name called and turned to see Leon waving for him. He knew this dream, even as he turned back, he knew she would be gone, felt the urgency of her being gone burning his throat. But she was still there, she had stayed where she was, looking back at him. She had always gone before, and he woke wretched and crying. Pathetic crying he could not control.

That's why you should wake up. They only start good.

But not today. This time, as he looked back, she was still there. They stood, looking at one another. Her hands caressing the tops of the flowers. The sunshine draped around her shoulders. She looked like she might have, if she'd ever made it there. Like she'd looked, stood in their kitchen. Tending her lavender plants on the windowsill and dreaming of an old, childhood home and long since gone grandparents. Nothing moved, nothing ended.

It will do. And you'll feel like shit.

Moth opened his eyes to the grim hotel room. To the fact that he'd woken up.

To the fact that she's dead. Dream or not.

He rolled himself upright, looking at the maps on the floor. It was a lie. She hadn't been there. The lavender fields had been empty. He'd wished his father dead a hundred times. Dreamt of it, imagined it, planned it, longed for it. Never thinking it would happen. Never thinking it would cost his mother.

You're going to end up crying.

Moth sat on the hard floor with the thin sheet crumpled around his naked body. His feet looking ridiculous and clean as they poked out under the end. They'd been as white as the Mont when he got to Ventoux.

It's no good looking backwards.

He picked up the strewn cards without looking at them. Feeling the absence of Guéthary like a wound. One precious memory gone. One anchor cast off. He left the card of the Mont, with its fields full of lavender, on the top as he put them back in the plastic.

If he could go back, he wouldn't change a thing. If bringing his mother back meant his father too, it wasn't a choice. There were things he'd do different, given a second chance.

But not that one.

Moth stood and stretched, the indecision of the day before gone. Converted into something hopeful. He looked at the printed roads that had been tangled spaghetti the night before. A phosphorous sharp line rose from the page and traced itself across the terrain to his fresh eyes. To Sillian by road, across the border then south to Cortina, and west through the mountains to Bolzano. Down through the Val Camonica along the river Oglio, to Iseo.

By road, in less than a week.

It would be brutal, hard miles every day and no proper rest. He might not make it. But it would keep him moving fast and hard.

If you're late he might be gone.

Whether Kit was there or not at the end was unimportant. He would go west, do the mountains, cut east, get a boat across to Greece. He liked boats. They ignored foot passengers.

Even bike toting ones like you.

Doubts dispersed. The plan settled into his head with a

clarity that was soothing. He could feel the miles arraigning themselves into days. The rough sketch of where to stop, when to eat, where he might find sleep.

You'll be back on plan within the month. Kit might even help.

He stretched again then bent to fold the maps up. He hadn't had the dream for weeks now. It came like a gift. He could do this. He could face the past and keep moving forward. He could face Kit and keep going.

You don't have to hide forever.

Moth felt energy flowing through him. Events reshaped themselves. Mila would get the package with the tickets in the next few days. If she didn't take the chance it would be her choice. There was nothing more he could do for her. Even the grim surroundings couldn't dampen his mood. He shaved in the damp blooming bathroom and felt wholesome in the sharp edges of the mirror.

The motel was quiet when he left. The road busy. Moth soon got off it and took the quieter roads west. The land was border country, confused by its own identity and belonging to no one. Signs in two languages. The bike was smooth on the tarmac and he felt fluid with it. Pulling towards the same destination. Mauthen a refuelling pause, lunch a roadside stop, Sillian passing in the early evening, a rush of traffic.

Moth pedalled south through the last few hours of the day. As his legs tired and the pace slowed, he pushed on beyond energy. Wanting those few extra miles south.

Stop when you pass the first sign solely in Italian.

In the end he took a detour off the main road, leaving the traffic behind, to cruise into the edge of Misurina in the settling dark. His tiredness echoed by the quiet houses, the end of evening lying upon the town. He passed through and stopped beyond the houses in a quiet wooded grove. Surrounded by the foothills of the Dolomites, knowing but not seeing the mountains looming away before him.

He spent the last half hour of his day studying the maps. Life hinting at him in the pinprick lights beyond the dark edges of the woods. He thought about Kit. Would Kit be any different? Would it be like the days they shared before. Days away from Riverdell, days when they had seemed genuine friends. Or would it be Kit when Isabelle had been around?

Possessive and spiteful. Putting you in your place.

Stirring everyone into a frenzy. Because he could. Perhaps the temptation of seeing Kit was the chance to say, 'I'm no kid. I made it this far by myself and I don't need you.'

And then leave. By yourself.

Moth put the map away, sure of his route. He wrote the thin line of his notebook into completion, Day 262, 20th March 2013. Misurina. Kit or no Kit. It didn't matter. He would go to Iseo because he could choose to, or not. And he would leave and move on.

Because you choose to.

The route was embedded in his mind when he turned the light off and settled down.

SHE WOKE BEFORE KIT AND, muscles tiptoeing inches at a time, crept from the bed.

She was beyond tired, every part of her wanting sleep, her body stiffened and aching. Kit's presence wreathed her in a fugue. She could smell him on her skin. Couldn't recall what she smelled like. How she felt in her own space. How time even felt, in its own space. He'd filled her every waking second from the moment he arrived late on Friday night.

Moments after Moth had left her with the unsettling news about Sunday lunch.

She sneaked from the room in her undies, clothes clutched to her body and, pulling the door to with a painful click, went three doors down to the empty bathroom on the second floor. Checking that Moth and Nat's doors were shut tight all the way, conscious of creaking floorboards, her bare skin shivering in the cold morning air of the corridor, locking the door behind her. The heater would make an infernal racket, but she needed heat, and hot water. She turned the shower on to lessen the noise of the heater and stood under its dusty electrical breeze while the hot water system convinced itself to summon water from the depths of the house.

She had no idea of the time. No idea how much time she had to herself. Her stomach clenched again. It wasn't James, or his new girlfriend – Asha, that was her name – or Asha that bothered her. It was the fact that Hester would be there too. Isabelle wasn't sure if it would be worse for her or Asha. Or James. Or her. The only thing she knew for certain was that Kit was going to love it all.

She took the soap off the shelf. It was old and split, and not the sort she liked, but it was that or the pine shower gel that belonged to Moth, or the fruity bubbles of Nat's. She let the water warm the old soap up and scrubbed it over her skin. She had to give up pride and used both the shampoo and conditioner the children had left. Her hair was going to look a wreck. The thought of her normal products lined up in her own bathroom added to the frustration.

She closed her eyes and pushed the anxiety back with the darkness. It was just another day. Family lunch. Nothing she hadn't endured before.

Out of the shower she realised she had no clean pants, and no socks at all. Her irritation deepened to a panic, she couldn't go back to her room, she might wake Kit. She dressed in a rush and dragged her hands through her hair. She had to get downstairs, where there would be clean clothes in the laundry, and out. Out and away, with coffee, up in the hills, on a quiet bench. She looked in the mirror one last time, turned the heater off and prised the door open, checking the hallway. The landing clock informed her she was trying not to wake the house at an obscene twenty minutes to six. Not even six o'clock.

The kitchen was empty. A post-it note on the kettle said 'Oven on from six am onwards if you're up, whoever you are, 150°C, write start time.' Isabelle checked the oven. A gargantuan joint of pork nestled in a tin, the pink meat streaked with grey and white fat, scored with deep cuts, the smell of its night-long resting place assailing her nose. She shut the door and turned it on. She had no more than ten minutes. Elsa would be up fretting about the day, and Kit would be two steps behind her.

She scrambled breakfast into a bag, heard the hot water pipes rattling behind the sink, scrawled 5.45 on the post-it note and ran for the back door. The boot room stone freezing underneath her sockless feet, grabbing boots from the racks as she passed them, her jacket off its peg. In the laundry she found pants, socks, a clean top, a washed scarf stiffened from the assault. She dressed in the workroom, snatched up her notebook and fled the house.

She snuck out the lower garden entrance, through the road gate, following the road across the bridge and over the river. The morning wind nibbling into her sore, Kit-festered lips. Walking uphill through tall trees and along sludgy paths

gorged with rain, her legs aching at the pace, but it was blissful, the wind loose around her. She unbuttoned her coat,
disentangling the scarf from her throat, stuffing it into her
pocket.

Leaf unfettered trees sketched the skyline with stark lines,
the dark shapes of conifers unravelling with tassels of lime
growth. She couldn't see her destination, the hilltop high
above the town, but her feet picked out the route, slipping
along known paths in blind confidence. She came to a fork in
the path. Either she could bend right, climbing up to a lesser
view, or she had to drop left, down to the stream at the valley
floor before starting up again to reach the highest vista. She
headed left, her legs enjoying the change, muscles slackening
as she tumbled downhill to where the stream coursed along
the tight valley floor, the path tucked between steep escarp-
ments. Isabelle crossed the rocky ford at the bottom of the
track and struck back uphill before her muscles had a chance
to complain.

When she came out of the tree lined path onto a high
meadow of uncurling ferns and rippling grass, she was
breathless. Puffing from the ragged pace, collecting herself
with hands pinching her sides. It was the view she had seen
the day she arrived, the grasses cascading off Climbing Jack.

Happiness surged through her, following the herring-
boned ruffles as they sledged off the distant edge, flinging
themselves into the valley below. The summit was glinting
between the lines of the new plantings. She was close to
the end.

She emerged onto the broad path that took her to the old
bird tower and the bench. Two years ago, the view westward
had been invisible, lost behind a bank of conifers. Now the
forestry commission had hacked away the uppermost part of

the slope to reveal the distant hills of the Welsh Marches creasing the landscape. Beyond, the sharp black scowl of Hay Bluff, and behind it the higher undulations of the Beacons festooned across the arching sky.

It was bliss. She felt undone, snipped free of life. She approached the bench, curled her fingers over its back, felt the tattooed plaque, chill beneath the warm, pulsing calluses of her sewn-out fingers.

'Hello, Mother,' she murmured, feeling ridiculous and comforted.

The words carved into the metal were worn smooth with weather but imprinted on her memory. Louisa Georgina Bethany Threlfall, 1944–1983. There was a space beneath, waiting for a quote. They'd left it for her to fill when she grew up, but she'd never known what to put in that blank harsh space. She couldn't get past the huge name at the top.

Isabelle tried to recall her mother, but there was no clear visual image she could possess. Nothing but the desperate garnering of second-hand images, creating a picture out of cast-offs. Her own memory limited to the sense of long hair falling around her. The burst of emotion that came with the scent of a gin and tonic. Memories that lived at the seam of sleep, or tacked across the depths of work, a wisp that dematerialised the moment she focused on it. Her mother, called Beth, because every other name shortened to a masculinity.

'Hello, Beth,' she tried instead. Neither felt right, words unsuited to the task.

This had been their favourite walk as girls, when the old bird tower stood beside the bench. They would haul a picnic basket up here and spend hours together, creating a secret den in the tower and enough noise to scare any interesting wildlife away. Kate called it the virginity hut, because that was where they'd all lost it. When Elsa denied it, Kate had laughed at her. And when Elsa complained that it wasn't true and she shouldn't speak about someone's parents like that Kate had laughed louder and apologised that she'd mentioned Isabelle's parents. Elsa had blushed, actually blushed.

The proud legs and square back of the tower were reduced to crumbling humps of mildewed wood, overlaced with brambles, festooned with gorse, but she could imagine it through Kate's eyes. Purposeful, solid, filled with giggling, irreverent girls.

Isabelle pulled out the coffee and the notebook, drinking quick sips of the steaming warmth in rapid succession. She peeled open the notebook, anchoring down the scraps that fluttered in the wind with her fingertips and looking over the sketches from her final days in India. Faint scents of chai rose from the pages, unfurling in the breeze.

In the chill sunshine India seemed so far away she couldn't grasp its intensity. Its warmth, its scents, its endless noise. How it anchored her to her mother in a way she could never grasp here.

She sipped coffee, thought of India and felt the great weight of life at Riverdell rolling down the hillside, unpicked in the wind. Even Kit seemed further away, something she needed to go back and put right. A pair of curtains that needed adjusting for the future.

Six hours after leaving, she strode back across the road bridge. Aching with lack of sleep and long walking, and replete from the bliss of a solitary hilltop in bright sunshine. Excited at the thought of the bustling house and their first family celebration since Moth and Nat had joined them. Hester would be all charm in front of Asha, determined to impress a newcomer with their family home. Isabelle knew her place today. Blending into the background, pliable as needed. She walked across the courtyard determined to enjoy it, her hopes expanding with the empty driveway.

Isabelle walked into the boot room and shed her outdoor skin. The house wore an aura of expectation. Beyond the kitchen door she could hear Elsa and Kate in the kitchen talking to Nat. Their swift tones stirring the shadows of the room around her, the dust rising from the worn stone flags and the muddy boots.

She stared at the paint-chipped door that led to the kitchen. It was time for a fresh face. Easter was the perfect opportunity for James to introduce his new girlfriend. She should feel happy for him. She was happy for him, and for Elsa, whose hopes of grandchildren must have soared at the earliest bud of a new romance, but she wasn't part of it.

She was cast-off, a relic from another life. She didn't fit the new form of the emerging family. Part of the past, like her mother.

Isabelle felt the distance between her and that ghost, which had reduced on the wild windy hill to nothing more than a plane journey, widen again. Leaving her a remnant of bygone days.

Her sense of guilt rooted her to the spot. She should leave now, disappear for the day, let them enjoy the new romance. She could sneak up the back stairs, freshen up and go, before anyone thought to miss her. What was there to keep her here, really? Though they would protest later, it would be easier for them all today.

She turned away to leave. Heard Moth walk into the kitchen, ask something, get a reply.

Moth's voice froze her feet.

Perhaps she could help him before she left. Yes, before she left. Because she would leave.

At some point. Not if. But when.

After she helped Moth adjust. That was all she was needed for. Tidy away the old, make fast the new.

The kitchen door opened into the passageway and Moth walked through. She looked up, startled by the opening door, her sense of peace radiating out towards him with a warm smile, blinking in the light he threw over her. He pulled up in surprise.

'We've been looking for you,' he said.

'We?'

'Well, me, the others keep asking and sending me to see if you're back. They're all a bit busy. Crazy busy.'

'Yeah, if you think this is busy, wait until Christmas!'

'You look windswept,' he said.

She could hear a tinge of jealousy in his voice, leant closer and whispered, 'You have to get up real early to get out before all this stupidity starts.'

'You could have warned me.'

'What, and have you miss all this?'

'You've had a nice morning, haven't you?'

'Amazing,' she said. 'I walked to the top of Climbing Jack and remembered all the things I love in life. It was so cold and bright up there.'

'Great, rub it in some more why don't you. I've been polishing silver and glasses.'

'Oh, you lucky thing, you.'

'Moth, have you found her?' Elsa called through from the kitchen.

'Tell them no,' she whispered. 'I was just going to sneak up the back stairs and...'

'Yes, she's right here,' he called over his shoulder, smirking at her.

'Oh, that's kind.'

'You owe me. I'm sure I've done most of your jobs.'

'Tell her to get in here and get washed up,' Kate called. She came to the doorway and peered into the gloom. 'Stop trying to walk backwards, Isabelle. Have you seen the state of your hair, and there is mud up to your knees. It's almost lunchtime. James will be here any minute, do come on.'

'I'm coming,' she said.

Moth stepped sideways and gestured for her to go first.

'You're on, I'll pay that debt. I have the perfect thing for you,' she told him, moving past.

'What's that then?' he asked.

'Oh, look, I have to go now, no time to tell,' she said with a vicious grin, and walked into the transformed kitchen.

She was hit by a wall of moist warmth, the windows steaming up from the combination of hot water, dishwasher, and both the oven and the Aga going. The smell of roasting meat, the sound of sizzling potatoes, the scent of sweet pears in pastry, and homemade custard. Her stomach churned in appreciation.

'Good heavens, look at the state of you!' Elsa complained.

'I'm sorry, I never slept well. I had to get out for a walk and clear my head and I ended up going a bit too far.'

'Go, wash up,' Kate told her. 'Make yourself look gorgeous too, they're all coming together. Hester and Rob have been at the farm this morning to meet Asha.'

'Oh great.'

'Yes, I thought you'd be thrilled about that,' Kate said. She eyed Isabelle up and down with concern, shook her head and moved back to the work surface. 'Moth and Nat have been amazing this morning, without them and Kit you would be in some serious trouble right now. Now, go, change, why are you still standing here? Moth, where is Kit?'

'In the dining room dusting the skirting board last time I looked,' Moth told her.

She handed him a stack of side plates and said, 'Tell him to get off his knees and get his arse in here now, I am not worried about the skirting boards, I have sauces that need stirring.'

'Yes, ma'am,' Moth said and disappeared into the hallway, rolling his eyes at Isabelle as he overtook her at the doorway.

'Isabelle, move!' Kate snapped at her.

'Everything's nearly ready Kate, stop fretting,' Elsa said.

'Yes, everything is nearly ready, except for Isabelle,' Kate snapped back.

'I'll be ten minutes, tops,' Isabelle said, heading for the far door.

'That's optimistic.' Kate, wiping her hands on a tea towel, moved to intercept her. 'I told you, gorgeous, not just passable, and put on that necklace your mother gave you, the India one. It always makes you look vibrant.'

Isabelle leaned forward and kissed her on the cheek, wiping a speck of custard from her nose.

'Yes, mother hen,' she said and darted away. Kate flicked the tea towel after her and caught her on the back of her thigh. She squealed and rubbed the spot.

'I'll send you back up to change if I'm not satisfied with the first effort,' Kate told her.

'I could go and assist her?' Kit offered, coming into the hallway from the east corridor.

'Get in here, now,' Kate said.

Kit passed Isabelle in the hall with a grin as she ran up

the stairs. He'd tidied her bedroom up for her, thrown the covers back to air the bed with as much precision as anyone else would make it. The bathroom was doused in detergents, both windows open and a strong breeze blowing through between the two rooms. She moved to close them, peeling off her dirty clothes as she headed for the bathroom, abandoning them on the floor.

She flipped the shower on, her sense of euphoria at the thought that she would leave mixing with thoughts of having to meet and greet the approaching party. Steam and scent capturing the confusion in bubbles that popped in the cool air. She rushed on, mindful of Kate's wrath, dripping on the floor as she struggled to dress, dry her hair, smarten her face. Her hands faltering as she began to pull a fresh pair of jeans on. Kate would not accept jeans. She rejected them, pulled leggings on, found an old pair of soft calf-length boots in the corner and dusted them off. Laced the long leather straps around her legs to keep them on. She shimmied into a thigh length skirt, pulled tops out of her drawers and built up a layered outfit of staggered hems. She topped it off with a bias-cut denim waistcoat that she'd oversewn with silk flowers, hoping they would sneak the loathed denim past Kate's judgemental eye.

She pulled her mother's India necklace off the mirror and was wiping the dust off it with the end of a nearby scarf when she heard a tap at the door and, answering it, found Moth and Nat outside.

'She sent us up to smarten up and get you,' Moth said. 'They've just arrived.'

'I'll be one minute. Will you wait for me?'

'We're not to come down without you,' Nat said.

'Oh, come in a sec.' Isabelle went back to her dressing

table. Brushed her hair one last time, put on her mascara and lip gloss and slipped a row of nine bangles onto her wrist.

'You look nice,' Nat said from the doorway.

'Thanks Nat, are you any good with necklace catches?'

'Not much.'

'I'll do it,' Moth offered. He moved across the room and stood behind her. She handed him the necklace and watched him in the mirror as he fastened it on.

'Moth used to do Mum's all the time,' Nat said behind them in a wistful voice.

Isabelle felt her breath catch with guilt and she looked for his eyes in the mirror. 'I'm sorry, I never thought,' she murmured.

He glanced at her reflected eyes, said 'That's alright, it's a nice job,' turned and walked back to Nat, playing finger tag with her, not giving her a chance to think about the memory.

'Come on,' Isabelle said, 'I don't think we can put this off any longer.'

'I like your necklace,' Nat said.

Isabelle fingered it self-consciously. It was a gleaming affair of multicoloured stones set between silver carved beads, the lapis lazuli, opal, amethyst and agate competing for attention.

'It was my mother's,' she said, looking at them both. 'Is it a bit much?'

'It's beautiful,' Nat said.

'It suits you,' Moth said. 'I mean, it is a bit in your face, but it does suit you.'

They walked down the hallway abreast but when they got to the stairs only two of them could fit at the same time. Isabelle gestured to them to go first but Moth grinned and said, 'I don't think so,' so she had to go first with Nat at her side, Moth following a few steps behind.

Below them they could hear voices in the hallway, talking across one another with that loud delight the family took in Sunday afternoons without guests around. The one evening of the week when Elsa refused to take bookings. As they turned the last corner and walked onto the mini landing beneath the stained lead lights, Nat slipped her hand into Isabelle's. Isabelle squeezed, wondering who was getting the most comfort from it.

They walked down the last run of stairs with the midday sun coming through the window behind them and watched the guests turning to see them. Isabelle felt her stomach churn. Hester looked straight past her and smiled at Nat. James avoided looking at anyone and fidgeted at the back. Rob smiled and moved to greet them. She gained a quick glimpse of the new girlfriend, Asha, stood next to James and speaking with Kate and Elsa. Her face had turned to look at them but carried on with her conversation. Isabelle had seen dark hair, a round face and a brave smile that looked nervous, and then lost the advantage of higher ground.

Rob gave her a peck on the cheek, saying, 'Isabelle, lovely to see you, such a gorgeous day,' before greeting Nat and Moth. Isabelle hid behind his presence.

'Natalie, come and meet Asha,' Hester called. Nat left her and ran across the hallway, leaving her hand empty. Moth came to stand next to her and shook hands with Rob in easy familiarity.

'I hear from James you're taking up cycling, an excellent sport,' Rob enthused.

Rob was so good at this stuff. Talking to everyone, always finding something to say, even if it was nothing, and managing to sound affected without condescending. His cord trousers, stiff-collared shirt and drooping V-neck sweater looking like he'd dragged them out of a charity shop or taken them off the back of a dead client. Rob wasn't unattractive. He avoided weight by attempting vegetarianism whilst being unable to socially insist on it, and though his hair was succumbing to a look of encroaching frost bite it was still thick and kept well-trimmed. As well as being a partner in a law firm in Shrewsbury, he was President of the local rambling club and Chairman of the Chess Society. Rob had always seemed destined for middle age, even in his twenties, and though he could have passed for handsome with just a little effort, preferred not to make it. She liked his sense of humour about himself, the way he put others first. The kindness in his hands, which were soft and gentle as they went about their work of arbitration and affirmation. The perpetual effort at cheer and calm in his voice, chasing away nerves and angst. She felt comforted listening to the two of them talking polite nonsense about cycling.

'Hoorah,' called Kit from the hallway. 'Everyone's here at last, wonderful. Come, come, let's have a drink in the sitting room to celebrate.' He came to stop beside Isabelle and took her and Moth's elbows and nudged them towards the sitting room, saying 'Umm, you look adorable,' as he corralled her down the corridor, 'Rob, old fella, how's the dreary life of a country solicitor going?' shaking hands with Rob and shunting him after them, 'Where's my two favourite grand dames, here you are,' waving away Kate's irritated complaint, shooing them towards the hallway. 'Hester, elegant as always,' Isabelle could hear the contempt in his voice from the sitting room doorway, Kit loathed beige, and Hester was wearing nothing but, despatching them all so that he could finish where he'd wanted to start. 'Ah, here's our guest of honour! Asha, darling, how wonderful you could make it, we're all so excited. James, do bugger off and stop hogging her, off you go, share and share alike. Come, let me show you round, they're all far too reserved to boast.'

Isabelle, passing into the sitting room, heard Kit start his litany about the house. 'Now, this is the grand hallway, original stained-glass window replaced with a far inferior imitation in the 50s when it blew out in a gale one night. The stairwell is Canadian maple, imported in the 20s to replace the original rotting one of French oak, and Elsa will show you the ghastly collection of ancestral portraits skulking on the first-floor corridor another time, I'm sure...'

She listened to his voice as James headed through the doorway with a resigned look of ineffective mutiny on his face, knowing Kit wouldn't let Asha into the sitting room until he'd given her the complete ground floor tour. They stood in small huddles, all pretending to talk, all listening to Kit as he headed down the corridor.

He opened the door into the study and guided Asha in, saying, 'Now this is the archetypal old-English study. Full of books never read, maps of places never been too and piles of paperwork that need burning. However, I'm banned from touching a single thing in here, so I feel no need to apologise for the result.'

'It's charming,' Asha replied. James had said she was Polish, but Isabelle could hear no trace of an accent. 'Are you so honest with your other clients?'

'They pay me for my professional opinion, not to be polite,' Kit told her. 'I do like to deliver to expectation.'

'I can imagine,' Asha said as they left the room. Isabelle

smiled at James as he stood alone by the fireplace. Asha sounded like she could handle herself, and Kit.

'Now, come, let's get that drink and kickstart this lunch party,' Kit said as he led the way into the sitting room, taking in the entire room with one sweeping appraising glance ending in a smile at her. It was lingering and satisfied, making her feel the most important person in that room.

For the duration of that look, her sense of inadequacy, her feeling that Kit was a job to be packaged away, and India a place to return to, tucked tail and ran. She was the woman he'd spent the night with. Her casual but colourful clothes marking her out. For that one moment she saw the room through his eyes.

James' hair sticking up awkwardly where he'd brushed it back in stress, fiddling with the cuffs of his shirt, trying to resist rolling them up, focusing on Asha in her black trousers and polo neck rib sweater. Rob stood in sagging clothes, collar askew, talking to Moth. Hester and Nat sat on one of the sofas, Elsa and Kate on the other. Elsa and Hester as middle class, middle age a mirror image as it was possible to imagine, the beige shades complementing the lilac. Isabelle looked nothing like them, she came closer to Kate for style. But where Kate looked smart and chic, with her trousers a sharp-pressed affair, a short, knitted jacket tossed across her shoulders revealing a bright sky-blue blouse that exaggerated her made up face and up swept hair, Isabelle was relaxed and subtle, hip and artsy. She could see Kit stripping the room with his eyes, she saw them all nude and exposed, and herself loved, desired, precious.

His glance moved on.

She was left adrift. Watching as Kit made sure everyone knew everyone, that all had a drink, talking over them, commanding them with his voice. Numb, watching the unavoidable moment come closer, as Asha was introduced to everyone in the room except herself. Isabelle tensed. Kit left Asha with James, who stood up straighter from the mantelpiece to encase her presence and went over to Isabelle.

'And this is Isabelle,' he said, putting out his arm and pulling her close to his side. 'Daughter, niece, cousin, traveller and seamstress extraordinaire. If it's made of fabric it's been through her hands, which means most of the house is stitched together by her.'

'Hi,' Isabelle said, 'nice to meet you.'

'And you,' said Asha, turning to Elsa and continuing, 'What an amazing house you have. What a wonderful place to live.'

Isabelle couldn't decide if it was a subtle put down or a tactful way of moving attention away from their individual greeting. Kit gave her a hug and moved away to stand on the other side of the fire where he could command the conversation.

'Well as I said, it relies on Kit to look this good, and Isabelle, and all the family. I couldn't have kept it together this long without them,' Elsa said.

'It's a good thing to have such a strong family about you,' Asha said. 'I miss my family very much living abroad.'

'It's not all sunshine and old English roses,' Kate told her. 'They can be bloody vile at times, don't be fooled by the ancestral glory around them.'

'Every family can be difficult,' Asha said. 'But better than having no family at all.'

'That depends a bit on the day with the family.' Kate drowned the comment in a sip from her glass and softened it with eyes that grinned over the top. Elsa poked her on the leg, but Kate looked at Kit with a grim smile, ignoring the rebuke.

The moment when Kit had looked at her was gone. Isabelle looked around the room feeling empty, they all had a place, except her. Kate and Elsa had grown together with the years, James inclining towards Asha, Nat flowering now Hester was back. She could see it in the fluttering hands that talked to each other as much as their voices, reaching out to make contact. Rob and Kit were like the glue that bound them, holding the tone polite or bending it with humour to keep them together.

She sank down onto the arm of the sofa beside Kate and listened to their conversation. Rob angling away from Moth to stand behind Hester and Nat. She watched as Moth pulled back a step at a time to stand beside the window. He made no effort to engage, no effort to draw attention to himself. He just sidestepped the moment in retreat. Her thought in the boot room returned with force. She was not needed here. She could leave. Even though Elsa might say otherwise. She looked at Moth. Except for him.

She stood up from the sofa and walked over to him beside the window. The river was glistening in the sunlight. She could feel his longing to be outside.

'Where have you been exploring?'

'I walked across to Bircher Common,' he said. 'Been up to the Clee, Croft Ambrey, all sorts.'

'You're going further afield.'

'I've gone about as far as I can and walk back in a day,' he said. 'I'm banking on getting that bike from James now.'

'Where are you planning to go?'

'Who knows?' Moth said. 'I've not cycled before. I don't even know if I'll like it.'

'I think you will.'

'How come?'

'You have the physique for it, for one thing,' Isabelle said. 'I remember when James got into it, he was part of a cycling club, he munched the other guys. Hardest part was finding a bike to fit him. Otherwise, height, muscle strength, everything, it always seemed so easy to him, and you're a lot like him.'

'Yeah, so you keep saying.'

'Physically, you're a lot like him. And you like being outdoors, and you like exploring. On a bike you can go places that cars can't, and faster than you can go on foot. Overall, I think you'll like it.'

'I hope so,' Moth said. 'He's making me work hard enough for it.'

'Oh well, not for much longer.'

'He hasn't said how long I have to work for,' Moth said.

'Yeah, but it doesn't matter now Kate has dibs on you,' Isabelle told him. 'James won't get much of a look in.'

'I get the feeling I don't have much choice in this idea of working for Kate.'

'Think of it like an initiation,' Isabelle told him. She turned to look at the room, standing closer to the window so she could see his face, and beyond him to the family chatting in their little groups. It looked like a vignette from a Wodehouse book. Generations of the same genetics pooling besides one another. Recycling words and rhythms of speech in comforting habits. 'If you want to be part of the family that is.'

'Who wouldn't want to be?' Moth asked in a neutral tone.

She couldn't say anything. Stood there beside him wondering how long it would be before she could announce to Elsa that she wanted to return to India and work.

Who wouldn't want to be part of such a family?

She could see Nat being absorbed into it one contented limb at a time. Surrounded by attention and love, a bright caring family backed by a wide circle of friends and acquaintances that would last her a lifetime. She knew the depths of that world, had swum in its shallows her whole life. Yet here she was, longing to leave. She looked at the back of Elsa and Kate's heads on the sofa nearest to them. Grey haired both, styled with a different hand, one gleaming with highlights, the other starched with spray, but both sat on top of rigid spines that had carried them through life.

That was her problem, she lacked the backbone for it all. The strength to stand tall and be proud of who she was. Where she was from.

'It's not for everyone,' she said. 'And it is a choice.'

'And you?'

'Me? Oh well, I was born fundamentally lacking in the balls department,' she said. 'I'm hoping you'll do better in that respect.'

He was about to reply when Kit spied them and said, 'What are you two conspiring about?' in a voice loud enough for everyone to hear. All eyes turned to them.

Moth looked at her in consternation, but she grinned and replied, 'Equality of the sexes.'

'Ha,' he said, coming to stand beside them. 'I knew you were conspiring. There is no equality of the sexes, women are infinitely superior. Why else would men have spent so many centuries and so much effort trying to convince them otherwise?'

'Oh God,' James said. 'Here we go. Moth, whatever he tells

you just ignore it.'

'Oh, please,' said Kate, with a tone that would have withered a fish fresh off the line. 'Male insecurity has ruined the lives of a whole gender for countless millennia and you tell him not to listen to the only specimen of secure masculinity within a ten-mile radius.'

'Fifty-mile radius,' Isabelle countered.

'At least,' Kate agreed. 'Moth, be a dear and go pop the Yorkshires in the oven to warm.'

'Me? I, I don't know how to cook,' he said.

'Well you won't learn standing there, will you?' she told him. 'It's self-evident, I set it out for the least capable of cooks to manage. Except, in this instance, I feel James should be excused.'

Moth grinned and left the room, shrugging his shoulders at James who was sighing at the ceiling.

'You can't cook?' Asha asked him.

'I can cook!' he protested.

Elsa, Kate and Kit choked a storm of disbelief between them. Asha frowned and looked at James.

'I can!' James tried to convince her. 'I do live alone, remember.'

'You can cook beans on toast and warm up microwave dinners,' Kate told him. 'That's not cooking.'

'Oh dear,' Asha said, looking at him with sympathy, trying not to smile, not wanting to approve at all.

'I do hope you like cooking,' Kit told her. 'James is terribly, how shall we say it, backwards, nay, Neanderthal...'

'Pre-Neanderthal,' Kate added.

'... in his approach to life.'

'Are you determined to set me out in the worst possible light?' James asked the room in general.

'Heavens, no,' Kate said. 'Just the most honest one, darling.'

'Honesty is not always the best policy.' Elsa defended her own. 'Sometimes we need to leave a little room for mystery.'

'Oh no, honesty, every day,' Asha said.

'Well, in that respect you have good taste,' Hester told her, in such cloying tones Isabelle struggled not to shudder. 'James is incapable of dishonesty. He is the most forthright person you will ever meet.'

'Spoken like a true sister,' Rob said.

'I'll say,' Kit agreed.

Moth came back, looking flushed from the warm kitchen.

'Well?' Kate asked. 'How did it go?'

'Done, Yorkshires are in.'

'Great, did you stir the gravy?'

Moth opened his mouth to reply, shut it and walked straight back out the room.

'Very bright young man,' Kate commented. 'He learns faster than any of you lot ever did.'

'Excuse me?' Kit complained.

'Well, at least on a par with you,' she said.

Hester, James and Isabelle all had the sense to remain silent.

'Well, I like cooking, very much, it is a great pleasure for me.' Asha told them.

'What do you like cooking?' Kate asked.

'All sorts. Foreign food, food from my home, cakes, everything. I like trying new stuff all the time,' she said.

'Well, you must come up to the bistro and show me something from Poland, I always like new ideas for the menu.'

'Really?'

'Yes, absolutely,' Kate said. 'It's a real challenge keeping fresh ideas flowing, input is much appreciated.'

'I would love to do that,' Asha said.

'Great, bring James. He's still learning how to peel veg but can occasionally be useful.'

Moth came back in.

'Well?' Kate asked.

'I checked the gravy and the veg, they're done, I think. Well, I've drained them anyway, but I don't know what to do with them next. I don't want to put them in the wrong dish.'

'See, fast learner,' Kate announced and got up from the sofa. 'Come on Hester, I need another pair of hands. You too, Nat. Kit, you can guide everyone to the table and sort drinks? I'm starving, anyone else getting hungry?'

Isabelle was feeling the effects of her long walk and a large glass of wine poured with Kit's usual extravagance was doing double time on her hunger and making her feel bubbly. Kit offered Elsa his hand and pulled her up from the sofa, with a deference that made her look elegant and pampered. James and Asha followed them from the room. She was enjoying the quiet moment as Rob came over to her and offered her his arm.

'This is all very formal,' she joked with him.

'I know, does feel a bit like best behaviour doesn't it?'

'You look tired Rob, are you working too many hours still?' Isabelle asked him, as they walked across the room.

'Yes, well, no, it's not really the work,' he said, pulling her up beside the fire and letting the others go ahead.

She looked at him in surprise. His face was screwed up in concern.

'Isabelle, I just, the thing is, I mean...' he looked at the door, back to her. 'Be careful, Hester is on the war path, she is so, so...'

Isabelle watched him struggling to get words out. 'So what, Rob?'

'I don't even know,' he told her, rubbing his temple. 'I can't make sense of it, she's so wound up, I don't know where it's going to come out.'

'But most likely it will come my way?'

He nodded, mute with discomfort, frowning with unhappiness.

'Oh well, best get on with it,' she said and made to move forwards.

He pulled her up again and said, 'What she thinks is...it's not what I think, I hope you know that Isabelle,' he stumbled over his words, 'but she's my wife, and she's desperately unhappy. I wish I could help her more.'

'Of course you do,' Isabelle said, patting his arm. 'Come on, Kate won't be happy if we keep dinner waiting.'

They walked into the dining room, where James, Asha and Elsa were sat at the table. Kit showed them both where to sit and Rob escorted her to her seat and pulled it out for her. As she sat down he squeezed her shoulder and went to his own seat, starting a conversation with Asha about her work. Isabelle felt anxiety creeping into her stomach again. When Kit topped up her glass she took a large gulp from it, putting it back down with a wobble on the tablecloth.

An awkward empty chair between her and Asha seemed to grow and stretch the moment. Isabelle focused on the amber-tinged glassware Kit had put out. How the different wine and water glasses created a neat spiral of height. The fold of the napkins as they lay aligned beside the cutlery. The line of stitching that peeped out where the layers overlapped one another. The room was rarely used, and often lay dusty with books and oddments piled up on top of the table protector. A low slipper chair sat to one side of the large window, looking out over the gardens. It was one of her favourite places to retreat to. A good shadow of dust had tempered the buttoned depths of its worn fabric and some of the button covers had rubbed raw to reveal the silver disc beneath. It looked in need of a good overhaul as it sat blinking in the sudden social limelight.

The time to think about it was taken from her as the door opened to a stream of people carrying dishes. Moth, Nat and Hester trooped in, dropped their loads and disappeared. Kit whirled around the table, commanding the dishes and the people into place. One by one the room filled, Kate and Moth walking in together with the last dishes.

'Everyone, help yourself. Dig in, Asha,' Kate told her. 'There's nothing fun about cold food that should be eaten hot. Come on, Nat, what do you want? Moth told me you love Yorkshires, here take two before they're all gone.'

Kit went one way round the table and Kate the other until they'd chivvied everyone into piling up a high plate of food. They sat down themselves and Kate began the meal by taking the first bite herself. Isabelle concentrated on her plate. Moth was sat right opposite her, Kit between her and Asha, and Kate to her right at the foot of the table. She was as comfortable as it was possible to be. Hester was at the far end, talking across its expanse and pulling James, Asha and her mother into her own circle of intensity. Rob was being adorable and chatting away to Nat, sat next to him, and ignoring his wife's efforts to pull him into her conversation. Kit, on the other hand, was butting in and contorting Hester's every other sentence, and giving James no chance to speak.

'You look tired,' Isabelle said to Kate, who was picking at her food, concentrating on the sustained effort of swirling white wine around the large globe of her wineglass, which hadn't left her hand since she sat down.

'I am,' she said. 'I always prefer preparing the meal to eating it. I pick at so much while cooking I'm never that hungry.'

'I didn't realise what a good cook you are,' Moth said around his forkful. 'This is awesome.'

'What, you thought I just told other people how to cook?' she teased him.

'Kind of, yes.'

'Well, I guess I do now, but when I first opened the bistro, I did everything. I had to. I couldn't afford decent staff so I had to know they would do it properly, which meant I had to be able to show them how to do it first.'

'Is that why you made them all work for you?' he asked, pointing with his head down the table.

'Partly. Partly I thought they were all lazy and spoilt, and needed a dose of reality.'

'Did anyone ever say no?' Moth asked.

'No, they didn't. Not even Kit, and I was vile to him for months before he decided to show some humility.'

'It wasn't one of my strong points as a youth.' Kit threw the remark down the table between an in-depth conversation with Asha about national property value differentials.

'It isn't now,' Kate muttered into her wine glass.

Isabelle and Moth grinned at each other, focusing on their plates.

'Why? Are you thinking of being the first?' Kate asked Moth.

'The first what?' He looked up at her.

'The first to say no?'

'I was just, wondering, if saying no was an option?'

'Why don't you try it and we'll find out,' Kate said.

'Eh, maybe not right now,' Moth said. 'But thanks for letting me know I can try.'

'I'm offering now,' Kate said. 'I might not be so amenable in the future.'

'Well perhaps if you could keep me updated, as it changes?'

'I think you might be spending too much time with Kit,' Kate told him.

'You're right, I should spend more time with Isabelle. She's a much better influence,' Moth said.

'I don't know that I'd go that far,' Kate said, her wine swishing in the glass.

'What?' Isabelle asked. 'What's wrong with me?'

'I never said anything was,' Kate told her. 'But I'm not sure that the general euphemism of a "good influence" would apply to you either. James would be a good influence, or Rob, for example. In the eyes of the world at large, at least.'

Isabelle looked up the table at both offerings for Moth's influencers and looked back at Kate with raised eyebrows. She shrugged and swirled her glass again, sitting back in her chair and giving up the pretence of eating.

'Kate, you've barely touched your plate,' Elsa told her from the far end of the table.

'I'm saving myself for pudding.'

'Again?'

'I do love pudding,' Kate retorted.

'This is delicious,' Asha said. 'You have done so much.'

'Thank you, my dear, you're most welcome. It's always a pleasure to cook for the family.'

'She doesn't mean that at all,' Kit said.

'She only cooks twice a year to prove she can do it, and so

much better than any of us,' Hester said.

'She prefers to be paid for her cooking,' Kit said.

'What's wrong with wanting to earn a living doing something you love?' Kate enquired.

'Nothing at all,' Kit told her.

'But you do much prefer cooking in the pub than doing it for the family,' Hester added.

'Not everyone is cut out for the family life,' Kate told her. 'It's long since been unfashionable to judge people for that crime.'

'Though it does happen,' Asha said.

'Yes, and more so in rural communities like this,' Kate said.

Isabelle could see her ruffled feathers in the enlarged swirl of the wine.

'I find women here see work as something they have to do before having a family,' Asha said. 'Many people at work keep asking me when I will marry and have family, expecting me to leave work when I do.'

'Don't you want a family?' Hester asked in a balanced tone.

Isabelle felt the whole table cringe. An invisible ripple of anxiety that pushed most of them back in their chairs, laying cutlery down over the last of their scraps, bringing napkins up to wipe their mouths. Kit, of course, sat forward in fascination, and Asha missed the warning flicker of enlarged eyes that came from Rob, Kate and Elsa. Nat continued oblivious too, but Isabelle noticed even Moth put down his fork and sit back, with a long look at her. She ignored him. Staring at the curving handles of the majolica dishes pulled from the kitchen dresser for the occasion, the green mixing with the amber glasses, pooling colours onto the tablecloth.

'Oh, yes, very much,' Asha said. 'But I love my work. I wouldn't want to give it up to have children, and I'd want to have children under the right circumstances.'

'Oh,' said Hester, stroking the edge of her plate, adjusting the abandoned cutlery to the side. 'And what would the right circumstances be, for you?'

'I suppose the same as for many people,' Asha told her, eyes fluttering around the table.

'In my experience people have very different ideas about the circumstances under which they will or won't have children.'

Rob squirmed in his seat.

'I think that's healthy, don't you?' Asha asked her, surprise at the tone of Hester's voice creeping into her own. She glanced at James, but he was silent and focused on the fire behind Hester, his fingers toying with the napkin by his plate. 'It's a very personal choice. Myself, I would want a secure relationship, a safe income and home to raise a family in, and a good network around me to help me do a better job of it. But other things matter to other people.'

'So, you'd keep working and have a family?' Kate asked, steering the conversation back to safe ground.

'Oh yes, definitely. I wouldn't want to give up my own identity to have children.'

'What if you couldn't have all those perfect circumstances?' Hester asked.

'It's not about life being perfect,' Asha told her, struggling to cover the irritation creeping into her voice. 'It's about making sure you're in the best place you can to give children the best chance of a happy life. I wouldn't want to have children if I didn't have confidence in myself, my life and relationship, that's all.'

Kate leaned forward and put her wine glass down on the table with a clatter against the water glass. 'I think that's a very wise approach myself.'

Isabelle winced at the sharp noise, and Nat looked up in surprise, glancing at Moth.

'I suppose it is, if you have the luxury of choice,' Hester said. 'Myself, I would be grateful for children under any circumstances. I know that's not how everyone feels...'

'Nat, how do you fancy helping me clear these plates?' Rob interjected, standing up and pushing his chair back, smiling at the young girl. 'I didn't do anything to get this fantastic spread on the table, would you mind giving me a hand?'

'Of course,' she said and stood up, glancing at Moth for comfort.

'Moth, fancy lending a hand?' Rob asked brightly.

'If you don't mind, I'll let my dinner settle,' Moth returned, matching his false enthusaism. 'I did help bring it in after all.'

'Fair enough,' Rob said.

Isabelle prayed he would ask her, but he never even looked her way. She would have pushed back her chair and stood to help but Kate kicked her leg under the table and frowned her best 'don't you dare' stare as Rob and Nat left the room.

Hester ignored them all and carried on past her husband's best attempt at diversion, '... but I do find it difficult when people actively choose not to have children under the best of circumstances.'

'It's a very personal choice,' Asha said, trying to end the subject.

There was a warmth in her tone that reached down the

table to Isabelle, and she wondered how much she knew.

'Are you a practicing Catholic?' Kit asked, interjecting in a tone that was trying to be curious. Isabelle wasn't convinced. 'I thought Poland was predominantly Catholic?'

'Yes, it is, and I am,' Asha said, her voice wary at the new subject.

'So, don't you believe it's up to God to decide about children, not people? You seem very progressive for a Catholic.'

Isabelle would make him pay for that comment later. He was enjoying himself, with an explicit grasp on the needling comments needed to inflame the simmering atmosphere.

'All people interpret faith for themselves,' Asha said. 'We live in a modern world. I don't think the question of family planning is a faith issue, though I'd prefer not to argue that with our local priest.'

'Hmm,' Hester grabbed at her statement, leaning forward to put an elbow on the table. 'Things do move on. I was reading in the paper the other day that in America they're moving towards changing the abortion laws in some states.'

Isabelle shuddered. The disquieting article from the train rushed back through her, she should have known Hester would see it too. She put her hands on the table to push away from it. Kate put her hand out and pinned her down, leaning forward to add her weight to the moment.

'Laws change all the time,' Kate said to Hester. 'That doesn't mean an improvement in moral or social certitude, it just means a swaying of the scales of mass opinion.'

'Oh, I know,' Hester batted back. 'And mass opinion is definitely swaying against the slaughter of innocent babies. In America, anyway.'

'Hester, I hardly think this is suitable dinner table conversation.'

'Why not, Mother?'

'I just feel that, well, perhaps, women's issues are hardly comfortable for men to talk about in public,' Elsa murmured, twisting the corners of her napkin.

'Don't be so sexist, Elsa,' Kit interrupted. 'What more could you ask for at a dinner table? Good invigorating debate about the details of social existence, don't you agree guys? James? Moth?'

'I agree,' Asha threw into their silence. 'I know it's very British to be polite but it's good to meet a family who aren't afraid to talk about politics.'

'Except when political discussion is really an underhand opportunity to punish those too reserved to argue back. Not everyone's a dinner table politician after all,' Kate added.

She said it with such nonchalance that Isabelle saw several heads nodding back in agreement but, through the firm hand pinning hers to the table, she felt a quivering rage building in the slender frame at her side.

'I think political diversity is healthy,' Kit said. 'How does society evolve if we don't question and debate the status quo?'

'It evolves politely?' Elsa suggested.

'No, that would be stagnation if I'm honest,' Kit told her. 'Asha's right, we're all so British, we need some decent Continental guts to liven us up.'

'It's about sensible interpretation of laws, rather than changing them,' Asha said, trying to be polite to all, looking to James with concern for what she felt she'd started. He offered her a useless silent smile, his hand twitching on the table.

'No, I'm pretty sure I'd change the laws, in light of the insensible personal interpretation that I've witnessed,' Hester countered.

'Well, if we're going to go about changing laws, how about we start with freedom of expression?' Kate backhanded. 'You shouldn't be able to freely express personal bitterness in the guise of political evangelism.'

'It's not personal bitterness to have an opinion,' Hester told her.

'No, but it is to spit it out at every opportunity without consideration as to who it might hurt,' Kate told her back.

'Who says I haven't given it consideration?'

'You might want to try remembering that you don't know everything about everyone,' Kate snapped. 'How do you know that you aren't condemning people at this very table to sitting on the other side of a law they followed themselves?'

'Kate, Hester doesn't mean to make it personal against anyone in particular.' Elsa tried to ease the situation.

Kate wrenched backwards in her chair in irritation, glaring in disbelief at the ceiling.

'Anyone else got any laws they'd like to change?' Kit asked the room. 'James, how about you, some obscure cattle legislation you dislike?'

'The law on badger baiting?' James offered with a grim look at him.

'Elsa?' Kit ignored the insinuation.

'No, I'm quite happy with the general law of life as it is.'

'Moth?'

'Well, as you're asking, I think they should change the legal age of consent.'

Isabelle watched as all eyes turned to look at him with amazement. She saw Elsa roll her eyes to the ceiling, Kate smile with approval, and Kit clap his hands in delight.

'Oh, I agree with that,' Asha said. 'They should definitely raise it.'

'I don't think that's what Moth meant,' Kit suggested.

'No, I think they should adjust it,' Moth confirmed. 'Not just the age, which is different all over the world, but they should change other parts of it too.'

'Now I think we really are stretching the boundaries of what's polite at the dinner table,' Kit said. 'Do go on.'

'Well, how about if two underage children are mutually consenting, is that illegal? And should there be a buffer zone, if one is underage and the other isn't but it's consensual? And, same as with abortion, which allows different rules on the grounds of rape, if a child is abused, should the legal age of consent apply to their choices afterwards?'

Isabelle couldn't help but look up at him, surprised by the intelligence and calm pondering he bought to the statement. She found him looking straight back at her, a lopsided smile wrapped round that Threlfall pout, locking his eyes on hers. She dropped her gaze.

'God, that is a good question,' Kit told him in the frigid silence which greeted his queries. 'I never thought about that.'

'We have these conversations at school all the time,' Moth said. 'Though normally in philosophy, or social studies, not in the dining hall.'

'How appropriate,' Elsa said with a testy tone to her voice.

'Kate? Anything other than freedom of expression?' Kit asked.

'Yes, I think there should be more mitigating circumstances for the murder of irritating arseholes,' Kate said.

'I think from the number of your customers you include in that category, it's probably better that one stays the same,' James managed to pipe up.

'Isabelle?' Kit asked.

'Yes, Isabelle, what about you?' Hester added. 'I think we're pretty sure where you stand on the subject of abortion anyway.'

Isabelle sucked her breath in with a shiver, narrowing her gaze to the white cloth space in the gap between plates, where the faint mark of a warm platter had left an oval ring on the damask leaves.

'Yes, we are,' Kit said. 'Isabelle agrees with the law as it stands.'

'As do I,' Kate added, leaning forward over her full plate, her silk blouse hovering close to the congealing gravy, its blue shimmer reflecting from the white china rim. 'Just because you can't remember the time when women died having shitty back street abortions, doesn't mean I don't. A change in the law on abortion would be the biggest backwards step possible for women, trust the Americans to pull that bullshit on us.'

'Yes, it's so much better for innocent babies to die in pristine clinics,' Hester said to her wine glass.

'You spiteful, little, bitch,' Kate said, throwing the napkin over her cold plate of food.

Everyone winced, James put his hand out to cover Asha's, and Kit expressed a deep 'Oooh' in support of Kate's emphatic dislike.

'Kate!' Elsa complained.

'Trust you to back her up,' Hester said to Kate.

'Did you ever think that I might be supporting myself?' Kate retorted. 'Or any other woman at this table who prefers to keep their legal choices to themselves? Or women in general?'

'I think we all know the truth behind that,' Hester told her.

'No, you don't,' Kate said. 'You really don't! Now, if you'll excuse me, I shall go and do pudding.' She rose with a sharp push of her chair, threw a furious look at Kit, and swept out.

Hester looked after her departing figure in confusion, her face flushed with guilt. In the gaping void of Kate's departure, finally released from her hand, Isabelle stood up and put her napkin down.

'Will you excuse me, Elsa?' she asked.

'Of course, my dear.'

Isabelle walked out without another glance at any of them. Kit reached a hand out to catch her but she evaded him with a sideways slip.

THE CHILL in the dining room frosted into a brittle silence. Kit waited to see if anyone else would break it, leant forward and grinned at Asha.

'Well, that was exciting! You are getting a real introduction to the family now, and we haven't even had pudding yet!'

Asha looked at him in astonishment.

'You are such a shit stirrer,' Hester told him.

'Me?' Kit roared with laughter. Her face was full of the discomfort of the too righteous. 'You're blaming me for that?'

'Yes, I'm pretty sure you started the conversation,' Moth said to Hester.

Kit looked at him in approval. Well, well, law on consent eh? He'd slipped that in like a murmur in the background of a storm, no one had noticed it, except him. Never mind what he'd been up to, what was he planning?

'I think it might have been me talking about family planning,' Asha said with a tinge of discomfort.

'Oh no, it was definitely Hester,' Kit assured her.

Rob and Nat came back in at that point and cleared some

more plates. The others sat in excruciating silence, which broke Asha first, rising from her chair.

'I insist on doing something,' she said, gathering plates up. 'Nat, will you show me where the kitchen is?'

'Yes, you can come with me.' Nat took a single plate off the table and led the way.

'Kate is in there whipping the living hell out of the cream,' Rob said to everyone. 'She really doesn't like cooking for the family, does she?'

'No,' Kit said. 'She really doesn't.'

'I'll help too,' James said.

'Oh goodness, don't put that crap on,' Kit told him. 'Since when did you ever do anything to help with dinner.'

'I'll do anything for a breath of fresh air,' James told him, following Asha and Nat out.

Rob sat down at the table again and smiled at those left behind. Kit raised his glass to him and took a large mouthful of the delicious wine. Elsa picked at the edge of the tablecloth and stared into the elusive private space hovering above the rim of her wine glass. Hester stared out of the window. Moth had his elbows on the table looking at Isabelle's abandoned chair. Kit tried to work out how this was going to end, with a final bang of fireworks or the inglorious fizzle of flat prosecco. Would Asha make polite excuses and slip away from James to a happier future, or shag him senseless in pity?

He took another draught, the berry richness of the liquid oozing into every part of his mouth, the alcohol tingling along his tongue. He held onto the warmth, feeling the fuller flavours relinquish themselves. The slight earthiness, the tinge of acidity, the rawness of burnt tobacco at the furthest edges. He closed his eyes for a moment, leaned back against his chair and swallowed.

Where had Isabelle gone? Booking a ticket to India whilst
they sat there waiting for the pear tart to caramelise? She'd
blame him, of course, she'd say he'd provoked it. Which was
bollocks. Hester had come with a mission. Lines to be drawn
in the family fray in front of this new arrival. He should have
a word with Asha. Tell her the greatest fault she'd find in
James was not his pre-Neanderthal domestic capability, or his
intolerable Saga lovemaking, or his disturbing obsession with
cattle. It was his inability to tell his fucked-up bitch of a sister
to go poison someone else's life.

He opened his eyes and looked at Hester. Oblivious to the
fact that her face was twisted in on itself, her mouth flaring at
the corners as she had a conversation in her head. Reliving
every word, no doubt, baking it into justification. Like some
long-abandoned, cold-set, rancid meringue, the white potential soiled by a crisped, burnt beige edge.

This child thing. It never went away. He couldn't understand it. Just fucking adopt. Children were great, he loved all
of them, even the little arseholes, at least you could have
some fun with them. Why did it have to be hers, only hers
that would make her happy? He'd known that fatherhood
was not for him. From about the time his mother had gone to
India and never returned. Making that choice had been liber-
ating, knowing he'd never be curve-balled by a pregnant
woman demanding paternity or expecting participation.
Parenthood was not for everyone, but it was like a red rag to
Hester's twisted horns. She wouldn't be happy without her
own child, and without it she would make sure everyone else
went down in flames too. She deserved the biggest kick up
her ice-blocked fanny.

Kit glanced at Rob, sat waiting for everyone to be polite,
his hand tapping the silverware, thinking about pudding.

Poor bastard, he had to live with her. No wonder he wasn't surprised by the atmosphere, he had to sit down to dinner with her misery daily. You had to admire him. The man could produce innocent contentment in the middle of a war zone. Born to be a solicitor. Elsa was looking down the table at Moth, full of deep thoughts she would never share with anyone, no doubt. Moth was staring at Isabelle's empty chair.

The sound of Nat and Asha chatting, coming back down the corridor, impinged. Everyone at the table sat up and put a smile on their face. A more insincere twisted set of bleak expressions he'd never seen in his life. Kit stirred himself and stood up as James and Asha came back in carrying puddings. Kate and Nat brought up the rear.

'Right, come on, family tradition, let's change seating arrangements,' Kit said. He walked over to the sideboard and opened another bottle of wine. 'Rob, come and sit down here next to Kate. Asha, you take a chair next to Moth. James, you can sit by your sister. Nat, you come up here and sit by Elsa. Hester, you... just stay put.'

She glared at him in response. He moved them all one by one, as Kate helped everyone to pudding. He refilled wine glasses and topped up water.

'Did you put coffee on?' he asked Kate.

She nodded in curt response.

'I'll go and check it,' he said.

He left the room and went to the hallway, glanced up the stairs. They reflected a wooden silence, the light from the window dancing through the banisters and mocking the ugly afternoon. It was doubtful she'd gone up there. He strode into the kitchen, tweaked the coffee machine, touched up the tray Kate had put ready. They both knew it was an excuse. He flew down the back stairs and ran along the corridor. Her workroom was empty, no lights on, not a sign of her. Kit went back up to the dining room. They had reassembled themselves and were talking in small groups.

He refilled Kate's wine glass, her untouched pudding on the plate in front of her. He laid his spare hand on her shoulder while he poured. She was tense with irritation but looked up at him and smiled, touched his hand in thanks. He went and sat next to Nat, aware of the empty chair between him and Rob. From where he sat the window gave him a wide view of the river running along the edge of the garden. The sunshine was enticing.

'We should go for a walk in this gorgeous weather,' he suggested. 'Show Asha the gardens. James does love his fresh air after all. We can have coffee in the sitting room afterwards.'

'What a good idea,' Kate said. 'You can all take a stretch and give me a chance to tidy up some.'

'Won't you come with us?' Asha asked. 'We could all help tidy up afterwards.'

'No, it will only irritate me,' Kate told her. 'I don't count endless expanses of mown grass as a garden. You go enjoy the river.'

They rose from the table, the idea invigorating. Kit had no intention of letting them go without him. If he couldn't comfort Isabelle, he could at least make sure Hester didn't get any more of an edge on Asha. He herded them towards the door to find coats. Moth looked reluctant to go and held back from his best efforts. Kate took plates away with her to the kitchen, but Elsa remained seated.

'Not coming?' Kit asked.

'No, I won't if you don't mind,' she said. 'There's something I remembered I need to do. Look after them Kit. Don't let Hester get too serious again.'

Moth began to edge towards the door under cover of their conversation.

'Moth, I'm sure you'd rather have a little time to yourself, but would you mind sparing me ten minutes in the study?' Elsa asked him.

He pulled up on his way out of the door. Kit watched his back resisting the effort to tell her to go hang.

'Of course,' he said, turning to look at her.

'Well, have fun, we'll see you in about twenty or so,' Kit told them.

She rose with effort, looking tired out, and walked past him to the study, Moth following her. Kit turned the other way down the corridor and went to the kitchen. Kate was stood at the sink, running hot water. He walked up behind her and slipped an arm around her waist, lay his chin on her shoulder. She didn't speak to him.

'See if you can find her,' he said.

She nodded but stayed silent.

'Are you mad at me?' he asked.

'No.'

'Not even a little bit?'

'No, you're safe for now, but once I stop wanting to ram this rolling pin up Hester's backside I may reconsider.'

'I think she already has a rod that needs pulling out,' he said. 'Not sure more stiffness up her arse is what she needs.'

He felt her shoulders relax a little. She gathered a sud of bubbles and put it on his nose.

'Where's Elsa?'

'Gone to her study,' he said and kissed her neck, moving

the warmth of his mouth up its curve towards her ear. She breathed out in a long sigh and let her shoulders relax.

'Go.'

'Yes ma'am.' He kissed her ear, left her, and went to join the others.

The freshness of the garden and river was matched by the lightness of Asha's conversation, determined not to return to muddier subjects. He herded them first one way, back the other, and home to the sitting room, where they were joined by Elsa and Moth in uplifted mood. He'd run out of energy at last though, and Asha's polite conversation was starting to grate on him. Rob decided the very same thing it seemed and suggested it was time to move.

As Rob took his car full of passengers out the door the family dispersed in relief. Moth and Nat disappearing upstairs together and Elsa retreating to her study with a firm click of the door. Kit walked through the kitchen, grabbed a bottle of wine and followed the path to the workroom. When he opened the door the lights were on, an empty bottle of wine sat on the pouffe. He walked past it, wove between the towering stacks of useless possessions and rounded the corner to the far back wall. Two sets of eyes looked guiltily up at him, empty wine glasses in hand.

'Oh, for heaven's sake,' he said. 'Not the crying corner again?'

'Don't you dare judge us,' Kate told him, pointing at him with her empty glass.

'Oh, and the old heirlooms of grief too?' Kit said, unscrewing the bottle and pouring.

Isabelle held out her own carbon copy glass. Irrresponsibly tall, with generous fluting cups rearing out from the slender stems, they were cut and etched round with filigree designs. They had once had silver work touched into the design, but they were old now and well worn. They were her favourite glasses. Her parents had brought them from Fortnum's when they were in London once. She tended to drag them out anytime she was miserable.

'Come on, move up,' Kit said, and shifted their shoulders apart. 'Is this the best we can do?' He sat down between them on the nest of old cushions and blankets, put his back against the wall where the warmth of the plumbing pipes rose up to the floor above.

'My bones are getting too old for this,' Kate said.

'Your bones are never going to get old,' Kit told her.

'Well maybe it's my skin getting thinner,' Kate said. 'I swear, if it wasn't for James trying to impress Asha, I would have hurled the gravy dish at Hester.'

'Elsa's rather fond of that gravy dish,' Isabelle said.

'Ugly bloody thing,' Kate retorted.

'The dish?' Kit asked.

Kate snorted in amusement.

'It's not Hester's fault Kate, she doesn't know,' Kit said. He wondered how many old wounds women nursed, thinking them unfit for discussion. Letting them fester, out of sight, ignored. It couldn't be healthy, one day it would implode for sure. 'You can't expect Elsa to choose between her oldest friend and her own daughter.'

'I don't, but I do expect her to arbitrate between her daughters.'

'That's even more irrational,' Isabelle said. 'Or, is that less rational?'

'Save me the grammar lesson,' Kate said. 'One day you'll get fed up with it. One day she'll push you too far. You'll stand up for yourself, you'll have to, something will be important enough to make you. You'd be surprised what you can do for someone else that you wouldn't consider for yourself.'

That was the truth of it, Kit thought. Mother instinct. Most powerful instinct in the world. He wondered if women one day realised that they were fighting for their daughters, not themselves, things might change. It was not having a mother that left Isabelle so adrift in the family, not being a mother that left her without a cause. Not that he would ever express that in front of Kate. Or Isabelle. Or any woman.

'I think she was trying to preserve the family dignity, as much as the gravy dish,' Kit commented, swigging from the bottle in absence of a glass.

'Well she failed. Miserably,' Kate spat out, chewing her lip and adding, 'Poor Asha, I do hope she doesn't tell James to go hang himself!'

'I get the feeling she won't,' Isabelle said. 'He's quite adorable, even with us lot.'

'Part of me wants to take her to one side and tell her to get Hester out of his life,' Kate said. 'Another part of me wants her to have to deal with Hester to give you a break.'

'I think you should stay out of it altogether.'

'Spoken by a woman hiding in the shadows,' Kate told her.

'I like the shadows, they leave me in peace.'

'Hiding or running, when are you going to stop doing one of those two?'

'I don't like confrontation.'

Kit sat in the middle and let them bicker across the top of him. At least they weren't crying any more, he'd missed the most maudlin stage.

'No one likes confrontation, Isabelle,' Kate said. Kit was tempted to argue otherwise but kept his mouth shut. 'I want to see you stand up for yourself. This is your life too, you can't keep running away to India when it gets shitty.'

'I like India,' Isabelle said.

'You like here too.' Kate pointed her glass across Kit. It had emptied again.

'Yes, but India is kinder, in general,' Isabelle retorted, bringing her own empty glass to bear.

Kit topped their glasses back up.

'It never suited me much,' Kate said.

'You never gave it a real chance,' Isabelle said.

'I've never been,' Kit offered, wondering what else had been said about India.

'Anyway, I can't leave her. She's lost too many as it is,' Kate said.

'Now who's taking the guilt trip?' Isabelle returned.

'Yes, but I'm not running away,' Kate said with smugness.

'Who said I am?'

'Aren't you?'

Isabelle remained silent. Kit bit his lip to keep the questions back.

'You made a promise to Elsa to stay,' Kate added.

Isabelle buried her head on her knees, said from the depths, 'Maybe I'm not as stoic as you. Maybe I can't keep that promise.'

Kit kept mouse-quiet between them.

'Stoic?' Kate said. 'Me? That's a strange choice of word. I would have put Elsa down as the stoic one.'

'Yours is just a different sort,' Isabelle said to her knees. 'You wouldn't break a promise.'

'Everyone breaks promises,' Kate said. 'You just learn to make fewer as you get older.'

'Or add more provisos in when you make them,' Kit

added.

'You could have told me that about two weeks ago,' Isabelle complained.

'As I say, I keep expecting you to stand up for yourself,' Kate said, in her most waspish tone. 'Besides, what is it you've promised?'

'To stick around as long as she needs me, to help with the children.'

'Well, why does she need you? I have no idea why, you're a bit unreliable. And as for the children, they don't need or want you.'

'Ouch, thanks for that.'

'We can all see who Nat's bonded with,' Kate said.

'What about Moth?'

Kit wanted to say, 'What about Moth?' too. Kate hurtled on.

'Moth isn't a child, Isabelle, and whilst he may need some support, he doesn't want any of us helping him. That lad has his own agenda, and we'll only find out when it suits him. You can't go basing your life choices on some misguided sense of responsibility to him.'

'I thought you were trying to persuade me to stay?' Isabelle said.

'I'm trying to understand why you want to leave.'

'I don't want to leave,' Isabelle said.

'What are we talking about then?' Kate said, squiggling on the cushion. 'Because my elderly skin is not getting any more comfortable here.'

'I don't want to leave,' Isabelle said. 'But I never feel right when I stay.'

'Oh, well that's a lot clearer.'

'I mean, I feel split in two. Like I'm always upsetting

someone with what I do. When I'm away I never feel like that. I miss you all, and I look forward to coming home, but I feel myself, and sort of an acceptable person.'

'Don't you ever feel like that here?' Kate asked.

'Sometimes, yes, of course,' Isabelle said. 'When I'm with you, or Elsa, or out walking, or down here working.'

'Well, you can't spend the rest of your life down here in the basement.' Kate snapped.

'I know.' Isabelle wailed.

'And you can't spend the rest of your life running away to India, I refuse to allow it,' Kit added, swigging from the bottle again.

'So what do I do?' Isabelle buried her head again.

'Get out of the basement, fool girl,' Kate told her. 'Stand up in the world.'

'You mean be mean back to Hester?'

'No!' Kate snapped. 'Absolutely not, no. I'm not telling you to behave like her.'

'But to toughen up?' Isabelle said.

'Look outside of the current situation, that's all. You don't always have to live here at Elsa's beck and call. You no longer have James keeping you here. Go stay with Kit for a while, go live somewhere else, try a new job. Try anything. It's always been here or India, at least try other options before you decide to go and live in India for the rest of your life. It's just so bloody far away.'

Kit was surprised she mentioned him as an option. Even if she did drown it in others. He looked down at their feet. They had both kicked their shoes off, and the mules and the soft boots had made a nest together on the edge of the cushions, right and left soles meeting where they'd fallen, looking like long-lost odd fellows, perfectly matched in length. Kate's toes sticking out from her trousers, Isabelle's tucked close to her body, pushing her knees into a triangle of support.

'And what about Moth?' Isabelle asked.

'Look, change nothing and nothing changes.' Kate spoke to her like a child.

'And it might just change in a way you don't like.' Kit added.

'I'm confused,' Isabelle said.

'What?'

'Well, if I change nothing, so nothing changes, how can it change badly? I mean, nothing's changing,' Isabelle said.

'Yes, because nothing has changed,' Kit explained.

'So, nothing changes means that nothing changes, not nothing changes,' Isabelle said, trying to grasp the words correctly.

Kate looked at Isabelle across Kit with a frown, turned her head away from the awkward angle and finished the glass of wine. Kit grinned, they were hammered.

'I don't know,' Kate admitted. 'I always assumed that it meant nothing would change, of its own accord, if you weren't the agent of change you would be the recipient. I never thought it might mean that nothing would change, that the set of circumstances would stay the same.'

'Oh,' said Isabelle, smirking. 'I'm glad we cleared that up.'

'We haven't cleared it up at all!' Kate wailed. 'Now I wonder if I've been misapplying the concept my whole life.'

'Can't we use it as we want?'

'Not if we're being idiots in the process!' Kate told her.

'Well, maybe we're just being drunk idiots,' Isabelle said, laughing at her. 'Maybe you'll work it out tomorrow with the hangover.'

'You've made me lose my point,' Kate said.

'I'm not sure you had a point,' Isabelle said.

'My point,' Kate said, 'was to shift your arse in a new direction.'

'Oh, well that's a lot clearer, I can grasp that,' Isabelle said.

'Yes, but can you do it?' Kate said.

'Ok, enough already.' Kit stood up. 'You two are going nowhere. Time to call it a day.'

'We're having a deeply existential discussion here,' Kate told him with a frown.

'You always do when you're drunk,' he told her. He offered a hand down and pulled Kate up, holding her as she wobbled and found her shoes, offered a hand to Isabelle. She was no steadier on her feet. 'Pair of drunken wenches, sat on the old crying cushion, licking your mutual wounds in the darkness.'

'I have reconsidered your culpability in the event,' Kate told him, hanging onto his shoulder.

He tightened his grip around each of them, they felt adorable, musty from the cushions and redolent of rich wine. Clinging onto their empty glasses.

'You two are going to have the most hideous hangover in the morning,' he said.

'Yours will be just as bad,' Kate told him.

'Come on, old skin, time to get you home,' he told her. He wobbled them both back to the sofa and released Isabelle onto it. She curled up in the depths, looking into her empty wine glass.

'Oh no, not yet,' Kate complained, clutching her glass as he peeled it out of her hands. 'We haven't finished our discussion.'

Moth opened the door and came in.

'Oh dear,' said Kate, voice awash with grape. 'We've been found.'

'Don't worry,' Isabelle said. 'Moth will keep our secret.'

'You're drunk,' Moth said, coming to sit on the pouffe and picking up the empty wine bottle.

'That's what I told them,' Kit agreed.

'It's my job to get people drunk,' Kate defended.

'Why do people drink so much?' Moth asked, twirling the dregs around the bottle's emptiness.

'People drink for many reasons, Moth,' Kate said. 'Some of them are arseholes before they drink, some of them are just arseholes when they drink, and some of them use drink to deal with all the other arseholes in the world.'

'What about you two?' he asked.

'I don't like myself when I drink, so hopefully a drunken not a sober arsehole,' Kate said.

'I'm using it now to deal with arseholeotheritus,' Isabelle said.

'I think I fit all three options,' Kit said.

They all agreed with him.

He pulled Kate towards the door. 'Moth, do your best to keep Isabelle awake until I get back.'

'I'll see you all tomorrow, for breakfast at my place,' Kate said. 'I'll need company for this hangover, and you, Moth, have work to do. 9 am, lean on the buzzer 'til I get up, please.'

'Do I get paid for that?'

'It's the only bit of leaning I will ever pay you for, but yes, that's a deal. Though I must say taking advantage of an elderly drunkard is disgraceful.'

Kit left with Kate leaning on him far more than she needed to. He would have rather gone back and found Isabelle comatose on the sofa than sat there with Moth. But life wasn't perfect, and Kate needed taking home and putting to bed.

13

To this day I don't know how Richard found the courage to ask Father for my hand in marriage.

I don't think I have ever been as scared as I was on that day. Not even now, all these years later when choices weigh so heavily on me. The options seem harder, the consequences grimmer, the fallout more far-reaching. But that day, just after Christmas '64, my whole future was on the line.

Richard arrived late on Sunday morning. We'd decided this was the best time. When Father would be in his study, reading the papers. Depending on the headlines, this would be as relaxed as we would find him. I told Richard to walk through the front gates, to make sure he crunched the gravel on his way in. I wanted Father to know something out of the ordinary was happening before we got to the study.

We met in the hallway, the door opening onto a courtyard whited over with fresh frost. The magnolia tree dressed in a festive snowy cloak. We were all holding our breaths that it wouldn't be another freezing winter like the one before. Richard's father had suffered hard that year. Losing not only stock but two fingers to frostbite and taking a blow to his health that he would never recover from, leaning ever more heavily on Richard to manage the farm. The benefit of this had been that Father had increasingly dealt with him about the farm business and spoke with respect of his choices.

Richard took my attention from the wintery courtyard. He was smartly dressed, a blazer tight on his wide shoulders, sitting over well-pressed blue woollen slacks, a white shirt straining against his neck muscles topped off with a red tie. Dusting off the snow from his polished boots, rubbing his hands together to warm them before folding mine in his. I was more used to taking his clothes off than seeing him this smartly dressed. Even though by then, our 'courting' had become public, we still spent most of our time out on the common or in his father's hay barn.

'Ready?' he asked.

'Yes. No. Yes,' I admitted.

'You're sure now?' he teased. 'I don't mind facing your father but I need to know you're sure this is what you want when I do so?'

'What if he says no?'

Kate came into the hall from making tea in the kitchen. On her way back to the sitting room fire with her nose in a book, swatting for her finals. She caught the tail end of my words.

'Fat chance,' she told us. 'He's not going to risk losing his only daughter, is he, numbskull? Besides, it's not him saying "no" you want to worry about. It's what he demands in order to say "yes".'

'I might have a few noes of my own to use,' Richard told her.

'Oh, please,' Kate rolled her eyes as she walked away. The

hallway was cold, the doors shut on cold rooms or warm fires. Father had refused to light the hallway fire, remembering how foolishly he'd tried to keep the whole house warm last winter, the terrible timber cost to the estate. 'Keep fooling yourself, sunshine, you're not fooling any of the rest of us.'

'Couldn't you just wish us luck?' I demanded.

'Sure thing, break a leg,' she said. 'Preferably not your father's. And remember, I'm maid of honour, right?'

She closed the door to the sitting room and left us shivering in the hall.

'Elsa.' He folded me up in his arms. Oh, how I miss those embraces. I was invincible in a hug from Richard. He always knew what to say to make me brave. 'We're going to have a long life together, with a truckload of crazy kids, and he's going to be the happiest grandfather because of it. We aren't leaving until we have his blessing. Are you still sure you want me?'

'More than life itself,' I told him.

He took my hand and led us to the study. Knocked three firm times on the door and waited to be invited in.

'Come in.'

Richard squeezed my hand as he opened the door.

Father was sat at his desk, the newspaper spread out before him, reading glasses on the tip of his nose. He looked up with a squint over their top to see who was disturbing him. Frowned, took the reading glasses off and folded them up with precision as we walked into the room, hand-in-hand.

'Ah, I see,' he said, leaning back in his chair, steepling his hands together and letting out a long sigh. 'You'd best take a seat, young man, my dear. It looks like we have a lot to discuss.'

Kate was right. Of course she was. When wasn't Kate

right? Father drove a hard bargain. With fierce words.

He demanded Richard take my name. That our children must bear it too. He told us he would not guarantee the inheritance of the estate, that his will was not settled on that matter. Richard told him he could give the estate to the Labour party for all he cared. He said a sound marriage was made on three things. Shared purpose, adequate money and good sex. He asked us if we were compatible. If we'd made sure we were compatible, in all departments. Richard never looked away from him and said he was entirely sure. I blushed to my roots and stared at the floor, Father said he'd take that as a 'yes' then. The only thing they argued on was that Richard refused to give up the farm. He said it was his life's dream to continue as his tenant as well as his son-in-law. When Father tried to persuade him to join him in the business of the estate Richard refused but said he would always support me to take on that role when it became necessary. In the end Father said he would not allow me to end up a farmer's wife; Richard could farm if he wished but that we must live here at the house and I would draw my own income from the estate. Richard asked for ten years of our own place. Father commuted that to five years or when the first child arrived. Whichever came first. Damned if it didn't seem like a business arrangement and make me feel like a piece of meat.

But when it was over my Father stood up, came round his desk and shook Richard's hand with a big smile on his face, said, 'Well done, lad, well done,' and gave me a hug filled with happiness. He called Kate in to the study and made us drink champagne together.

'So, maid of honour then?' I said to Kate.

'Too right,' she grinned. 'And make sure your brother's coming home for the wedding.'

14

It was a warm day to tame the mountains. Spring volatile as it hit the slopes.

He left Misurina before the sky was bright. Playing with the road in the shadows of the weak light. Pushing hard for twenty yards, easing off and loosening up. Enjoying the pressure in his thighs as they read the steady rise of the road coiling through the valley floor. Passing in and out of thick, light-stealing forests. Through spreading noisy farmyards. Between dew glistening meadows.

Out of the shadow of the trees the wind stung his face even as the sun warmed his back. He slowed, let the heat battle the chill, winning, sliding up his spine and across his shoulders.

Crossing the feathered line stretched across the road and falling back into the enclosing trees Moth sucked the frigid air into his lungs and pushed harder to keep warm.

He made it to Cortina as the shops were opening. Fuelled up on coffee and fresh pastries warm with sticky syrup. He sucked the life out of three oranges, set off again.

The holiday villas were waking as he passed them, late skiers eager to catch the last of the winter. Their excited calls piercing the air. Moth ignored them. He sped up through the villages, slowed down on the isolated patches. Watching the mountains rear up ahead. Stretching upwards with every curve of the road he consumed.

You can do this.

It had been a long while since he felt this unsure of himself. Getting on the bike might often be an effort, but this sense of doubt, the scale of the task ahead, he could remember being this daunted. It took him back to those first uncertain efforts. The attempt to master something external to himself that was leaden and unresponsive.

That had been the first challenge of cycling.

The change when he began to see the bike as an extension of himself. The extremities of his body forged to the frame, the curve of his spine echoing the road. Swinging round the narrow roads of the Shropshire hills. Riding for the sake of a new pleasure.

Able to choose where you go.

When he wanted to.

Fourteen and owning the freedom. He succumbed readily. Hurt muscles eagerly. Pushing energy over the handlebars into exhaustion. The first time out on the bike. The first time following a map.

Elsa had given him the maps a few days before, in her study, after Easter lunch. A pile of dogeared, bulging OS maps, tidied away in one of the neat collection of boxes that lined the shelves. Cradled on her lap long enough that he wondered if she really wanted to part with them.

'If you're going on a journey,' she fingered the maps with a distant look, 'your grandfather always said it's best to have a destination, even if you don't get there.'

It was as close to approval as he thought she'd give him for going off on a trip by himself. She put the maps out on the desk in front of her, placing them one at a time, until the box was empty, and she closed the lid with a sigh.

'Why are you giving them to me?' he asked, not reaching out.

The maps sat between them. Moth as reluctant to pick them up as she seemed to let go. Reluctant to be asked into the study by himself in the first place. Jittery in his chair on the far side of the desk.

'I find it helps, during these... difficult times,' she tapped her fingers on the table as she found her way around the distress, 'to recall better memories. It saddens me you never got to meet your grandfather. He was a loving, kind person, with a wicked sense of humour.'

Moth reached forward to the nearest map, turned it towards him, flipped back the cover.

'I think he would be pleased to know these went to someone with a similar love of exploring, Moth.'

Afterwards, after that awful lunch, after Nat was in bed, after Kit took Isabelle upstairs in a drunken state, he laid them all out on the floor in his room. The county laid out, and beyond it the bordering counties, stretching away over creased, conquered squares. Markings peppered across them. A rating system. Skulls and crossbones in some places. Little beer glasses. Rainbows. By the sea, where the maps stretched that far, awful pictures of dolphins. Scribbles in the margin, a rough script in fading ink. Dates, companions, miles walked, pints drunk.

Moth read the maps for hours, pulled outwards into the

worlds they held. Woke in the morning asleep on the floor, reaching out a hand guided by sleep-blurred eyes, touched a rainbow marked on the page and decided, there.

You should go there.

And gone there, only a few days later.

Cycling out of intense irritation, away from the sulking wreck of Easter dinner. Irritated with Kit and his provoking ways. With Isabelle and her hiding in the basement. With Kate and her work orders. With all of them. Glad even to be away from Nat for a short while, guilty with the relief of it.

The roads had been the second challenge of cycling.

Roads wide enough to take good traffic at decent speeds did not like cyclists. Artic lorries going past him so tight the bike wobbled in their tail wind. Cars roaring past him without warning, close enough to crush each other in the space they thought he left on the road. Bikers coming from nowhere and passing him in a sarcastic rush that left his heart pounding, his mouth dry and tasting sharp. Moth learned fast that cyclists were scum on the roads of the world.

He turned onto narrower roads that wound themselves through convoluted hills with short-lived thanks. Here, the drivers seemed enraged to see him. As though he alone were taking all the space in the world. They rarely slowed or stopped. Glaring at him, swearing as they passed. Or hitting the horn right behind him. Sound warping in the rush of wind around his head. It was enough to put him off.

Except for the arrival. You remember that too.

The fact that he'd taken the day in his own hands, gone somewhere on his own achievement. No money needed. No public transport. No lift, no favours, no licence. A destination. Arrival.

All by yourself.

He put a shaking foot down from the pedal in a quiet stone car park, hidden in the fold of two hills, looked at the woodlands rising above him and claimed the land for himself. The sun warm on his sweat drenched t-shirt, his hair damp on his neck. Grinning so much it made him laugh.

He found himself on the larger map, refolding it to make a smaller area focused around the rainbow. The creases of the paper fluid as the map rippled beneath his fingers into a reduced version of itself. Like a memory.

The memory of the man who owned it before you.

There were no photos of the grandfather he'd never met at Riverdell. It was as though Richard had never lived there, let alone raised a family of three children in its walls. At the farmhouse he was everywhere. James kept his father close by. Walking sticks, photos, rusting tractors loitering in sheds, barometer still tapped morning and night in an echo of the man he'd grown up watching. The two men echoed in each other. Masters of their own destinies, one demanding day at a time.

James was so different to his own father. Watching him work on the farm, Moth wondered what it might have been like, to have a man like that for his father. A man like his grandfather. He looked down at the map. James had followed in this man's steps in so many ways and turned out sound. His father had been nothing like either of them.

You don't have to be like him.

He could follow a different example.

Moth looked at the land in front of him. The path from the car park dipped its way through an excessive puddle and broke up, drenched senseless, into five or more smaller paths that headed in different directions into the wall of woodland.

You don't have to be what he made you.

No one here, in this moment, in this car park, knew him as Moth. No one knew about his dead parents, or his sister. No one knew how old he was or cared why he was there. He was a visitor to the hills, escaping the towns to find some peace in climbing hills or walking the valleys.

Free to be whoever you want.

Perhaps not for long, but for that moment at least. He plunged through the puddle and into the trees, chose the path that looked right on his grandfather's map. Rode across the soft ground, wondering how far he'd get before his walking grandfather's route proved unsuitable for the bike. But the rainbow was on his side.

The path led him onwards. The line on the map and the track in front of him calling to one another. The map pulling him into its language. The trees pulling him into their padded world. Noise reduced to wildness. He felt his heart in his chest, the unfamiliar ache of his arse from the bike seat. A sense of fear mixed with happiness, fuelled by excitement.

Away from everything. Everyone. You're on your own.

Emerging from the trees, to see the wide solid track all the way up the hill. To take the bike up it, to the towering rocks at the top, and the view that stretched all the way to Snowdonia, to the tips of mountains smoking out the far horizon, and the wild thatched fields between him and them. They'd seemed huge.

Moth looked up from the road to the Dolomites towering ahead.

Like hillocks compared to these bastards.

But huge on that day. He'd pitched the tent, cooked his first ever pot of campfire porridge and settled in for the night on the top of the hill.

You can do anything. You're invincible.

The thought had not lasted long. He spent the night in a rigid battle with fear. Twitching at the snap of the tent fabric, at each scuffle, hoot and shriek. Been cold like he'd never known cold, at 3 am when his breath was chilling on his face and sending the shakes down his spine. Huddled in a ball beneath the duvet pulled off the bed at Riverdell. The ground hard beneath a folded blanket. Cocooned. Petrified. Sick with his own weakness and inadequacy. Knowing he would never leave the county, the house, the people again.

You're going to be stuck there forever. Like Nat.

Hating the fear. Its taste in his mouth, the taste of self-loathing and chickenshit. Sleeping at last in a huddled ball.

Waking to the simmering sunlight. The clarity of each bird note. The wind rippling the surface of the tent. He unzipped the opening, lay exhausted and watched the day take shape. Finally warm in his cocoon.

Alone, on a hill.

Colours bleeding into the frosted air.

Turning the world beautiful.

It's not a rainbow, it's a sunrise, you idiot.

The moon shining on the dark edge of the sky.

The fear of the night gleaming alongside the brilliance of the morning.

In that moment Moth started again. Everything that had gone before was left behind.

You can do this. No one can stop you.

Cycling into the Italian mountains Moth remembered that sunrise as the first day of his life. The first time he'd known who Moth could be. He was nothing, invincible. Young, ageless. He was his grandfather, and his father. He was neither. He was himself.

Chickenshit scared, and doing it anyway.

Moth grinned in memory and flew across the main road heading to Venice, carried on west into the mountains, pumping the bike forward. Motorbikes and cars passed him, ignored him, windswept him, tooted him. It didn't matter where you went, a cyclist was always the lowest moving matter on the road.

Some things never change.

Perhaps it was why he was going to meet Kit. Perhaps that was part of the need to keep putting the past down, to face it, and move on again. To claim life, fresh, in the face of fear.

Perhaps, if he made it to Iseo in time, if he saw Kit, he could say, I'm good, piss off, I don't need you. I don't need anyone. I can do this on my own.

And it will feel as glorious as that rainbow sunrise.

ISABELLE LISTENED to Kit leaving Riverdell in the dying hours of Easter Monday.

She'd nursed her hangover all day through his enthusiasm, grown weary by teatime. A relaxed affair that was all the happier for Hester's absence. The memory of Sunday lunch lingering only in Elsa's sensitivity to noise and Kate's refusal to cook so much as a bean. Kit cooking with Nat and Moth, the three women curing their hangovers and their irritations with another dose of wine around the kitchen table.

She was breathless by the time he left. Dizzy from the fury of his final lovemaking. Surrounded by his packing while he buried himself inside her. The intensity of his muscles holding her, his lips sucking her skin into his mouth, his dick persistent, lasting beyond pleasure while she tried to find the orgasm he needed to know he'd given her. In the end, for it was beyond her capacity to fake it with Kit, she murmured enough and lay beside him as he masturbated, stroking his chest and kissing his shoulder. She'd retreated to her bath and not gone downstairs to say goodbye. Not wanted to stand next to Moth feeling this bone-weary exhaustion.

From her bathroom she could hear the crunch of tyres as he drove off. Her ears straining for some knowledge that he hadn't changed his mind. Her muscles relaxing into the steamy room and her shoulders sinking into the water with a long out breath. She propped her toes on the ridge of the bath and submerged her body out of sight.

Sex with James and sex with Kit were like the difference between sitting down to a bowl of porridge at breakfast and facing a full undressed lobster on your plate at dinner.

James had never kissed her all over like Kit did, consuming her skin like a tender steak falling apart in his mouth. James had never wrapped her leg around his chest to penetrate more deeply, or turned her sideways, scissoring her legs, using the full width of his penis to arouse them both more. James had never coated her fingers in lubricant and encouraged them inside his arse. James had never sat astride her and locked tongues until they drowned in saliva. James had never made her come with his fingers before masturbating himself to orgasm. James had never much got out of the bed, Kit seemed to think every surface fair game.

Her body wasn't used to this level of muscular challenge. She wasn't sure she wanted to get used to it. She and Kit had explored intimacy without penetration enough times that she'd never thought there would be more, so much more, to Kit as a sexual partner. That he had held back so much of himself while waiting for her to decide. Whilst James could have been more creative in the bedroom, she felt like Kit had dragged her naked to a modern art exhibition and they were the display.

Between the hangover and Kit's energy she was pretty sure she wanted to lock her bedroom door and sleep for a week.

A cup of tea would have been divine, but the fear of bumping into anyone convinced her to stay upstairs. She picked up clothes, straightened the bedsheets, tidied away the evidence of Kit's presence in her space, crawled into bed with a notebook and pencil, and let her mind find peace in the scrawling of ideas.

SHE WOKE next morning to warmth between her legs, the headache in her head increased to a bolt of pressure through her pelvis. The trickle of blood increasing, waking her. She groaned as pain grabbed her stirring body and crabbed to the bathroom, her hand tucked between her legs. Sitting on the toilet the pressure increased, and the first gush of her period released itself.

It had been months. Her erratic menstrual cycle worsened by the heat in India, her lack of appetite, her body adjusting to the months off the pill, adjusting post-op, trying to figure itself out again.

She sat on the toilet, letting the stress in her body wash through. Unwinding the loo roll, sopping up the mess, reaching for the pads. In fits and starts, from toilet to underwear drawer to second pad, to bed, she let her body adjust. Sinking back into the covers and pulling herself up against the pillows. She reached into the bedside table, pulled out the packet of pills.

It had been eight months since she took them. The day

she'd woken up with sore breasts and known something was wrong. She hated the tiny yellow orbs. They promised so much yet had failed her twice. If she'd kept on with the pregnancy, she would have been nearly due by now. Isabelle closed her eyes and let her head fall against the bars of the bed. Where had that time gone.

August last year. James in the depths of harvest. The thin blue line of horror.

Timing was everything. She was sure of that. The first mistake, when they were so young, when so much was happening, she could put down to youth, fear, the fresh grief of being parentless, overwhelmed by expectations.

But the second. She wondered what the outcome might have been if timing was different. If James hadn't been so busy. Frantic with work, out day and night on the kit, struggling with the contractors and the weather. She'd felt abandoned again. Alone night after night, her hands on her flat belly, trying to fathom the invisible life inside, out. Seeing herself a mother, at the farm, tied to the house while he disappeared into the vortex of it all. If he'd been there, those long nights, talking to her, sharing it, perhaps it might have happened.

But he hadn't. James couldn't be there. And she'd had to face that she didn't want the life. Didn't want the farm. Didn't want the relentless destiny that it made of James' days. Didn't want the great expectation that sat in her belly. Didn't want James' child.

How could she ever explain that to him, to his mother or sister? What she hadn't been able to face herself until it took hold in her belly and made her realise. She couldn't do it.

How could she explain the grief of abortion? The wondering thoughts that had been added to those about her lost parents. Explain it to a woman who couldn't conceive.

Hester's dislike had hardened to hatred, served up in ever increasing portions like it had at Easter lunch.

Isabelle opened her eyes, raised the packet to her face. She'd stayed off the pill since the abortion. Run away to India. Stayed away from sex, until now and Kit. Knowing that with him, it would only ever be sex. Not this relentless weight behind it, waiting for her to be ready. She'd left the pills in the drawer. Waited for her body to find its own rhythm after all those years of denying it. For no bloody reason. She'd hated being on the pill, the way it controlled her emotions, flatlined her feelings, dictated her body. And she'd still conceived.

She knew that every reason they might have failed rested on her. The odd missed day, her lack of ability to stick to a routine life, with set time scales, with that perfect three-hour window, accepting James' dislike of using condoms on back up days, not arguing with him, praying silently in her head.

They all rested on her. As did the final decision. She'd known not to ask him to share it, known how disappointed he'd be. She hadn't been prepared for how he'd shared it with Hester. Regardless of her own miseries about children.

Isabelle might have put a brave face on for Elsa but, at heart, knowing that she was on her own with that decision hurt the most.

Well, she was on her own for it now. Completely on her own to choose. She rattled the pills in their packet, they looked like hormonal drops of poison to her. Felt her body aching with natural purging.

She couldn't do it. Couldn't start taking them again. That was one advantage to Kit. He was obsessed with birth control and sexual safety. No lover was going to dictate life, health or paternity to him. He'd made double sure of that. Kit had never had any doubts about following his own preferences.

So, she'd given up the pregnancy, lost James, disappointed Elsa, alienated Hester.

Put herself outside the family with the outcasts, Kate and Kit.

Kate was right, the future was her own to choose.

She threw the pills toward the bin. Watched it hit the side, rattling as it slid into the abyss. Isabelle curled her hands across her aching guts and felt at peace. Stretched out and revelled in the emptiness

No James, no Kit. She did have choices, and right now, she wanted to keep them. Excitement bubbled up in her. She rose, dressed and stripped the bed. Life needed to be released. Old stuff let go of. It was a rhythm deep inside her. Detritus flushing out.

SHE WORKED to take her mind off the worst cramps of the first few days. Ticking off jobs and piling them up beneath the table. Each vibrant line crossed off the list adding to the sense of ending. Each throb of pain suggesting something fresh might be there when she got to the end. Each wrapped job making her think about what came afterwards.

When she moved from the machine to the table the great map of India caught her eye, holding her poised like the old names, crafted in place, but she moved on, picking up what she was seeking, returning to the orange lines above her machine. India seemed less urgent, now she wasn't swamped with people. Always there if she needed it.

Upstairs, when she went looking for a late breakfast on

the Wednesday, the house was quiet. Elsa's car gone from the garage, Moth nowhere to be seen, not back from his overnight camp. She stood in the kitchen doorway, holding its closing pressure open with her shoulder, feeling the weight bearing against her, listening to the house. She could hear nothing. No guests, no residents. It was eerie and blissful at the same time. She shook off the strangeness and went back into the kitchen, letting the door close with a solid clunk.

Back at the sewing machine she focused on the cushions she was mending. The simple task of fixing a zip had become more complex. Turning them inside out she found that the seams were bare breaths apart from the stitches and would soon collapse past the holding line, there was nothing for the zip to hang onto. She reduced the zip seam by an inch to strengthen them but that made the pattern of the fabric unbalanced, so she had to unpick and sew round all the sides, reducing the cushion down to a smaller size, and only at the end managing to fix the zip. The inners were so old and soft the cushions would feel plumper for being tighter. From the outside nothing looked different, on the inside the invisible new strength of the seams was holding the cushion together.

She turned from the job and looked across the room. At all the boxes and chests, baskets and bags. It looked ramshackle and sprawling. She'd never noticed how much it had piled up. How much of it wasn't hers, how much wasn't needed.

She stood, eyes drinking in the sheer vastness of the room and the contents. It was the strangest of feelings. Memory, stirring hope, catching fear, holding breath. She could do anything. Even within her work, she could do something new. It didn't always have to be this, alterations and repairs when home, or costumes for the production teams when in India. She looked up at the distant map on the far wall. There was all this space in between, all this choice.

The hollow torpid breath left her. What else could she do?

Never mind where she lived, or who she shared that with, or what anyone thought of her. Right here was a whole part of herself packed away in boxes. Her fingers stilled in her lap. Hearing the emptiness of the house above, floating in its own dream of dust and sunlight, the hollow spaces of life waiting to be explored.

She rose, pushed the cushions aside. Wondering where to begin.

Because that was how it felt.

Beginning again.

She padded through the pathways, her hands caressing the corners and edges of the piles and pulled an old hamper basket out. Because it asked her to. And then, then she began to rummage. Rummage in a way she couldn't contain. Rummage until the boxes were piled around her in chaos and she'd lost the network of alleyways. Rummage until she'd smudged the dust lines that declared her foot habits and lack of vacuuming. Rummage until piles began to form on the table. Rummage until she ran out of table space.

More memories surfaced. She found some trestles, cleared some space. She was stood, hot and sweaty from the effort, her innards aching, her hair full of dust and spider dressings, looking about in frustration when Moth opened the door and came in. She looked across in surprise, her mind too focused to switch tracks.

'You've been busy,' he said, walking into the room and

finding no passage, looking around in bemusement. 'Did you lose something?'

'Yes, I think I did,' she said. 'I lost my sense of fun, and I'm pretty damn sure it's in here somewhere.'

'Ok... do you need a hand or want me to go away?'

'Oh no, definitely, help. I have another table here somewhere and I could do with a hand to put it back up.'

'Eh, where are you going to put another table?' he asked. 'There wasn't any space in here before you made, this, eh, thing you've been, sort of, doing.'

She glanced across the chaos, it looked like an explosion.

'I know it looks a bit chaotic, but I can feel something good coming out of this. And I made space right here for the table.'

'Right there?'

'Yes, right here,' she said, stretching out her arms to suggest the space she was stood in the middle of, between the two large trestles that she'd dragged into place. 'James made these for Hester and me, when we first started. I think he made them from some old feed troughs at the farm, they weigh a tonne, but they're so sturdy and there are boards that fit together and make a table top.'

'Ok,' he said. 'Any idea where they might be?'

'I've been looking for the last twenty minutes. I have a bad feeling they're underneath something and I can't think where.'

Moth walked towards her, negotiating a difficult path between piles of fabric and bits of ribbon, buttons, tassels, old dresses, blankets and bric-a-brac. Upended boxes teetering on top of each other as he passed. Arriving to stand in the middle of the space she was so proud of.

'I'm glad I got my bike tent out before you started all this,' he said.

'You were gone a while, have you only just got back?'

'No, I came back this morning but went straight to the farm. I've been helping James out with fencing,' he said. 'There's no one else here, haven't they come back yet?'

'Can't have if you haven't seen them, unless they've come home and gone back out again. I don't even know where they were going today, do you?'

'Something to do with shopping, for school stuff I think.'

'They'll come find us if they need us.' Isabelle glanced around again. 'Did you enjoy the camping?'

'Yeah, it was cool,' Moth said in his indifferent tone. 'What do these boards look like?'

Isabelle could tell when he was evading her. He didn't want to talk about his trip. Well, that made sense to her, she didn't want to try and explain what she was up to either. Because she didn't know yet, not quite. Maybe it was the same for him.

'Really long and about two feet wide, should be six of them. It was enough for two tables, but I only want three boards, I'm only putting up one table for now.'

'Why do you need another table?'

'Have you seen this?' Isabelle asked. 'I can't do something with all this and keep up with work on the same table. I'd forgotten how messy creative work is. It used to drive Hester mad. I need space to work this through, to work out what it is I'm trying to find, and I don't want to have to put it away to finish off the jobs I have to do.'

Moth grinned at her.

'What?' she asked.

'Nothing,' he said, grinning some more.

'If you're not going to tell me what, stop grinning at me like an idiot.'

'It's just, you're not usually this, well, ehm, energetic, about stuff,' he said, gesturing at the room and its dishevelment.

Isabelle looked at the room, it did look wild, but full of tantalising promise, and back at Moth, who was as roughed up as the room from his day at the farm. His beanie hat pushed back, his clothes dirty, his face flushed from the sunshine.

'No. No, I suppose I'm not. I'd forgotten what excited feels like. It's like this when I'm away, working, but not quite like this.'

'Like this?'

'Yeah, this. This, I really, really, really want to do something, you know. Don't you feel that?'

'I guess,' he said. 'About some stuff.'

'I didn't even realise it had gone,' Isabelle said. 'How shocking is that?'

He grinned again, staring at her, so that she raised a hand to her hair, smoothed at her top and wondered how trashed she must look, like the room.

'What stuff?' she asked, focusing on him. 'What stuff do you get excited about?'

'Oh no, let's just stay with you,' Moth said.

'Come on, one thing,' she insisted.

'I'm still thinking!'

'Bollocks, you're hiding,' Isabelle said.

'Ok, this biking thing,' Moth said. 'James said today the bike's mine now, if I work for him the rest of the month before working for Kate. I'm excited about that.'

'You enjoyed your trip away?'

'Yeah,' he shrugged.

'But why? What's exciting about it?'

'Why are you excited about this?' he retorted.

'I don't know,' she said, chewing her lip and shrugging at him. 'But I am.'

'Crap answer.'

She scowled at him, thought about it and tried to find words. 'It's something I've forgotten, or lost, something to look forward to. Something I might enjoy again. And, by the way, your question instead of an answer was an even crapper answer.'

'I like the idea of it being mine, and it's new to me. Nothing like I've done yet.'

Isabelle watched him look away from her, he was being careful, but he was excited, she could hear it in him. The same thing she could feel in herself. 'I guess that's about the same for both of us then. Something new, that hasn't been part of what's gone before.'

'So, are we looking for this table or standing here talking about it?' Moth asked her.

'Evasion,' she told him.

'Absolutely.'

'WHAT WERE you two up to last night?' Elsa asked at breakfast. 'You were downstairs making a lot of noise until long after I went to bed.'

She was making toast and stirring scrambled egg. A smell rich with nutmeg that had pulled everyone in the house from their beds. She was flitting between the guest dining room and the kitchen, passing food out in all directions. Nat was helping her while Moth and Isabelle were sat at the table. Isabelle looked up with a guilty face.

'I'm sorry, did we disturb anyone?'

'I don't think so,' Elsa said. 'I'm not complaining, just curious, darling.'

'Isabelle was spring-cleaning,' Moth suggested.

'She hasn't cleaned that room since she moved, Moth,' said Elsa. She was not fooled.

'Moth was helping me rearrange some furniture,' Isabelle said. 'I decided I needed another table up, and it was a bigger job than I expected to make space for it.'

'Have you got another of those awful oversize jobs to do?' Elsa asked.

Moth looked at Isabelle with raised eyebrows, she shook her head a fraction as she said, 'It's not too bad, but I won't manage it on the main table, and it will give me a reason to take down the old silks and replace them.'

'That'll be nice, you've been meaning to do them for years. Have you found a fabric at last?'

'I might have, it's all a bit ahead of itself, but I was taking advantage of having Moth, to help me move stuff,' Isabelle said, focusing on her coffee cup. She always struggled to lie to Elsa. Let alone in front of Moth's scrutiny, aware she wasn't setting him a good example.

'Perhaps we should look at the sitting room curtains? There are so many jobs you can only do with that big table, and now you've gone to the trouble of putting it up we really ought to make the most of it,' Elsa stood at the Aga stirring her eggs, and talking to the tiles. 'I wonder if we dare consider the guest dining room? I shall have to speak to Kit about this year's budget again. Oh, how exciting!' she said with a burst of enthusiasm and a tap of the spatula against the rim.

'What's exciting?' Kate asked, coming in from the hallway, her hands full of the post. 'Morning all, what's going on now?'

'Isabelle and Moth have been putting up the big table. She could be available to consider some of the curtain jobs we've been putting off for years.'

'Elsa, we need to consider your general excitement level,' Kate said with a raised eyebrow.

'Don't be superior. Not all of us aspire to be international celebrities, you know,' Elsa told her, moving past her with two plates in her hands and Nat in tow with extra toast. 'Anything interesting?' she asked of the post.

'I don't know, I haven't looked yet,' Kate told her. She held the door for Elsa to leave the kitchen and, after waiting for it to close, looked over at Isabelle. 'Well,' she said, 'now you've done it.'

'I didn't think that through,' Isabelle said with a blush, squirming on her chair.

'Why have you put that table up?'

'You need to see the amount of mess on top of the table before you start giving her a hard time,' Moth suggested round his toast. 'Then you'll have some ammunition.'

'What on earth are you doing down there?' Kate asked, throwing the post onto the table in front of her normal chair. She moved to make a flat white with swift precision.

It was Kate who'd insisted Elsa install the industrial quality coffee machine, pointing out that people would not accept average coffee at the prices she was charging for her B&B. It had a lot more to do with the family having an addiction to decent coffee, but it had been the argument that won the battle.

'I don't know yet!' Isabelle complained to the room in general. 'And I didn't want to say that to Elsa, you know she likes something a bit more solid than 'I don't know, I'm trying to work my way through it'.'

'Oh dear, not that old creative curse again,' Kate said as she came to sit down. She looked across at Moth. 'I had a visit from James yesterday, Moth. I really came to see you. He's asked me to forgo having you to work for me until the end of the month.'

'Yes, he said he was going to speak to you.'

'We've negotiated a deal, which we would like to offer to you for consideration,' Kate said as Moth opened his mouth to complain.

'Ok,' Moth said.

'James requires your help until the end of the month, and I believe you've already accepted payment for this.' Isabelle looked across at Moth. The sly dog, he must have known Kate would try to buy off his agreement with James. They'd outfoxed her. She hid a smile. 'I've asked him to spare you on a Friday and Saturday morning, so that you may begin training while I have some of my best staff back from uni for a few more weeks.'

Moth remained silent, thinking.

'I can offer you an hourly rate of £6.50 whilst you're in training, rising to £7.50 when you can join me properly. We do need to pay this as cash for now, for all sorts of sticky scholastic, legal, ethical reasons that I don't really want to discuss in front of Elsa.'

Moth, again, stayed silent. Isabelle got the feeling that working for Kate wasn't part of his plan, whilst he had nothing particular against the idea.

'I don't normally take anyone on under sixteen,' Kate

added, with a casual flick through the post. 'Generally, I find them too immature to handle the public.'

'Why are you making an exception for me?' Moth asked.

'I rather like exceptions to the rules.'

'Should I talk to Elsa about this first?'

'I'll do that,' Kate said. 'But I didn't want to until I'd spoken with you. I'd like it to be your choice.'

'I thought we didn't get a choice in this?' he asked, looking from Isabelle to Kate.

'We didn't,' Isabelle said.

'I think it's alright,' Moth said, his words slow with lack of certainty.

'That doesn't seem very adamant,' Kate said.

'If James is happy with it, it's fine by me,' Moth said. 'But I don't know how long it will be before I have to go back to school. It's a bit hard to make arrangements about other things.'

'I understand that, Moth.' Kate said, 'This will be a week-by-week arrangement, for both parties. I shall talk it through with Elsa later.'

'You've come with a mission this morning,' Isabelle said.

'Yes, I have,' Kate agreed. 'On which note, what are you doing next, Isabelle?'

'Finishing my breakfast and going back downstairs to make more sense of my creative curse,' Isabelle told her, draining her coffee.

Kate looked at Moth.

'I'm off right now to go help James,' he said and stood up from the table, without a single scrape of his chair.

'See you later,' Isabelle said.

'Will do,' he said. 'Can you say bye to Nat for me?'

Isabelle nodded in confirmation, seeing Kate watching

Moth grab some food from the kitchen cupboards and heading for the boot room, her head cocked like a curious bird inspecting a worm before turning to opening the letters in front of her. Sifting through the post-Easter weekend pile-up which Elsa had ignored for several more days in her focus on Nat. She put bills to one side, bookings and enquiries to another, making precise piles. She took the time to read the handwritten contents of several letters, mostly thanks from happy guests. These formed another pile. She was part way through this process when she outed a long slow 'Oh' of surprise that brought Isabelle's attention back.

She'd been lost in thought about the task she was heading downstairs to. Moth and she had, finally, managed to locate and erect the table. It had been messy, and noisy. She hadn't wanted to admit to Elsa that several boxes had tumbled in the process and there had been a bit of damage to some of the contents. She hadn't realised she had an old collection of teacups down there. Even Moth had grimaced at the carnage inside the box and asked how she was going to stitch that back together. She'd thrown a cracked cup at him in response. He'd thumped her with the nearest cushion to hand and it had started a stifled war that ended in tears of laughter. They'd not gone to bed until gone 2 am. Which explained why she was sitting there trying to wake up under the glare of Kate's searchlight. That long 'Oh' pulled her from her reverie.

'Oh?'

'Ohhh.' Kate laid the thrice folded letter central, isolated from the rest, in front of Elsa's chair. 'Miss Shorrock has died.'

'Oh,' said Isabelle. 'Oh.'

'Yes, exactly.'

'How old was she, anyway?'

'I have no idea, must have been late nineties at least,' Kate said. She sat back in her chair with an irritated sigh. 'That's another job that's going to need sorting.'

They sat in silence, looking at one another. Isabelle thought Kate seemed pensive. It was only a tenant, Elsa had to deal with tenants leaving all the time. Though she wasn't sure a tenant had ever died on them before. Miss Shorrock was a legend, albeit a distant one. Isabelle had never even met her.

Elsa and Nat came back in together.

'That's it, they're all done,' Elsa said with satisfaction. 'The day is ours.'

'What are you planning today?' Kate asked, watching Nat help Elsa wash up and tidy the kitchen.

'We have a free day,' Elsa said. 'For a nice change too. What about you two?'

'I have the morning free to help you,' Kate said. 'Which appears fortuitous, you have a lot of post and banking to sort through.'

Isabelle could see her frowning at Nat's back, trying to work out how to remove her from the news.

'I have the day in the workroom, but, if you fancy, Nat, I could do with some help to sort some stuff out,' Isabelle said.

Nat looked at her grandmother for approval. Looking less than overwhelmed, Isabelle thought.

'That sounds like a nice idea,' Elsa encouraged her. 'Isabelle might show you how to do some sewing too, if you want to.'

'Of course we can,' Isabelle said. 'And you can come back up anytime you like, to help Elsa and Kate.'

'Oh, ok,' Nat said, her voice smaller than Isabelle would have liked.

She stood up from the table and smiled at Kate. Kate raised her eyebrows back. Elsa was sitting down with a contented sigh as Isabelle and Nat left the room, picking up the letter that Kate had left in prime position for her attention. By the time they started down the stairs she heard the faint echo of another long 'Oh' from Elsa.

She was starting down the corridor when she became aware that Nat was looking up at the cobwebbed ceiling.

'Are you alright?' she asked.

'Ehm,' Nat hesitated, daunted in the corridor. 'I don't like spiders.'

'Ah.' Isabelle stopped and waited for her. 'I know it looks bad here, but Moth helped me chase them out of the workroom last night. And I have a nice high stool you can sit on and sort stuff on the table. Trust me, you'll be fine.'

Isabelle held her hand out to Nat. It was a natural enough gesture but the moment she did, it felt weird, like an unexpected request that Nat didn't know what to do with. Isabelle squirmed inside. She'd seen Nat take Hester's hand so often in recent weeks and there had been that offered hand when they walked down the stairs before Easter lunch. Her hand stayed stuck out in the corridor, neither of them knowing what to do with it. Isabelle pulled it back in embarrassment.

'I don't mind if you want to go back upstairs,' she said. 'Elsa will understand you don't like spiders.'

Nat stood in the corridor looking at her, her face uncertain. The dusty ceiling, draped with cobwebs wasn't helping Isabelle's case, she really must get it swept off.

'I'd like to come for a bit,' Nat said.

'Great,' Isabelle smiled enthusiasm back at her courage, 'come on.'

She turned and led the way down the corridor, wishing

she had the morning to herself, instead of feeling like Kate wanted some time with Elsa to think about the letter from Miss Shorrock. She should be less selfish, they had a tougher morning, working out what needed to be done next.

'Wow,' said Kit, looking around in horror, mouth agape.

'Well, this should keep you busy for a while,' Kate said, picking her way across the dust-covered carpet, following a thread worn passageway that led to the curtains at the back of the room.

It put Isabelle's workroom to shame. Now this, this was a hoarding habit of distinction.

'How old was she?' Kit asked, peeking into boxes and looking round piles of magazines and books.

'Ninety-four,' Elsa said. She was looking up at the grey tinged ceiling with a frown, as though the grime that had collected there was the most disturbing part of the house. 'Though it looked like this when we were all living here.'

'Not quite like this,' Kate muttered.

She'd made it to the curtains, giving one side an almighty shove and watching as a cloud of dust, dead insects and rotting fabric flew to the far end of the pole with a clattering of brass rings. She wiped her hand on her coat and waved the dust filled air away from her. Sunlight tried to crawl through the thick filth on the windows.

'Jesus, you don't need Kit,' she told Elsa. 'You need environmental services.'

'I feel awful,' Elsa said, staring at the piles on the floor. 'I didn't realise she was living like this, I should have come and seen her.'

'Yes, whilst trying to manage your own life, house, business and multiple family deaths, you should have found some time for her as well,' Kate agreed.

Kit got the impression they'd already had this conversation. Despite Kate's salty comment Elsa remained silent.

'How long had she been living alone?' he asked.

'I'm not sure,' Elsa said. 'I knew she'd stopped taking in new students a few years ago but I didn't realise she was on her own. The university wrote to me, I think social services got in touch with them.'

'And she has no family at all?'

'She was a spinster professor,' Kate said. 'She never had any family. That was how Elsa's dad talked her into selling the house.'

'She had her private rooms down here, and the kitchen and communal rooms on the upper ground floor,' Elsa said. 'I did try to offer some refurbishment costs about ten, maybe fifteen years ago, but she said she didn't want the trouble of it. Oh, I feel awful, look at this place.'

Kit and Kate exchanged glances, Kate rolling her eyes. It was pointless to offer any comfort, Elsa would berate herself regardless. And it was a shock to see how the old bird had ended up.

'You've agreed to pay the funeral costs, I don't see what else you can do.' Kit poked through a pile of leaning magazines that had curled at the edges and sunk in the middle. 'More to the point, you two need to make sure this isn't how you end up.'

'Kit!' Kate remonstrated.

'Well, I'm just saying, single old women don't always end up too good. I mean, how long was it before she was found?'

'When I make it back over there, I shall kick you for that shitty comment,' Kate told him. 'It was only a few days. The local shopkeeper raised the alarm when she failed to collect her daily papers for the second day.'

'Papers?' he asked. 'How many did she read?'

'Two a day, three on Sundays,' Elsa said, looking at the accumulated towers of *Guardians, Telegraphs*, and *Times*. 'Her whole life.'

Kate pushed aside the other curtain and stepped back from the dust fall, wiped a hole in the dirt on the windows. 'There's a large garden, it accesses onto the woodland at the... oh, dear, God.'

'What now?' Elsa asked.

'I think you might need some assistance with the garden too, Kit,' Kate said. 'Even I feel bad now.'

Kit came over to stand beside her at the French doors that led out to the garden. They were stood in the lower ground floor rooms of the Swansea house, in Miss Shorrock's sitting room. He wiped a larger hole in the grime and peered out.

'Hmmm,' he said. Whatever garden, or view, there had been was obscured by foliage.

'We'd better have a look upstairs,' Kate said. 'If this is what it's like down here, I dread to think how the unused rooms have fared. Besides you might stand a chance of seeing the garden.'

'It's a lot like my house isn't it?' Kit mused as he wandered back to the door. Kate and Elsa looked at him in bemusement.

'I mean in layout, it's the same layout, but bigger. Living accommodation on two floors with two floors of bedrooms above.'

'Three floors above, there's an attic with two large rooms in it,' Kate said. 'Rose and Beth shared one of them, they always liked the top floor.'

'And it's wider, more generous on the room proportions,' Kit was still thinking aloud. 'This is a substantial property Elsa. Admittedly, it needs a massive overhaul, but it should have a huge letting income when it's done. I mean, I had no idea it was this big. From the pitiful rent it brought in I thought it was some appalling student squat.'

Elsa looked upset again. Kit knew all her accounts, he managed the entire estate budget, apart from the farm, which James never let him anywhere near. Only Mrs Staines' house was larger than this one, though in a worse state of neglect.

'I don't think Father ever charged her properly for it,' she said. 'He wanted to know there was someone here keeping an eye on us. And he bought it for a song of course, it was that long ago.'

'The houses on this street fetch in excess of half a million now,' he told her. He'd done some research on the area. 'You might want to think about selling it and reinvesting the money in the estate. Either way, rent it out or sell it, it's going to boost the income stream.'

'Yes, but you'll have to pay for the refurb first,' Kate reminded him. 'And I don't think you budgeted for that this year, or next.'

'Or both together,' Kit added.

He led the way out of the sitting room, back along the corridor to the stairs that led up to the ground floor. Taking in all the details, building a picture in his mind.

The house sat in the middle section of a back street of The Mumbles, upon the brow of an intersecting road, looking out across the sweep of Swansea Bay. It was the only house on the road to get the full view of the sea. The hill continued to rise behind it, so that the lower ground floor had tall front windows, and at the back French windows dug into the rear garden. The rear upper ground floor hovered over the garden like old petticoats flirting some ankle. The front door and generous hall accessed up a short flight of steps from the pavement. It was an awkward house, and it knew it. Awkward floors, awkward access, all compensated with generous proportions and pretensions of grandeur.

'The garden alone will be a ten grand job,' he mused out loud.

'Stop it, you're frightening me,' Elsa said.

They followed one another up the stairs, Elsa ahead of Kit as he wove his way past the mountains of leaning magazines and papers that sat at each side on every step, Kate bringing up the rear and falling behind them. He'd have rather had Kate's backside wobbling up the steps in front of him at eyelevel than Elsa's, but she was being aloof. All wrapped up in her black woollen coat, avoiding eye contact, her hand trailing across the tops of the stacked magazines with an unhappy frown on her face when he looked back down to her, stirring the grey dust into the air. He had great memories of Kate and Swansea, but she didn't seem so enamoured.

'Come on, old girl,' Kit called back to her. 'You've a few stairs to go yet.'

She looked up at him in surprise, pulled from some deep thought, her face blank, without the vim he'd hoped to prod her to. Kit felt bad. She was subdued, like entering the house had taken her a step closer to the old woman she would become. Memories of the young girl she'd been fossilised in the student house. She climbed the last few steps without retort and he offered a guilty hand when she made it to the hallway, but she brushed him aside and followed Elsa.

The three of them had attended the funeral that morning. The weather as dull, flat and lifeless as the reason they'd come. No family members and a handful of local people who'd known the old girl. Kate and Elsa her only former student lodgers. It had been a hectic week arranging the details and making time to come to Swansea, Elsa anxious to get it all done before Nat started school on the following Monday. When he arrived to pick them up Moth was out, Nat and Hester on their way out, and Isabelle had put in a brief appearance but slipped off to the workroom while Elsa fussed over Nat.

Kit had maintained a determined cheerfulness in the face of such a solitary life and death, provoking Kate to ask as they left the funeral, if he'd be this cheerful at theirs. They found the student sitting room looking out over the front of the house, and towards the sea glimmering in the distance. Kit looked at the grim array of sofas and chairs stacked around the outside of the room.

'It looks more like an old people's home than a student house,' Kit said.

'It felt like that forty-seven years ago,' Kate said, standing in the doorway and glancing around, resisting taking another step.

'Good heavens, is it that long?' Elsa asked.

The wallpaper was dismal, the furniture cheap post-war veneer, the carpet motheaten and patchy.

'Was it always this depressing?' he asked.

'No, it was a wonderful place,' Elsa protested. 'And we were so young, so carefree. All of us together away from home. It was such an exciting time of life.'

Kit tried to think about his mother there, Isabelle's mother, all of them at university together.

'Your mother was our gang leader,' Elsa told him, her voice full of fond recollection. 'She spared us no experience, it was a new life, new city, she was amazing. Didn't give a hoot for the sexism or the rules, she was our hero. Your mother was born for the sixties.'

Kit looked at the silent Kate, whose face was not glowing with the same enthusiasm of happy memories. She looked away when she caught his gaze and pulled her coat once more around her shoulders, stepping away from them and into the hall, straightening the pale silver scarf puffing out around the collar. He wanted to get her away from Elsa, pull her into a long cuddle, warm her up. But there was little chance of that.

'Why did your father end up buying it?' Kit asked, as they toured room after room of abandoned furniture.

'She inherited it from her parents and, on her wages as a professor, she couldn't afford to keep the house. It went on the market but didn't sell. After our first year, Father bought it from her for a reduced price on the understanding that she pay a small rent. He liked knowing where we all were, he didn't want us moving into other accommodation.'

'Was he shagging her on the quiet?' Kit asked.

'You are so...' Kate began to say but Elsa interrupted her.

'I thought so myself,' she said. 'Well, he was a widower for so much of his life, and the arrangement did seem rather odd. She came to his funeral, terribly upset, kept talking about how she would miss him. How he'd always taken the time to visit her. It set me thinking, even with the age gap and all, and when I found out in his will Father had given her the right to live her life out in the house, well.'

'What's wrong with big age differences anyway?' Kit asked.

'Well, nothing,' Elsa said, a catch in her voice. 'I suppose I just...'

'But you said it was all rather odd,' Kit needled. Kate sent him death ray stares.

'Well, yes, but I mean, she was what, maybe late forties when he died, and he was in his seventies,' Elsa said defensively. 'I can't imagine wanting to have sex in your seventies, let alone with someone so much younger.'

'Perhaps you lack imagination,' Kate suggested.

'I'll say,' Kit added.

'Can we talk about something else?' Elsa asked.

'Yes, let's,' Kate agreed.

'How about the kitchen?' Elsa asked.

'What, sex in the kitchen?' Kit asked.

'Oh, stop it,' Elsa told him.

'I'm just trying to keep up,' he protested as they walked into the large kitchen at the back of the house. 'Oh good, bloody God,' Kit complained, hands going to his hips in disgust. 'You cannot tell me anyone has cooked in here for at least two decades. I mean what the hell is this oven?'

Kate and Elsa looked around. Kate shuddered.

'It hasn't changed one jot since she used to cook our dinners. She'd stand and stir it into mush while she read some longwinded paper or book. Oh and, do you remember Elsa, she'd pull that pencil out from behind her ear and scribble some comment down, forget she was holding the pencil and stir the vegetables with it before popping it back behind her ear. We used to have to pick her hairs out of the supper.'

'She used to look for all the world as though she was a witch brewing a potion,' Elsa said.

'Ugh, I can smell boiled cabbage again,' Kate said. 'I'm sure four years of this hell was what inspired me to turn from history to food.'

'Four years?' Kit asked.

'I honoured in mine,' Kate told him with a prim tone. 'I stayed a final year by myself. Elsa had gone home and married, Rose and Beth travelled to India together in the year I finished.'

'Well, I didn't know that,' Kit said.

'There are many things you don't know about me,' Kate told him, 'and quite frankly, I like it that way.'

'You are so tetchy today,' he told her.

'Funerals always upset her,' Elsa told him.

'No, they don't,' Kate snapped.

'Yes, they do. You've never been good with death. I remember Ted's memorial, you were in bits, and he was my brother!'

'Not everyone gets to be an expert at it like you,' Kate told her. Even Kit blinked and Kate's face dropped in anguish. 'Oh, that was vile, I am sorry. It's this place, gives me the creeps.'

Elsa went and put her hand on Kate's arm, a light touch of forgiveness, before moving towards the table. It was a useless drop of what she needed. Kit felt frustrated. He wasn't used to seeing Kate like this or being unable to do anything.

'I think we could sell the fittings in here as vintage,' Kit said, wiping his finger across the surface of the Formica shelves.

'What about the grease, is that vintage?' Kate asked him.

'Adds authenticity,' Kit replied, opening doors and checking functionality.

'Father installed the kitchen when he bought the place, back in the 60s.' Elsa said. 'Heavens, Kate, this is like stepping back to our youth.'

'Yes,' said Kate. 'An altogether uncomfortable experience.'

'What were you like in the 60s?' Kit asked, looking up at them from the floor where he was squatting down looking into cupboards. 'Virgin eighteen-year olds?'

'My virginity or lack of it is none of your business,' Kate told him.

'Well, I never had eyes for anyone other than Richard,' Elsa said with a lift of her chin.

'Not for lack of Rose trying to persuade you otherwise,' Kate said.

'Oh, she was a shocker, even then,' Elsa agreed.

Their eyes met in a moment of recollection, passed on in awkward silence. Kit stood up and dusted his knees down, pretended he hadn't seen it.

'Well, if she was a virgin past thirteen, she beat my record,' Kit said, his tone brighter than the kitchen.

'Yes, well, that's another subject best left alone,' Kate said with a high tone and a flash of her hand to push the discomfort away.

'Why are we talking about sex just after we buried a nonagenarian?' Elsa asked in distress.

'Fear of death,' Kit said. 'Huge aphrodisiac.'

Kate laughed, a brittle sound that hit the high ceiling and shattered in discomfort.

'Does the kettle work by any chance?' Elsa asked. 'I could kill a cup of tea.'

'Spoken like a true Englishwoman,' Kit teased her, but he did find the kettle and get it going, rattling around for some cups and teabags. He opened the fridge and gagged, banging the door shut and turning away.

'Jesus, holy cow,' he breathed out. 'If you two ever have a fridge like that I shall abandon the pair of you. I don't even know what died in there. Or how long ago.'

'No milk?' Elsa asked.

'I'll nip down the end of the street and get some,' he told them. 'It will take that long for that kettle to boil.'

'Get some biscuits too,' Elsa told him and began to fumble for her bag.

'Do put it away,' Kit told her. 'Now, no more exploring without me.'

'We wouldn't dream of it,' Kate told him.

He left them stood in the kitchen, heard his own feet clattering across the wooden hallway in the barren quietness of the house. Great wide planks. Old oak. They'd come up a treat. Limed, they'd look great limed. Lighten up the space too. He pulled the door shut behind him and jumped down to the street level two steps at a time, heard the door had failed to catch behind him. He turned in mid-stride and went back, was pulling the door too when he heard Elsa say from the kitchen, echoing through the still house, 'I can practically hear them.'

'Hear who?' Kate asked. Followed by a silence, in which Kit could imagine Elsa's face, and a long sigh from Kate.

'You're terribly maudlin today,' Kate accused her. 'I hear the wind in the weeds in the garden and the creaks of an empty house that needs a lot of TLC.'

'You're so determined to push the past away,' Elsa said. 'I feel like they're sat right here with us. I can see Rose, whipping her hot chocolate until it froths, and Beth, her skinny knees up against the table. I can't even remember how many nights we spent here together. Whispering away, trying not to wake Miss Shorrock down below.'

'Rose was never a whisperer. I do hope Kit hurries back.'

'I seem to be surrounded by ghosts,' Elsa said. 'Every time I see Moth, I see my father, and David. Every time I wonder what to do next, I miss Richard. Now, here, I feel them as close as ever too. It's such a strange feeling.'

'I'll say. You want to stop this nonsense. You'll turn your brain soft. People die, Elsa, you have to move on.'

'Perhaps I'm tired of moving on. I'm getting terrified of who I might lose next.'

'Well, it's better than the alternative,' Kate said.

'What's that?'

'It might be you next. Do cheer up, your mood is as grim as the smell of cabbage.' Kit heard a chair being pulled back from the table. 'What are you going to do with this place anyway? It's an awful lot of work to put right.'

There was a silence that stretched, and Elsa replied with a strange catch in her voice, 'Do you know, this is the only house I own.'

'How on earth do you figure that? You have a whole heap of houses.'

Kit glanced down the street, he should go get milk, but it was hard to leave such a statement as that. It was hard not to walk back in and ask what she was talking about, rather than straining to catch the trailing ends of their voices.

'You aren't making a lot of sense,' Kate said in a softer tone. 'I think you really have been to too many funerals. It's starting to distress you.'

'Oh shush,' Elsa said. 'I'm not entirely soft yet you know.'

'Well, what do you mean?' Kate asked. He heard another chair pulled across the floor. 'Only house you own indeed.'

'I don't really own Riverdell,' Elsa said. 'My father... my father explained that to me. It's only passing through your care, for the next generation. When Miss Shorrock died, this house became mine. It was left to me in his will with her having a lifetime interest in it. I've never felt like this before.'

'Like what exactly?'

'Like I can choose,' Elsa said. 'It's the strangest thing.'

'But you choose what happens with Riverdell. I mean I know you would never sell it, but you can choose what you do. How is this different?'

Silence stretched down the corridor to Kit. He felt like a kid, spying on his mother, trying to figure out their adult world. Except now he was trying to figure out their youthful world. He pulled the door to behind him and ran down the street to the corner shop. Kit shivered as he ran, his dark funeral jacket was more than warm enough, but Kate's vibes were affecting him. He shopped in high speed, hopeful of getting back before they'd finished the conversation. He ran back up the hill, the plastic bag of emergency shopping held high in his hand, and back into the kitchen to catch Elsa saying, 'I need a little time to consider it, that's all.'

'To consider what?' Kit asked trying not to sound breathless. 'Look at you two, sat there reminiscing about your wicked youth. I don't suppose you thought to look for teabags?'

'Do tell me you bought coffee?' Kate asked him. 'I don't want to consume anything from the cupboards of a dead woman.'

'Yes, I bought coffee. They even had unbleached sugar, gem of a shop. This is a cracking location Elsa. I've been looking at the houses as I came back. This street is rather upmarket, you must own the most dilapidated house on it.'

He deposited the bag on the table and went looking for cups.

'Well that's a comfort,' Kate said. 'Elsa is getting very attached to this dilapidated pile.'

'Well, it might be dilapidated, but it is mine,' Elsa told them both with smugness.

Even Kit looked round at her with an odd expression.

'Oh don't,' Kate said. 'I can make no sense of her. I'm hoping you can.'

'What's going on here?' Kit asked, a bright false sparkle in his tone. 'Have you two fallen out while I was gone?'

'No, of course not,' Elsa said. 'I was trying to explain to Kate, but she doesn't want to hear it, that this is really mine. My own house, to choose what I do with.'

Kit looked at Kate with raised eyebrows. She stared back at him and said, 'Do make some coffee.'

'You'll have to do better than that, Elsa,' Kit told her, going back to his rummaging.

'I had the solicitors check my father's will before we came down,' Elsa said. 'I'd sort of forgotten about it, but on her death it's become entirely mine. Separate from the Riverdell estate. I can choose what to do with it. To sell it, to use the money for something else, to keep it, to use it even, maybe as a holiday home or... something.'

'Or... something?' Kit asked. 'But, besides that point, you choose what happens at Riverdell, it's yours too.'

'Apparently, it's *different*,' Kate told him.

'I shall refuse to talk to either of you for the rest of the day if you aren't nicer,' Elsa told them in a petulant tone.

'Here, have a biscuit, darling,' Kate told her in a sour tone, pushing a packet of Bourbons across to her.

Elsa took the packet and unwrapped it without responding.

'Hang on, hang on,' Kit said. 'Let's have some plates and be civilised. You're not students now you know.'

'Thank God,' Kate said.

'Oh, I'd go back any day.' Elsa embraced the diversion. 'Wouldn't you?'

'Heavens, no,' Kate said. 'I much prefer life now.'

Elsa scowled at her. Kit watched, close as a hawk, tiptoeing around and trying to reduce his presence.

'You all left on a wave of glory. You to marry an adorable man, remember? Rose and Beth tripping off to India together after your brother,' Kate said. 'You forget I was here by myself for a year after that. She wasn't the same delightful landlady.'

'I would hardly call her delightful,' Elsa protested. 'But we did have happy times here.'

'She was a different woman without you around. Cold and unpredictable, and she had nothing but contempt for any pretensions I had about achieving a masters. Telling me to be grateful if I got my honours and go home and marry. I'd never be a professor like her.'

'She probably didn't like competition in the scholarly department,' Kit offered. 'It must have been pretty hard for a woman back then.'

'Which justifies her being vile to all others who tried?' Kate asked.

'Of course not,' Kit said, putting a coffee in front of her and squeezing her shoulder with a kind hand.

'It wasn't the same without the rest of you, that's all,' Kate said more softly to Elsa.

'I miss those days,' Elsa said. 'Us girls together, Richard was so young and energetic. I felt alive, full of joy and hope for all our futures.'

'And now?' Kit asked, coming across to the table with plates and unpacking them a mini-feast.

'Now I feel a bit stuck,' Elsa said. 'Like my options were

taken away one by one, along with the people I loved so much.'

'We're still here, thank you,' Kate told her.

She jumped when Elsa reached across the table and held her spare hand, rattling her coffee cup in its vintage saucer.

'And I am so grateful for that,' Elsa said, her voice thick. 'And I don't tell you often enough, both of you, how much you mean to me. Or that I am thankful every single day that I still have you with me.'

Kate turned her hand over and squeezed Elsa's in return. Kit could see that tightness in her chin when she was avoiding emotion. He went and gave Elsa a shoulder squeeze from behind, ducked his head to hers and leaned in to give her some support. He pulled a tissue from his pocket and handed it to her, and she dabbed at the corners of her eyes.

'Oh dear, I am a bit emotional, aren't I?' she said, laughing at herself.

'A bit,' Kit agreed. 'It's charming though, you do it so well. Kate, can you unload the snacks, or do you need some comfort too?'

Kate glared at him.

'I thought as much,' Kit said and went back to the kettle, glad to have provoked a more normal reaction. Kate feisty he could deal with any day. Kate brittle and distressed was making his charcoal funeral tie feel tight.

'Right, so let's accept that for whatever strange reason you cannot explain, this house feels different to you,' Kit said from across the room, washing off the spoon, wiping the surface with a piece of absorbent kitchen towel. 'We need to make some decisions on what to do.

'I've still got loads to look at but, already, I can tell you most of the windows need replacing, the roof needs repairing if not replacing, the entire interior and exterior need painting, the heating system needs overhauling and the electrics are illegal. That doesn't even address any layout alterations to bring it up to modern expectations.'

'Oh dear,' Elsa said. 'My strange feeling of happiness is rapidly diminishing.'

'I knew you'd talk some sense into her,' Kate said with approval.

Kit joined them at the table.

'The contents alone will raise some money,' he said. 'Look at this tray, its vintage, massive market appeal. As is all the crockery. I swear we can sell this entire kitchen. Plus, there's all the furniture too, and those books must be worth something. I mean, it won't make a dent in the total bill, but it'll return something. But you need to think hard about those choices, Elsa. Renovating will take a huge amount of money, and it's a minimum six-month job. Sell it now, and it's all someone else's problem and you have the cash for yourself. Even at a low selling price you'll get a substantial figure.'

'Plus, you have Nat and Moth to focus on,' Kate told her. 'You're not in a position to take on another project.'

'But I don't need to do it all immediately,' Elsa said. 'Do I, Kit?'

'Well, you won't get a tenant in it like this,' Kit said. 'At least not the sort of tenant you're going to want.'

Elsa stared into her cup. Her eyebrows raising a frown between them.

'Look, you don't have to make an immediate decision,' Kit relented. 'Let me do a complete assessment. Work out some costings and options, that will help you make a more informed choice. I'll get the team in and get all the furniture and personal belongings moved out and disposed of. You're sure there are no relatives or friends who will want anything?'

'You saw them all at the funeral,' Kate pointed out.

'It was a bit depressing,' Kit said.

'Shouldn't we go through some of it ourselves?' Elsa asked. 'It seems so callous to dispose of it. Maybe there are some other old students who would want something? Or the university?'

'No, absolutely not!' Kate told her. 'I refuse to let you take that on, and I can assure you I will not be helping if you insist. You have enough to focus on. Miss Shorrock was not your responsibility Elsa, she was a tenant. Don't assuage some ridiculous sense of guilt in taking on a job you have no reason to do.'

'Ok, ok,' Elsa, said, laughing at her.

'She's right though,' Kit said. 'It's a miserable job, you don't need to put yourself through it. Let's just be glad there's no will and you have a free hand on the house clearance. I'll make sure I know who's doing the sorting. Perhaps Jamie, she'll flag anything odd up.'

'You are such a help,' Elsa said. She reached for another Bourbon.

Kate drank her coffee with both hands around the cup, warding ghosts off her adored caffeine.

'Great coffee,' she told Kit. 'Just what we needed.'

'We might need a bit more yet,' he said. 'We haven't even looked upstairs. You can show me where Mother used to sleep.'

15

W e were married in St Laurence's Church on the last day of July.

You would think I might have missed my mother on such a huge day of my life. Looking back now, I realise I wasn't given the chance. The girls woke me at half past six on that morning.

'It's revenge time,' Rose sang as she waltzed through the door.

'What on earth?' I was still dazed with sleep, struggling against my nerves the night before.

'Get your slacks on, Queenie.' Kate threw my walking trousers at the bed. 'All those trips up Climbing Jack are about to bite you in the arse.'

'I am not getting married in my trousers,' I protested, glancing with fear at where my dress was hanging on the wardrobe, sheathed in thick plastic, peeping out below the hem of the protective cover. Billowing in the draught their entrance had caused.

'Oh, Elsa,' Beth plonked herself down on the bed and

beamed. 'You aren't getting married until 2 pm and you're not spending the whole day waiting.'

'Come on, we're taking a hike up to the bird tower,' Rose told me. 'Last time we'll all be single.'

They all looked at me with a challenge. Even Beth was sparkling with fun, and she'd been ill for most of the last year of university. My dress had been waiting for weeks to be worn. But they were right, I would only spend the whole day worrying. I grinned back at them.

'What a great idea.'

Kate and Rose led the way. They'd prepared a pre-wedding breakfast and had to haul it all the way up Climbing Jack Common in two baskets. Swearing and bitching in equal measure. I walked with Beth, our arms entwined. Talking about the hills, the trees, the flowers. Beth was even softer than she had always been. A year of three-week long cramps, menstrual bleeding so excessive she'd been hospitalised twice for blood infusions, anaemia she now had to take medication for, and the resistance she'd had to show to the overwhelming appeal of her doctors to have a hysterectomy had taken their toll. And not just on her health. Kate and Rose had both achieved First's in History and Sociology, and Politics respectively. Beth had missed most of her last year and been awarded a Pass in her Geography degree. My third in Literature had been in some ways a reflection of my desire not to leave her behind. Though I had enjoyed my last two years of University, it had been more for the time we'd had together than the desire to prove myself academically. For Beth, whose love of geography had always been quiet but deep, it had been the twist of the knife in her back.

We stopped often to look at the view, to give her time to rest.

'Have you thought any more about going home?' I asked her.

'Home?' she asked, squeezing my arm with a twinkle in her eye. 'Elsa, Riverdell has been more home to me than any I've ever known.'

Beth's family consisted of aunts and uncles, distant cousins who had grown up without her. Her parents' work as archaeologists had taken them away from their family before disease had snatched them away from her too. So that, orphaned at ten by the ancient city of Troy, sent home from Turkey to live with a family she had hardly met, asking to go to boarding school once her parents inheritance was released to her, Beth truly was on her own in the world in a way that worried us all.

'And you know Father is very happy for you to stay as long as you want.'

'You've both been so kind.' We walked on. Beth casting her eyes to the ground, searching for things only she could see. 'And Rose and Kate want me to go back to Swansea, resit my final year.'

'And you?' I asked her. 'What do you want to do'

'I think I want to travel,' she said. Looking ahead to where the other two had tossed down their baskets and were arguing over some minor detail with great enthusiasm. We grinned at each other. 'Perhaps I don't have a great degree, but still, I have one. I've been looking at English Language courses too. I can do one in a few months and be qualified to teach anywhere in the world. And I would like to see more of the world...'

Beth trailed off absently. She had developed the habit over that last awful year. As though she felt the edge of limited chance more keenly than the rest of us but didn't want to add '... while I can' to the end of her sentences.

'And as I'm lucky enough to have such good friends to come home to, I think I might see if I can't travel my way around the world.'

'Come on, you two slow coaches,' Kate turned back and yelled down the path. 'I'm starving, hurry up.'

'Where would you like to go?' I asked as we made our way more swiftly.

'I really don't mind,' Beth said. 'I rather fancy some out of the way places, like Siberia, or Iceland, and perhaps the Himalayas, eventually. But, to start with, I think I'll go wherever opportunity allows me.'

'You know we'll all miss you terribly,' I gripped her arm tighter. The thought of Beth travelling alone filled me with dread, impinging on my wedding thoughts like a cloud. 'And Rose, Rose will be...'

I looked ahead to where Rose had arrived at the tower first. Her black hair swishing around her shoulders in delight as she came to a rest. If I was dreading the thought of Beth going away, how on earth would Rose cope?

Beth looked ahead to where Kate had caught Rose up and smiled to herself.

'Don't tell her yet,' she asked me. 'You've all been so busy this last year, with finals and weddings. I've had a lot of time to think about what I wanted to do. Let me tell her in my own time. I've made no solid plans yet, so there's no rush. And besides, what we really need to talk about is your wedding. I do wish there was a bench at the top of this hill. You'd think someone would have thought to put a bench there to appreciate this wonderful view. Did you manage to get much sleep last night? I was awake all hours.'

Beth distracted me readily back to what my heart really wanted to talk about. It's only now, looking back, I realise that what seemed no more than the seed of an idea was already pushing its way to the surface of Beth's future. But on that fresh beautiful morning, drinking tea, and eating scones and bacon sandwiches on the common, all I could think of was my day ahead.

I had peach anemones and lilac in my bouquet and a dress made of antique lace repurposed from Mother's wedding gown. Hers had been hand made in London in the earlier years of the Second World War and still bore traces of a hope and luxury that would soon disappear. I had it tailored in Swansea to suit me, with a cream satin bodice to modernise the skirt. A small piece of the lace from Mother's gown girded the ruched bodices of the dresses for my three adult bridesmaids and made cuffs for the dresses of the two little flower girls on Richard's side of the family.

It was without doubt the happiest day of my life. I had my proud father at my side, my three dearest friends with me, and my brother stood as Chief Usher. At the altar stood the man who was to be the love of my life. We were not a huge party, at our request, though I think Father would have filled the church if we'd let him. And we walked through the town on a gorgeous Saturday afternoon to take our bridal tea in the gardens at Riverdell, with the bells of St Laurence's ringing us home.

It is strange how, worrying about the future so much that I lie awake as I did the night before my wedding, I am transported back to those days like I could reach out and touch them. I would give my home up without a thought if it could bring us all back. How I miss Father, Ted, the girls. How deep an ache it still is that Richard will not be home at teatime, to sit with me and listen to all my woes and help me make the decisions that weigh upon me. Though I know what he would say. He would tell me if I have all the options, I already know the decision. I just need a drop of conviction and a cuddle to help me. And maybe now, at last, I do have all the options. But how I long for that cuddle.

16

As the roads got steeper and the pace slower Moth couldn't think beyond the agony of making his body do what it was battling him to stop doing.

Life reduced to the physical. The screaming leg muscles, the biting ache deep in his buttocks, the tension in his arms, the stretch at the base of his spine. All straining to keep the bike steady as the pace slackened. Vehicles grew rarer.

Never thought you'd want to see cars.

Craving their distraction as the effort grew harder. It was limbo time in the mountains. The skiers on their way out, the walkers and bike tours not yet arrived. The air getting colder as his body warmed with the effort. If he stopped, cold descended on him with a bite.

Best you don't stop. Go slow, but maybe don't stop.

So he didn't stop. The effort of getting going again so much harder than the demand of keeping moving.

The space between his thoughts growing shorter. His brain grasping at distraction. The flashing stripes of the paint. Each bend of the road. A marking tree.

That boulder ignoring your efforts.

They helped him climb. With each grinding wheel rotation, he questioned the necessity of everything aboard the bike, resisting the urge to throw weight out of the bags in the vain hope it would help. The sun grew warmer as it swung round to the south. He gritted his teeth and pushed on. Then the cold of the shadows bit in and his muscles fought the chill upon them. His battle intensified.

Why, why, why? Stop. He should stop.

Don't you dare stop.

Idiot idea. Mountains, who cares anyway?

Don't be so weak. You're pathetic.

One day, when he was older, he would buy a motorbike. Park this old bitch against a wall and walk away from it. Without a backwards glance. He promised himself the upgrade with each upward turn of the pedals that peeled his soul away from his muscles.

Then came the downhill reward. Freezing wind biting his face so that he pulled the snood back up around his mouth. The bike flying through the air with him sat upright on it. His hands a vice control upon the brakes. The view piercing him with its violence and glory, glistening victorious from the jagged frigid peaks.

You're as free as they look.

Everything from the start of his life until right then, lost, irrelevant. He was part of the bike.

Greater than you can be without it.

Faster, stronger, freer. His power alone taking him higher. He would never leave the bike. It was who he was.

Until the ride slowed and the road inclined again. He bent back over the handlebars and hated them anew, the only thing in sight the sweat dripping from his brow onto the road.

By midday he was numb. Burnt out and hollow with the fight. He gave in, his legs falling numb off the pedals. Drenched in sweat he drew painful breaths and let the sun beat down on him. He'd cycled through thick forest for the last hour and the heat was like honey on his muscles.

The road had levelled and carved a thick swathe out of the woods, trees ceding ground to a large rock face in the crook of the road. He wheeled the bike behind it. His fingers stiff and cold, curled round the handlebars in a grip that hurt to loosen. He fumbled with the panniers, dragging out food, his sweater.

He stood at the base of the rock and looked upwards. It was not that steep, barely a leap and a hand hold on a normal day.

It's not every day you cycle up a mountain.

He threw the stuff up first, with sore fingers hauled himself up to the top. Lay down inert. Basking in the warmth. His muscles shaking and jolting as they relaxed against the stone.

Moth jerked out of the lethargy that was slipping towards sleep. The stone beneath him had turned cold, his bulk depriving it of the surface warmth. A shiver going through him as the monolithic chill seeped upwards. He forced his aching body upwards. Wriggled into the sweater and crossed his legs, leaning forward over them as a prop.

You need food. Rest.

Moth forced food into his tired system. The bike might be free, but he still needed fuel to run it. Listening to cars and cyclists on the road below. The easy purr with which they ascended mocking his exhaustion. The food hit his empty stomach with a vengeance, pulling his eyes down, making his head wobble. He lay back, eyes closed. Listening to the strange pops between the fissures of his organs. Watching the tree tips swaying over him. Thinking he might never get back on the bike this time.

You will.

He might have to admit defeat, turn around, go an easier route.

You won't.

He'd known this before. The crippling sense of self-doubt.

You overcame it before. You will again.

It had been Nat before. Wondering how to leave her. Where. If anywhere could be safe. Watching and waiting to work out the family. From the moment he and Nat first arrived at Riverdell, rolling into the gravel driveway with the social worker. Delivered to their unknown grandmother from a short period in care facilities while social services worked out what to do with them. It had only been a few days, and they were taken to Riverdell.

A few days were all you needed.

To decide that care was not a place he would ever be able to leave Nat.

Moth had learned a lot about Isabelle from her work-room before she even arrived, more as he watched her work. He'd come to understand James from being at the farm. Known Kit from watching him gear up into a work frenzy that shut out all else. He'd absorbed his dead grandfather when he unfolded the map and began deciphering the scribbled thoughts in the margins. He'd come to terms with Elsa through seeing her as James' mother, not his father's. His grandfather's wife, not his great-grandfather's daughter.

It took you a while, mind.

It was the study that had been the problem. Turning up at

Riverdell, seeing that wide olive door nestled in the crook of the house, going through it holding Nat's hand, he had refused to believe anything good would come from where his father had. Even when Nat's mouth had opened in stunned amazement as they walked into the hall.

The study near finished you off.

He thought about the study. Walking in behind Elsa. All those books lined up with such arrogance. Rising from floor to ceiling in commanding order. Arranged by subject, by author, by age. The maps on the walls, the oil landscapes. Imperialism condensed. Himself reduced to a child. He never realised, until Riverdell, what his father had been recreating in his modern four-bedroom suburban life. The map prints in regulated matching frames, the low-level bookcases, the same smell. The centrally placed desk, opposite the door, which Elsa retreated behind. Where his father would look up and greet him, Little Timmy. Entering the study at Riverdell brought it back to him like a slap.

Yeah, it took a while to change your mind about Elsa.

In the OS maps of his grandfather he'd found a different script. A man who valued sunrise, sunset, pints and mountains. Who put skulls and crossbones over his disappointments. Who went home to Riverdell, farm and family. He couldn't find a link between this man on the maps and the son he'd raised. It broke a link in the distrust, let Elsa in. Moth had written his name on the map, beside the first sunrise.

Moth.

Not Timothy. Little Timmy.

That name had died with his father. He would see it never got used again.

Moth.

Isabelle had tried to tell him about Elsa, but it was his grandfather who changed his opinion.

Which left Hester.

He'd never worked her out. Hated how Nat grew straight towards her like sunshine. He'd been struggling with Hester even before Isabelle arrived.

You were struggling with the funeral.

Perhaps he had transferred it. His anger to her grief. The funeral hadn't been the problem. When Elsa had given him the awkward choice, he'd loved that it fell on Leap Day.

Perfect.

He'd only have to remember it once every four years.

But you did struggle with it.

He'd struggled with Hester weeping. What right did she have? A brother she'd not seen, his mother she'd met once. They were his parents and he hadn't shed a tear.

You shed enough before.

Hester. Hester and Nat. That had been the crux of it. Looking over his grandfather's maps Moth had seen it annotated with thoughts and wishes he could feel himself. Perhaps this was as far as he'd ever made it from home and duty, bogged down with family and farm. Just like James.

'Just go, and travel,' she'd said.

He would, he swore to himself. He would.

But how to leave Nat. When he couldn't trust Hester.

Could he do it. He couldn't do it. How could he do it. Leaving Nat. Conquering the mountains.

Same doubt. Different question.

The motivation equal to the fear, hung up on blind doubt. Hung up on the woman Hester was with Nat, the woman she was with Isabelle. Not knowing which one to trust.

And every day you lingered you got sucked in.

He had.

Moth lay on the rock in the Dolomites, weary with mountain battle, lethargic with food, drifting off into the rushing thoughts of Isabelle. How she talked. How she thought before speaking. How she moved with the same consideration. How she held a needle between her fingers with more certainty than she did anything, wove it back into the jumper above her chest, forgetting it was there. How he wanted to tell her to be that person, upstairs, outside of her workroom. To fight back against Hester, so he'd know Nat was safe. How he wanted to touch her.

That became the real problem. Not leaving Nat. Leaving her.

Moth had wanted to touch her so much. He'd wanted to know what touch was. Real touch. Chosen touch. To hold a hand. To feel skin. To kiss lips. To push her hair away from her face. To feel the fineness of her neck in his hand...

Moth jerked awake in a sweat, feeling the fingers on his neck. The table against his cheek.

'No!' He jumped up and roared. Shaking with fear and fury, legs turning to jelly, his voice emptying away from him into the fractured air.

He crumpled on the rock, felt his bladder threaten and tried to grip his muscles. A dribble came anyway, staining his groin.

You pissed yourself. Jesus.

He was damp, shaking, sweat-drenched. Sick to the stomach, stunned with memories and sleep. A car eased below the rock and carried on down the road, taking his glazed eyes with it towards the tree line and the decline.

You need to focus.

He wiped sweat off his face with the sleeve of his sweater.

Yanked it off, trying to cool down. Wanting the shiver of the wind to grab him. He couldn't do it. He couldn't keep going.

You can't go back.

He looked up past the tress, saw the mountains rising.

It's just a mountain.

He looked down at the sweater in his hands, the soft yarn underneath. His own fingers holding it, his own fingers, holding the top, not, not...

... not that.

The memory faded. The fingers lost their touch.

They always start with her.

But they never ended there. The good thoughts all got dragged downwards. He pushed all memories away.

Think about the road. Nothing more.

He slipped down from the rock, pissed interminably against the trees behind, recoiling from his dick in his hand. The dark groves of trees moving. The ground unstable beneath his stiff legs. Moth gripped the bike, one hand feeling the cold leather of the saddle. Lines worn into creases, stretched taut over the hard nose. His other hand gripped the handlebars, steadying himself as he pulled it away from the rock.

He remembered their faces. Moving through them. Isabelle, Hester, Nat. Nat had been the hardest. He drained himself into the bike. It was everything he needed, all that he was. He stayed there, in the cool darkness between the rocks and the trees, the wind stirring his hair, clutching at his moist shorts. Stayed until his heart calmed and his stomach levelled.

It's all gone. Done. In the past. This is your life now.

He'd done what he could for Nat. Seen her safe as he could.

You made your choice.

He didn't belong to anyone and no one could claim anything of him. The law that said otherwise wasn't a law that touched him.

You're a free man. Not Timothy. Not Little Timmy. Moth.

The best revenge he could conjure. His life. Lived his own way. The one thing his father didn't have.

Moth looked at the bike, flexed his fingers. The only decent thing about memories was...

... they always fade.

Good or bad. Some might take longer than others. But they all faded.

You don't look back. Keep looking forward.

He put his helmet on, turned the wheels to check them, rotated the chain. A car drove by, he ignored it. Waiting until it passed and checking the road behind. Pushed the pedal round and placed his foot, gliding onto the tarmac and swinging his leg over the frame in one smooth motion. It was a sweet curving downhill that sharpened into a few switch-backs, slackened into straights. He guided the bike with the lightest touch. The wind rushing past him a soothing chill that took the last sweat off his skin.

You can do this.

It was a good ride through the afternoon. Rich alpine meadows. Sunshine bouncing off the high snow. Fields of soporific cows. He loved that afternoon ride, the night alone in a meadow, conviction spreading into the next day, feeling powerful, counting his first victories. Not for the gradient, or the speed, or the passes. Or the sweat, agony, gritted teeth and painful breath.

The fact that you keep going.

Moth loved that not even the mountains could get in his

way. By the time he got to Iseo, he would never fear them
again, he would know he could master anything.

ISABELLE FELT the change inside her grow into a need when
Nat went to school after Easter.

The house rearranged itself around the new routine,
dragging her in. Nat rose early with Elsa, helping her with the
guests' breakfast while getting her own. Moth got up to be
part of their life before school, disappearing off to work as
Nat left. James had sidled out of his agreement with Kate for
handing over Moth at the end of April, claiming that he
needed help with late planting following the enduring drizzle
that month had been. Moth suffered their haggling with a
good grace, either option kept him out of school, except,
Isabelle suspected, for the niggling doubt that the bike might
yet become his. Going where Elsa mediated, and coming
home for when school finished, or biking over to the school
and making Nat walk home with him. She moaned at him for
that, preferring to be collected by car, especially on the days
that Hester did it. Those days when arriving at the breakfast
table from upstairs before Hester did from Shrewsbury was
the only victory Isabelle would claim, her elbows swept off
the table with the crumbs, making it clear who was in charge.
Hester talking about what they had planned for the day, what
Moth had been doing, what she was cooking for their dinner,
so Isabelle could make her excuses for not being there.

Isabelle threw herself into finishing off the pile of work
that Elsa had amassed for her. She wrapped it, invoiced and
delivered it, and refused to take any new orders. As April
blossomed into a drier May she opened the doors to the
workroom, the last few lines on her sheet promising an

empty month ahead. She promised Elsa she would renovate the large sets of curtains upstairs and even took down the old silks in the workroom, throwing about lengths of fabric she might replace them with. But she was procrastinating, trying to work out how to take apart her old self, repurpose it, coerce her new life to shape.

A processing of material she should have excelled at and was shocked to find terrifying. A sense of panic gathering inside, as the outer unfettering of the workroom spoke of carnage, not creativity. She would look at the map of India and think she should answer the emails from the film company, book herself down for the upcoming projects. When she dropped her eyes to the chaos there was a stronger urge, to unpick, to cut away, to find what was lurking within.

Each box unpackaged dragged her down a creative sidewalk. Discovering canvases, paintbrushes, acrylics, that felt lost and alien in her hands. Old domestic machines buried with shrouds of machine embroidery, reminding her hands how to guide fabric through the footless aggression of the needle, charming her for days until she remembered how the lack of usability of the end product annoyed her. Looms she'd made from oak planks off James, hammered through with enormous nails at regular intervals, and basket after basket overflowing with wool. Knotted pots and baskets woven from rags, and the Viking longship she'd created from knotted rag skeins. Its sails like wings, ragged and creased from the box.

Hester's canvases, together with the box of her scrapbooks tied with a neat bow of parcel string, she separated from her own and tidied away to the side of the door along with anything else she found that wasn't hers. Questioning the validity of its presence in her realm. Hester's stuff she left, unable to force it further than the door, hoping it might walk out of its own accord. But, in her forays upstairs, she deposited the other unwanted items in the kitchen. On the lesser used end of the table, or leaning against the windows where it was visible, but not obtrusive, a note scrawled as offering, 'Nat, I thought you might like this,' or, 'Elsa, useful for the guests?'

The items found their way onward, as though the owner had found it and wondered where it was the whole time. These cast asides that had gathered themselves to her by accident but knew they belonged to someone else in the world upstairs. The neat and sensible world that ran to set routines, mealtimes, school-times, bedtimes. Counting through the weeks that warped and meandered in her mind.

Moth was the only one who visited her in the downstairs realm. Either when Nat was busy with Hester, or after supper, when she was with Elsa doing homework, or after bedtime if he had been busy all afternoon. His opening of the workroom door the sole marker of her own life, as she tiptoed around the upstairs routine.

One day he came even later than normal. Her hands were busy trying to pull together a basket of woven strips of linen. Tussling to keep the rounded shape she wanted by pulling the strips closer together as they rose from the base, wrestling the oddity under the machine foot, while the machine tried to spit it back out. Wanting straight lines and flat surfaces, not curves and dimensions. She had been there for hours, counting each stitch that pulled the shape out of her head and onto the fabric in front of her as a step toward the unknown destination.

'Hi,' he said, voice weary, as he came through the door and shut it behind him.

'You sound tired.'

'Nat only just went to bed.'

Isabelle looked at the clock. It was almost ten. On a Wednesday night. Late for Nat to still be up.

'Is she alright?'

'I don't know. I think so. Just needed to talk a lot,' Moth made his way from the room to the machines, a hand gliding across the fabrics thrown across her table. 'She's finding school hard.'

'In what way?'

'I think she's not at the same level as everyone else,' Moth said. 'She's having to work extra hard to keep up and feels a bit stupid.'

'Did she talk to Elsa about it?'

'Yeah, talked about nothing else, all evening. To Elsa, to Hester, to me.' He perched on the end of the small table that lay beside her machine, looking at the basket she was making with a bemused tilt to his head, trying to decide what it might be, lying sideways beneath the needle.

'Did they help?'

'I don't know. They say it's the difference between private and state school systems, and she's ahead on some stuff, and sideways on others.'

'Sideways?'

'That was Hester, I think she was avoiding using "behind", not that Nat was convinced.'

'It's a big change going to a new school, it takes time to adjust,' Isabelle said. 'She's doing well, it's only been four weeks, not even that.'

'Yeah, they said all that too,' Moth said.

'You're not convinced?'

'Nat's not convinced.' Moth glanced away from her around the room, his face full of concern. 'She needed to talk about mum a lot before she'd let me go. Hopefully she'll be fine again tomorrow.'

It wasn't the first time Nat had missed her parents and it was only Moth she would talk to about it. Isabelle focused on the thing they stood a chance of fixing.

'It's only a trial,' Isabelle said. 'If she ends up not liking it Elsa will move her somewhere new and try again.'

'I know.'

'I guess that's not much better though, is it?'

Moth remained silent. She sat back in her chair, the streaming linen rags trailing from their becoming form, hemmed under the needle, holding it with her hand to avoid any pulling on the fibres. He looked crushed. His hair scuffed up from the anxious fingers he'd raked through it, his fingers playing with the loose thread on the corner of the table where she'd worn the calico cover through dragging curtains over it.

'Did you finish working with James today?'

'Yes,' he said. 'Finally, I'm all paid up on the bike.'

'Well, that's pretty amazing.'

'Yeah, I was pretty buzzed up about it earlier,' Moth said, smiling at her. 'Nat kinda took the edge off it.'

'You're feeling bad because she's having a hard time today?'

'Yeah, that, and I'm going to stay with Kit tomorrow.'

'And now you don't want to go because of Nat?'

'Partly, I don't want to leave her,' he said, taking a breath as though to continue, letting the air wash out of him, not wanting to voice it.

'Partly you want to go and feel guilty?'

He shrugged his shoulders, not wanting to admit it. She felt wretched with his turmoil. Elsa and Hester would sort

Nat out, she had no worries about that. Elsa would be there, same as she had for all of them, competent hands on the helm, making sense of confusion and finding a cure to every woe. Moth, however, he needed help he wouldn't accept and carried the weight of Nat, as she felt the weight of helping him. It was after all, why she was there. Why she was still there.

Isabelle released the needle from the fabric and pulled the fabric out from under the foot. Moth followed her over to the table, looking at the various shapes she was amassing.

'You seem to be going with baskets and... jugs? Is that a jug, a giant jug?'

'I think so,' she said, prodding the linen shape into something more upright. 'I wasn't sure myself to start with, but it does seem to be leaning towards the idea of useful unusable vessels of some sort.'

'It's leaning, that's for sure.'

Isabelle prodded some more, watched the effort slide back to where the fabric wanted it. Non-resistant wasn't always malleable.

'I like that one,' Moth said, pointing towards the back where a tall waisted basket in vibrant jewel-toned silks, shot through with thick knotted spines of earthy tussah, sat.

'I made that one way back,' Isabelle said. 'After one of my first visits to India. I found it a few days ago and keep coming back to it.'

'What does it make you think of?'

She'd told him so many times how her thoughts had meandered that it had become the question he asked, what did her days work make her think of.

'Of India,' she said. 'Women carrying baskets, strong

women with upright backs, baskets of food, baskets of clothes, of colour, of spice, of potential.'

'Potential?'

'Hmm, like it all comes back to vessels, and what we're meant to carry. What we're meant to do,' Isabelle said.

He didn't respond. On some days he would challenge her thoughts, probing deeper into them, or teasing her about how obtuse they were. Other times, he was bemused, but didn't like to say he hadn't got a clue what she was talking about. Which was good, because those were the days when she didn't know herself and was fragile with the frustration of it.

'You ever feel like you're not meant to be here?' Moth asked.

Isabelle held the question in her head. There were so many ways in which she could relate to the question, so many multi-layered, interwoven ways in which she doubted her validity, her purpose, her presence. Thoughts which hung in the frightening disarray of the workroom, where her identity was stripped from her, along with any conviction for the future. One where she was looking out at others who seemed so confident, like Kit, or James, or Elsa. But that was not what Moth needed to hear in this broken moment.

'Sometimes,' she admitted. 'But not now.'

Moth remained silent.

'What about you?' she asked.

'I like the idea of being like that,' he said, nodding at the basket. 'Knowing I have a purpose to find.'

'That's all a basket is,' Isabelle said. 'Made with a purpose in mind, but its true purpose is revealed by the user, not the maker.'

'That sounds deep.'

'It wasn't meant to.'

'I liked it.'

'Yeah, me too,' she said, grinning at him.

'Maybe what you're doing is philosophy, not craft?' Moth's face was smoothed by the humour, less creased with concern.

'I don't think I'll make a living out of philosophy,' Isabelle said.

'That's alright, Kate doesn't think you'll make a living out of craft either,' he told her.

'Cheers, thanks for that,' she said. 'Now, I do believe I owe you one.'

'What?'

'Easter Sunday, family-lunch-from-hell, in the boot room when you stitched me up?'

He thought back and recalled the moment, said, 'Oh yeah, I'd forgotten about that.'

'Well, I hadn't,' she said.

'Cool, so what are we doing?'

Isabelle looked out of the French doors. A slim wisp of moon was hanging in the clear sky, catching starlight in its curve. The perfect evening for it. The day had been mild, the skies clear for a change, and the water would be perfect, ice cold and still deep enough for best effect. She had a wobble thinking about it. A curve of fear around the lining of her stomach that told her she should be more sensible. A curve that reminded her how it used to feel, being young, when excitement and fear nestled in the rim of the hanging moon. She looked at Moth. He needed to share that with someone. Maybe she wasn't the right person for the job, but she was the only one there. She pushed the fear aside and seized hold of the purpose.

'I'm not telling you,' she said. 'You have to trust me and just do it.'

When he grinned at her, she felt her fear and his worries disappear. James had never grinned like that. He'd tended to sigh and wonder what idiocy she and Hester were about to get into that he would need to drag them out of.

She found a length of fine soft silk, a gorgeous peacock blue, the vibrancy of it seducing her hand as she hovered over a pile. Calling her out into the night, reminding her of warmer climates and the soothing feel of cool water. Moth would love India, it was so intense, none of the frigidity of England. You could lose yourself there.

'One day, I hope you get to India,' she told him.

'Why?'

'I think you'd like it,' she said. 'When I imagine you travelling, I think about you being there, amongst other places. I think it would suit you.'

'Where else do you imagine me going?'

'Oh, all over.' She waved her arms to suggest the entire world.

'Really?'

'Hell, yes,' she said, looking at him in surprise. 'When I see a great place on TV, or on a map, or in a book, I think how much you'd like it.'

'That's cool.'

'Why?'

'Sometimes I think I won't make it past the county line, let alone out of the country.'

'That's just today.' She caught his hand and pulled him towards the windows. 'Not even all of today. Now, you feel shitty, because of Nat, and can't imagine leaving her, right?'

He followed her, mute. His hand limp in hers, the weight

inside him falling into her palm, voicing what he was too weary to battle or acknowledge.

'It won't always be like that, Moth,' she told him. She dropped his hand to open the doors, rattling the swollen windows out of their tight frames, reluctant to be opened again now the warmth of the day's sun had gone. Took his hand to pull him outside. 'I have no doubt you're going to go travelling. You have this real clarity over what you want, so you'll do it. When you're ready. When you know you can trust others to help you look after Nat.'

She stopped beneath the edge of the verandah. Most in the house would be heading for bed if not already there, but there might be a few eyes watching the garden and the tempting clear sky. She hoped they would be dark shadows, diminished by the bright inside lights.

'I need you to take your shoes and socks off,' she told him. 'And take anything out of your pockets, leave it here.'

'Why?'

She sighed and looked at him pointedly. He shrugged and did as she'd asked. She stepped back a few paces, out to where the grass began to roll away from the house, beckoning him forward, holding up the band of silk.

'I have to blindfold you, are you going to be alright with that?'

'Do I have a choice?'

'Yes, you can choose to go back inside.'

'That's a crappy choice,' he complained.

'Life's a bitch,' she sympathised, holding the silk up, taunting him with it.

'Yeah, go figure,' he said. 'Ok, you can blindfold me.'

She was tying the silk behind his head, trying not to catch

his hair, when he asked, 'Is this an adventure we're going to share at breakfast?'

Her hands froze with the words. Her stomach churned again. She shouldn't do this but doing this was the only thing she could think of to help him.

'You keep saying stuff like that and I'll go back inside,' she said. She finished tying off the silk and came to stand in front of him. She lifted his hand and put it on her shoulder.

'Now, you need to follow me,' she told him and took a slow step forward. His hand pulled away from his body, but he stayed immobile, until his fingers were about to leave hers, then took a hesitating step forward, then another one.

'This is weird.' His voice hushed in the darkness. Curiosity mixed with discomfort.

'I haven't done this for so long,' she said. 'Later, you can do it to me. I need to remember how scary it was, we used to come up with the weirdest things to do.'

'We?'

'Hester, James and I. Sometimes Kit too, even once or twice we did it with Kate and Elsa, though of course we were relatively tame with them.'

'And tonight?'

'I told you, I'm not telling you.'

Isabelle began to walk towards the river, turning him left and right, confusing him, before heading towards the weir.

'I know you're trying to confuse me,' he said.

'Hush,' she said, squeezing his hand, guiding him to stop. 'Now, you cannot speak from this moment forwards, until I take the blindfold off. Afterwards you can call me every name under the sun. The moment you speak, that's it, your time is up.'

'Then I get to blindfold you?' he asked. 'Same rules?'

Isabelle's stomach flipped again.

'Exactly the same rules?' Moth asked again, grinning out from under the blindfold.

'Yes, yes.'

'Cool, that's a deal,' he said.

'So, from now on, silence?' she stressed.

He nodded silent compliance. She poked him hard in the ribs with one finger. He flinched and went to open his mouth, but pulled the words back in at the last minute and clamped his mouth shut, covering it with his spare hand. Good, she had his attention.

She looked up at the house, the stone around the windows glowing where a hint of light crept through curtains, spreading into a darkness swallowing up the walls that connected them. She turned back to Moth. His hair protruding above the now colourless blindfold. A pale reflection of light, silvered and dim, highlighted by a warm glow from the house above them, by glinting reflections from the river beside them, fading into the darkness where his face was but a dim shadow.

She gripped his hand to her shoulder again, set off for the weir, guiding him back along the path they'd taken so many weeks earlier, when they first met, helping him across the metal race bridge. She kicked her shoes off, pulling him behind her as before. His arm wrapped around her waist, confident, he knew this trick. The water was cold to the bone, cutting into their senses. In the darkness she felt Moth all lean and angular around her, firm bone, and slight muscle. His height reminding her of James, his slenderness more of a fit in the darkness and the cold. James had always been taller, wider, huger than her.

They reached the point where the weir was broken. It

would be natural enough to turn back. She could end this right now, stop and take his blindfold off. Be sensible. God, Elsa would freak if she could see this.

Isabelle drew them up beside the gap in the stone. Her skin prickling with cold and his closeness. Her mind rushing with the waters over the weir and bubbling into the river below. Like one of the vessels she'd left behind on the table, full of the hope of purpose. It wasn't only Moth who needed this. She needed to remember how it used to be, to feel like this. Like life was that moment and nothing more. No oughts or shoulds or mights or musts. Doing what came next until there was no next left. She turned her head and spoke over the noise, close against his ear.

'Sit down, on the edge.'

She lowered herself down onto the last bit of stone that sat beside the gap, her breath a shocked gasp as the cold water soaked her jeans. Moth sat down beside her, knocking against her in his sightlessness and grunting at the same cold but he didn't speak.

'Hip to hip, move sideways as I do.' She shuffled her weight through the rushing water, waiting for Moth to follow, until the water was rushing over her up to the waist, her top soaking up the water, pulling the chill up to her chest. She felt Moth sliding beside her, muttering under his breath. She laughed with wicked delight. He wasn't worrying about Nat now. You couldn't think about anything except the intensity of the water, the chill licking away at your body. They shimmied into the middle of the gap and she stopped, Moth bumping into her. He'd expected them to keep going. To cross the gap and back up the other side, but that wasn't what she had in mind.

'On the count of three, let the water take you forward.

One,' she began to count, wondering if he would speak, stop her, resist, 'two,' she grasped his hand in hers, they would go together, 'three.'

She slipped away down the long rush of the weir, feeling Moth come a timid instance behind her, breaking his silence as he did so with a curse that carried him down the weir and into the water gushing across the rocks at the bottom. Banging them both several times until they were dumped in the full river. She went in under her head and felt him do the same, the water churning around them. Isabelle felt the bottom beneath her feet and pushed off. Up into the beaten metal surface, rising for breath, lifting off the slippery stones.

She gasped, stunned by the cold. Moth came up with the blindfold in his hands and tried to take the same sharp breath of stunned air. Trying to speak and managing a frozen 'fuuuu' of cold, the water rushing past them, the current pulling at their bodies in the water. She reached out for him, laughing, and tried to catch him. But he was stronger than her and it was him who pulled them together as they bumped along the bottom of the river away from the weir and out into the wide basin where they stood up to their shoulders in the ripples.

'I'm guessing that's how you broke your leg before?'

'Yes. Oh, please tell me you only bumped yourself! I really don't want to have to explain your broken bones to Elsa.'

'No broken bones, don't worry,' he told her. 'That was weird. Jesus this is cold.'

'Keep moving, it helps,' she told him, stretching out, and holding onto his arm.

The lights bobbing nearer and the pressure of the river slackening as they drifted before the house. Knees and legs and arms jangling against one another.

'How long since you did this?' he asked.

'A while, though I often walk down the river at night, when I'm home in the summer.'

'This isn't summer,' Moth told her.

'No, but the river needs to be full to do the weir thing, else it does hurt. And I haven't had anyone to do this with for a long time.'

'I can't imagine Hester ever doing this.'

'She did, but it does seem a long time ago,' Isabelle said.

'And James?'

Isabelle smiled at him and said, 'you and James aren't quite the same.'

'He never did this?'

'No,' she said. 'James never let us do this when he was around.'

'I think I'm feeling warmer,' Moth said.

'Your body adjusts to the cold,' Isabelle agreed.

'So, is it my turn now?' he asked, and pulled the blindfold up out of the water, wringing it out.

'I was hoping you'd lost that in the water.'

'Yeah, I bet!' He pulled her closer, held the sodden cloth around her head and turned her round to tie it.

'Right, lie down in the water,' he said. 'And remember, no talking.'

Isabelle felt the cold dampness of the cloth covering her eyes, the intense absence of sight, the slow awakening of all her other senses. Awareness diminishing to the river sluicing past her. Round her, through her. She lay back, let her legs rise, the weight of her soaked jeans resisting the lift. She felt Moth beside her, his hands rising under her back, settling against her soaked top. Supporting her shoulder blades, her hips. Points pinning her.

'Now, be silent, and float,' he said, and pushed her down the river.

She felt the water lapping against the side of her face. The strange rush of the current where it swirled around Moth and nibbled at her. Her ears numbed beneath the water line. Sound a gurgle of movement, of pressure and presence. Focusing on it, she lost it. The river disappearing, she afloat on the warmth of his nestling arms. His hands turning her. Pointing down river, toes first. His arms fluttering loose, like fish slipping past, moving parallel under her shoulder blades. His face hovering beside hers. His submerged shoulders protecting her from the current.

She thought he could let go and she would slide away, full of a sense of purpose that was replete.

They moved again, Moth pulling her against the river and guiding her to the edge of the water.

'You'll need to stand up in a moment,' he said. 'I'm going to let go, we're back to shore.'

She felt the river recede from her body. Falling away from her with his hands, taking repletion with it. Grief rose up in her, twisting in her chest, cold descending. An out of hours visitor she couldn't understand or refuse. Dredging up a host of memories and regrets released by the water. She stood up, stumbled, pulled the blindfold off in panic. Watched Moth wading towards the shore, moving towards the lights of the house while she was swamped by the darkness.

'Moth.'

He looked back at her, saw the blindfold in her hands, heard the crack in her voice. He turned back, reaching out a hand, took two steps towards her. Voices rolled out across the garden towards them and the shock of being seen surged across them, pulling their anxious hands together. Moth tugged her drenched and speechless from the water as two voices descended the steps from the verandah. Heading out to the river and directly towards them, with only the great old chestnut stood between.

He pulled her towards the thick trunk, and they huddled behind it, trying to disappear. Freezing and shaking together, their clothes clammy and dripping round their ankles. The voices taking shape. Elsa and, as her senses tried to catch up, she recognised Rob too.

'What are they doing out here?' Moth whispered.

'Shhh,' she said, cringing. Wondering what they would think of her and Moth, dripping wet and hiding.

Elsa and Rob settled on the bench on the other side of the tree, oblivious of their presence. Moth and Isabelle pressed together into the trunk. His chest pinning her back against the bark of the tree. His arms wrapped around her head, muffling all sound, shaking with the cold as well. Her arms wrapped around his waist, trying to stop his shivering. Both trying to diminish themselves smaller behind the tree.

Isabelle wanted to go back to that moment in the river, floating free of all awareness. She was shaking inside and out, throat tight with panic, overwhelmed by the cold. She couldn't focus on anything, as though the water had got inside her and was still rushing. The only solidity was Moth. Tight up against her, trying to warm them through. She could feel her face pressed against the sharp curve of his collar-bones. Feel his hips slim against her, sitting higher than her own. Feel the chill of her clothes on her skin, and the warmth that radiated through between the points where their bodies met. She could feel the slow increase of his hard on against her hip. The lump in her throat increased, squeezing out a gasp.

Moth pulled her head closer against his shoulder, wrapping them up even tighter as she shook beside him, horrified and lost in a moment she couldn't comprehend. His erection pressing against her and the two intimate voices murmuring in words she couldn't grasp from behind the thick trunk of the chestnut.

She buried her head in denial. If they could only go back to the river, it would be fine. It would be like it was then, washed clean of all thought and feeling, as pure as the river itself.

Taking them away somewhere senseless. Not like this moment that felt so hideous and wretched and all her fault.

When Moth pulled away from her, to the point where she could feel only the press of his wet clothes against her arms, she couldn't look up at him. She couldn't not. She'd started this, it was her fault. She looked up, his face right next to her.

'Did you hear any of that?' he whispered.

'No.'

He pulled further back, stepping away, peering round the tree. 'I have to go,' he said. 'I have to get ready for tomorrow.'

Isabelle looked at his outline, his face submerged in the intense dark beneath the tree. Did he know she'd felt him hard beside her? Could they walk away from the moment and it would be like nothing had happened? She couldn't ignore it, she was the adult here, she'd started this.

'Moth,' she said, desperate to put it right. 'I'm sorry, this was a bad idea.'

He stepped back, right next to her, and cut across her words, 'Do you mean that? Really, are you sorry?'

She sucked her breath in. He was so close, his voice so intense.

'Yes, no,' she said, swamped with guilt, and fear, and

something else she didn't understand. 'I don't know, I'm, I'm...'

'What?' he asked. 'You're sorry? For being where you might get caught out, or for being here with me? Which are you sorry for?'

'No,' she said. 'No. I'm not sorry for being here with you. I'm sorry for making us hide. I wanted to do something good for you.'

'You did.' He pulled away, looked across the lawn at the lights of the house. 'But don't take that away by being sorry,' he said. 'I'm not sorry one bit. It was... amazing. Thank you.'

'Thank you?'

'Yes, thank you,' he said. 'Thank you, and I have to go, and I'll see you, and don't freak out, and thank you.'

He looked back at her, hand lingering on the gnarled curve of the chestnut, she could see the whites of his eyes and his grinning teeth etched in silver reflected from the river. When he ran across the lawn away from her, she was left with nothing but glimmering water and her own searing cold against the hard trunk of the tree.

KIT LOVED BRISTOL TRAIN STATION. In truth he loved any train station, the buzz, the emotions, the indifference, but Bristol station had been part of his life for so many years, recording so many critical departures, that it had become a philosophical indulgence in the manic flow of life.

It too had changed a lot. The old stone that made up the station buildings had been cleaned to a false virgin smugness, a shade he liked to call 'buff' for its evocative skin tones. The approach road, which was now wide and expensively paved, awash with fresh painted lines and strict instructions, keeping pace with its facelift while failing to provide adequate parking. The restoration conferred on the premises a worthiness that warmed him with its financial bottom line as he sipped coffee from a takeout cup and waited for Moth's train to come in.

He checked his watch, ten minutes to wait, if the train was on time, which the arrivals board was pretending it might be.

Drafts from the long corridors and high ceilings caught the close-trimmed hairline of his neck, fluttering through the back of his hair. It was unsettling, this longer length. Tossed, not tousled, a trial agreed between him and his stylist. He'd promised to give it a week and had spent three days itching to get it cut off. He should have known better than to listen to someone else's opinion, but he'd been tempted by the sly suggestion that not many men his age could handle a longer cut. Plus, the photo of the model with the suggested cut had been teeth-achingly fuckable. After all, perhaps there might not be that much longer before he had to cut to suit what was happening on top of his head, not what was inside it.

He tweaked the collar of his jacket higher, uncrossed his legs and switched them over. The gleaming toe of his shoes swinging an idle pleasure as fresh blood rushed through them, his roving eyes dredging the scraps of life before him. Sieving out the dross, the poverty, the litter skittering into corners and hiding beneath benches, narrowing in on the essence of what was beautiful and tempting, decanted into the other worldliness of the station. Seeing the swish of a full skirt, hearing the click of high sharp boots on the stone, the warmth of aftershave floating past him, teasing. Noir. He could smell it anywhere. It reminded him of an ex, a warm and intense memory. Lust and happiness rising, evaporating as the scent meandered away.

A young woman with cinched-in waist and expanding breasts walked by, her back curved over to hide the development. Her shoulders hunching into her bag. She would end up with terrible posture and insecurity, and the breasts would not stop growing for it. Kit grimaced. He'd tangled with a pair of 38GG once and that memory had been a long time leaving him, well after the face and name had faded. Kit tried to recall the Noir memory to drown out GG, but it had trailed away to a cold recollection.

He looked elsewhere, pitying the young girl with the too full chest. Seeing the eyes of other men following her long after he'd abandoned the view. Natural selection was a mean old bitch. You had no say in the hand you got dealt and all the surgical skill in the world was dealt out on either financial capacity or emotional distress, with a wasteland of unhappiness in between.

His gaze shifted to the lad serving at the Burger King checkout, shifting in and out of view as he went back and forth behind the counter. His narrow frame lost beneath the apron. His sharp cheekbones ridiculed by the hat perched on his head. The uniform crushing Kit's fleeting spark of interest. He never could look twice at a person who would allow commercialism to pervert them. He knew it was an unkind contempt, but he did, he hoped, manage to keep that to himself. Someone had to work in Burger King after all, or how would the nation feed itself?

His eyes flickered back to the arrivals board. The train had developed a five-minute delay. He raised the coffee cup to his lips and took a seductive warm mouthful in, savouring the heat, the froth, the second shot of bitterness he'd asked for. It was good to stop. He felt his body uncoiling, enjoying the break from incessant thought. Elsa's house in Swansea had become a huge ball ache, exacerbated by her reticence to make any clear decisions over it.

He'd had three estate agents value it and, when she'd murmured insubstantial clucking sounds at him for another week, he'd gone and met another two agents at the property himself. It hadn't made any difference; she wouldn't make a decision. Leaving him to grit his teeth and begin the process of getting quotes for the work. The noughts kept creeping upwards.

The garden surveyor had found Japanese knotweed and trebled the quote. Kit went in person to investigate. The extent of his botanical knowledge incorporating cut flowers and the invasive variants of knotweed, balsam and hogweed. He'd found no evidence, and the garden surveyor had been difficult to get hold of. He'd dragged in another two. No knotweed, but their clearance quotes had still taken a bit of swallowing.

The house had damp issues in the basement, the front façade windows were rotten, and woodworm was rampaging through the attic and roof rafters. The dining room and kitchen floors were spore infested, the stairs in need of patch-work replacement and most of the doors had warped out of line to their frames. There was one bathroom in the whole house and the kitchen was a biochemical health hazard. The electrics were uncertifiable, the gas boiler redundant, and there wasn't a room that didn't need repainting, re-carpeting and refurnishing, with most of them, in his opinion, needing re-plastering. He looked at the phone in his hand, he'd been about to call Lou and ask her how the clearance was going. She and Jamie had been there three days and were on their fourth skip.

The coffee sliding down his throat reminded him he was

supposed to be switching off for the day. He put the phone away.

A man approached him at the bench he'd taken a central position on, but he was not in the mood for sharing. Kit looked up at him, a stout middle-aged businessman with no taste in suits. He spread his arms along the back of the bench and opened his legs, thrusting his hips forward, smiling and gurgling suggestively in his throat. The man reddened with a speed that made Kit laugh out loud and hurried away, his feet scuffling along the stone in distress while Kit smirked.

He returned to his placid and watchful pose. Smoothing the chinos back down, loving the train station even more. Even the coffee had improved.

He could remember the last time he saw his mother, leaving the station on her way to Southampton docks. The details of her thick dark curls wrapped up in a messy chignon. Her summer coat hanging off her shoulders, it's vibrant striped lining kicking in the breeze. Her hand holding the takeout cup, long manicured nails wrapped around it for warmth, scowling at the steaming contents with distaste. The social change that had swept coffee passion through the nation had happened long after she left. Kit thought she would have approved being able to get a decent cup of well-made coffee wherever she went. She always had preferred coffee to tea, even when milky tea in a Styrofoam cup was all you could get at the station.

Kit was lost in the reverie when he sensed another bench seeker stop before him. He leaned back again and was about to do the same insidious stretch when he realised it was Moth. He snapped back into a more appropriate position and smiled a contrite welcome.

'Well, you were miles away,' Moth told him, hitching the bag across his shoulder.

'Wasn't I!' Kit admitted and stood up. 'Moth, fantastic, you're here. Drag me from this place before I lose myself in history.'

Moth looked around. 'Well, I suppose it is old.'

'It wasn't that sort of history I was struggling with.' Kit stretched his shoulders out. 'Come on, let's go get some food, I'm starving. You hungry?'

'Yeah, starving,' Moth said, glancing around. 'Though I don't suppose we're going to get a burger, are we?' he asked, nodding his head in the direction of Burger King.

'Too bloody right we're not.' Kit dropped the coffee cup in the bin a stride away from the bench and started to walk backwards as Moth caught up with him. 'I need meat, proper meat, a steak, and some serious balls of a salad to go with it. And some bread, hot bread, dripping with salted butter. With onions, fried onions sizzling on the plate. And a pint to wash it down with, maybe two.'

'You aren't making me any less hungry.'

'Good, come on, let's go.' With Moth beside him Kit strode out of the train station. His car was parked in the waiting bay outside. He grabbed a card off the windscreen as he got in, ignoring the irritated looks of other drivers circling the car park.

'How do you get away with parking here?' Moth asked.

'Advantages of working for royalty.' Kit waved the card at him.

'Is that the royal crest?'

'Yes, but not our royal family.' Kit jumped into the car. 'I have to arrange collections for terribly self-important people, who pay through the nose for preferential parking arrangements.'

'At Bristol train station?' Moth fumbled his way into the passenger seat around his bag.

'Oh, you have no idea,' Kit told him. 'So, what news from Riverdull? Anyone been stabbed yet? Or is Hester being delightful for a change?'

'Eh, well, it's interesting you should ask,' Moth said.

'Ooh, what now? Do tell all,' Kit insisted, pulling out into the traffic.

'Eh, I think maybe I shouldn't.'

'You teasing bastard,' Kit said. 'Spill now or I'll tip you straight out the car.'

'Well, I sort of accidentally overheard the information,' Moth said.

'You were eavesdropping?' Kit asked, his voice admiring.

'No, I was not eavesdropping,' Moth said. 'I happened to be somewhere doing something...'

'... doing something you shouldn't have been, hmmm?'

'... quietly when two other people assumed the same space and spilled their guts in front of me.'

'My God, this is exciting stuff!' Kit pulled the car up in the middle of the traffic and switched the hazard warning lights on. 'When did this happen?'

'What are you doing?' Moth asked as traffic screeched past them hooting.

'Waiting for the goss. I did warn you, I won't accept being teased.'

'We're about to cause an accident!'

'Well, yes, you are,' Kit told him.

'Jesus, alright, I'll tell you,' Moth said. 'Just move the bloody car!'

'Tell, tell, tell, tell, tell,' Kit chanted at him as he moved back out into the traffic and flipped a finger at an irate driver.

Moth sighed. A long, worried sigh, and glanced sideways at Kit.

'And don't bother asking me to swear to secrecy,' Kit told him. 'It'll be a waste of time and I'll only end up disappointing you and feeling bad myself.'

'Don't you ever keep a secret?'

'Only my own, buddy,' Kit said. 'They're the only ones that count.'

'Oh, that's nice.'

'Stop procrastinating and spill.'

'Rob told Elsa he's leaving Hester,' Moth said in a rush.

Kit looked at him in stunned shock. Flicked eyes back at the road, back to Moth to see if he was kidding. Moth was chewing his lip.

'Holy cow fucking a priestess.'

'I told you it was big,' Moth said, raising his hands in defence.

'Wow,' Kit said. 'I mean, like, frigging, frigging wow. How? Why?'

'I don't know the full details.'

'Or if you do, you're not telling them?'

'I don't know them,' Moth said. 'I was trying hard not to let them know I was there. Inadvertently there, inadvertently listening. I didn't hear everything.'

'So, are you sure this is what you heard?'

'Totally.'

'Holy cow...'

'Yes, fucking a priestess, I heard. Nice image, thank you for that,' Moth said.

'I mean, this is like, not big, this is huge.'

'Yes, I kind of figured that.'

'Does Isabelle know?'

'I don't think even Hester knows,' Moth said. 'I only heard last night, and I got the impression he was telling Elsa first, to warn her in advance. He seemed to be apologising a lot.'

'I'll bet!' Kit said. 'I don't know if you're well out of it for a week or if we should both go haring back up there right now.'

'Don't say that,' Moth groaned.

Kit remembered what Elsa had said. Shit, he'd lost his head with this news. Moth was struggling to leave Nat as it was.

'No, we're definitely best out of it,' Kit said. 'In fact, we should make sure you don't go back until the shit has finished hitting the fan and spreading as wide as Hester can make it travel. And, trust me, she has an international diploma in that department.'

'What about Nat?'

'Nat's at school, and Hester won't shit shovel in front of her.'

'She did at Easter lunch.'

'Nah, that was shovelling to impress Asha, stop fretting.' Kit moved off the dual carriageway, flicked a glance at Moth who was watching him.

'It's not going to help Isabelle's cause, is it?'

'Nothing bad happening to Hester is going to end well for Isabelle,' Kit said.

'Should we tell her?'

'Who? Hester or Isabelle?' Kit asked with a grin.

'Isabelle, obviously.'

'No, we stay out of it,' Kit said. 'We stay well out of it, and pretend we have no knowledge of the events until we are told by Elsa.'

'Uhm,' Moth said, looking out of the window away from him.

'Uhm?'

'I just, what if Isabelle thought, afterwards, that we knew, you know, beforehand, and didn't tell her?'

'Why would she do that?' Kit asked, trying to look at Moth around focusing on the road. He was staring out of the window, a study of innocence.

'I don't know, but what if she thought we'd known first?'

'I don't think we should tell her first to make sure she doesn't think we could have done,' Kit said. 'If that makes sense.'

'I get your drift,' Moth said, looking uneasy, turning away from the window and back to him. 'What about telling Kate?'

'If Elsa knows, Kate knows,' Kit said.

'You're sure?'

'Look, stop fretting about it,' Kit said. 'You're here for a week, and you need it. All this shit at Riverdell is turning you into an old woman. You haven't been away from Nat since, well, for months. And God knows I love Elsa, but she can be such a clucking hen sometimes.'

Moth stayed silent. Jesus, he was sensitive today. Had he picked up on that slip about his parents? Kit gripped the steering wheel and looked forwards, even more convinced that Moth needed this trip. His own thoughts about the house in Swansea were gone, smashed out the arena. Hester and Rob, eh? He hadn't seen that one coming. Hester single again? Hmmm. What was the matter with him? He could see Kate smirking at him.

'Well, I'm even hungrier now,' Kit told him. 'I'm taking you to this great bar, down by the old docks, they do the best steaks.'

'And afterwards?'

'Ooh, so many plans,' Kit told him. 'You wait and see. You won't give a shit about any of this by the time you go back. You'll be glad to get away from me for a break.'

Moth smiled, looking away from the side window and straight at Kit.

'I could do with that.'

'And that, buddy, is what we'll do.' Kit revved the Bentley and switched it through the busy traffic like a cat flicking its excited tail.

'ALL THIS?' Moth asked. 'For you?'

'I'm not always on my own,' Kit told him, cracking open a bottle of wine in the kitchen.

Moth was walking away from him towards the wide windows that made up the end wall of the lower ground floor. The garden lights were lighting up the terrace and long lawn as it spread away and down to the large trees that framed the end wall. Beneath the birch the city lights were twinkling through the dancing branches. They'd spent the day in town before arriving home. Kit had given him the grand tour, showing him the master suite on the second floor, the guest bedrooms and music room on the first floor, the drawing and dining rooms on the upper ground floor, the basement gym and kitchen cum living room on the lower ground floor.

Kit was hungry again. He went and opened the double doors of the American fridge, pursing his lips at the contents, judging his needs with a keen glance. The fridge had cost a packet, but he'd had to order one in for a client and got a deal on two more. By the time he'd redesigned another client's kitchen his had been paid for.

'You must be earning some serious packet to afford all this.' Moth walked towards the kitchen units, running a hand along the marble counter. 'Money is freedom, right?'

'Not always,' Kit said. 'I prefer the idea that money is money, freedom is freedom, sex is sex. Don't mix up your notions.'

'Rules again?'

'More politics.' Kit rummaged through the tidy shelves. Alcohol at the top, ready made in the middle, raw at the bottom. 'Politics would be so much more effective if we stuck to the principles. Too many lefties trying to lean right and the middles have gone all hard core.'

'So anyway,' Moth said. 'Back to the original question.'

Kit looked at him, a blank stare rising over the armful of cold meats he was taking back to the counter.

'Your wage.'

'How vulgar,' Kit protested.

'You talk about sex the way other people talk about money and turn your nose up at money as though it's an obscenity,' Moth said.

'Survival skills,' Kit said. 'Never divulge past lovers, clients, finances or future projects. Anything else is fair game. I told you, poverty's not for me. I run a big little business for a niche market. I make the money to look after this place. I didn't buy it. I was left it, by Granny.'

'You inherited this?' Moth pulled a stool out, sat down and swivelled round to test it out.

'Amongst other things, yes.'

'From your grandmother?' He came to rest facing the counter.

'Great-grandmother, actually, though I always called her

Granny.' Kit pulled a shining knife from the foam packed top drawer and began running it over a sharpening rod.

'You opening the packets or killing the cow?' Moth watched him sharpen the knife with concern. 'Why not from your parents?'

'My mother died before Granny, and my father was a technical necessity, nothing more,' Kit said, paring away the details with each pass of the blade. 'Granny left me the pile when she died. Most of it a load of tasteless crap, with the odd gem hidden in the midst. I tell you what, clearing out old ladies' drawers is not a gentlemanly task.'

'Not when you put it like that,' Moth said.

Kit pointed the sharpened knife at him with a distasteful frown and turned it to open the packets.

'Didn't she have any other children?' Moth asked. 'No aunts or uncles?'

'Not that she mentioned in her will,' Kit said. 'Thankfully.'

'Wow, some windfall, huh?'

'I would have settled for having her around a little longer,' Kit said. 'I missed her when she died, she was always my escape route. I grew up here, then, when I was living with Elsa, I would come here to visit, she was so much fun.'

'Yeah, but at least you didn't end up poor, as well as bereaved,' Moth said.

Kit looked up from what he was doing. Moth had turned away from him, looking through the far doorway into the gym. He went back to pulling the slivers of beef from the wrapping.

'I CAN'T HEAR YOU!'

'I said, relax,' Kit boomed in his ear.

'I am relaxed.'

'You look like a virgin sacrifice about to face the altar.'

'I'm taking it in.'

Kit watched Moth scanning the busy club. Poking the straw through his ice and letting it melt into the murky waters of the bubbling Coke. It was a good job the drink drive laws were so strict these days. A decade ago, no one would have been convinced he was legal age if he'd ordered a straight Coke. At half eleven on a Saturday night. In a rammed gay club. The best one he knew of in Cardiff. He couldn't have found a more stringent testing ground.

Moth looked freaked out to the limit, though cute with it. He had a pair of new trousers on and a shirt, open at the neck, if only one button. He'd resisted the shopping expedition, but Kit had insisted. The attention he was catching in his new kit wasn't helping his discomfort level. Moth had a rugged freshness that was straight off a clothing catalogue. Apricot hair or not, he was fit, and he was noticed. Kit grinned.

'What's so funny?'

'It's like looking in a time mirror,' Kit yelled. Even though they were right next to one another. The DJ had got the sound rocking the roof off.

'Don't think there's any such thing,' Moth told him.

'Yes there is, it's sat right next to me,' Kit said. 'I remember being your sort of young, but it feels a fucking long time ago. Spending time with you is refreshing, Moth, but it's also rather ageing.'

'Refreshing?'

'Uhm, like diving into the pool of youth,' Kit said. He felt the three cocktails kicking through his system with delight.

The barmen were skilful little fuckers. Each of them drop-dead gorgeous and unfettered by uniform. 'All those options before you, all that choice. So much unknown, unconquered territory.'

'You sound like Isabelle,' Moth told him.

'Do I?'

'She's always going on about potential too. Makes a lot of jugs and baskets.'

'Oh God, she's not going through that again?' Kit frowned at his drink, stabbing it with the umbrella. Moth seemed to know a lot about what Isabelle was doing.

'Why, has she done it before?'

'Oh, every time she has a crisis,' Kit said. 'She starts pulling the workroom to bits and trying to decide what she should be doing. Baskets, pots, jugs even. I think there was a jug one year. A fabric bloody jug, what's that about?'

'Finding a purpose?'

Kit burst out laughing. Slapped his hand on the bar and sat back huffing with suppressed laughter.

'What's so funny about that?'

'It suggests we have a purpose to find!'

'Don't we?' Moth looked back from the heaving club to the wall of mirrors behind the bar, struggled with the lacing of the aprons tied across the nude plaster models that stood in front of them, revealing their pert buttocks in the mirrors, and turned back to look at Kit.

Kit grinned. Making Moth blush was a sport he ought to grow out of, like gravel spurting.

'Those mirrors rock, right?'

'If you like the look,' Moth said, stabbing his Coke. 'Seems a bit excessive to me.'

'No, they're crucial. According to Jay, and he should know.'

'Who's Jay?'

'A mate, rescues pubs and bars for a living. Reckons mirrors are the biggest difference in a place. We argue over it all the time. You can ask him, he'll be here in a bit.'

'Weren't we talking about purpose?'

'Hmm, yes, purpose. The only purpose in life is the one we craft for ourselves. It's something you decide, not something you find, Moth,' Kit said. 'A direction to cling to in the great purposelessness of life. That was a big fuck arse word. Purposelessness, purposelessness. You can sure get your lips round that fucker.'

'I guess she has a different opinion.' Moth ignored his rambling.

'And you?' Kit asked.

'Still thinking,' Moth said, stirring the ice in his drink.

'And back we come again.' Kit picked the umbrella up out of his empty drink and twirled it in his fingers, watching the rainbow colours merge into one another and turn to sludge.

'To what?'

'You, sitting on the fence.'

'I'll get off the fence when I know which direction I'm going in,' Moth told him.

'Well, I'm heading in the direction of the dancefloor,' Kit told him.

He looked out over the heaving mass of packed bodies. All that flesh, so warm, so close, so odorous. Writhing limbs detached from bodies, a mass feeling of desire. Moth looked too.

'I'll stay here for now,' Moth said.

'Your choice, buddy.'

'Kit!' A voice called out as he pushed his empty glass across the bar.

'Jay!' Kit turned to see his friend squeezing through the tight space, looking as peeved as Moth. His hair short and choppy, his sharp frame shoving folk aside. His pokerfaced indifference smoothed over by an easy Asian smile to anyone who complained. For a fellow with little happiness, Jay could produce a smile to win contracts. 'You made it, at last, what too so fucking long? Jay, Moth. Moth, Jay. Shit, you two sound like some kind of kinky animalistic double act.'

'You're drunk already, you tosser.' Jay told him, turning to Moth. 'Hey, yeah.'

Kit watched Jay greet Moth with his customary fist pump, looking round the club.

'Man, I hate your taste in clubs.'

'You hate my taste in nearly everything,' Kit told him. He flicked the collar of Jay's shirt away from his dark skin. 'From the man who still thinks it's cool to wear a pink shirt.'

'Lydia likes this shirt.'

'Oh, fuck, tell me you didn't bring her,' Kit complained. He couldn't stand the bitch. 'I told you it was a boys' night out.'

'Yeah, she said hi too,' Jay quipped back at him. 'Fuck, it's loud in here.'

'Tell me about it,' Moth said.

'Get yourself some Cokes in,' Kit told them. 'You two boring asses are cramping my style. I'm going to dance.'

'Coke? What? Wait a minute, do I even want to know how you're getting home?' Jay asked, narrowing his eyes as Kit began to sashay away. Kit pretended he couldn't hear. 'You fuckwit, I'm not your free taxi ride.'

'You don't even like drinking!'

'That's not the point!'

It was a point they argued about regularly. Kit maintained that Jay's dislike for social drinking was a residue of his upbringing rather than a reflection of his own taste. And Jay pulled the racist card in defence every time.

'What is the point?' Kit put a hand to his ear?

'I like having the sodding choice.'

Kit sashayed back, leaned on Moth's shoulder and mock whispered in his ear, 'He's the bestest best friend, you two are going to get on like a house on fire.'

Jay turned to Moth and said, 'He's the shittiest shitty friend. Tell me you can drive?'

Moth shook a negative, asked, 'How come you like him then?'

'Because I'm the very best of people,' Kit told Moth.

He danced his way out onto the dancefloor. He had no worries about leaving Moth. No one would go near him. He looked as straight as the Virgin Mary. Kit giggled. Which was to say, not as straight as she should have been. Immaculate conception her holy arse. And Jay would soon warm up. He always arrived with a bad mood. Standard practice at weeding the chaff from the wheat of folk. At least it was only the bad mood tonight, not the bad bitch girlfriend too. He felt the warmth of the dancefloor flow out and pull him in, the hard rub of bodies as he shimmied his way into the centre, caressing his body from all angles. Kit felt shivers of excitement and relaxation running through him. It was gorgeous, just gorgeous. Back at the bar he could see them, watching him, working on conversation. Both as fucked up as each other. Both freaked out by the club and pretending it was nothing to do with their own confusion. One day he would have a straight up conversation with both of them about their sexual hang ups. Straight up. Kit laughed. Nope, it wouldn't be a straight conversation. He'd put money on Moth not being straight, despite his best efforts to avoid facing it, but as for Jay, he still couldn't figure out what issue he was avoiding.

'IS THIS REALLY A GOOD IDEA?'

'Relax, no one comes out here at this time of night.'

'I was more worried about your car.' Moth said.

'It's well insured, don't worry.'

'For underage driving?'

'Well I wouldn't actually tell them it was you driving, duh,' Kit said.

He stretched back in the passenger seat, lowering it into a semi-recline, and watched as Moth steered the Bentley around the empty park-and-ride on the western side of town. At two in the morning, deserted, though well lit. Why didn't they just turn the lights off after a certain time? Save the council a fortune. Kit felt he could do some serious work in the civil service. Except he couldn't be arsed to work for someone. Not without the opportunity to tell them to shove it up their arse.

'Go around that post, back through the lines,' Kit instructed him.

'This is really weird,' Moth said again. He'd already said it several times.

'Driving is not weird,' Kit said. 'Driving is awesome. Driving is freedom.'

'I thought we weren't supposed to mix our notions?'

'Don't quote me back at myself, it's irritating,' Kit said. 'But fair point, driving is a step on the road to freedom.'

'Why?'

'In charge of your own destiny.'

'Only if you can afford the car, the insurance, and the petrol,' Moth said. 'Only if you're over seventeen and have your licence.'

'Details.' Kit waved his comments aside with a lazy hand.

'Three years' worth of details.'

'Well, yes, but at least you'll be able to drive as soon as that time is up,' Kit said.

'I think I prefer the bike.'

Kit looked across at him in pity. Moth was staring out of the window in concentration. Clutching the wheel with both hands, fumbling with his feet on the pedals, hunched forwards in his seat. 'I must remember to kick James's arse,' he said and closed his eyes.

'Why? I like the bike, it's cool, and I can do it now,' Moth said. 'I mean, this is obviously cooler...'

'... and faster!'

'... but I can't do this for years. I can get on the bike tomorrow and go anywhere I want.'

'Is that what you're thinking of doing?' Kit asked, keeping his eyes closed.

'What?'

Moth was focused on the driving. Kit kept his relaxed pose neutral.

'Taking off on the bike?'

'No, of course not,' Moth said. Too quickly, Kit thought. 'Not off, off. Just away for a day or so, go exploring you know.'

'Is this before or after you go back to school?' Kit asked.

'I don't know,' Moth said. 'I'm ignoring school. Until someone makes me face it. Wouldn't you?'

'What, milk any opportunity possible to get out of school?

Course I would, I did!' Kit peeked at him. 'Sit back a bit,' he said. 'Try and relax, it will be easier if you do.'

Moth sat back and stalled the car again.

'Oh great, yeah, big help.' Moth turned the key over, and the engine thrummed back into life.

Kit watched as Moth wiped his hands on his trouser legs and regrasped the steering wheel.

'Just relax,' Kit said, closing his eyes again. 'We're not going home until you can drive us, so we have all night to get this right.'

'What?' Moth squeaked. 'No way. Are you crazy? Drive this car through Bristol. No way we won't get pulled over.'

Kit didn't respond, he could feel his eyes getting heavier. Christ, it was boring going in circles at 10 mph. He could never be a driving instructor.

'Who's going to pull us over?' he mumbled. 'It's not like you're going to break any speed limits.'

'Are you falling asleep?'

Kit mumbled at him.

'Kit?'

'Kit!'

Moth poked him hard.

'Both hands on the wheel, Bugsy,' Kit told him and fell asleep, the soothing glide of the car too hypnotic to resist.

'WHAT ARE YOU DOING?' Moth asked Kit.

'Thinking.'

'In your underpants?'

'It's my place, I can do what I want,' Kit said, turning his head to look up at Moth peering out of his bedroom window. 'Did I wake you?'

'Eh, yes,' Moth said. 'Along with the neighbour's dog.'

'I couldn't sleep,' Kit said.

Moth's voice had pulled him up in the middle of the garden on the way down to the birch trees. There was a soothing nonsense to pacing down the length of the lawn, letting each light pop on as he passed, waiting until they went off and doing it again. From the house to the trees, pause, from the trees to the house, pause. He'd forgotten Moth was in the house. His skin was prickly, his toes were wet and cold, even his dick had retreated in irritation. Which had been the plan.

'Ok, I'll go back to bed,' Moth said. 'As long as we're not being burgled.'

'Nope, not being burgled.'

Moth pulled the window back down and shut the curtains. Kit threw another out-of-date sausage over the fence to the barking dog. It was nice to have company in these prowlings and the frequent descent of food kept the dog awake for longer. Plus, it messed with his digestion, so that the irritating neighbours next door had to deal with the results on their extensive, wooden-decked sun terraces. It was a small revenge for the frequent screaming of ill-managed children in the summer. The only problem with owning a family-sized home was that the houses in the rest of the street tended to home families.

He paced back to the house. Moth had disturbed his reverie. At least the persistent hard on had gone. More to the point, the endless dreams that spun a web between Kate and Isabelle had gone. They'd been keeping him awake for nights, pleasantly enough, until Hester started popping up in them. Undressed. Ghostly white in the flesh, as though it hadn't seen the light of day for too many decades, her stomach sagging from a pregnancy she'd never known. Kit shuddered. He didn't like dreams. Not night dreams anyway, they had too much life of their own. He liked fantasies, the ones he controlled.

He went into the kitchen, pulled the glass doors shut behind him, and put the coffee machine on. It felt closer to getting up time than going down time. His short dressing gown was hanging off the back of a kitchen stool. He put it back on, enjoying the sounds in the deep quiet of the night. The coffee machine coming to life, the cup being placed on its saucer, the spoon clinking as he pulled it out of the drawer, the vacuum rush of the fridge door, the gurgle of milk going into the pot.

The week with Moth was going well but it had seemed oppressive tonight, in the depths of the bad dreams. Somewhere in those dreams Elsa's house in Swansea loomed. A dark corridor of dreary rooms going nowhere and, whenever he opened a door, there were endless pots. Isabelle's bloody pots and baskets, littering the corners of the corridors. He must have dozed off and woken up four times before he gave up and took the inconsolable hard on out to the garden and walked it off.

'Mind if I join you?' Moth asked from the stairs.

Kit turned and looked at him in surprise. 'Of course not,' Kit said. 'Though I might be rather dull company, I have work issues boring through my skull like a jackhammer.'

'I can piss off if it's a bad time.'

'Thanks for the offer, but have a drink first, then I'll tell you when to piss off.'

'Thanks.'

'Tea, coffee, chocolate?'

'Hmm, I'll go chocolate.'

'So, what really woke you up?' Kit asked. 'Lights turning on or your own thoughts?'

'Not sure,' Moth said, sitting down on the third step. 'Woke up and there you were. Pacing the lawn in your pants.'

'Man's gotta do what a man's gotta do.'

Kit found another cup, more milk. He needed to get back to work. A sense of urgency was looming on him. Coupled with an uneasy sense of things he couldn't get into place.

'Do you mind if we take a trip to Swansea tomorrow?' he asked, scooping the milky froth off the top of the jug. 'Today, that is.'

'I don't mind what we do,' Moth said. 'I thought you were determined to do a complete mystery tour for the whole week?'

'I was, true,' Kit said. 'I have this job in Swansea that's playing on my mind and I need a day there to put some stuff right. I know we only have two more days, but if you don't mind...'

'You can send me back to Riverdell if you need to,' Moth said. 'I understand if you need to work. I don't want to be in the way.'

'You won't, you're not,' Kit said. He wasn't engaging in that teenage emotional bullshit. 'And we have one day left afterwards. We'll pack up today, head over to Swansea, then sleep on the beach. Perhaps Cardiff again too? You can catch the train back from Wales.'

'What, two days of advance notice?' Moth quipped at him.

Kit turned and pointed the spoon at him. 'Mocking little prick.'

'Less of the little,' Moth said.

'Hah!' Kit said. 'That's the truth of it. Well, there we go, one hot chocolate and a plan. You coming to sit down, or you drinking on the stairs?'

'Here's good for me,' Moth said.

Kit took it over to him on the stairs, loading a couple of biscuits onto the side of the saucer.

'You really know how to look after people,' Moth said to him as he took the saucer out of his hands, a buttoned t-shirt open at his neck and a pair of pyjama slacks on. An edge of vulnerability to him in the nightly garb and the compliment.

'Thanks.'

'It's like your purpose in life.'

Kit looked up at him from the bottom of the stairs. Moth's voice was tired and unguarded, full of appreciation.

'It's been cool, staying with you,' Moth said, dunking the biscuit in the hot chocolate. 'I've enjoyed it.'

'That's a shocking thing to do to a biscuit,' Kit told him, hand catching the end of the balustrade as it curved down to the final wider step.

'Snob,' Moth said, mouth around the soaked goodness.

'But thanks, I'm glad you've enjoyed it,' Kit said. 'It's not over yet, mind.'

'Yeah, no doubt,' Moth said. 'When you say, "sleep on the beach", do you mean actually "on the beach"?'

'Wait and see,' Kit said. He moved back to the counter and picked up his own coffee, sat on the barstool and took a slow sip from its loveliness. 'You know, you're welcome to come and stay anytime.'

'Part of the family, huh?'

'Stuff the family,' Kit told him. 'Family are alright, but it's friends you need in life. Family do what they think is right by you, friends do what you think is right by you, or they're not a friend.'

'Thanks,' Moth said. 'Anytime it gets a bit too Riverdull, I'll remember that.'

'Or too Riverhell,' Kit said.

'Yeah, that one too.'

'Any time, you're always welcome, Moth.'

'I think you mean it.'

Kit looked at him in surprise.

'Yes, I do, but I think you need your own space too.' Moth soaked another biscuit and scooped its dripping form into his mouth.

'Oh?'

'I don't think you'd cope if I descended on you too often,' Moth said. 'You're a lot like Isabelle in that.'

'I am?' Kit felt the unpleasant creep of an honest opinion about to descend on him.

'You both have a need for personal space. Like a lot of it. Her, the workroom. You, this house, your job.'

'I suppose so,' Kit said, hiding in his coffee cup. 'Feels like life to me.'

'Yeah, it looks good. I'm jealous,' Moth said.

'Jealous?'

'Uhm,' Moth said, sipping his chocolate. 'You do what you want, and not if you don't.'

'I wish,' Kit said. 'It might seem like that, but we're both wrapped up in our own set of obligations. Now you, you seem truly free to me.'

'Me?' Moth asked. 'You must be kidding right? I've got no home, no family, except a kid sister to look after, no money, not even any rights for another two years, minimum. I literally belong to Elsa, and if not her, the social services. How's that freedom?'

'Because you have all your choices before you,' Kit said.

'Even with those slight issues. How you react to those things, how you make yourself the person you become, that's all yours.'

'You and Isabelle had that too.'

'Yes, we did,' Kit said. 'Still do too, though she doesn't always see it. But it gets harder and harder to shake off expectations and remember you have choice. I never felt like that when I was younger. I knew I was going to do whatever I wanted, and no one was going to stop me. No matter who it affected.'

'What I do affects Nat,' Moth said.

'Does it? Really?'

'She needs me.'

'I think you need her more,' Kit told him. 'After all, without her, who are you now? She needs to know you're there, you're her only link to the past, but she needs more than you can give her. Nat needs a home, Moth, and people to care for her. She needs people to help her build a new future. You think you can do all that?'

Moth stayed silent, sipping through his thoughts. A dark line of chocolate framed his upper lip, a shadow of the man that would come, the shape of childishness itself.

'Don't take upon yourself something you can't do as well as others,' Kit said. 'Be honest about what you want, and don't hide behind oughtisms you can't fulfil.'

'Oughtisms?'

'Yeah, life gets fucking full of them faster than you can imagine,' Kit said. 'Don't stack the decks against yourself before you need to.'

'What if what I want isn't a good or a right thing to do?'

'Good or right by what rule?' Kit had the feeling that the

ground between him and Moth, which last time he looked had been made of solid Canadian maple, was turning marshy. Elsa wouldn't appreciate him screwing up the picture with some careless words, he'd be dragged in for a cup of tea and a bollocking.

'By other people's rules, I suppose.'

'As long as it's just you, as far as I'm concerned, it's your life.'

'What if it includes other people?' Moth asked, looking into his cup.

Kit was pretty sure the contents were gone. A gnat couldn't have licked it any cleaner.

'If you're taking other people along for the ride, make sure it's consensual, whatever the ride is.'

'Consensual?' Moth asked.

'That's the only guide you can take, in my humble opinion.'

'Not legal?'

'The law is there to defend the innocent,' Kit said.

'Defend the innocent?' Moth looked at him with a scowl. 'Don't you mean, protect the innocent?'

'I wish I did,' Kit said. 'But from what I can see it fails to do that. It can defend afterwards. In my eyes, the only thing that can protect is our own choice not to cause damage. That's where I draw the line, at non-consensual behaviour.'

'What about the bystanders?' Moth asked, changing tack. Running his finger round the edge of the cup to catch the last bubbles of froth.

Kit tried to keep up with the weird conversation. 'You mean those not directly involved, but perhaps affected?'

'Uh-huh.'

'That's public opinion,' Kit said. 'I don't think you should live for that, but it's a choice we all have to make. Give a shit, or not give a shit.'

'I think I'm more not give a shit,' Moth said.

'Well at last, a toe off the fence,' Kit said.

Moth looked up at him. 'No matter what the consequences?'

'That depends on how brave you are.' Kit looked into his own cup. It had come to a frothy end. He stood up to make another one. 'Another chocolate?'

'No, thanks, I can feel the 'piss off' coming on,' Moth told him.

He walked down the stairs, swilled the cup out, put it in the dishwasher. Kit was glad something had rubbed off on him during his stay, he was getting more domestically capable, even if it was only a toe off the fence and not a foot.

'Get some more sleep, I'll wake you when you need to pack up,' Kit told him.

'Sure thing,' Moth said, heading back to the stairs.

Kit watched him walk back up, his body curving out of view with the steps. Bare feet sticking to the wood. That had been weird, very teenage angst. Kit shrugged aside the discomfort and stretched his shoulders and neck out.

A couple of hours work, a blast in the gym and a bloody hot shower. He would feel himself again by the time they hit the road.

MOTH LOOKED bemused as he drove the van out of the lock up.

'Not taking the Bentley?'

'Nope, I'm in work mode. Besides, we need it for the beach.'

'It's a campervan?'

'It's an everything van,' Kit told him, getting out of the van. 'Work van, overnight stop van, camping van, shagging van, shopping van. If anything can, this van can.

'Sort of like the 007 of vans?'

'Good image,' Kit said. 'I like it.'

'What's this logo?'

'It's not a logo, it's a coat of arms.'

'Seriously?' Moth asked.

'Yes, family name, de Lavelle,' Kit said. 'Inherited from Granny, who was the daughter of an Earl, via my illegitimate mother.'

'What?'

'Ok, now focus,' Kit warned him, mock dancing into a boxing warm-up on the tarmac in front of the lock-up. 'My grandfather spawned my mother from an affair with a Spanish aristocrat whilst he was British ambassador to Spain, back sometime, like, whenever. The aristocrat was married so she gave the child to Grandpa to raise. His wife refused to have anything to do with it when he brought her home, so he left her, my mother, with his divorced mother, Lady de Lavelle. Granny having resumed her own name following divorce. Mother was given the matriarchal surname and gave it to me in turn.'

'Granny who left you the house?'

'Yep.'

'Is that true or did you make that up to justify putting a coat of arms on your van?'

Kit stood in the lock up doorway and grinned at Moth approvingly. It was just after 9 am and Moth looked weary in the dull light of an indifferent day. He had his bag hitched over his shoulder again. Kit remembered going away to

London with Kate with nothing more than a toothbrush and a pack of condoms in his jacket pocket. He'd been about four years older than Moth, but that was a long time ago. He pulled open the back doors of the van and looked at the stacked interior. Travelling light was something that only the young or the indifferent could get away with and Moth made him realise he was no longer either.

'Does it matter?' Kit asked.

'Wow,' said Moth, looking into the back of the van. 'That is a lot of stuff.'

Kit resisted the urge to defend himself. 'Chuck your bag in, make yourself comfortable up front. I've got to get a few extra things.'

He grabbed the measuring tools in their fabric holdall, the camera and the tent, along with its two boxes worth of associated gear. Camping stove, portaloo, water bottle, kitchenware, sleeping bags. Kit could load and unload the van in an instance, whatever the demands of the day, because he'd trained his staff to leave the lock-up in pristine condition at the end of the day.

He parked the Bentley inside, cast a critical eye about to make sure all was in place, turned the lights off, pulled the doors too behind him and set the alarm.

'Spawned?' Moth asked as Kit climbed into the van.

'Huh?'

'You said your grandfather spawned your mother,' Moth said. 'Makes her sound like the devil's child, or a frog.'

'That was how Mother described it.' Kit settled himself behind the steering wheel, chucked the Bentley keys at Moth and indicated him to put them in the glove compartment. 'Illegitimacy was a stigma then, but she didn't care a hoot about it. Loved using it to make others uncomfortable.'

'Of the "not give a shit" variety?' Moth asked, buckling his belt.

'Like you would not believe,' Kit told her.

'Is that where you get it from?'

'Straight from the breastmilk, buddy, hot from the teat.'

'Oh God,' Moth groaned, turning his face away from Kit in disgust. 'That is too gross.'

Kit laughed at him and said, 'Guess you're not a breast man?'

'Not a mother's breast man. Jesus, who is?'

'There are some,' Kit said. Moth gagged at his side.

THEY PULLED up outside the house in Swansea, adjacent to another monogrammed van parked in front of the house.

It was like coming home, but bigger. Only without the wide road and generous front parking space of Bristol. The house too big for the space around it. The view of the bay detracting from this imperfection. If he'd been looking to buy, he might have been tempted by this.

He lingered with the thought. It hadn't occurred before. Was he looking to buy?

Kit had never thought beyond the home he had. He could certainly afford to, if he sold the house in Bristol. He shook his head. No, that would never happen. It would be a betrayal. Kit frowned. He'd never thought about his own choices, or lack of them, until Moth had started him thinking about it. He looked at the house again. It was so full of potential. Perhaps he could raise the money anyway, it wasn't beyond him. Shook his head again. What was the point? Shame though.

'You done?' Moth asked, from his side.

Kit turned to look at him, saw his face pursed up in amusement and curiosity.

'Hmm?'

'You seem to be having a conversation with yourself.'

'Was I talking to myself?'

'Not quite, but almost there.'

'Thanks for the save,' Kit said. 'Well, we're here.'

'Yeah, I figured,' Moth said, pointing at the identical van. 'You run a regular fleet of these things.'

'I know, but they look so good together, don't they?' Kit said.

He looked at the gleaming dolphin-grey van, with its matching charcoal crest on the sides. Oozing class from the low alloys, tinted windows, encased headlights. It was his marketing strategy; identity without names, like a secret club. When he had all four lined up, on the odd days that the whole team were together, his, Jamie and Lou's, Henri's, Ed and Fred's, it gave him a thrill like seeing Kate naked, bent over and arching her back in expectant pleasure. His van had a thin line of chrome wrapped round the bodywork. Even thinner, wider tyres. A highlight of silver touching the under-curves of the logo. The slight emphasis that said he'd arrived. He unbuckled and jumped out, trying to forget Kate.

'So, who's the client?' Moth asked. 'Do they live here? Do I have to be on best behaviour?'

'No, it's empty. Client's deciding what to do with it, we're clearing out the previous tenant.'

'As in eviction?'

'As in deceased,' Kit said. 'I'll show you round, not that there's much to see, then we'll work out what you want to do for the rest of the day.'

'You going to be here all day?'

'If you can cope with it?' Kit said. He felt a twinge of guilt, leaving Moth to himself in a strange place.

'Sure thing.'

JAMIE AND LOU nagged him to stop at 4 pm.

'Ok, I get it,' he said.

Kit looked around the pitiful upstairs kitchen one last time. The dims were doing his head in, but not as much as the fact that Elsa's oddity about the place had got under his skin. He was starting to try and work out what to do to the house. How to change it, what the cost would be, what the structural implications were, how to divide it, how to create an income.

'Seriously, boss,' Lou said, pointing at the notebook he'd opened again.

Kit shut it again, twanged the piece of elastic shut around its leather cover and put the tape measure down on top of it.

'We're not leaving until you do,' Jamie told him. 'And we're finished, which means you're paying us to stand here looking at you.'

'Which becomes double-time if we get back after hours,' Lou said, leaning back against the doorframe.

'That was the focus I needed,' Kit told them. 'I must find Moth anyway.'

'Poor lad. Spent the whole day in Swansea by himself,' Jamie said.

'Oh, please,' Lou complained. 'Poor lad my arse, did you see the wad Kit gave him?'

'It's a bit piss-poor,' Jamie said. 'You're supposed to be looking after him, and you send him packing so you can work.'

'He needed the space,' Kit said. 'We've spent all week together and he's soon got to go back. He needed something fresh to do as much as me.'

'So,' Lou vied for his attention, scuffing the floor with her soft trainers. Grey, like the clothes they wore too. He'd had them specially made. Hoodies, tank tops and trousers, and boiler suits for the boys. Nothing but top quality, mono-grammed in a matching thread. Hardly a uniform, more a statement, like the vans. It wasn't like he insisted they wear them. Not all the time. 'What are you doing with this place?'

'It's not up to me,' Kit said.

'Oh dear,' Lou said.

'That's going to put you in a bad mood for a week,' Jamie added.

'That's the problem with working for family,' Kit said. 'They think they're entitled to an opinion.'

Lou and Jamie laughed at him.

'Working for someone who has an opinion?' said Lou. She quirked her eyes in outrage at Jamie, an evil grin curling her strong jaw into a softer look. Blue eyes sparkling as lines creased the corners. Short blonde hair one snip longer than spiky. Lou had an athleticism to her that could take her looks between no-nonsense determined and intimidatingly sexy. Not unlike Steffi Graf, he always thought. But pissier.

'Yeah, who'd do that?' Jamie asked. Jamie was the softer counterpart. Her hair longer, mousier. Her eyes a duller, darker blue. Her waist thicker, legs shorter. They made a good team. Jamie happy to follow, quick to lead if needed and swifter to hand back.

'You're both dismissed,' Kit told them. 'I'm not paying you to mock me.'

'Best stop giving us so much opportunity,' Jamie told him

as she walked towards the door. 'Come on Lou, let's go. We'll make no difference to what he does. Try and remember to find Moth.'

Kit watched them walk out of the kitchen, bickering and laughing as they collected their bags and loaded up the van. He sent Moth a swift text. All done here, where shall I meet you? Glanced around again, what to do, what to do?

Put the kitchen downstairs like he had. One huge family room, better access to the garden, but the house was too big. You could make a decent bedsit from the downstairs rooms and there was a separate access from the side. But the rooms upstairs needed major reshuffling to create a more modern living space. It pushed the costs right up. If Elsa was looking for a holiday home it was too much money, too much space. It needed splitting up somehow, some part of the house needed to earn a regular income. If he put the two top floors into a flat the access went straight through the middle of the house. The central hallway would have to be massacred. Kit frowned and tapped the pen on the side of his head.

Moth hadn't replied. His frown deepened.

He paced across the kitchen towards the garden windows. The garden, now you could see it, was big. Rising to a high cliff wall of natural rock, topped off with old woodland. What was she going to do with such a garden? She already ignored the one she had. Kit drummed on the window with agitated fingers.

Where the fuck was Moth?

He turned away and walked out of the room. Jamie and Lou had stripped the house, sold, binned or recycled the contents and cleaned it to within an inch of its life. Their greatest achievement, finding a buyer for the piles and piles of old books. Some classics collector who'd practically wanked off over them, according to Lou. The emptiness had the dismal effect of making the house look worse. He needed to see Elsa. He had to pin her down, work out what the hell she wanted to do with this place before he went mad. Lou was reversing out of the drive when he pulled the door too behind him.

His phone buzzed. Ten minutes away, walking back along the front. Kit took a deep breath. Well, at least he hadn't lost Moth.

He threw his stuff in the van, took one last appraising look at the house. He was irritated with its size. It was too big for what Elsa might be considering. Too big for what he might be able to do with it. But it might be the right size for him and Isabelle. She could use the basement as a workshop. They'd have enough space upstairs to live. It was close enough to Bristol to make his business manageable.

Kit shook his thoughts off. He needed Elsa to make some clear decisions, before he made some stupid ones. He pulled the van away from the kerb and went to look for Moth.

'How was town?' Kit asked as Moth jumped in the van.

'Yeah, good, townish,' Moth said. 'I caught up with a school friend.'

'Really?' Kit asked. 'Here?'

'No, not here,' Moth said. 'Computer café, we Skyped.'

'I didn't think you had any schoolfriends,' Kit said. 'I was under the impression they were a load of stuck up wankers.'

'Ben's a former school friend,' Moth said.

'As in friend from a former school, or formerly of school?'

'As in, he left,' Moth said. 'As a result of his unacceptable behaviour.'

'The older guy?' Kit asked.

'What?' Moth said.

'Your bad experience?'

Moth looked across at him. Kit could feel the stare, but he kept his eyes on the road, both hands gripping the steering wheel.

'No, not him.'

'Oh, so expelled, left?'

'Hey, what's with the Spanish Inquisition?' Moth asked. 'I just said I spoke with a mate, thought you'd approve.'

'Shit, sorry,' Kit said, and let out his exasperation with a long breath, sat back from the wheel and repeated the deep sigh. 'Been a frustrating day.'

'I can tell, you are well wound up,' Moth said, his voice fluffed up with irritation too.

'Did you do anything else good?' Kit asked.

'Spent most of your money at McDonald's,' Moth said.

'I deserved that,' Kit said, smiling across at Moth who had his bag clutched to his chest in annoyance. 'Sorry for being an arse, I'll make it up to you. Let's get some supplies and go camping.'

He pulled up outside the Tesco Express.

'Come on, come choose some food,' Kit said to Moth. 'Ignore me being a dick and help me relax a bit. I could do with forgetting this job.'

'Do you normally get this wound up with work?'

'I can do,' Kit says. 'It depends a lot on the client.'

'Now, THAT,' said Kit. 'That is a view. What do you think?'

'Are we allowed to camp here?'

'Who gives a shit? Look at this, it's awesome.'

'It won't be so awesome if we get kicked out halfway through the night.'

'We won't. It'll either be this evening or first thing in the morning,' Kit said. 'Dog walkers. Bitching about rubbish on the beach while their dogs shit on the sand.

'You've done this before?'

'Once or twice,' Kit said. 'It's been a while though, it's amazing how the time goes by.'

'Old man,' Moth mocked him.

'Get the fucking tent up,' Kit retorted.

'Grumpy old man.'

Kit looked out across the bay, listening to Moth open the back door, to the sound of boxes gliding along the carpeted floor. The sun was lingering, turning the sky deeper blue and lighting up the horizon with the start of an impressive sunset. He hadn't been here since he and Kate camped. Years ago, during one of her trips down to the university, the famous alumna giving a speech.

Afterwards, driving round the headland, they had camped on the deserted beach in their ball clothes. Making love in the tent with all her petticoats getting in the way until he'd thrown the underskirt out of the tent. The morning dog walkers had not been impressed when they found it skittering down the beach. Kate had been so polite about having it back. Humiliated them standing in front of the tent in just her pants in the early morning light. Coming back in with her nipples pert enough to hang a coat off. Overwhelming him with her confidence. He still wondered if he should have... but no, no point having regrets.

He went to help Moth unload the tent.

The intense blue was giving way to the dying flame of the sun by the time they had the tent up, fading their chilled fingers into blurred edges. A brief spurt of anger had turned to laughter as they got it upside down twice. Done, they stood back with beer, Coke and pride in their achievement.

'Now, food. Let's get that camp stove going.' Kit handed Moth his beer and went to the boxes arrayed on the ground. 'Go find some stones for the fire.'

Moth put the bottles down on a large stone that rocked them at a precarious angle and walked away from him along the beach, bending down to pick up what stones he could. Kit unloaded the camp stove, found the saucepans. The sea breeze was blowing the cobwebs of the old house off him and memories of Kate were making him feel good again. She had been younger too, moaning at him for making her camp but full of fun with it too. They had bathed naked in the night sea, screaming at the cold and streaking back up the beach to warm each other up.

He watched Moth walking in the sand, his shoes kicked off, his trousers rolled up to his calves. He had an armful of stones and was searching for more. Whatever he'd been up to all day he looked chilled out. Kit lit the stove and listened to the fizzing escape of gas as it waited to catch the light. The blue wavering flame dancing in the wind round its orange centre. Moth wandered back along the beach towards him.

'Hope this is enough,' he said.

'Great, see how big a circle you can make for a fire,' Kit said. 'Put it there, near enough to keep us warm, it's going to get bloody cold as soon as that sun disappears.'

'You don't seem to give a shit much about whether we're allowed to do this or not,' Moth said.

'I try not to worry about stuff until it comes up,' Kit said. 'You can spend too much time doing that.'

'I'd like to get to that place,' Moth said, building a circle of sea-worn stones in the sand.

'You make a choice, Moth,' Kit said. 'Do it, or worry about it and don't do it.'

'That simple?'

'No, not simple, determined,' Kit said. 'If you want something, make your mind up to do it, and be prepared to take the consequences. What's the point in thinking about it from every angle, worrying about it? You'll just find another reason not to do it.'

'Some might say that was selfish.'

'Yes, and people do, have, will.' Kit tipped the carton of soup into the pan. 'The ones who didn't, because they couldn't grow a set, and resent anyone else who has. Public opinion or personal destiny? Your choice.'

'So where are you going right now?'

'What?'

'How's this personal destiny policy of yours going?'

'Hah,' Kit said, stirring soup. Watching how it parted round the spoon, reverted to the mass in its wake. 'Interesting, actually, thank you for asking. Right now, I'm on the cusp myself.'

'On the cusp?'

'Hmm, sort of stuck between two possible routes, deciding which way to go. Life-changing sort of shit, you know?'

'Yeah, I know.' Moth knelt on the sand, began building the fire inside the stone circle. The sun was setting on the estuary behind him as it dived into the Irish Sea, lighting up his hair.

Kit grabbed his beer from the rock, raised it at Moth. 'I need a reason to do stuff like this Moth. You're a good reason, thank you.'

He wondered if that was what he'd been to Kate, a good

reason. If that was all he'd been. He looked up at the night sky chasing the indigo down.

'We'd best get some headtorches. It's going to get dark quick out here.'

'IT'S BEEN A BLAST, THANKS.' Moth hoisted his bag onto his shoulder, looking around Cardiff train station.

'It's gone too quick,' Kit said. 'Hope you're not knackered.'

'In a good way, I think,' Moth said.

Kit put his hand out and took Moth's. He was sad to see him go. It had been good having someone to kick around with, even if he was itching to get back to work. Moth shook his hand and started to walk away.

'I'll be up at May bank holiday, see you then,' Kit said.

'Yeah, will do.' Moth turned and walked towards the platforms.

Kit dragged a hand through his hair, there was sand in it. He needed to get home and have a shower. He glanced towards the entrance and, when he looked back at the platforms, Moth had gone. How easily he came and went. Youth itself.

17

After the wedding guests left we were a happy home. The bungalow Father was letting to Richard and I was not to be ready for a few more months and we filled Riverdell with laughter and joy. I had found a man who would be the mould we all tried to beat and I believed then, as I did for many years after, that the same joy was due in course to my friends.

Ted lingered on with us that summer.

He was thirty-seven the year I married and had long since left the army to build his own business in India. The ravaging anger he had felt at the damage done by partition had faded as much as his youth, and disappointments in life had brought him closer to forgiving Father, if not quite to the threshold. Even the antagonism between them seemed reduced in the scale of our family happiness. It was as though, through bringing Richard into the family, and with it his own network of uncles, cousins and siblings, we had padded out the seams of what wore thin between them. Father's grief at losing two wives, Ted's and mine at losing our mothers, and their disappointment with each other were smothered by the new wave of family and optimism.

Rose and Kate would argue politics all evening long with Father and Ted. Rose passionate about feminism, socialism, human rights. Bitter about racism, nationalism, colonialism. Determined to prod at Ted, to see where his true thoughts lay. Was he the anti-colonialist he protested himself to be, or just the rich son playing at independence? Kate backing her up with all the research of her dissertation specialising in the intricacies of colonial independence. Father and Ted finding themselves sometimes in agreement, sometimes at odds and wondering what to make of the two fierce young women harassing them. Which left Richard and I in peace to listen, cuddling on the sofa and wondering how long we must stay before we could retire to bed, and Beth, curled up in a buttoned slipper chair in the window of the great drawing room. Looking out across the balcony towards the diminishing sun where it slid behind the curve of the valley. Listening to us and refusing to engage when she was called on for an opinion.

It was Ted who took the picture. The one I pass daily on the piano in the hall.

Richard was out working on the farm and Father was locked up in his study. I had been reading in the drawing room and needed a snack so headed out to the hall. Beth was sat at the piano, her fingers soft on the keys. With uncanny exactness the kitchen door opened admitting Kate, heading to change from a swim, and the front door opened to admit Rose, who had been up in town.

'Come play with me,' Beth insisted. 'I can't remember the last time we played together, can you?'

'Pretty sure it was about the time you got your arse

covered in cowpat by Richard,' Kate tossed at me. 'You know how distracted she's been since then.'

'No, it was definitely that night you told Father the Conservative Party was full of right-wing fascist murderers,' I tossed the insult over to Rose and reluctantly put the book-mark in *War and Peace*.

'Oh, please,' said Rose. 'We all know it's Beth's fault we no longer play together, ever since we tortured Greensleeves she can't bear us to try.'

By turns we all got to the stool. Rose going to sit at the far end, Beth shunting along to make space for Kate, myself last. Rose and I were the weaker players by far.

'What shall we play?' Rose asked. 'Please let it be simple.'

'How about a rousing political march?' Kate said. 'That should suit you.'

'Father's in the study,' I added. 'Why don't we play the USSR anthem and be done with it?'

'What a bloody good idea,' Rose said.

'No.' Beth put a hand over hers. 'I'm heartily tired of all your politics and vigour. How about we play something sweet and romantic for a change.'

'Ick,' Rose said.

'There's nothing ick about romance,' Beth nudged her in the ribs.

'What do you suggest then?' Kate asked. 'We're all a little rusty.'

'Let's do Clair de Lune then,' Beth suggested.

We all groaned. Out of the limited pieces which Beth and Kate had managed to adjust for our four hands, this had always been one of her favourites and our least accomplished.

'You know it's going the same way as Greensleeves, right?' Rose teased her.

But we all tried, for her sake. It took several practices. My hands hitting Kate's where the close notes overlapped and Rose managing to get the wrong notes entirely at her end. But still, we got smoother. In the end we managed several runs through which were not bad and, laughing at each other, decided to give it one last go.

Ted came through from the kitchen, camera in hand, knowing we wouldn't break off in the middle. I've wondered since if he had been hiding behind the door until we were well into it. Kate pulled the plunging neckline of her robe self-consciously up and missed a few notes. Rose plonked even harder on her few keys with a scowl at his presence and irritated me immensely. She seemed determined to dislike Ted that summer. Beth never missed a note. She played her part beautifully, a smile on her face hidden beneath her cascading hair. Her neck crooked over the keys as though she could hear something the rest of us couldn't.

When it was over and Ted scolded for sneaking photos, Kate rushed off to dress, Rose went to rouse Father and I went to get my snack, *War and Peace* tucked back beneath my arm, and never thought any more of it. Leaving Beth in the hallway to close the piano, talking to Ted.

That was the last time we ever played together. If I had known that, I would have lingered longer, made them play more. Chased Ted away myself to leave us in peace. But hindsight is cruel like that. It teases you with your own stupidity.

Because I was stupid that summer. I was so wrapped up in my own romance that I never noticed the one beneath my nose until it unfolded in the first days of September like a late blooming rose.

Beth had found the first place she wished to explore, courtesy of my brother's blushing invitation to travel to India. From the smile on Beth's lips and the warmth in her cheeks we all realised too late what was happening. Rose exploded with anxiety, just as she was about to go back to university. Father, worried about Beth's health, was dead-set against it and the old turmoil between him and Ted flared back up in an instant. Richard tried to get me to stay out of it, but the arguments were so awful, I couldn't bear that our perfect summer was being ruined. I tried to reason with Beth, reminded her of the language teachers' correspondence course she had signed up to do, which she had a week in London to attend in commencement. Spoke with Ted that her health was not suited to it yet, to give it time, let her recover first. Pleaded with Father to not fall out with Ted.

Rose screamed blue murder at us all, barely softening her tone for Beth. 'You can't go to bloody India by yourself. You've never travelled further than the end of the corridor without one of us. And what the hell are you going to do out there?' Refusing point blank to accept what was happening.

To no avail. Beth had decided for herself and would not be swayed. It was not just the thought of India that inspired her. She had fallen in love with Ted himself.

In the midst of it all, swamped with guilt about my own happiness and distraction, I never noticed Kate.

Kate it seemed had watched us all more closely than I, and saw it coming before the rest of us. Kate was quiet, keeping her own counsel as the household descended into chaos.

It was Kate who insisted Ted go home to India while Beth gave it time to consider. She told him it would be more clearly her own decision if she came afterwards and he would not be seen as the scapegoat.

It was Kate who told Beth she was a fool if she didn't do her course. How could any of us support her throwing away her own decisions to run off to India after a man she hardly knew who was sixteen years her senior?

It was Kate who told Father 'better the devil you know' and persuaded him to look into the financial resources available to Beth if she became a language teacher, to think about the painful reality of Beth's lack of assistance in life.

And it was Kate who told Rose to calm the hell down and stop thinking about her bloody self, which shook her into silence.

'You're right about one thing, Rosie,' Kate said, patting Rose's hand where she sat dumbfounded by the vehemence of the statement that she was being selfish. The three of us were in Kate's bedroom late one evening. Beth had gone to bed already and Rose was too wound up to go to their shared bedroom. Ted had left that morning and Rose couldn't bear Beth's moping over his absence. 'She can't go alone.'

'You're talking like this is actually going to happen,' Rose complained. 'It will all blow over now he's bloody gone.'

'You keep trying to convince yourself and you're going to be miserable for longer,' Kate said. 'This is happening, whether we like it or not. Have you seen Beth this summer? Have you really looked at her? She's lit up like we haven't seen her in years. And what about Ted, staying longer than he ever has before?'

'But I thought that was...'

'What? You thought she was being swept along on Elsa's wave of happiness?' Kate teased, a strained edge to her voice.

'Well, you weren't the only one wrong about what was lighting Beth or Ted up. Get over it.'

'And you honestly think this is okay?' Rose demanded, bouncing off the bed and over to the window. 'Beth and Ted, for Christ's sake? No offence, Elsa, but he's practically old enough to be her father!'

'So what if he's older? Maybe she needs a father figure in some way. Anyway, he's a sound man, and a good looking, intelligent, charming one at that,' Kate said, throwing herself backwards on the bed and staring at the ceiling. 'Hardly surprising one of us fell for him, is it?'

Rose stood at the window in bitter silence.

I felt guilty all over again for loving the man who was causing the misery.

Kate stared at the ceiling, thinking, waiting.

'What do you mean, then,' Rose finally turned to look at us. 'She can't go alone?'

Kate sat up on the bed, a brave smile on her face. 'I mean that one of us is going to have to go with her. I've checked with the course she's doing. If she does the first week in London, she can do the remaining five weeks by correspondence. There's a cruise ship leaving Southampton for Bombay three days later. It's a five week journey with stop-offs. She can finish the course by the time she arrives. But you're right, she can't go alone. Elsa can't leave now and her father won't set foot in India over his own dead body. So it's either you, or me.'

'But you're both due back at Swansea,' I pointed out.

Rose and Kate ignored me. Staring at one another across the curving metal bed end of Kate's bed. She'd shared with me right up until Richard and I were married and moved into a room of our own on our wedding night. Accepting her solitude with a bright smile and practically throwing me and my clothes out of my own bedroom door. Now here she was, facing an even tougher abandonment.

'You can't afford to miss months off your Masters, you'll never catch up.' I tried once more to protest.

'Five more weeks with Beth, or a Masters?' Rose asked. 'That's the choice is it?'

'Looks like,' Kate said. 'Not the choice I would have asked for, either.'

'I guess it's not the choices we get, but the decisions we make that count, right?' Rose asked her with a sad smile.

'Something like that,' Kate said, wrapping her arms around her waist. And we all cried together. The world felt like it was ending, and we were the ones ripping it apart when all we wanted was to hold it together.

Very much like now.

But, as they showed me then, the choice of how we react is all we are ever granted in life.

18

He was alone for breakfast. Driven from his bad night in the dorm by their rising air currents. The last few days a blur of fatigue and victory. Stretched out like the buffet meats, salted and pungent.

The slog of battling up hill, cruising back down. He'd passed through Corvara he knew, but the details of it were hazy. Looking at the notebook, trying to think where he'd slept on nights 263 and 264.

You slept in the tent.

It mattered that he filled them in. He didn't like their emptiness, the way it emphasised the date he would rub out later, today's date with Kit. He was nowhere near Lovere, and not even heading that way. He was heading south, east, to Venice. If he could just remember where he'd slept.

You slept in the tent in the mountains.

Moth wrote Day 263. 21st March. Dolomiti. Day 264. 22nd March. Dolomiti.

You spent last night with a bunch of farting wankers.

Day 265. 23rd March. Campolongo Pass.

He'd spent the long afternoon crawling his way up the mountain to the Campolongo Pass. The day had been a trance of pain and focus. Ending in a shared dorm with five strangers who were asleep by the time he dragged himself out of the shower and into the lowest bunk. The room a cocoon of foot odour, farts and twice-worn underwear. The scent of men a wall he walked into behind the door, making him shudder.

For once you smell better than the rest.

He sat on the side of the bed, feeling the strangeness of his feet in socks on the warm heated floor. Marvelling at the freedom of his toes, trying to push away the crawling skin on his back. Lay down rigid with discomfort.

This bunk feels smaller than the tent.

Trying not to move, to disturb them. Every time his eyes closed the guy in the bunk above stirred and made him jump. He slipped in and out of an exhausted numbness between their movements. Lying frozen in the early hours when the guy above him slackened off his morning wood, turned over and went back to sleep. Not trusting sleep afterwards, too tired to get up and leave.

They were still snoring while he filled himself to the brim with hot food. It would slow him down for the start of the day, but he'd paid for the pleasure and didn't want to waste it. Hot porridge, meat, cheese, fresh bread, juice. The guy cooking and serving was on autopilot when he walked into the dining room, but he soon woke up to having an audience

'You're early for your season,' he told Moth.

'Trying to avoid the crowds,' Moth offered, trying to avoid engagement by looking at his food. The guy was too cheerful for that.

'Yeah, there's a reason they don't come this early,' he said.

'It's a toss-up,' Moth agreed. 'Bad weather or empty roads.'

'You don't like company?'

'Prefer my own.'

'Well, who doesn't,' the guy agreed as he headed back to the kitchen. 'But be careful too, the weather is not good on the passes today.'

'I'm hoping I'll miss the worst of it.'

The guy shrugged at his optimism. He was tall, spilling out of the kitchen apron he'd chucked around his body. His back muscles straining against the fitted top as he walked away. Contours rippling down his back like altitude lines on a map. Moth bet he could out-ski any of the guests struggling out of their drink-laden torpors.

'Make sure you take the numbers off the board.' He pointed at the general notice board on the far wall. It had a large blown-up map of the area on it, with hotels and phone numbers, emergency contacts and shelters shown on it.

They're no use to you.

'Will do,' he said.

He took extra fresh bread, fruit and meat with him from the sideboard whilst the guy was in the kitchen. Headed down to the basement lockers for the panniers and out the back of the building to find the bike.

He was warm through by the time all was set. Unused to the thin merino base layer he'd filched off the end of the bunk next to him. It fitted a treat. After hearing the weather forecast, he was grateful to the benevolence that had put it in his path.

Never turn down a gift from the Gods, or fools either.

The man asleep in the bunk had an excess of expensive clothes thrown all over the bed and floor. Flaunting his worth. Needing his buddies to know he could do better and was only tolerating the lodge for their sake. Labels facing outwards as Moth's eyes clocked the value in the weak morning light.

He'd resisted buying one before leaving England, collecting his cache of belongings. Each one a deliberation over cost, weight, space and multiplicity of purpose. He was careful. Never buying more than one thing from any shop. Careful to spread his purchases around the various towns he visited. Bristol, Swansea, Shrewsbury, Hereford, Rugby. The merino an indulgence he couldn't afford.

Moth wriggled his toes in the trainers. Loosening their stiffness up as he headed down the side of the building towards the road. Getting the feel for the pedals. The shoes had been by far the hardest choice to make.

Bike shoes and trainers. Bike shoes or trainers.

The experts said he needed proper bike shoes to do long-haul cycling. His inexperience, his need for flexibility and the imperative to fit in, to look local, not a long-distance athlete, these weighed more mightily than the experts' advice.

None of the books mentioned what Moth considered to be his best advantage. Moth's morality was less picky than the writers of those books. His financial resources more limited. His theory towards the 'acquisition' of belongings and food, along with his plan, motivated every choice he made.

Steal and be free. Or not steal and be dependant.

Stealing from Elsa had been hardest. Until he realised that nothing he ever took was missed. And Moth was careful with what he took. Isabelle's amassed goods a lesson in the invaluable essence of so many valuables.

Whose is it, where did it come from, will it ever be used?

Stealing from Elsa had been useful for bolstering the

account and buying provisions. But more than that, it had been an education in how other people lived. Stealing from Mrs Staines had been no more than helping Marge with the overwhelming housework. A spate of crime so petty that it was put down to poor memory or decluttering. Covered by working for James at the farm and Kate at the pub.

Stolen goods no one can tie you to selling.

That was the beauty of Ben. Ben had taught him about chain removal of evidence. Send everything on several stages. Never be connected to the further stage.

One day Ben will do serious time.

There was no way Moth could see him avoiding it. Even with all his removal stages.

Doesn't mean you need to share the invoice.

That was why it worked for now. Once he hit sixteen, he wouldn't be a young offender, it would be serious time if Ben dragged him down too. Moth had twelve months left before he'd have to find a real job, a real way of living.

Choices and consequences. Like Kit said.

The guy in the dorm had been an arrogant slob with his gear. Now he'd have to pay the consequence.

You'll be over the summit by the time he knows it's missing.

Looking forward to the view down into the next valley and the haul of the day. Across switchbacks and back up to the Passo Pordoi.

Your final big one.

The Campolongo pass came. The view did not. The vista of earth and heaven lost in the void. Moth warm inside with exertion and his stolen base layer. Crisp on the outside at every point that his skin contacted the air. Face, neck, knees, calves. He stopped as soon as he reached a layby. Pulled trousers on over the shorts. Pulled the waterproof cape from his bag. Fixed glasses over his helmet. The cold would turn to moisture as he dropped. It was no good stopping when the weather turned foul.

He swept down from the hidden pass into Arabba. Keeping the pace controlled, testing the road for ice. The chill air looming overhead. Kilometres swallowed by gravity. He ignored the town, cycling on, sweating and suffering. Stopping. Resting. Eating. Starting again. Uphill. Kilometres stretched out by effort. The final summit pulling him back into pain.

The incline up to the Pordoi Pass rippling through his leg muscles and into his pelvis and back, asking more, a little bit more...

... extra effort, you can find it, don't stop...

... the ache deepening and hurting.

The bike began to slip as ice caught on the road. Flurries of stinging snow whirling like crazed butterflies. Driving against his face, biting his hands, whipping the cargo trousers against his calves. He pulled the glasses down for relief, put his gloves on. His knees stiff with cold where the cycling shorts stopped under the cotton trousers. Clarity and vision fading to nothing more than the narrow strip of road in front of him.

The world reduced.

To nothing. Nothing can touch you.

Compressed by the weight of his foul weather gear, the vicious sky and impossible incline, to himself, the bike, and a road that was threatening to disappear.

To nothing.

Numbing chill and fear threading through him. The tyres

skidded on the road and he wobbled sideways, his gut twisting and hands clenching as he tried to correct the bike.

You could ride straight off the top of the world.

He straightened up and the wheels gripped again. Relief flooding through his veins. He grinned.

You're insane.

Only an idiot would be out here on a bike.

In a snowstorm.

On a mountain.

Going higher.

Moth whooped, a great gust of breath that froze as it left him. He straightened up from the handlebars and put an arm out to feel the clouds. His fingertips seemed fainter at the end of his arm.

You really are disappearing.

The wind screeched at him. He roared into the storm. Feeling the warmth of the breath rising through him. Fear mixed with defiant glee. He was here, all alone, nothing between him and God.

Well that's perfect.

He had a few choice words he wanted to exchange anyway.

As the tyres stuck in the snow gathering on the road and the visibility dropped, Moth crept closer to the middle of the road and the pallid anchor of the white line. The threat of an oncoming vehicle filling him with energy. He pushed on harder. Bent over the bars and made his legs work to bursting point. Time warped to a rotation of the wheels. The seconds unhinged by the weather. He didn't dare stop.

You must get through the pass soon.

Breath gasping inwards. Colder than imaginable. Cutting into the heat from his lungs and stinging the back of his throat. The snow sticking on the road. The white line wavering into the background. His eyes straining to focus. Glasses clogging with the snow. He pushed a hand up to wipe them.

Lights came from nowhere, pulsing towards him and erupting with screams.

Jesus. Fucking. Christ. MOVE.

The snow plough shattering his hidden world of wind and snow. He lunged away from the white line, skidding across the lane with the bike, throwing a leg down to stop himself from toppling as the tyres and brakes fought each other and the snow. Jamming. The rear tire locking, rising, curving round him with a thin squeak of rubber. The crossbar slamming into his body, crushing his balls. Agonised breath stuck in his chest, pain exploding upwards, grappling with panic as the rising rear wheel threatened to tip him over the handlebars. Feet slipping in their trainers. Toes trying to grip the road. A cloud of stirred snow billowing towards him. Covering him over, settling into the space behind, the air sucking at him in vengeance. Pulling the bike back down. Behind, several cars crawled along, tooting contempt at him.

Go fuck yourselves fucking sideways...

'... you wankers,' he screamed at them. Spitting out snow.

He steadied himself, righted the bike. Pushed off on shaking legs, his arms rigid with shock, locked on the handlebars. The lane he rode was covered over, the centre line gone, but beside it lay a clear expanse of tarmac. Tempting him. He wobbled closer back to the middle and carried on.

You need to get off this mountain now.

The risk stayed liquid in his muscles. Exhilaration turning to cold fear and reality. If a plough came up behind, he'd have to risk swerving into the other lane and pray nothing else was coming at the time. There was only one way off. No shortcut. Over and down.

Yeah, well, you've been in worse places.

Because he had. Before Riverdell. Before his parents died.

They didn't die. He killed her.

Before all of that.

Fear pumped his legs harder. Memories like treacle threatening to drag him backwards. Snow and fear pushing him forwards.

Keep going. Keep going.

It had felt like this. Impossible. Undoable. A grimness he could never escape.

The subtle nuance of pain shifted. The muscles gearing down a notch before he could see the change. Life, land, fear, levelling off.

Keep going. You're there, you're there.

He pushed on, missing the signs that told him it was done. The view that was his reward. The mountain that was his glorious achievement. The achievement declining without glory. Indifferent to him. Feeling the loss in the increasing speed of the bike and the ease of his legs.

You missed it.

He swept out from the clouds feet first. Felt the sky lighten and the cold retreat. Every pedal turn taking him lower, the bike picking up speed. The victory lost in bad weather.

One more shitstorm sweeping you aside.

He wanted to go back. Bury himself in that moment. Feeling alive on the verge of death.

You can't go back.

When he swept off the open mountain and back into the trees he stopped. The morning was gone. His breakfast was burnt out. Cold seeping in the moment he stopped. Fingers stiff and shaking in relief as he peeled them off the handlebars. He pulled the tent out of the bags, threw it over the bike and crawled in. Focused on food, on drinking, on resting. Crushed with gratitude for the merino top. Recovering in its invisible shell. His throat swelling, blocking the food, when he remembered the softness tempting his hand that morning.

It was late afternoon when he pulled the tent down. Eased sore toes back into the trainers and laced them up. His fingers were looser now and managed the knots in the hacked-off laces. There might be no trailing ends to cause a hazard...

... but they're a pain in the arse to tie.

The clouds had retreated, peeling off the top of the mountains. They danced above him. Typical. Just after he cycled through it.

You still did it.

All those days ago, when he left Riverdell and Nat, he could not have done what he did today. He would have doubted himself. Two-hundred-and-sixty-five days on the road had taught him a lot about making decisions and facing the consequences.

He'd left England a pissed-off kid. Wanting his own choices. Hating the place everyone kept trying to put him in. A wall of ugly truth so high between what they thought of him and what he knew, it had seemed unscaleable. He'd just cycled over a mountain in a snowstorm and made it down the other side. He was a lot closer to the future he was building than the past he'd left behind.

He got back on the bike in silence. Looked down the road. So, it hadn't been what he'd hoped. Cycling over the mountain. He remembered this feeling too. The sense that you were moving towards something immense. Something that would change you. Something that would make you new. Within your hand reach. Fingers touching. Someone.

Snatched away by the clouds of others. Swept up and dragged off.

And what was left for you?

Choice. That was what he'd seen. You could whinge about it. Or you could keep going forward. Adjusting. Recalibrating. Letting go of a wild hope. Realising there never was anyone else to do it with him. He had to do it alone.

It was a small step you had to take, from one place to another.

But it was the hardest one.

Walking away from something imperceptible. Into something unknown.

You keep looking behind you, that snow plough's going to come back.

Moth looked down the mountain. Well, he'd done it. Proved his own worth. It was all behind him now. What was the point in looking back?

It's what lies ahead that counts.

He pushed off. One foot lingering, the other taking leave of the road. Gravity taking hold, pulling him down the mountain. Regret pushed out of him by the wind. Determination a sharp line on the tarmac.

You always make such a fuss about that first step.

ISABELLE WALKED into the kitchen with her breath held. It was becoming the norm. The house had become shark-infested waters to swim through. On either side, the safety of her attic bedroom and her basement workroom. In between, the silt of Hester's misery.

The morning light was dull, heavy clouds hanging over the castle and shadowing the courtyard windows. Elsa, Nat and Hester were all there.

Hester had all but moved back into Riverdell. From the limited amount of information Isabelle had gathered from Kate, there was no need for this. Rob had left their home, walking out with a bag and his favourite chessboard. He'd filed divorce papers on the grounds of unreasonable behaviour and was making no claim to any of the property. In Kate's opinion he was an idiot. The precise nature of his idiocy changed from day to day, but Kate's irritation with Rob was swallowed by her greater fury with Hester's martyrdom of the event. That her desire for children could be considered unreasonable. It was like Rob had taken her mallet away and handed her a sledgehammer instead. Kate might be caustic for it, but at least she broke up the atmosphere when she was there, which unfortunately she wasn't.

'Morning,' Isabelle said to the room in general.

'Good morning,' Nat said.

'Morning,' Elsa said, stood before the sink. She'd dropped the darling from her greetings. Isabelle had noticed it like an anchor hitting concrete. 'What's your day entail?'

'The usual.' Isabelle moved to get a coffee. 'More sorting, more sewing.'

Hester watched from the kitchen table as she walked across the room. She was drinking tea and helping Nat get her bag ready for school.

'Kit's promised to assess the budget for replacing the curtains when he's here.' Elsa placed a dripping plate in the rack on the draining board.

That was about another ten days of trying to pretend she had any intention of remaking those curtains. May had disappeared. Into a storm released by Rob. In Moth's absence in Bristol. In Hester's presence at Riverdell. Two days left before the start of June and the school half-term. If it wasn't for the last-minute holiday Elsa had booked, Isabelle would have packed her bags for India. The horrifying thought of Hester in the house solidly with Nat off school seemed to arrive in her head on the same day that Elsa announced she was taking them all to Swansea for a week's break. She couldn't remember the last time Elsa had taken a holiday. Ever. Was still stunned into breathless amazement when Elsa added she'd cancelled all the guest bookings for the same week. She knew that had never happened. Ever. It was like another current in the river that Isabelle couldn't see. Only the waving of weeds to tell her something was going on.

'Why do we have to wait for Kit to make the decisions?' Hester filled her silent pondering.

She really needed to be more focused for these morning incursions into the kitchen.

'Kit knows the budgets inside out, darling,' Elsa breezed. 'I don't spend a penny unless it fits in with the big picture.'

'You should let me look at the budgets, Mother,' Hester said. 'You've been doing this all by yourself for long enough. It shouldn't be Kit's job to help you.'

Isabelle focused on the coffee machine. On the dripping of the coffee into her mug, on the shiny grid of the drip tray, on the curve of the cup handle.

'Well it is his job,' Elsa chattered away to the sink full of bubbles. 'I asked Kit to help and it's allowed you and James to run your own lives. Thank you for the offer, darling, but we don't need help. The house is managing so well entirely thanks to Kit's enormous experience.'

Isabelle let the fizzing air warm the milk and turned the handle of the cup so that it lay aligned with the interwoven vine design on the saucer. She counted the seconds of silence as they ticked by, interspersed with Nat rummaging through papers and books, the clunk of Hester's cup returning to the table.

The reason Kit did it all was because of David, which Elsa wouldn't say in front of Nat. Kit had been called in when Elsa and David first fell out. After Richard died, and David had wanted to sell it all, distribute the estate amongst the family. Kit had been Elsa's means to prove she could cope. But none of that could fit in the tight air of the kitchen. In the vortex of David's daughter needing to get to school.

'Come on, Nat,' Hester said, standing up. 'Time to go.'

'I'll get ready,' Nat said.

She stood up, gathered her bag and went to give Elsa a quick hug by the sink. Elsa returned the hug with a surprised, soggy hand, held high. Suds dripping onto the floor. These hugs were a recent and unpredictable occurrence. Isabelle had yet to experience one but, right then, she was glad for Elsa.

Nat took her bag through to the back hall. 'See you later, Isabelle.'

'Hope it goes well today,' Isabelle said. 'Remember, two more days and its half-term.' Nat grinned back at her.

Hester went and put her cup on the work surface beside her mother, claiming intimacy, making sure her voice spread as far as Isabelle but not through the back door to Nat.

'I know why you got Kit involved, Mother. I know what happened with David. I'm just saying, we could change things now. My... life... has changed. Maybe it's time to start thinking about what happens with Riverdell, about who has to look after it next.'

Isabelle couldn't drag out making coffee any longer. She went and sat down at the table, pulling a chair out, willing it not to scrape. She sipped the coffee and let its intense flavour infuse her, tried to let her breath out. Somewhere around her third rib, right where she was holding her breath, a faint fluttering was demanding her attention.

Two months ago, when she first came home, this fluttering would have been anxiety about being in the same room as Hester. Even two weeks ago it would have been looking at the door. But Hester had a point, after all.

Maybe it was time to think about the future.

Maybe they were all thinking about the future and not talking about it.

Thoughts that sidled up to the fluttering and stirred it further.

It had started during the week Moth had been away with Kit. When the fallout of Hester's separation from Rob had evolved into her constant presence at Riverdell. When Isabelle faced again how little she was needed at Riverdell if Moth wasn't there. When she began to consider that her endless sense of not belonging at Riverdell was just that; a place she didn't belong.

'I think Hester's right,' Isabelle said.

She gulped as it came out. She hadn't meant to say it. The thoughts and the words had run together. She pulled a knee up to her chest on the chair as the two women turned to look at her. Hester looking as though she was choking on a fish bone, stuck between irritation that Isabelle had dared to comment and confusion that she'd backed her up. Elsa stunned, her arms poised above the bowl of crockery, her mouth trying to respond.

'I'm just saying, I think she has a point.'

Nat walked into the room and said, 'I'm ready.'

Hester looked at Nat and smiled. A smile that dispersed like sun behind a cloud as she looked back at Isabelle. Isabelle returned the look, one knee hugged to her chest, the coffee cup raised between the table and her lips. The inner flutter increased. It was exhilarating. To sit there, perched in the eye of the storm and feel so liberated.

Hester walked past her, talking to Nat about her classes that day as they left the house. Elsa turned back to the washing up. As the sounds of Nat and Hester leaving diminished, Isabelle could hear the clink of china against itself, the swish of water, and the distant rumblings of guests upstairs. Isabelle watched Elsa's back, her methodical elbows, her hand placing cups upside down on the draining board, retreating behind her body. Tones of ochre infusing the russet skirt today. A remnant of a dining room set she'd upholstered. Isabelle remembered keeping back the pieces for her. A mustard line knitted in around the maple back of her cardigan.

'Where's Moth today?' she asked to break the silence.

'Up at Kate's, I think,' Elsa said. 'It seems to be getting harder to know where he is or what he's doing. Kit gave him a taste of independence, I fear.'

'He already had the taste for it,' Isabelle said. 'Kit gave him a break from worrying about Nat.'

'Perhaps,' said Elsa. 'He does need to try and stop worrying. I must make some decisions about him soon.'

'I'm not sure they're your decisions to make,' Isabelle said. In the weeks since Moth had come back, she'd noticed a change. He asked less, said less. Laughed more, did more. A change that she feared Elsa was missing.

'Do you know what he wants?' Elsa raised her hands from the bowl, staring out the window. Suds dripping down her elbows and onto her skirt.

'No,' said Isabelle. 'I don't think anyone does, but I feel like he's getting closer to knowing himself.'

'I envy him his confidence,' Elsa said. She noticed her dripping arms at last, tutted, and moved to find a tea towel. She came and sat at the table, taking her usual chair at the head and scrunching the tea towel up beneath her hand.

'It's hardly something you lack.' Isabelle looked at the faded pattern of the town printed on the linen. The map appearing and disappearing in the folds of Elsa's restless hands.

'I steal it,' Elsa said. 'I hide behind others. It used to be Richard. Now it's Kate, and Kit, and you. It's never been something I had a lot of myself.'

'You do a very good impression,' Isabelle said. 'I've always envied you.'

'Me?' said Elsa. 'Silly girl, what have you got to envy? I could never do what you've done. Take off for months at a time, travel, work, live away.'

'That always seems so easy.' Isabelle laughed. The sunlight lifted from behind the clouds and came in weak streaks through the windows, tilting itself upon the unsteady old stones of the floor and trying to prove itself. The rays were stragglers through thick cloud though and soon chased away. 'It's people that I struggle with.'

'You have confidence a-plenty, and don't let anyone tell you otherwise.' Elsa planted her elbow on the tea towel and hovered her hand over the table at Isabelle. 'I've known you since you were this high. You have strength that never wavers, a quietness in the way you carry it, kindness in the way you use it. Don't change that, darling, it serves you well.'

Isabelle blinked at her, swamped with warmth for the sudden approbation, eyes wrinkling in puzzlement, and asked 'Why so serious?'

'I'm worried, that's all,' Elsa said. 'I remember this from before, and it caused all sorts of misery.'

'This?'

'Yes, this, this sudden thinking about Riverdell. About what's going to happen with it.'

Isabelle put down her cup and reached a hand across the table to put it on Elsa's, where it had returned to scrunching up the tea towel. Elsa looked up at her, her brow caught in a crease, her eyes trying to smile.

'It's not like it was, before, with David,' Isabelle said. 'Maybe all this is happening for a reason. Hester's life changing, Moth and Nat's life changing, mine and James. Maybe it is time to embrace change and see where it takes us all.'

Elsa looked at her with a strange twist to her lips, holding her response back, so that Isabelle had to prod her with a reassuring smile and ask, 'What?'

'Change.' Elsa let the word out on a huge sigh. 'Oh, change is coming, I agree. I can feel it coming at me from every angle. It's scary Isabelle, and exciting. I have this strange feeling in my chest.' She reached a hand and tapped herself above the stomach, in the same place Isabelle had come to notice on herself. 'I keep thinking I ought to go see the doctor about it, but it's just that I haven't had it for such a long time, I've forgotten what it feels like. Excitement, and anxiety mixed in, because I can't see the future. I know things are going to change, but I can't see how. That's scary when you're my age.'

'It's scary at my age too,' Isabelle said. 'And no doubt even scarier for Moth and Nat.'

'I know things are going to change, darling.' Elsa moved her hand round beneath Isabelle's to squeeze it before releasing it. Folding up the tea towel into a tidy line, laying it over the edge of the table so that the far end dangled out of sight and pinning it down with her hand. 'The problem is, I'm not sure we're ready for it. Or that we'll like the changes that come.'

'Well, maybe it's time we got on with it and found out.'

The bell in the hallway rang. Elsa stood up, a habitual swift response, laughing at herself. 'Well some things stay the same, the guests still want their breakfast.' She moved to the door, looked back at Isabelle. 'Change rarely brings us what we want or hope for. Try not to be too disappointed, Isabelle, with what comes of it all. Very little of all this,' and she raised her hand to sweep across the room, encompassing all of their lives in the circumference of the kitchen, 'very little of it has ever been up to me to decide.'

'I'll try to remember that,' Isabelle said.

Elsa smiled and left the room, the closing door shushing into the gap behind her.

LATER THAT DAY Isabelle was holed up in a corral of boxes, feeling like the sole survivor of a town under attack, surrounded by decisions she couldn't make.

What to get rid of, who to give it to, what to repack and add to the growing pile of boxes that sat towered in an area marked in her head as 'moving'. She wasn't clear on where they were moving to. Plus, she had the strange feeling that their moving involved her moving. Looking at them increased the fluttering inside.

The door opened. She didn't have to look up to know it was Moth. The confidence with which he turned the handle, opened the heavy door, stepped inside. Moth had lost timidity in Bristol, his habit of staying back from the fray. She popped her head up over the boxes on the floor.

'Hey,' she said, giving him a direction to look in.

He walked across and stepped over the boxes into the circle in the middle.

'This all looks of the "staying" variety,' he said, as she pushed some fabrics aside and made space for him to sit down.

'Yep, this is all from India. Some of it's my mother's.'

'I guess it's going straight back in the boxes?'

'I'm struggling to weed much of it out,' Isabelle admitted. 'Though I have managed to put a few things aside.' She pointed at a small pile sat to the far edge of the circle.

'Big deal,' Moth said.

'Pretty pathetic, huh? What you been up to?'

'Training with Kate, went to see Mrs Staines, did some jobs for them, went for a ride, spent some time with Nat, avoided Elsa who's nagging about school, so went for another ride.'

'How's Nat?'

'Better,' said Moth. 'Looking forward to their trip away.'

'They all are.' Isabelle toyed with a piece of embroidered crewel, a scrap of green velvet with golden white embroidery that wouldn't be large enough for the face of a cushion. 'Even Hester seems buoyant about it, and I think Elsa needs the break.'

'I didn't realise the house in Swansea was hers,' Moth said. 'Kit didn't tell me that when we went.'

'You went to Swansea?' Moth had been circumspect about his time with Kit, as had Kit.

'Kit had to work one day.' Moth looked away at the various piles of fabric. 'He seemed a bit wound up about the house, but I didn't realise it was Elsa's.'

'Perhaps if she's down there for a week he might get some decisions out of her,' Isabelle said.

'Will she sell it, do you think?'

'I have no idea,' Isabelle said. 'I don't think even she knows what to do with it.'

'Nat can't wait to see the sea. It's been ages since we went.'

'Wish you were going?' She folded the tiny scrap of crewel and put it on the keeping pile.

'No, I'm glad they're going.' He picked at the dusty rug fibres they were sitting on, toying with the pile, smoothing the colours back and forth from shade to tone. 'It'll be pretty cool to have this place to ourselves for a change.'

'I can't remember the last time there were no guests in the house,' Isabelle said. 'It's going to be weird.'

'Exciting.' He drew a line down the pile with his forefinger, separating the tufts.

It was exciting. That Elsa had cancelled all bookings was an extraordinary event. She and Moth were going to be on their own for a week. Daunting too.

'You got any plans?' Isabelle asked.

'Nope,' Moth said. 'It might be my last chance to do nothing. I think Elsa's gearing up to send me back to school.'

'I get the impression you were hoping to avoid that until September?'

'That would have been pretty cool,' Moth said. 'But I guess it's up to her, after all.'

Isabelle looked at him. There was not one ounce of conviction in his voice that Elsa had any right to tell him what to do. He had Kit's influence written all over him.

'You got any plans?' Moth asked.

'Try and finish off this lot,' Isabelle said.

'Oh, how exciting!' Moth told her with precision-enunciated sarcasm.

She kicked him with her foot. He fell over in a mock death roll.

'Come on, is that the best you've got?' he asked. 'We could do anything! We could tear the whole house up and no one would know. We could eat breakfast in the study, camp in the garden, bathe in the river, and you want to spring clean?'

'I want to get it finished,' she protested. 'I meant to find something in all this, instead I've got side-tracked sorting it out. I want to pin down the purpose I thought I was hiding in here.'

'Maybe it isn't hiding in here?' Moth said. 'Maybe you need to go through all this to realise it's sitting out there in plain sight the whole time.'

'Yeah, thanks for that, Confucius,' Isabelle said. 'You've been spending too much time with Kate.'

'Has Kate been down here recently?'

'No, she refuses to come down until I stop wasting my time,' Isabelle said.

'Wow, that's sharp.'

'Yeah, you should be grateful you only have Elsa on your case about school,' Isabelle told him.

'If you insist on wasting the week away down here, I may go off doing some longer rides,' Moth said.

'Well, wasting or not, that's what I'm doing,' Isabelle said, sorting another scrap that was handkerchief size into the keeping pile.

'So, you won't mind if I go off for a few days?' Moth asked.

Isabelle looked back at him. Her chest tightened up again. The memory of their night in the river, of how they hadn't spoken about it since, sitting alongside the coming week alone, all of it made her feel unsettled. But the idea of him going off when she was left in charge felt more tremulous. She wanted to tell him he couldn't go but was too scared to insist on his staying.

'I want you to do what you want to do.'

'Really?' Moth asked, looking straight at her.

'Within reason.' Her hand reached into the box at her side, hoping for distraction, finding it empty.

'Whose reason?'

'Elsa's,' she offered. 'I don't want to get my arse kicked when she gets back.'

'You're no fun.'

'Where are you thinking of going?'

'Pardon?' Moth asked, blinking away the question.

'Next week, if you go off for a few days, where are you thinking of going?'

'Not sure,' Moth said, twiddling with the fabric pile nearest to him. 'Maybe see how far I get before I have to turn back.'

'That is a "no plans" policy,' Isabelle said. 'If you could just let me know where you go, I need to be a little bit responsible after all.'

'I'll tell you when I know.'

'You have a phone, you can keep in touch, that's all I'm asking.'

'Deal, on one condition,' Moth said.

Isabelle groaned and buried her head on her crossed knees.

'I'm serious.'

'What condition?' she grudged from her knees.

'We have to do some fun stuff too,' he said. 'Else I shall go off and sulk and refuse to get in touch.'

'You nasty little shit.' She looked up to see if he was joking.

'Why, thank you,' Moth said.

'Fine, counter condition,' Isabelle said. It was Moth's turn to groan. 'You have to help me get this finished.'

'Oh, come on,' he moaned. 'You can't even sort this out, how is anyone else supposed to do it for you?'

'I don't care, you have to.'

'Fine, see this piece here?' Moth asked, picking up the nearest piece of fabric. 'You should put that in the bin.'

'I can't, not that one,' Isabelle said. 'It was my mother's.'

'Then you must keep it,' he said.

'But I have too much already.'

'See!'

She threw a piece of fabric at him. He might be right, but that was not the point.

ISABELLE STOOD BAREFOOT on the front porch on the Saturday morning of half-term, with the camellia scent heavy in the late morning sunshine.

It had been a tense family breakfast as Hester loaded the car and refused to sit down and join them, Isabelle longing to trip her up as she traipsed in and out of the house. She would have given a lot for Kate's presence, but Kate was hectic with the bank holiday flood of tourists.

Now Elsa was putting her handbag in the foot well of the passenger seat, Hester loading the last few bags into the boot of her car and Nat talking to Moth through the open window of the back seat. Nat was full of excitement, released from a school she wasn't enjoying, and teasing Moth about all the seaside fun he was going to miss out on. Elsa walked back over to her.

'You're too old for me to tell you not to wreck the house,' Elsa said.

'But you're going to anyway?'

'I don't know what to tell you,' Elsa admitted. 'I've never left the house like this before.'

'Nothing is going to go wrong, try not to worry.'

'And you're sure you and Moth will be alright?'

'We'll be fine, trust me,' Isabelle said. 'As soon as you go, we're going to rearrange the furnishings, paint a wall in each room and mow a tennis court in the garden.'

'Don't tease me, Isabelle.'

Isabelle stepped forward, her toes hovering over the flagged brink, and gave her a hug. 'You need teasing. It's a holiday. Go away and enjoy yourself. Great hotel, pool, beach, what's not to look forward to? Even the weather's on your side.'

Elsa hugged her back. 'You're right, I know. This is going to be good for us, but it feels strange.' She stepped backwards off the porch and held Isabelle's hand as she pulled away. 'You enjoy it too. It's a rare, rare treat to have the house to yourself. Make the most of it.'

It felt like a parting shot, a warning that grabbed at Isabelle's flutters and churned them. But if it was, well, better that than no warning at all. If this was Elsa's way of giving her one last relaxed dose of her life at Riverdell, she would make the most of it.

'I'll try not to get used to it.' Isabelle grinned at her.

Elsa went to respond, squeezed her hand instead and walked away. Leaving Isabelle thinking she'd said something wrong.

Hester said goodbye to Moth and got in the car without so much as a look at her. Moth said goodbye to Nat and Elsa, staying out on the drive as Hester backed the car away from the garage and drove round the magnolia tree. Its flowers had long since decayed on the gravel, its shiny green leaves broad and vigorous, glinting in the sunlight. She watched the car disappear up the hill into town. Moth walked over and shut the gates behind them.

'Turn the sign around too,' Isabelle called.

He walked over to the right side, reached a hand through the metal bars and turned the heavy slate sign to CLOSED.

'I don't think this side is used to seeing the light of day,' Moth called back.

'No shit, Sherlock.'

He sauntered back over to her, standing on the gravel, kicking a few stones away from him. Neither of them spoke. Listening instead to the sound of traffic on the road, passing over the bridge.

'How long before we know they haven't forgotten something and are coming back?' Moth asked.

'No more than ten minutes I reckon,' Isabelle said. 'Though, from Hester's bad mood, I'd be surprised if she let them turn back.

'She did seem particularly sweet this morning.'

'I don't think she trusts us in charge of the house.'

'I'm not sure I trust her in charge of Nat,' Moth replied.

'Look, big brother,' Isabelle said. 'Like them or not, Nat is with family, and they will look after her. You need to stop worrying for a bit.'

'Family doesn't always look after one another.' Moth scowled at her as though she were being a fool.

She opened her mouth to protest and thought about breakfast, and the last few weeks of Hester's behaviour and David's decision to drive his wife to a drunken death. Kit and Kate, had they been there, would have passed a far more contemptuous comment.

'Fair comment,' Isabelle conceded. 'But those three will, they're like the Three Musketeers. Away from here for a week they're going to have a ball.'

'Are we done standing out on the drive yet?' He didn't look at all convinced by her opinion.

'Yep,' Isabelle said. 'Let's go see what the house feels like empty.'

They walked into the hall, Moth pushing the door to behind them. Standing on the rucked rug, Isabelle smoothed its haphazard corner with her toes, and listened. Nothing stirred. Anywhere. She felt Moth's height beside her.

Light was angling through the coloured glass on the landing, bending round the town to fall over the river. It streaked golden hues across the floorboards, a sliver sashaying around the banister and up to the door of the guests' dining room, reminding her of the day she'd come home. Isabelle walked across to the room, pushed the aperture wider, letting the sunlight within. The tables lay empty. She crossed the threshold. It was spotless. Gleaming wood, glistening windows, glitzy furnishings. She walked across to the wide windows.

'I've not been in here much,' Moth said from the doorway.

'I love this room,' Isabelle said. 'I remember when I first came here, before Elsa went into B&B, this was the formal drawing room. I was so overwhelmed, it seemed huge.' She turned from the wide bay, with its balcony supported on huge stone corbels. Moth was leaning on the doorjamb looking at her. 'I remember holding my father's hand, meeting Elsa for the first time, and Kate. Right here,' she pointed to where the furniture sat, 'there used to be the sofa that's now in the sitting room, but it was a different colour.'

'How old were you?'

'Six.'

'That's when you came to live here?'

'Hmm,' Isabelle said.

'That's pretty young to be left with strangers.'

'I suppose they thought they were doing the right thing,' Isabelle said. 'My father wanted the best for me, and he felt that was here in England, and he wouldn't leave India. Besides, I felt lucky. At our school there were children my age boarding who only saw their families once a year. I felt so lucky, living here with my own family. Having cousins at last.'

'You're not angry, when you look back at it?' Moth said.

'Not at all,' Isabelle said. 'Come on, let's move some furniture around.'

'Seriously? I thought you were joking about that?'

'Hopefully, so did Elsa.'

'We painting rooms too?'

'Maybe. Well, no, perhaps that's a step too far,' Isabelle said. She moved over to the tables, hefted the side of one and nodded at Moth to come and pick up the other side.

'And the tennis court?'

'I don't even know how to use a lawnmower.'

They moved the first table over to the far interior wall,

then another, then more. Stacking the chairs as they went until they created some space. They moved the gilded, ornate three-piece suite. The one that Kit had chosen for the guests because it looked great and felt awful, so they wouldn't be persuaded to spend too much time lingering in the sitting end of the room. They grunted in unison when they lifted the colossal sofa and staggered across the floor with it, dropping it just shy of their toes in front of the stacked chairs. Straightening up from it they surveyed the results. From the door to the space was a wide corridor they could move through. Beyond it, the room was cleared right into the bay window with its French doors. Moth moved to claim the space first.

'Awesome view,' he said, standing in front of the windows.

'I know, right?' Isabelle said.

'Why did they choose to use this for the guests?'

'Biggest room downstairs, only room by itself, grandest impact. Besides, Elsa always did prefer the sitting room. We hardly used this room. Christmas and important occasions only. She'd given it to Hester and I for a year as an art room.'

'All good reasons,' Moth said. 'Seems a shame not to keep the best room for yourself though.'

'Elsa would freak if she could see this,' Isabelle said, looking around.

'Getting cold feet?' Moth cocked his head to the side and cupped an ear. 'Is that the sound of wheels on gravel I hear?'

'Very funny,' Isabelle told him. 'Come on, you can help me move another sofa for that.'

'What?'

'You're the one who said no rules, come on, I want to sleep in here tonight,' Isabelle told him, heading out the door.

'What?' Moth said.

'Why not, when are we going to get the chance to do this again?'

He followed her through to the sitting room. Isabelle looked at the enormous four-seater sofa at the back of the room. They looked at one another and frowned. There was no way they would be able to lift that, they moved toward the nearest of the smaller two sofas, taking an end each, grunting at its weight.

'You sure we can't drag mattresses downstairs instead?' Moth asked.

'Brainwave, you genius!' Isabelle declared, dropping her end of the sofa. 'But we need some chairs. Which is your favourite chair in the house?'

'Eh, don't think I have one.' Moth said.

'Right, well mine's the one in the dining room, so let's get that. Then you can try out every chair in the house until you find one.'

'Every chair?' Moth asked. 'Even in Elsa's bedroom?'

'Might be a step too far,' Isabelle admitted.

'How about the study?'

'All yours.'

'Cool.'

'WE NEED A TV IN HERE,' Moth said.

'Am I boring you?'

'Don't you like watching TV?' he asked.

'Never done it much. I'm more of a film person.'

'Well, let's watch a film,' he said.

'I ought to do something more productive.'

'There must be a TV we can sneak in here from somewhere?'

Isabelle sighed and gave up. Moth grinned and sprung out of his chair, offering her a hand.

'Let's try the one in the morning room, though I have no idea how to connect aerials or stuff,' Isabelle said.

They walked into the morning room. It was dull with no sun on the window, cooler than the corridor.

'Does anyone even use this room?' Moth asked.

'James, sometimes, to watch the news, or Kit likes a television to himself. It's used if you want some privacy.'

'Instead of hiding in the dining room like you?'

'I don't hide in the dining room,' Isabelle protested. 'I retreat there, for solitude.'

'Honestly, there is such a small difference between those two things, it's like, not there.' Moth pulled his finger and thumb together to emphasise the point. He looked at the television on its low table beside the small fireplace. 'Right, let's do this.'

Isabelle watched Moth pulling the complex nest of wires apart behind it and winced. 'I hope you know how to put those back.'

'I do,' he said. 'Come on, grab that side, and hold the wires up.'

It wasn't heavy, but awkward, and Isabelle felt nervous about its fragility. They put it on the floor in the guest room and Moth set about looking at cables. Isabelle felt useless and went to make snacks. When she stuck her head out of the kitchen door, he was stood in the hall trying different cables out and laying a trip-hazard that stretched from the morning room into the guest room with numerous odd-looking connections on the way.

'I don't think this is going to work,' she told him from the doorway.

'Thanks for the support.'

'Do you know you talk to yourself when you're thinking?' she asked.

'Do you have any idea how you look when you're sewing?'

She went to reply, thought better of it, and went back to the kitchen. When she'd piled a tray up, she started to tidy up. Realised she didn't need to. There was no one else here to consider. No one who might come along afterwards and be annoyed. It struck her so hard she froze, hand poised to grab a dishcloth. She could leave the mess if she wanted to. The house frowned down on her as she courted the thought. Slowly, she pulled her hand away from the cloth. Quietly, she picked up the tray and walked for the door.

Moth was at the back of the television when she walked in, muttering and connecting.

'Can you find the remote?' he asked.

She put the tray down, went and found the remote tucked down the side of the sofa in the morning room and returned.

'Great, turn it on,' he asked, from behind the black outline.

She pressed the button and the lights flickered and turned blue and solid. The screen flickered into life.

'I made brunch,' she said.

'Great,' Moth looked round. 'Where are we going to put it?'

They both looked back at the chairs, now arranged in front of the television.

'We need a coffee table,' Moth said.

'And pouffes,' Isabelle added.

'OK, REMIND ME,' Moth said.

'Great-grandmother, on the paternal side,' Isabelle said, looking at the portrait. 'I think.'

'You think?'

'I'm getting confused,' she admitted. 'The more you ask me the harder it is to be sure.'

'What's the point of all this?' Moth said, looking back down the corridor at the long row of portraits. 'If the family can't even remember who they all are.'

'Kit says it adds eminence to the house,' Isabelle said. 'He says using the Clive family name is marketing gold.'

'Even though that's old history? I mean did a Clive ever live here, even?'

'Kit's not that fussy about the details as long as he can use it for his marketing strategy. As far as he's concerned it's enough that the family are descended from them. Plus, Elsa can't get rid of anything, so they have to go somewhere.'

'Where's Elsa's portrait?' he asked. 'I assume she has one?'

'It's in her bedroom,' Isabelle said.

'Why's it not in the hall?'

'I'll show you, come on.'

They walked back along the first-floor landing and into Elsa's bedroom, which looked out over the garden, above the sitting room. It was large and bright, aged but immaculate. The old, muted chintz curtains drawn to protect the worn carpets and furniture from the midday sun on the two large windows. The pale faded floral bedspread tucked into place. The surface of the dressing table dust free. Spaces showing in the careful alignment of brushes and mirrors where Elsa had taken her favourites with her on holiday. Books and photos aligned on every surface. Matching water glasses and alarm clocks on the pair of Queen Ann painted bedside tables. You wouldn't know that Elsa was a widow. It was as though

Richard had gone to work on the farm, and she had made the bed ready for them both in the evening. Isabelle sat on the upholstered ottoman box at the end of the bed. She pointed to two portraits hanging either side of the fireplace. One was of Elsa, the other of Richard.

'She likes keeping them together,' Isabelle said. 'And to herself.'

'I recognise him from photos at the farm.'

Isabelle watched him walk over to the picture of Richard, looking up at it. It was a kind portrait, unlike some of the other austere ancestors. Elsa had chosen to get a soft likeness, more modernised, looser in the detail. It aged them both with the style, so that despite their youth in the pictures they did not seem too different from what she remembered.

'My father never kept any pictures of his family in the house,' Moth said. 'Apart from the odd one Mum used to show us, we hadn't got a clue what any of you looked like.'

'He was a lot like James, in temperament,' Isabelle said, looking at the portrait of Richard. 'I loved him. He was so easy to like. He never got old or faded, he just died. Happy with his life.'

'He looks nothing like James, or my father,' Moth said.

'Or you,' Isabelle added. 'You all look like Elsa's father.'

'You too,' Moth said, 'but the girly version.'

'And Hester took after her mum. It's hard to remember he was with us sometimes.'

Moth looked round the room. Isabelle followed his eyes. He seemed to be looking for something to dislike, but couldn't. Elsa's bedroom showed softness, a gentle touch wherever you looked. It was the side of her she felt compelled to conceal, one of the consequences of turning your home into a business. His eye settled on a rough wooden chest that lay between the windows, dark wood banded in iron, with large rough rivets knocked into it, intricate designs carved all over it, silver etched into the carved hollows. It was the only thing that looked out of place.

'What's in there?' Moth asked.

'I don't know,' Isabelle said.

Moth looked over at her and grinned with raised eyebrows. Isabelle blushed.

'I tried, yes,' she said. 'When I was younger. But it's locked, always has been.'

'You didn't ask her?'

'Maybe, once,' Isabelle said. 'I can't remember what she said, but it wasn't an answer, more of an evasion.'

'Elsa has secrets?' Moth asked.

'Everyone has secrets, Moth.'

'Even you?' he asked.

'Even you,' she said, looking round the room in discomfort, standing up from the ottoman, moving toward the window.

'It's like she's still here.' Moth voiced her thoughts. 'But it's a nicer version of her.'

'One she doesn't show?' Isabelle said. 'I often wonder what she'd be like if she wasn't running a business from her home. The house feels different to how it did when we were growing up. We used to run through the halls screaming as kids.'

'Nat says it feels odd,' Moth said.

'Really?'

'She says sometimes she likes it, all the people, and doing breakfast and stuff with Elsa. Other times she finds it a bit scary. She doesn't like to go somewhere unless she knows Elsa will be there, or me, or Hester.'

'And you?'

'And me what?'

'How do you find it, living here?'

'I don't feel like I'm living here,' Moth said. 'Stopping for a while, a bit like a guest, I suppose.'

'That's a shame,' Isabelle said. 'Elsa wants you to think of it as home.'

'Do you?'

'I suppose so, yes.' Isabelle thought about how she felt about the place, moving back to the ottoman but feeling bad about sitting there again. 'Or at least it's one home to me. Home is maybe more moveable to me than others, it doesn't need to feel like one place.'

Moth didn't reply and she began to consider that her response had not addressed what he'd asked, and to wonder what she might have missed when he interrupted her thoughts.

'I don't envy Elsa. I wouldn't want all this, that's for sure.' He nodded round the room. 'Everyone falling out about it, not talking, what's the point? You have to fill it with people, so it doesn't feel empty, until it doesn't feel like a home.'

'I suppose,' Isabelle said. 'Different things matter to different people.'

'My father liked the idea,' Moth said. 'All he ever told us about his family was this house. What it was worth, how it should be his already, how it would be one day.'

'You don't have to hate the house because you hated the way he was about it,' Isabelle said. 'It's not the house's fault.'

'I suppose,' Moth said. 'But anyway, rather Elsa than me.'

'Or me,' Isabelle agreed.

. . .

'WE MUST BE GETTING close to finishing this?'

Isabelle rocked back on her knees and looked about them. It looked a wreck, with more boxes left than there should be. Even with the rejection pile bolstered by Moth's brutality and boredom.

'I begin to wonder if we'll ever finish it,' she said in despair. She looked at her phone. 'Wow, 10 pm, have we been down here all night?'

'Yes,' said Moth. 'Yes, we have, since after we last ate.'

'When did we last eat?'

'Last time we ate, obviously,' Moth said.

'Shall we stop for food?'

'How about we just stop?' Moth asked.

'Are you tired?' she asked, with a saccharine tone.

'No, just really, really bored.'

'Right, point taken. You go get food, I'll try and wrap up for tonight.'

'I'll be back in less than twenty,' he told her. 'Make sure you're done. Where are we eating?'

'Bring it down here,' Isabelle said. 'We'll eat out on the lawn, it's an amazing night.'

'Right.' Moth moved towards the door, turned and looked back at her. 'Twenty minutes, tops!'

'Yes, sir!'

When he'd gone, she stood up, stretching her back and looking around. It was more impressive when she looked at it this way. Progress showing at last in the empty stretches of wooden floor and old rugs showing their colours. The walls loomed in the distance and the light from the windows reached all the way across to the fireplace.

Isabelle went over to the dresser, looking for a bag to put some small pieces in. Rummaging through the drawers she found her old CD wallet. She was so used to working in silence she couldn't remember the last time she'd played music down here. The CD player was buried on a small table over by the fire, long since lost under collections of magazines, books about fabrics, and travel books. She'd only recently rediscovered it. The large open windows enticed her to look outside, inspiring her and, by the time Moth came back, bringing with him the subtle odours of cooling Chinese takeout to stir her hunger, she'd moved the player over to the window side of the room, connected it up and had music playing out of the windows. She'd dragged a large rug outside, and laid it on the lawn, piled up two walls of cushions and opened a bottle of wine. The effort had made her thirsty so that, when Moth came out of the workroom windows, she was refilling her glass and glowing with enthusiasm.

'Ta da!' she said, delighted with her efforts. There were majolica plates and forks on the rug ready for him.

'Not bad,' Moth said. 'Eh, are those the plates off the dresser?'

'I know, they're hideous,' she agreed. 'But we've run out, they were the only clean things left I could find. We have some serious washing up to do.'

'Yeah, I figured the same thing,' he said, walking out and kneeling on the rug with the bag in his hand. 'This is cool, and I didn't have to drag you out of the middle of a load of boxes.'

'Bonus, right?' Isabelle said. 'What do you want to drink?'

Moth held up a fresh bottle of Coke, and said, 'I'm good, thanks.'

Isabelle sat down on the rug, and took the boxes out of the bag, opening their tops one at a time, and putting spoons in the boxes. 'I think I've forgotten what a proper vegetable looks like.'

'Yeah, it's great isn't it?' Moth said, dumping a fortress of rice onto two of the majolica plates and handing her one.

They ate with focus, dibbing their forks into containers and piling the dripping contents inside the rice. Leaning back on the cushions and watching the lights of cars passing over the bridge, the streetlights curving away around the corner and ending where they merged into country darkness. The town lay, unseen behind the house. They listened to the music coming out of the workroom. When Isabelle finished her glass of wine, Moth poured her another one, propping the prawn crackers in a bag between them.

'Why are these things so hard to stop eating?' Isabelle said.

'One of life's little mysteries.'

She poked him in the rib in response.

'Ow,' he complained. 'Jesus, your finger poke could be a new form of torture. You should licence it to the SAS or something.'

She poked him again. He grabbed a cushion and flung it at her head. She yelped and ducked to avoid it, tried to right her wine glass and he ended up catching her shoulder instead. She put her wine glass down while he was laughing, grabbed another cushion and swung it back. Moth threw himself sideways on the rug, grabbed his own cushion and they clawed their way onto their knees swinging at each other, shouting abuse and laughing. Isabelle managed a massive thwack against the shoulders that sent him reeling, and when he yelled dire retribution she scrabbled to her feet and ran down the lawn. He rugby tackled her to the ground about ten feet away.

'That's not fair!' she complained, wriggling to get out from under him.

'Sod fair,' he said. 'You hit hard.'

They tussled on the grass in the darker shadows at the far end of the garden, Isabelle trying not to admit defeat. But Moth was tall, and though he was a lightweight compared to James, he was man enough to end up pinning her down.

'Ok, ok, you win!' she shouted, her arms pinned either side of her body, her legs pinned down by his. 'No more poking.'

'Promise?' Moth asked, his face hovering over hers, his shoulders struggling to keep her pinned down. 'Or next time I'll throw you in the river.'

'You wouldn't dare,' she said.

'Oh, I'm sorry, did you just dare me?'

'No!' Isabelle shrieked. 'I said you wouldn't dare, not I dare you!'

'Seems mighty close to me,' Moth said, looking at the river with a judging eye.

'It's going to get ugly if you try and wrestle me into the river,' Isabelle warned him. 'I shall scream blue murder.'

'Spoilsport,' Moth said but he took the tension out of his arms.

She could feel the lawn hard beneath her, see the lights of the house behind them, hear the river as it came over the weir. She looked up at him, his face full of shadows in the darkness. The memory of that sodden moment beneath the willow tree closer. He rolled off, lay on his back beside her and tucked his arms under his head, looking up at the dark sky, at the stars moving behind the clouds. She lay back, the warmth of food and wine and the rowdy tussle dizzying her senses, unbinding her body. The clouds rolling over, stars peeking out above the pale amber glow of the town. The house windows peering down at her.

She held her hand out, over his body, leaning her arm against his ribs where he could feel them. The back of his hand came against hers, and they laced their fingers through until the tips of their fingers met. Not holding or squeezing but resting, entwined together with a gentle connecting pressure. Perfect gravity and form holding their limbs connected. Their breath rising into the chilling air, their bodies imprinting upon the ripe grass.

Isabelle filled with a lonely wonder that Riverdell had never brought her more moments of intense and joyful peace like this.

THEY SAT IN THE CHAIRS, their feet up on the pouffes. The windows were open, the Thursday late-afternoon sun teasing the ruffles of the river, dipping down beneath the arcs of the bridge.

A warm breeze was dancing the heads of the wisteria that hung along the stone balcony outside. On the low table between them were the remnants of a takeout pizza. Arrayed on the floor were a mess of mattresses, cushions, blankets. They were drinking milkshakes through plastic straws from crystal wine goblets. A cut-glass jug was filled with the frothy remnants they hadn't been able to get in the glasses, a box of chocolates passing between them.

They were part way through *Indiana Jones and the Last Crusade*. Having already worked through films one and two. Film selection was an arbitrary process, composed of a medley of 'Hmm, nah, uuh, yes,' that brought them to a decision. They had watched documentaries, films, series, and kid's animation. Isabelle found she was avoiding anything that had the potential for sex scenes in it. They had watched at least five Disney films before Moth had told her 'enough already', half way through *Pocahontas*. They moved to Japanese animation and found it energising by comparison, and onto Bollywood, which she sank into like a feather duvet. But Moth said she was driving him mad analysing the infinitesimal details of the costumes, and the actors, and the sets, so they agreed to try *Indiana Jones*.

Isabelle stretched, her body aching. Tired from the strange hours it was being made to keep, even by her standards. Last night they had stayed out on the lawn, talking, dancing, dreaming silent dreams beneath the stars, until the rising sun feathered the roof tiles. Fallen asleep on the mattresses in the guest room, their fingers reaching across the inch of wooden floor that separated their mattresses and touching as they fell asleep. Not woken until midday when hunger prevailed.

Isabelle sensed Riverdell moving away from her. Afloat on a boat, time had wrapped her up and moved her downstream. Moth afloat next to her, their oars resting from one to the other, binding them with the lightest of touches. She was aware of the house retreating, aware of Moth riding the river with her, of herself looking forwards and the flashing ripples of the waters teasing at the fluttering in her chest.

'Are you falling asleep again?' Moth asked.

'No,' Isabelle said, opening her eyes. 'I was daydreaming.'

'Let's watch something else,' Moth said, grabbing the remote and flicking switches.

'No, I love this one. It's the best film!'

Moth was sitting up to argue when the doorbell rang. They froze together. It wasn't the first time it had happened,

but they had locked the door and ignored it until now. It rang
again. They stayed looking at each other. The buzzer started a
third time and didn't stop. Someone had put their finger on it
and wasn't taking it off.

'Oh, shit.' She handed the box of chocolates to Moth and
got up. 'I better answer it.'

She walked into the hall, as an afterthought pulling the
door to the room closed behind her, kicking aside the heavy
velvet prop. She straightened her rumpled clothes off as best
she could and, realising she needed a good bath and a tidy
up, opened the front door with a polite smile on her face.

'WELL, FINALLY!' He took his finger off the buzzer and
straightened up from his pose leaning against the door. 'I've
never known this door be locked before. What the hell are
you up to?'

'Kit?'

'The one and only.' He walked towards her, trying not to
chase her as she retreated two steps into the hallway,
sweeping her up in a crushing embrace. 'I know it's a
surprise, but I couldn't resist having a few days with you
while Elsa's away. Oh God, I've missed you. I've thought about
you night and day, all week.'

He felt himself unwind as he held her. She smelt divine,
as though she had spent most of the week in bed, musty and
warmed through. Her hair falling across her make up free
skin. He kissed her lips, her cheeks, her neck.

He'd driven straight from a job in Cheltenham, stumbling
between thoughts of work and thoughts of seeing her. Of
making love to her. Wherever they wanted it. In a house
devoid of guests and family. He'd been so turned on by the

thought of sex on the desk in the study he'd had to take a moment out from the meeting with his clients and have a quick wank in their downstairs bathroom. In need of a complete refresh, he added it to the list when he went back to deciding budgets with them.

His desire had been inflamed by the sense of her distance on the phone. The sense that she was not missing him. That Moth was in the background, where Kit couldn't pin him down, or see what was happening. It had not been easy to rearrange his meetings, his customers were not the type to be rearranged.

'You're staying?'

'I am, darling.' He walked past her into the hall. 'And I'm gasping for a coffee, and a glass of something else. I have worked my arse off to get here.'

She looked even more stunned than he'd hoped for. He grabbed her again. Christ they could do it right now, right here in the hall, on the wooden floor if they wanted to. He raked a hand through his hair, backed away from her. He needed to calm down, give her some space. Groaning he pulled away from her, headed for the kitchen.

'You look amazing, just let me get a coffee and I'm all...' he backed into the kitchen chewing on his knuckles in frustration, turning away towards the coffee machine, '... Jesus Fucking A Fire Brigade! What the hell happened?'

Isabelle came and stood behind him in the kitchen door as he surveyed the carnage.

'I mean, have you lost your mind? What are you, a savage?' He took shocked steps closer. The sink, overflowing with dirty plates and food not scraped off. The bin, lid sticking up in protest against the rammed in contents. Above it, takeout containers stacked high and greasy. The table, smeared plates, frothy cups and opaque dreg marked glasses abounding. 'What the hell have you been doing? Have you had a party every bloody night?'

'No, of course not,' Isabelle said. Her face looked flushed and stressed. 'It's just Moth and I. I guess we got a bit too relaxed.'

'Too relaxed?' Kit asked. 'Too relaxed! Upside down horizontal, I'd say. Where is he? I thought he was going off on his bike?'

'We've been busy, he's been helping me sort the workroom,' Isabelle protested. 'I guess we lost track of time.'

'Well you both better regain a sense of time and tidy this fucking mess up,' Kit said. 'I have not got away from work to spend it tidying the fuck up!'

'Calm down,' Isabelle said. 'I don't expect you to tidy up, and I didn't know you were coming.'

'So, what, I need an invitation now?' Kit asked. His sense of arousal had floated away on the scum lining the kitchen sink. 'You think I can relax? Knowing all this needs doing?'

'Look, no, of course not. I'm thrilled you're here, but it's just a surprise,' Isabelle said. 'Look, I'll start right now. Why don't you unload your stuff? Ignore it, it'll be sorted in no time.'

He watched her move past him, towards the sink. Stop, her back to him, thinking. Kit narrowed his eyes, his shoulders hitching a ride up to his ears. It was that same sepia shade of bullshit he couldn't identify.

Isabelle turned back to him. 'I'll get Moth to help.' She walked towards him. 'It's lovely that you're here, Moth will be thrilled too. Go get your stuff in, I'll find Moth, we'll clean up.' She kissed him on the cheek, put her fingers through his, squeezed. Slipped past him and out of the kitchen door.

His shoulders went even higher. He moved towards the hallway as she disappeared out of view and caught the closing kitchen door in time to see the door to the guest dining room close. Kit took a step into the hall. He should go and get his bag. He shouldn't follow her. He took another step towards the closed door. Every instinct he had for a relationship told him to leave her alone. His hand grasped the handle, inside he could hear her murmuring to Moth. He opened the door and walked in.

His eyes tried to focus on it all at once, unable to grasp what he was seeing. There was too much furniture where it shouldn't be, his brain trying to relocate it. He could see Moth and Isabelle stood up talking in the bay window, they both went silent, looking back at him. Moth with a face like he'd sucked on a lemon. His brain couldn't move beyond the misplaced furniture.

'Why are all the chairs stacked up?' he asked, taking another step forward. Saw the chairs arranged in the window. 'Isn't that supposed to be in the study?'

Kit knew he was missing a key point, but he couldn't reach it. There were too many details distressing him.

'Hey, Kit,' Moth said, frowned and stopped whatever else he was about to say.

'Why on earth are there mattresses on the floor?' Kit asked, moving towards them down the tunnel they had made of the furniture and letting the full vision of the bay window open to him. He looked up at the ceiling, with its ornate decorative plasterwork. 'Has something gone wrong with the house?'

'No,' Isabelle said. 'Of course nothing is wrong with the house. I can take care of it, you know.'

'Why's there a television?' Kit asked. 'There's no television in here.'

'Kit, I told you,' Isabelle said, moving towards him. 'Moth and I mixed things up a bit, had a bit of fun. We'll put it all back, you need to chill out. You've been working too hard.'

She took his hand again, tried to pull him back to the hall. Kit pulled his hand away. Watched her look at Moth, smiling false comfort. 'Looks like our holiday's over Moth, we better get everything back to normal. It's a good job Kit's here, he'll make sure it's all back before they get home!'

Kit looked at Moth, waiting to see if he would take the light-hearted jest she was trying to cover the situation with. Moth looked back at him with a stony face. Kit looked at the mattresses again, saw the rucked sheets and blankets. Looked back at Moth, standing tall and unrepentant. Had they been...

His sense of outrage went through the plasterwork ceiling.

'What the hell is going on? What have you been up to all week?'

'Kit!' Isabelle protested. 'You're blowing this out of all proportion and spoiling our week. Calm down. Come on, I'll make you a coffee, and you need a beer. Moth, you start in here, I'll start in the kitchen. Let's get everything shipshape and Kit can stop freaking out. He's no good with a mess around him. Come on, you,' she grasped his hand and pulled him out of the guest dining room.

Kit was too stunned to resist. Moth? Isabelle and Moth? He couldn't get it in his head. The little shit, asking for advice about his love life, and getting his dick where Kit had already staked a claim.

Isabelle dragged him into the kitchen, sitting him down at

the table, clearing the mess away in front of him. She was talking. Pointless nonsense. Keeping him focused. His mind was trying to straighten itself out, drowning in the endless babble she was trying to pull out of herself. Small talk never had been her strength.

'Are you two fucking?'

'Kit!' she said, stopped dead in her tracks by the statement. 'What is the matter with you!'

'Matter with me?' he asked. 'I turn up to find you two have made a cosy fuck nest and you ask what's the matter with me?'

'Get a grip,' Isabelle said. 'Don't you dare let Moth hear you say that. That's your problem, not ours.'

'Ours?' Kit asked. 'Ours? Who is ours? Who are you even talking about? I thought we were ours.'

'Oh, grow up,' she said, throwing plates around on the work surface. 'I've just got out of one load of relationship guilt, and here you are dragging me back into another. You deal with your jealousy issues, don't offload them onto me. Moth is a teenager. I'm not a child molester, thank you very much for the suggestion. You turn up here unannounced and mouth off because you don't like how we choose to chill out. Well, thank you very much indeed, for ruining what has been a once-in-a-lifetime chance for me to enjoy this house for myself.'

Kit watched as she gathered up a head of steam. Crashing crockery and clanging pans around. Trying to pretend she was cleaning up rather than making the mess worse. The edge of guilt nibbled at him.

'Like it's even going to be part of my life for much longer anyway. Like Hester isn't going to slam the doors of Riverdell shut in my face as fast as she can manage it. Like I have any clue what I'm doing with my life, or where I'm going, or who with. One bloody week of peace with someone who isn't always trying to get something out of me, and you come in here like a spitting tomcat and piss all over it.'

Kit stood up and went up behind her, took the pan out of her shaking hand and tried to wrap her in his arms.

'Get off!' she said, pulling away. There were tears in her eyes, she scrubbed them away. 'You go and apologise to Moth and clear this mess up. That's your job right, clearing up other people's mess? Well, go clean your own up first.'

She pushed him away and walked out of the room, heading for her workroom.

Kit watched the door slow close behind her and surveyed the carnage. Well, maybe he had come in a bit heavy-handed. He opened the dishwasher, it was full of dirty, stinking crocks. He snarled. They'd bloody deserved it though.

He put it on, began organising the dirties on the work surface and table into piles. Cleaned the sink with bleach and vigorous dislike for the scum, and ran a bowl full of scalding hot water.

It wasn't easy letting go of his own interest when it had been building a several days head of steam. To finally get here and find that den they'd made. He slipped the dirtiest dishes into the soapy water and soaked a cloth until the heat hurt his skin, wrung it out with the heat biting into his fingers, and wiped down the table.

Restoring a slow sense of order to the room and gritting his teeth until his temper cooled. He sensed movement at the door, looked up to see Moth standing there. His hands in his pockets, looking around the kitchen.

'She's downstairs,' Kit said. 'Gave me the most almighty

bollocking, told me I'm a complete wanker and left me to clear up.'

'Nicely handled.'

Kit wasn't sure if he meant himself or Isabelle. He flexed his shoulders and went back to the washing.

'Did you get that coffee yet?' Moth asked.

'You can make coffee now?'

'I'm working for Kate now.' Moth moved across to the coffee machine.

'Oh, excellent woman,' Kit said. 'I'd love a coffee.'

'And a beer?'

Kit could hear the disdain in his voice. He wiped the last scum off the table, wrung out the grime in the cooling sink. 'It's been a long week,' Kit said, feeling defensive. 'I've worked my arse off day and night to get a few days away before Elsa came back. Not to mention having to trek to Swansea three times to try and work out what Elsa's doing with that bloody house.'

Moth turned his back on the coffee machine, looked at him in boredom. Kit felt the cry for sympathy fall flat on the floor between them. Apologies had never been his strong point. And here he was making them to a teenager with a degree in indifference.

'I might have been a bit out of order. I... I apologise, if I misjudged the situation.'

'Hey, join the club,' Moth said, turning back to the coffee machine. 'A lot of people wonder what I'm doing, or aren't doing, or should be doing.'

Kit grimaced at the sink. He'd deserved that. 'You should take it as a compliment,' he said. 'It's not everyone I get jealous of.'

Moth remained silent. He took the cup to the table, found a beer in the fridge, opened it and put it next to the coffee.

'Pretty sure the only clean glasses left are in the dining room,' Moth said. He moved to leave the kitchen. 'I'll go tidy up, but I could do with a hand to move the furniture.' He stood in the kitchen door, looking into the hall. 'That was a pretty crap apology. I hope you did better with Isabelle.'

Kit watched his back disappear out of view. The cheeky bastard. He gritted his teeth and sucked his breath in to hold back the retort. It had been a pretty low-level apology. The thought of Isabelle downstairs in the workroom made him feel worse. He growled and kicked the wooden kickboard of the sink unit, did it again harder. Checked he hadn't scuffed his toes. Or split the creaking board.

He walked across and looked at the coffee. Moth had made the shape of a dick in the froth. He had to smile. He picked up the beer, wiped the neck of the bottle and took a long swig. Felt the acidity and the bubbles rush down his throat. The bitter after sting and the slow warmth of alcohol.

Between them they'd made him feel the guilty party, but his neck was tingling, his shoulders trying to take flight. Kit knew when he was being shafted by someone else. No matter what they said. He took another long swig from the bottle.

He'd arrived just in time but screwed up with his response. He emptied the bottle, let a bit of its relaxation gain hold of him. He picked up the spoon Moth had put with the coffee, wiped the dick off the froth. Kit drew in a deep breath and closed his eyes with it, let it fill him all the way down to his stomach. Let it out and straightened his shirt, flexing the neck muscles that were trying to sit up round his ears.

There was no one, but no one, who could out shaft him.

He took a slug of the coffee, scalding hot and bitter, full of vim. Drank it all down and put the grainy bottom of the cup down on the saucer. Left it alone on the fresh wiped table, claiming turf.

Right. First Moth. Then Isabelle. Divide and conquer. Conquer and rule.

He walked out of the kitchen, into the guest dining room.

'Right, where do you need me?' he asked. 'What do you want to move first?'

Moth was stood in the bay window, looking out over the garden. He turned when Kit came into the room, looking at him with a guarded face. Kit put on his most open, winning, engaging smile. What Henri called his million-franc-smile.

'I've been a dick, I get the message,' Kit said. 'I was jealous of you two chilling out here after the week I've had. I'm sorry. Genuinely, sorry. Neither of you deserved it. I shall help you tidy up and go grovel for forgiveness to Isabelle.'

'I can't imagine you're very good at grovelling,' Moth said.

'It's not my strongest skill.' Kit couldn't argue with him. He kept smiling. Break you little shit, break. Stayed silent, watching Moth back. Added a long slow languorous blink. Moth broke the gaze and looked away, his shoulders sagging. Kit's smile widened to victory. All those years with filthy rich, impossible clients and he could outstare a teenager. Great.

'I suppose the chairs first,' Moth said, looking at the chairs as though they were the last thing he wanted to move.

Kit moved to join him closer to the window, standing a little distant from him, looking out over the garden.

'Best room in the house,' Kit said. 'It was a sacrifice when we had to give it up to the guests.'

'I'll say.'

'I can see why you two picked it,' Kit said. 'It's a room

none of us get to enjoy, you always feel like it belongs to them now.'

'How was Nat?'

'Hmm?'

'You said you saw Elsa. How was Nat?'

'Loving it.' Kit turned to look at Moth. 'High as a kite, bouncing round the house waiting for them to go back to the beach. I've never seen her so confident.'

Even Hester had been a different person. Light-hearted and chatty, if indifferent to her mother's attempt to engage her in the house. Assuming she would sell it, tolerating her strange reluctance to finalise the decision without pampering to it. Hester had been wrapped up in Nat. Kit had watched her, and watched Elsa watching her, and wondered what on earth was going through the older woman's mind.

'They were all loving it,' Kit said. 'They needed a holiday.'

'I don't think she's been missing me,' Moth said to the floor.

'I tried to tell you,' Kit said.

'Yes, you did.'

'There must be some sense of relief in that?'

Moth didn't reply.

'But I guess that's not the easiest thing to admit,' Kit said. He looked round the room, focused on the mattresses. 'Are those king-size mattresses?'

Moth grinned at him, 'Yes, from the guest bedrooms.'

'Oh, you wankers,' Kit said. 'Do you have any idea how much harder it's going to be to get them upstairs than it was downstairs?'

'It wasn't that easy getting them downstairs.'

'Fuck's sake,' Kit muttered. 'I thought I'd finished work for the week.'

'Are you going to stop moaning or what?'

'Get the other end,' Kit said, moving to throw the duvets and blankets off the mattresses. 'We'll see who's moaning by the time we're done.'

KIT FOUND the note that Moth left when he went to make coffee the next morning.

Gone off on the bike, got my phone. Moth.

He tried not to crow but couldn't restrain a fist pump, straight out from his gut and into the crotch of the empty room. Excellent. He would take her the note up with breakfast. No, they would have breakfast on the verandah outside the sitting room and he would give her the note there. Before they made love on the floor of the sitting room. There was a deep pile rug there that he'd wanted to feel beneath his naked butt for years.

He was going to get her to come down and stay with him. She needed time away, time to focus on them. Moth needed time without her. To realise how much Nat didn't need him, to realise he needed to either go back to school or get himself expelled and get a job. After all, it had worked for him, why not Moth?

He'd woken in the early hours of the morning, lying next to Isabelle in the dimness of her bedroom, trying to work out where they were going, feeling restless. He'd crept out, holding his breath when she turned over, walking through the silent dark rooms of the house in his underpants, opening doors and experiencing the empty house like never before. It felt bleak, devoid of life. A coldness in the vast empty spaces. It had sent shivers through him, the eerie search for something that refused to reveal itself.

He'd ended up in Isabelle's workroom, sifting through the piles on the tables, prising open boxes, closing them again in bemusement. The disarrayed packaging of the room more unsettling than its clutter had ever been. A lack of purpose where there had always been one, its identity put in uncertain boxes, in unconfident piles. Returning to the kitchen for his fourth coffee he found the note.

Gone off on the bike, eh? Moth must have been creeping around while Kit was in the workroom. You could lose all sense of time and life down there.

Kit took his coffee into the guest dining room, sat down at the table they'd used the evening before, strewn with empty wine glasses and the cards they'd ended up playing. Kate had been waspish when she arrived, ever so close to telling Kit he was a presumptuous little prick for sending Moth up to drag her down, let alone demanding she bring four dinners with her. The atmosphere of the house had worked its magic on her too and they had all ended up lighter.

This morning, the room was cold and dull. All the bright morning summer sunlight focused on the opposite side of the house. He drank his coffee, leaning back in the chair and stretching his legs out. Silence descended on him, like dust sifting down through the ceilings. No squeak of floorboards, no clatter of steps on the wooden floors, no senseless murmurs of people that you could hear but not discern.

Nothing but emptiness between him and Isabelle asleep upstairs on the top floor.

His bare legs goosebumped in the air. The house felt wrong. It wasn't peaceful, or purposeful, it was abandoned. He looked at the pile of chairs gawping in disarray. The empty room said loud and clear that Moth and Isabelle had shared that sense of purposelessness and found it harmonious. Well, stuff that.

He drained his cup, went and grabbed the first chair, rebuilding the pattern of the room as it had been laid out. Making small tweaks and changes that improved the footfall. Until he was warm through, and all sense of doubt had been pushed away. He finished off with the vacuum, sucking up the sense of degradation and leaving the pile of the rugs upstanding and glowing.

Kit dragged Isabelle groaning out of bed at 9 am, woke her up with bacon sandwiches and sex, until she was all out of groaning and lying on the sitting room rug. Leaning back against the sofa, the used condom slumped on the slate hearth.

He lay on the opposite side of the plush rug, naked on its softness, his fingers teasing their way through the pile beneath him. Adoring the subtlety of the colours that ran back and forth. At heart they were blue and yellow, a combination he refused to engage in for his clients, but the rug was Indian, and stunning. The blue like the binding edge of a fine bone china plate, the yellow a primrose tone as soft and mild as spring flowers in shade. He'd have picked out some of the other, gentler tones to decorate with, the smoky mauve, silvery ash or hushed celandine, and let the rug stand out. Dichromatic colour schemes appalled him. But Elsa had insisted, plastering the walls, furnishings and décor with those two predictable shades. The china blue and primrose as comfortable to her as her tweeds and twinsets.

Despite the irritation of the décor Kit felt relaxed. The tension of the week drained away in the second, or third, or was it fourth shag, the distance between them gone. Like Moth was gone. His note lay on the floor beside her, where her eyes kept drifting to it, while she balanced the saucer on the thin, silky dressing gown she wore, holding the cup in her hand.

'Give him a call later,' Kit suggested.

She looked at him in a poor show of feigned misunderstanding. He didn't bother trying to believe her, watching, stroking the luxurious rug. The thick pile made of copious strands of fine wool, given to Elsa by her brother on a trip back from India. Isabelle stopped pretending.

'I'm sure he'll appreciate the peace,' she said. 'He's been stuck here all week helping me with the workroom.'

'What are you doing with the workroom?' Kit straightened from his casual elbow position, leant back against the sofa and crossed his legs at the ankles, liking how it emphasised his balls by pushing them up above his taut thighs, his dick preening on top.

'I'm not sure yet,' Isabelle said. 'It started as a search for creative purpose, but now I'm near the end I have no idea what it was I was looking for.'

'Found anything else along the way?'

'A sense of doubt?' Isabelle said with a wry smile, and another stolen look at the note, pulling the gown closer around her. It stuck beneath her bottom and tautened across her lap, emphasising the triangle of her thighs as a tunnel that reached up beneath the gown.

'Doubt about yourself?' Kit asked. 'Or about others?'

'Oh, a loose, general, all-pervasive sense of doubt,' Isabelle looked across at him, her eyes glancing across his body, across his crotch, finding his face. 'You know the sort where you feel completely frigging lost.'

'Why don't you come stay with me for a while?'

She blinked in surprise, her eyes dropping downwards,

and back to his face. He smiled at her, trying to cover his own shock at the words. Out there, in the world, no longer churning in his head. Kit felt his own doubts smack him in the back of the teeth as they rose up with a vengeance from his tightening stomach.

'I mean, for a break. Get away from here, think through what you want to do next.'

'Maybe,' she said. 'It's been ages since I stopped at yours. What a nice idea.'

He didn't believe her. Whatever she was looking for, it wasn't at his house. His doubts rocketed around the room and came back at him from the side. Maybe it was the idea of Bristol, maybe it had nothing to do with him.

'Have you ever seen this house of Elsa's in Swansea?' he asked, trying to keep up with his own thoughts.

'No.'

'I was thinking about buying it off her,' he said. 'Perhaps somewhere new might be exciting for both of us?' His doubts reflected in the odd expression Isabelle gave him.

'Can you afford to do that?' she asked. 'I never thought you'd sell Bristol.'

'I don't need to,' he lied. 'It's possible to restructure the finances. We could try it, that's all I'm saying, see how we like it. We can always sell it if it's not right.'

'Does Elsa want to sell?'

'She might be more persuaded with a firm offer on the table,' he said. 'Besides, I can't see what else she's going to do with it. It's far too expensive to keep as a playhouse and she can't afford to renovate it for income.'

Isabelle looked puzzled. Kit could have sworn. His own contradiction was so obvious. Like they could afford it as a playhouse any more than Elsa.

'Perhaps we should wait and see what she decides?'

'That's all you ever do.' Kit dragged his fingers through his hair, wrung the watch on his wrist, the only thing he ever kept on. 'I'm sick of watching you wait to see what this family does and trying to fit in. Hester isn't going to want you here Isabelle, you must see that. It's time to ask what you want to do.'

Kit was roiling inside, he'd chased his own good mood away with a series of dumb statements, and now he was trying to cover it up with turning on her, needling her about decisions only he wanted her to make. Her eyes rolled across the hand scrawled note again.

Kit rolled onto his knees. He crawled through the pile towards her, took the empty coffee cup out of her hands and the saucer off her lap, pulling her down to lie on the rug. He hovered over her, his dick growing against the silky, ruched up hem of the dressing gown, teased her eyes shut with kisses, not wanting to see the doubt in them, and grabbed the piece of paper Moth had scrawled on. He tucked it under the cushions on the sofa, distracting her by rubbing his hips against her, pressuring her legs apart with the hardening nub of his erection.

'Kit! You're insatiable.'

'And you're irresistible.'

He hovered millimetres off her, feeling her body vibrating through his skin. The strength of his arm muscles holding him up, the silky fabric slipping apart, teasing him with its shiver.

'I can't wait any longer for you to work out what you want to do. I want you. I've waited for years. Come on, Isabelle, it's our time now.'

He kissed her face, her neck, her ears, her naked shoulders, easing aside what was left of the gown. He pushed his hips even harder against her, seeking her out, feeling her moistness. She groaned, a low rumble from behind her sealed lips, the guttural tone making him harder. Her hips rolling beneath him with interest.

'I want to make love to you in every room in the house,' he whispered beside her ear. 'I want to make love in the garden, in the kitchen, in the fucking boiler room. By the time we're done I want you to be sick to death of this house, and come away with me, somewhere new.'

'Really?'

He could feel her warmth on the straining slit of his dick, he struggled against the urge to push her legs that little bit further apart, feeling the grip of her muscles resisting him. He pressed a millimetre further, felt his skin stretching over the head, the curve of her vulva kissing him. She was warming up. She wanted him. He had only to push inside, and they would be together, nothing between them. The ecstasy unfettered by a condom. But that was Kate's preserve, and only Kate's. He'd have to tell Kate if he went commando. It was the first rule, her rule, their rule. He might as well marry Isabelle as tell Kate he'd had unprotected sex with her. He reached up to his trousers, abandoned on the sofa, pulled out a condom.

'Really,' he said, marvelling at the confidence in his voice. He pulled onto his left arm, and she watched him slip the rubber over his dick with one confident hand. Her fingers stroking down the length of it, tracing down his thigh.

She kissed him back. Gentle kisses on the lips, hesitant. He twisted to lie back over her, encouraging her with his tongue, rolling across the surface of hers, pulling her lips away with his, teasing her mouth until their kisses grew

stronger. His arms rigid with the pressure of holding himself
off her. His muscles, taut as his dick, honed in the gym for
this one skill, to keep himself hovering above the person he
wanted, for a length of time that would drive them mad. The
perfect plank.

Her hands cupped his buttocks, tensing him against her.
He toyed with her, teasing her swelling lips, opening her up
without pleasing her. She pulled harder, her legs relaxing,
her warmth swallowing the head of his bulging dick. She
moved her hips up off the floor and took him inside her. Kit
let his muscles relax, sank down onto her and, with long
lingering strokes that pulled out of her to the tip of his shank,
that made her grip his buttocks and draw him back in, began
to build a rhythm inside her.

He wanted this. He knew that much. The rest was a bit
unclear. But this, oh how much he wanted this. To feel her
legs wrapping round his thighs, her warmth swallowing him
inside. Kit closed his eyes and let the disturbing consequences of what he'd said flow away.

Every room in the house, that was a challenge he could
rise to. They would christen them all, pack their bags and
leave.

He would make her come, one way or another.

Kit flipped the television on. It was early again. Sunday
morning programmes were the worst. His sleep was all over
the place. He missed his garden and the neighbour's dog. He
had no idea how to soothe himself, and Isabelle sleeping
beside him made him horny as a frog all night long.

He flicked from programme to programme while gathering a stress snack, needing the noise to sooth his agitation.

They'd conquered the attic floor, though she'd refused to make love in Moth or Nat's room, every bedroom on the first floor, including Elsa's, though there she'd insisted on the floor and vaginal sex, despite his desperate pleas for anal on the floral bedcover. He'd recreated a favourite movie scene over the study table and, when she wearied of his pace, finished it by masturbating himself between her thighs standing up against the fireplace. Ejaculating onto the wood Elsa had piled there ready for winter. Thinking what great fuel to start a fire.

He went back to looking for meat in the fridge. His hunger had ramped up to match his holiday and their sex fest. They had made out on the stairs, on the hall sofa, on top of the kitchen table – where he'd given her hopeless giggles with his erotic plans for a pot of Nutella – and in a stinking nest of coats in the boot room. She had refused to engage in the guest sitting room. Elsa was due back later today, Moth had sent a text message but no news of his return, and Kate would soon demand to know where he was and why he was ignoring her. He still had the basement, the boiler room and the garden to tick off and he wasn't convinced they were any closer to Isabelle making a decision.

He flipped the channels over again. News, more news. Enough of that depressing shit. He flipped the television off, sat and waited for the morning sun to seep in through the kitchen windows over the rim of the castle wall. Six am. Hours before he could go wake her. He grabbed at ideas to keep himself busy. Bedsheets. They had messed up a lot of bedsheets. He pushed the chair back and headed for the laundry room. He opened the door to the boot room and jumped back in shock as a figure came towards him out of the dark.

'Jesus!' Moth swore, jumping back himself. 'Christ, you shocked me.'

'Shocked you!' Kit said. 'I nearly took you out.'

'Looked like you were running backwards to me,' Moth said.

He walked through the door, his rucksack in his hand. He was covered with mud, like he'd been sleeping in a bush for two nights. His hair dragged out of the beanie hat, springing up rumpled and windswept. He looked rugged as hell. And ten years older. Like a model about to rip his clothes off for a sports shot. Kit squinted through the dim light, seeing a different Moth in the shadows. The man he was going to be. And soon.

'You look wrecked.' Kit tried to sound calmer than he felt.

'Yeah, it was a bit wild.'

'Where did you get to?'

'I have no idea,' Moth said. 'Here a bit, there a bit. Just went where I fancied, then tried to work out where it was, how long I'd need to get back.'

'Have you seen any water since you left?' Kit asked.

'Yeah, seen lots, not used much.'

Moth put his bag down on a chair, went and got a glass of water, drinking it in one long draught and refilling it. From the back he looked even dirtier. Mud had spattered up his clothes, sitting in a curved line around the base of his trousers where whatever jacket he'd abandoned in the coat room had pulled up as he cycled.

'You're up early,' Moth said, turning to look at him, sipping from his second glass.

'Early bird catches the worm.'

'Second mouse gets the cheese,' Moth retorted.

'I'm trying to fit in housework for Elsa before she gets

back.' Kit pulled out a chair, not liking the idea of another mouse getting his cheese. The washing could wait a little longer.

'Due back later, huh?' Moth asked.

'You've spoken with Nat?' Kit watched him take his bag off the chair, putting it beside his feet as he sat down.

'Yeah, couple of times, and Elsa.'

'What did Elsa have to tell you?'

'Not much. Asked me to be back for when they got home,' Moth shrugged disinterest, the sort teenagers seemed to acquire with puberty. Kit wasn't used to seeing it in Moth.

'What's that about?'

Moth shrugged again, drank some more water.

'She might have decided to toughen up on your return to school,' Kit mused. 'I was going to talk to you about that.'

'Don't worry,' Moth said. 'I don't need another one of your lectures. I get it.'

'Get what?' Kit asked, marvelling at how Moth could get under his skin, wondering if he'd ever been as annoying at this age. Couldn't have been, Kate would never have tolerated it.

'I'm going back to school.'

'You are?'

'Yes, you're right.'

'I am?'

'About Nat, anyway,' Moth took another sip. 'Nat doesn't need me, she needs to become part of this family. That's all she has now, isn't it?' Moth stared into his glass, keeping his voice steady. 'I can't give her what she needs. All this, this home, and care, and all the stuff she needs as a kid. I don't know how to do that.'

'I don't how to do that.' Kit was impressed at the change in him. 'I don't think you got this from me. I think you found it out in the mud bath you took.'

'Maybe,' Moth said, looking at him with a quick grin. It warmed his eyes, took away the frown, retreated, let the frown back in. 'Maybe I needed to be away from her a bit too, and to hear how happy she is. Away with them. With Elsa.'

'And Hester,' Kit added, because he wasn't convinced. He needed to know how committed Moth was before he decided to give him an alternative. 'How do you feel about Hester?'

Moth was silent for a moment, twisting his glass on the table. Water had dripped down the sides in his rush to fill it and left a widening damp circle on the wood. Kit resisted the urge to get a cloth.

'Hester's alright,' Moth said. 'I think she's not so bad, when Isabelle's not around. And she cares for Nat, doesn't she?'

'She does,' Kit said. 'Maybe she needs Nat as much as Nat needs her. That always helps build a relationship, and you're spot on about her and Isabelle.'

'Anyway, even if Hester's not perfect, Nat thinks she is. She doesn't need me hovering over her, doubting everyone.'

'That doesn't mean you have to go back to school,' Kit said. He wasn't convinced it was the right thing for Moth. 'There are other options you could consider.'

'I know,' Moth said. 'I've thought about them. But if I go, Isabelle will leave too.'

'Where did you get that idea from?'

'She's only here because Elsa made her promise to stay,' Moth said. He rushed on over Kit's raised eyebrows. 'Oh, I know she loves this place, but I don't think she wants to be around Hester, and she knows Nat's not that sure of her. If I go, maybe she will too. Then Hester will be happier. Which will help Nat, right?'

Kit tried to follow the logic. It was extraordinary. Moth had convinced himself that if he went back to school it would benefit not only Nat, but Hester and Isabelle. Kit opened his mouth to quash all over the presumption of his power of influence. Opening his mouth was as far as it got, the words dumbstruck by the possibility that Moth might have a point.

Not that he was right. Nothing so simple would influence Isabelle making a decision about her life. But, if Moth wasn't here, and Hester was, well, at least it gave him the sparkle of a hope, glinting off Moth's twisting glass, that he might be able to push Isabelle in the direction he, more or less, wanted them to go.

The thoughts raging in fast succession, toying with his watch, Kit was struck by an irritating sense of responsibility.

'Not that I'm arguing with your logic,' Kit said, because it got more appealing as the seconds lengthened. 'But have you thought about yourself in all this?'

'Of course.'

'And is this what you want?' Kit asked. He leaned forward in his chair, put his hand on the table, opening the palm out to Moth. 'I thought you hated that school?'

'Last few months, I've pretty much hated everything.' Moth drained his glass and put it down on a fresh patch of wood where it began to spread a new stain. 'Most of all, I've hated feeling like I had no choice in anything. How, just when I think I'm sorting stuff, something, or someone, comes along and messes it all up. At least now I'm making a choice.'

Kit went to speak, stopped. Moth wasn't watching him. He was twisting his empty glass. He opened his mouth, again nothing came out. He clenched his open hand on the table, opened it and tried hard to make himself speak. Moth's absence in the last few days had been good for him. As much as he wanted to be a good mate, he wanted Isabelle to himself more.

'Well, seems you've made your mind up.'

'Yes, so don't try and persuade me otherwise,' Moth said, looking up at him with a wry smile on his face. 'I know how much you like having me around.'

Kit tried to smile back. It came out weak and uncomfortable. Moth stood up and took the glass to the sink, got his bag and headed for the door.

'I'm going to wash up and get some sleep,' he said over his shoulder. 'I'd like to tell Elsa myself, if that's alright?'

'Of course,' Kit said. 'Your decision, your news.'

Moth walked out of the door without any response, letting it glide shut behind him. Kit watched the soft close hinge work in the silence he left behind, waiting for the door to catch shut. It was a tad too slow, needed to be quick enough to be invisible, he'd adjust it later. He drummed his fingers on the table surface. So much for the final rooms he'd planned to conquer, Isabelle wouldn't come near him now Moth was back. Back and going back to school.

Well, revelations at the kitchen table and it wasn't even breakfast time, what else would the day bring?

KIT WENT INTO HYPERDRIVE. He'd done the linen, moving between washer, dryer and ironing board for an hour, done fifty burpees, showered and was dressed, pressed and ready to impress by 10 am. Moth was nowhere to be seen and Isabelle was fast asleep.

He walked up into town, let himself into Kate's flat and

found her stumbling round her kitchen looking crinkled and spoiling for an argument, her hair as adrift as her nightdress. He had to kiss her for an hour to adjust her mood, beginning with her face, where he tried to kiss away the lines of exhaustion etched into her skin, following the curve of her shoulders down to her breasts, circling her hardening nipples as he pushed aside her nightdress and her irritability, and moving all the way down to her gorgeous toes before heading back up to her dripping crotch. Pushing her back until she leant against the kitchen table and snaked her hands through his hair. Afterwards he ran her a bath and ordered her to soak for an hour.

He opened the bistro, let the staff in, pointed out ten jobs he wanted doing and prepared breakfast in the kitchen around the chef to make sure he was also awake. He took breakfast back upstairs to the flat, pulled her out of the bath, dried her off and wrapped her in her morning robe. They ate in the warm morning sun on the roof terrace, where he'd laid the table with all her favourite china.

'You know how to pamper a tired old lady,' Kate said as he buttered her croissants.

'You're no old lady,' he told her. 'You're a workaholic.'

'People in glasshouses,' Kate said, but she held her hand out to him, and let him caress her fingers.

'Elsa's back later,' Kit said, passing her chunks of croissant. 'Moth turned up this morning, covered from head to toe in mud, went straight up to bed.'

'Well, he knows how to have fun,' Kate said, with no conviction. 'Elsa rang me yesterday, asked me to come for supper. I had to say no.'

'Why?'

'It's the final evening, I have all the tables fully booked.'

'I thought Sunday evening was quiet?' he said, with-holding a piece of croissant and giving her a sharp look. 'Haven't they all gone home by tonight?'

'Well, maybe not all the tables,' Kate admitted. 'But I'm too exhausted to face Hester and Isabelle squaring off. I promised to go up in the morning instead, after a late breakfast.'

Kit focused on his caresses. Elsa seemed to have spoken to everyone near enough, bar him. 'Have you been using that skin cream I bought you?'

'Religiously.'

'As in abstaining, religiously?' Kit said.

'I have a terrible memory.'

'You have a prodigious memory,' Kit said. 'About as strong as your indifference to looking after yourself. Skin needs more help as we get older you know.'

'Let me know when you start using it.' Kate took her hand away from his critical gaze.

'I already do,' Kit said, reaching across and taking her other hand. He took the rings off her fingers, laying them on the table, and put one fingertip into his mouth to suck the buttery grease from her skin. She watched him with steady blue eyes.

'You're very devoted this morning. Have you been rebuked again?'

'Only by my own sense of guilt in ignoring you.'

'Oh good, I do prefer your devotion when it's self-generated.'

He took her finger out of his mouth and pulled her hand until she had to stand up, made her sit upon his lap. He cupped her head in his hand and turned her mouth towards his, pushing her blue robe aside at her knees. He reached his hand inside and stroked her thigh.

She took his hand and pulled it higher. Kit let his fingers find her hair, soft from the bath and teasing round his fingers as they ferreted their way through. Her clefts were dry and though he teased there was no moisture in return.

'I ought to go and see the staff,' she protested, beginning to pull away.

'The staff are fine,' he told her, wrapping an arm around her hips to keep her on his lap. 'You need to worry about me right now.'

'Selfish bastard,' she told him with another deep kiss.

He pulled his hand out and reached across to the butter on the table, streaked two fingers through where it lay collapsing in the sun, and furrowed back beneath her robe.

'Too right,' he said. 'I have a mighty head of guilt to lose. Now, focus will you, old girl.'

She cuffed him across the head, reached her hands into his hair. His butter-slick fingers reached deep inside her and made her groan through her kisses. They grinned at each other. He twisted her round on his lap, pushing aside the belt of the gown, lifted them both off the seat, pulled his erection out of his pants and let his trousers slip down onto the ground around his ankles.

They sank down onto the small metal chair together, her lips closing round his naked dick as she slid onto him. The gown billowing round her shoulders, her feet straddling the chair, wrapping round the rusty iron legs and pulling him deeper inside. She pulled his head down to her breasts, where he circled a nipple with his tongue. He felt her moisture rushing out to encircle him and took long slow pelvic thrusts up into her, his hands gripping her hips down onto him.

'Well, what do you know?' she quipped. 'Life down there after all.'

They let the pleasure build, their movement restricted by the chair, the depth of his penetration reduced by his position, but savouring the idle pleasure. Kate enjoying his toying tongue on her breasts. Kit relishing the freedom, the joy of knowing there were no barriers. She came with small tired shudders, wrapping her arms tighter around his head and pulling his hot mouth closer, letting the joy of it wash away her weariness. Kit held back until she'd finished and let the same warmth flood through his own tensions. They sat replete, hugging each other on the chair, wrapped together in her robe and lost in satiated calm and a pool of sunshine.

'Now you need to bathe again,' he told her. He lifted her off his shrunken dick, catching the leaks with the tea towel from the table before they hit his trousers. 'Come on, I might let you go back to work now.'

'Typical, use me and abuse me and send me back to the grindstone!'

'You love it,' he told her, flicking her with the tea towel as she pulled her robe tight with a great show of dignity. 'Go, go bath and dress. I'll tidy up.'

She reached down for his trousers and pulled them up, kissing his stomach as her head rose. 'You're adorable, today,' she said and walked down the steps.

Kit felt another notch of tension leave him. He sat back down at the table for a moment, pouring another cup of treacle coffee and finishing off a croissant.

.   .   .

THEY WERE IN THE KITCHEN, flustered and cooking, when they heard the car pull up on the drive.

Isabelle was trying to get potatoes to brown and taking instructions from Kit on making Yorkshire mix, Moth was laying the table and unpacking the emergency shopping, Kit was trying to put a pudding together from the ingredients he'd thrown in the trolley, complaining about the meanness of the small supermarket.

'They're back,' Moth noted.

'Shit.' Kit notched up another level.

'Moth, go distract and procrastinate for at least another ten minutes while we try and look more organised,' Isabelle said.

'At least!' Kit added.

'How am I supposed to do that?' Moth asked, stood with a hand full of cutlery.

'Be enthusiastic, terribly, terribly enthusiastic,' Kit told him. 'Bombard them with questions the moment they get out of the car, Elsa can't multi-task. Wind Nat up to the hilt.'

'Enthusiasm?'

'Yes, I know it's not your strong point, but find some hidden unexpressed depths and get out there,' Kit emphasised, taking the cutlery out of his hand and pushing him towards the hall. He finished laying the table while the door was swinging shut behind him, tweaking details that Moth had done badly, or not at all.

'Dig out the gin,' he told Isabelle. 'Pour them both a stiff drink they can't argue with. Load it up with ice and lemon, make them look irresistible.' He listened to the noise out on the drive, everyone talking at once. 'At least Moth's making an effort.'

'You gave him the hardest job,' Isabelle said, heading for the glass cupboard.

'I know,' Kit said. 'But he couldn't have done this at all.'

'We're not that late.' Isabelle looked at the clock. 'I'm sure Elsa will be fine.'

'I know,' Kit said, poking the multiple saucepans full of vegetables, willing them to come to the boil. He went back to putting the cream and fruit tart together, and getting the strudel rolled up. Purchased puff pastry, it felt false beneath his fingers. He wanted to look the picture of effortless domestic calm that most irritated Hester. Being late with dinner was not what he wanted at all, better it was sitting going cold for their late arrival than they were sitting waiting for it.

The kitchen door opened, Moth walking in backwards. Questions spinning out of his mouth that he stopped to listen to each response. In his hands a painted pebble large enough to cause a head injury, a stick of candy and a terrible model of a seagull roosting on a lighthouse. He'd even demanded gifts to help slow Nat down, but he could hold out no longer, he had to let go of the kitchen door and let them in. Elsa came through, in a wave of warm greetings and hugs. Isabelle first, a long embrace and a happy acceptance of the gin glass pushed into her hand before she came to Kit, her arms open.

'Kit, darling, wonderful man,' she said, full of energy. She gave him a warm hug, held it long enough to make him relax. 'I am so glad you got my messages. My phone has been so sporadic all day. I think it's on the blink, you'll have to look at it for me. I dropped it on the sand too many times. Oh, I'm so glad you're here and this smells divine, you angel!'

'You look invigorated,' Kit told her, trying to keep the

huffiness out of his voice, his hands holding aside the sugar drencher he'd been about to assault the strudel with.

'It's been wonderful,' Elsa said, 'just wonderful. I hadn't realised how much I needed the break.'

Kit watched Isabelle walk over to Hester, hand her the gin and tonic, say a gentle 'Welcome home' and watched Hester smile in return, take the glass, sip from it. Well, maybe a holiday had been what they needed.

'Kit,' Elsa murmured, leaning towards him. 'I must ask if you can stay tomorrow? I have some answers for you, and I want to get the ball rolling. Is there any chance you don't have to rush off for work? I know how much you have on.'

He'd been planning to leave in the morning, first thing, with clients to see in Cheltenham and Bristol. He smiled, said, 'No, of course I can stay.' He would have to call Henri, make rearrangements.

Elsa moved across to speak with Moth. Kit pulled his phone out of his pocket, sugar drencher poised, tapped in a reminder, scattered sugar all over the rolled and scored pastry and put it in the lower oven of the Aga. He moved back to the fridge, pulled out the plate of hors d'oeuvres, called Moth over and gave him the plate to hand round. Walked over to Hester, who'd sat down in her usual chair, put his hands on her shoulders and surprised her with a light kiss on the cheek.

'You look as restored as your mother,' he told her when she looked up in muted surprise.

She patted one of his hands in gratitude.

'Nat,' Kit said across the room to where Nat was chattering to her brother. 'How was the hotel?'

'Amazing,' she said. 'We had a pool, and a hot tub, and a

little pool, and a sauna, and a, a, what was it called?' she asked Hester, looking across at her.

'A steam room,' Hester said.

'Yes, a steam room,' she rushed on. 'When you opened the door the steam puffed out and it was so hot inside and there was a restaurant right on top of the bay, you had to go up special stairs to get to it, and there was a...'

She turned away from Kit and carried on talking to Moth.

Kit orchestrated, herding them into place, armed with drinks and feasting on nibbles, getting them out of his space as he pulled the meal together, encouraging the flow of conversation at the table, carving the joint of beef into fine slivers, despite it needing a little longer to rest and resisting the task.

'Kit, this looks wonderful,' Elsa said. 'It's such a joy to come home and have a lovely meal waiting for you. Thank you again.'

'My pleasure,' he said as he sat down. 'Dig in, do.' He wiped a discreet hand across his sweaty brow, disguising it for a hair adjustment, picking up his wine glass with relief.

He ate less than he drank, watching Hester through the warped sighting of his glass. Her calm demeanour focused on Nat, and on her dinner, but as the meal wore on, and conversation ebbed, her eyes refused to engage with Isabelle and she pushed her unfinished food to the side of the plate, barricaded against the aligned cutlery. Isabelle was moving food around the extremities of her plate, one hand holding her own wine glass. Kit stabbed the fork into the last of his beef. It had been a brief lull, a glimpse of an alternative existence.

The meal ended with a whimper, far preferable to the bang of Easter. Isabelle excused herself first and disappeared upstairs, Hester went to unpack, taking Nat with her to get ready for bed and school in the morning, Moth was helping him with the washing up and Elsa was looking through her backlog of post when she sighed, pushed the post aside, and stood up.

'Moth,' she asked, a hand tapping the table. 'Can I trouble you for a few moments in the study?'

Kit felt Moth freeze beside him, set the dish he was washing down on the rack with a hand that turned into a clenched fist. Kit was surprised, he'd seemed sure enough of himself this morning. Perhaps he was having a change of heart after all. Kit stayed quiet.

'Would you mind bringing some tea for us?'

Kit felt conscious of Moth's silence beside him. 'I'll put the kettle on,' he said. 'Go settle yourself.'

'Thank you,' Elsa said, oblivious to Moth's reaction. 'Delicious meal, and I'm so glad you can be here in the morning.'

Kit watched her go, dried his hands on the way to getting the kettle. 'Not too late to change your mind.'

'What?'

'About school,' Kit said.

Moth looked at him, eyes unseeing, his jaw taut.

'You look like you've lost your courage,' Kit said.

'What?'

'You seem less than happy to talk to her now it's come to it.'

'Oh,' Moth said, his eyes returning to the dishes. 'No, it wasn't that.'

Kit put a tea tray together. He felt the urge to influence Moth rise to the surface of his moral compass again, managed to swing the needle away and kept his mouth shut. 'Here you go,' he said, 'go face the music.'

Moth came and took the tray off him. 'Tea tray, I mean, who does this stuff?'

'Heathen,' Kit said. 'All civilised people, if you ask me.'

'Snob,' Moth muttered, heading for the kitchen door.

'Well-paid snob,' Kit retorted, but the door was already gliding between them. His phone buzzed, he checked the reminder, ring Henri, cancel Monday. Kit pressed the fast dial. Henri would not be happy.

ON THE MONDAY morning Kit joined them in the study last. Enjoying the sense that they were all waiting for him when he did walk in.

Arranged around the room in various poses of unease were the rest of the bemused family. James and Hester in chairs on the window side of the fireplace, Isabelle with her back to him on the door side. Moth, aside from them all, in a solitary chair behind the door where he could see everything. Kate was sat on the far side of the room, close to Elsa at her desk. On Elsa's other side were George, senior partner at Rob's firm of solicitors, and Rob.

Hester had received Rob's arrival with a look that would curdle custard as he disappeared into the study with Elsa and his boss for an hour. An hour which passed like treacle dripping through the eye of a needle. Moth hovering in the alcove of the kitchen windows, refusing to be engaged. Isabelle hiding in her workroom until Kate arrived and dragged her out. James hiding behind a newspaper and clearing his throat. Hester sat at the kitchen table, her foot twitching a tempo in time with her drumming fingers that appeared to match the executioner's thud with which she was visualising Rob's repeated death.

Isabelle wilted in the atmosphere with a rapidity that increased his doubts about what he was going to say if Elsa announced she was selling the house in Swansea. He had a price in mind to offer her. A low price, but what he could afford, if all things went wrong, and sell it on for a profit. His own need to drum fingers on the table was kept in check by the sense of superiority not doing so gave him over Hester. Instead he filled the painful silence with long phone calls to Henri full of loud work talk, enjoying his voice bouncing off the walls and making even Kate wince. When Elsa opened the kitchen door and asked them to join her, he loitered on his phone in the kitchen, so that when he did enter it was with a sweep of the door, and all eyes on him. He knew it was petty, but the wave of irritation that rolled off James was worth it.

He took the last free seat by Isabelle, in a chair by the fireplace where he could see his previous efforts in here still gleaming on the wood. He grasped Isabelle's hand, locking his fingers through them. Watching the ire rise off both James and Hester. He smiled at them, passing over Kate's watchful glance. When all eyes had turned away, Isabelle pulled her fingers free and folded them together in her lap.

Kit's uncertainty increased with the removal. He hoped he wouldn't have to make that offer here, in public. It would be much better delivered in private. He looked at Rob, who was maintaining a studious gaze of fascination with an obscure facet of the patterned rug at his feet. His boss cleared his throat to get full attention of the room, offered his palm with pompous flair to Elsa.

'Thank you, George,' Elsa said, her voice stilted, breathless.

She fumbled with the papers on her desk and took one

last look at Moth. There seemed to be a final question in her eyes, one that he acknowledged with a faint smile. A teenage shrug that ill-suited the moment.

Kit glanced at Kate, she tutted and said, 'Do get on with it, Queenie, you've built up the drama more than enough.'

'Thank you as ever, Kate, for the support,' Elsa said, shuffling her papers once more, though the caustic nudge seemed to give her voice its normal clarity. 'Though I do appreciate you've all been patient with me, and my apologies for the delay, I needed to... to make sure I was completely ready.'

'And are you?' George asked. 'Entirely certain?'

Elsa looked at him with a wan smile but when she spoke the tremor in her voice had gone. 'Thank you for your concern, George, but I am.'

George nodded and turned his legs sideways in his chair, crossing them over, absolving himself of what was to follow. Kit was quivering with curiosity. He would give Moth some grief for keeping whatever part of this mystery he knew about to himself.

'I've valued the time away, this last week,' Elsa began. 'It has enabled me to come to a decision I have been struggling with. For whatever difficulties this decision causes all of you, I apologise in advance, unreservedly.'

Kit resisted the urge to sit forward, or to look around the room. The look of astonishment on Kate's face sufficient to convince him that she had no clearer idea of what was going on. He tried hard to compose his own face into the polite, detached, bored blank he used to befuddle his customers with.

'I made a promise once, a long time ago, to my father, who I adored. A promise I have long come to regret, but a promise is a promise. On his deathbed, when I was ill-equipped to deny him, my father insisted that the details about the dispersal of his estate, which I had not then seen, never be revealed to the family. He told me it was for the best for Riverdell and our family. I stupidly agreed and for this I have often cursed both myself and him.'

Kate opened her mouth to speak, but when Elsa shot a glance at her, converted it to a hefty sigh and swallowed whatever she was about to say.

'However, now, for many reasons but most notably the importance that I place on being able to provide a secure and loving family home to my grandchildren, Nat and Moth,' Elsa drew a breath, glanced at Moth again, and said, 'I have decided to release my custodianship of Riverdell Estate to the successor named in my father's will.'

She dropped the sentence with slow, precise enunciation into a deep and impenetrable silence, where the impact of the words began a slow percolation.

James frowned, Hester moved her hand to her throat, Kate's trousered legs uncrossed and re-crossed. Beside him Isabelle twitched her foot, lifting it and resettling it back on the ground. Kit blinked in furious self-control, refusing to be the one who gasped.

Custodianship?

Kit thought he'd known everything about Elsa's estate. He looked at Moth in outrage, if the little shit had known about this and not told... but, no, Moth had sat up and was blinking in surprise too. Whatever they'd talked about, it hadn't included this.

'It is an absolute relief to end this promise,' Elsa said. 'My silence cost me my relationship with my son, and with my grandchildren, and has caused me nothing but grief.'

She looked around the room with steady eyes, meeting all

of them and holding their gaze. 'I love you all dearly,' she said. 'I am grateful for the support you have always shown me and pray that you will continue to do so. I will now ask Rob to read the details of my father's will.'

She sat back, twisted her hands together in her lap, lowered her eyes to her desk. Rob rose from his seat, holding a yellowed piece of paper in front of him. He looked once at Hester. A look Kit couldn't believe came from such a dull man and returned his gaze to the writing.

Kit could feel his throat tickling with the urge to laugh and, from Kate's exaggerated glance, knew she found the situation just as ridiculous. As Rob began to read the will, their eyes, twitching in amusement, locked on one another, blinked, narrowed and widened to shock together. He saw Kate blanch, turning from healthy and amused to shocked and pale in the handful of breaths it took Rob to finish.

He looked around, as understanding rose through the layer of obscure legal jargon, watching the family discern the sense, or idiocy, beneath that vapour, and turning eyes one pair at a time on the sole inheritor to the entire Riverdell estate. The impact of the news on him ricocheted from amazement, to disbelief, to calamity, to opportunity, with such swiftness that he even disliked himself, whilst all the time Kate grew quieter and whiter across the room from him.

Kit turned to look at the benefactor, sat in stunned silence in the chair next to him, the last to reach comprehension, unable to speak, confusion etched on her face.

'What?' Hester asked first, Kit's delight withering in the sound of her frailty. For all her venom, this lost, confused whisper of a voice was more stinging than any rage she could have thrown out.

'The remaining entirety of my estate to be left to the first-born child of my firstborn child,' Rob repeated.

'But he disinherited him,' Hester said, trying to fathom it with stumbling words. 'Surely you mean Moth, Mother? Does it not mean Moth? The firstborn child of your firstborn child?'

'It does not.' Elsa told her with swiftness, glancing at Moth to deny any hope he might catch from her words. 'My father disinherited his own son, but left the estate to his child, to Isabelle. With myself to have a lifetime interest or until I relinquish it.'

'Why?' James asked. 'Why did he have to keep it a secret?'

'He never wanted my brother to know,' Elsa said. 'He didn't trust him.'

'That's a shitty reason to keep us in the dark all these years,' James said with anger. 'Though I suppose we weren't all in the dark, were we?' he added, looking at Rob.

'I have never read this document until today,' Rob said.

Kit looked at Kate. He could feel Isabelle frozen in shock beside him. Kate needed to catch up, they needed her to take control before the situation crumbled.

'I don't want it,' Isabelle said, her voice stumbling over itself. 'It's wrong, it can't be me, Elsa. Give it to Hester, to James. It's not mine, I don't want it.'

'Well, there's a surprise,' Hester spat back. 'She doesn't want it.'

Kit winced, tried to find something to say, anything that might stop the widening chasm gaping in the middle of the room. Glaring at Kate, why wasn't she reacting, doing something, saying anything?

'That's not possible,' George interrupted. 'There conditions upon the trust in which it is handed on. The decision is tied up. Only Isabelle may dispose of the estate. It isn't your mother's choice what happens to it, just when to relinquish her right.'

'This isn't fair,' Isabelle said, her voice anguished.

Kit watched Kate flinch at the tone, curl her hands around her chair arms into white-knuckled claws. He was aware of Moth tucked away behind them, watching the drama unfold. Unable to turn and see his reaction without making it obvious.

'No, it isn't fair,' Hester said, standing up, batting away James' attempt to catch her hand. 'All of it to her, and what about you, Mother, what do you get to live on now? It isn't just unfair, it's ridiculous.'

'I know this is hard to grasp.' Elsa leaned forwards and put her hands on the desk before her. 'Please, all of you, understand my reasons for relinquishing my interest now are governed by Natalie, by what's best for her. Please let's try to keep her, and Moth, in mind. To remember the loss of their parents, the loss of David to us all. Riverdell is just a house and what counts now is our family.'

Hester looked at her with tight-lipped hostility, threw a look at Rob that would freeze the melting ice of Antarctica, glanced in Moth's direction like trying to catch an anchor. Looking for help, until her eyes fell upon Isabelle, sat frozen in her chair. Kit watched the scathing hatred return to her face, rising from a well that had filled over too many years.

'All this heartache, because of you. Well, I hope you're happy, I hope it's worth it.' She stalked from the room, frustrated by her inability to slam the door. They sat and listened to her heels twitching down the wooden floor of the hallway.

Kit watched Rob resist the urge to follow her, wiping a tired hand across his eyes, sitting down in a despondent slump. He looked across at Kate, she was staring at Isabelle, thought about taking charge, caught James glaring at him and decided perhaps he'd wait a little while longer.

'This is wrong, Mother,' James said, standing up. 'Not because of you, Isabelle, I bear you no grudge. But for yourself, to have worked so hard to care for it, and be left what? Nothing? No provision at all?' He looked across at George.

'The terms of the will are absolute,' George told him. 'Although there was some separate provision which passed to your mother on Mr Threlfall's death.'

'The house in Swansea,' Kit said, as pennies dropped into place.

'Indeed,' George agreed. 'With some partial life interest remaining in a few properties, although there is no doubt it leaves Mrs Threlfall in a considerably reduced position. One of some dependency upon the successor.'

Kate spoke, her voice sharpened by shock and irritation, rasping on an uneven breath. 'Isabelle is not about to evict the woman who's raised her from her own home.'

'Of course she's not,' Kit said, reaching a hand out to take Isabelle's, limp and clammy though it lay in his. 'It's all a nasty little shock, but it's nothing more than a change in ownership, not a change in management.'

'Actually,' said Elsa, her hands flexing in front of her on the desk, her voice slow with weariness. 'I feel it's exactly time for that. I promised you an answer today Kit, about the house in Swansea. In consultation with Moth...'

Kit turned sharply to glance at Moth with a frown. But Moth was looking at Isabelle, his face guarded, his eyes refusing to budge, waiting for her to look up. Chewing on the knuckle of his middle finger. The whole world was crumbling at their feet and he was staring at Isabelle. If he didn't know about this, then what the hell had they talked about?

'... I have decided that Natalie will be much happier raised in a quiet home that is not a business. I feel this will be better achieved in my own home in Swansea than here at Riverdell. I have decided to retire to Swansea.'

'What?' James asked.

'What?' Kate asked, her voice a stunned gasp.

'You can't leave,' Isabelle whispered in shock. 'I can't... we need you, I...'

Oh shit, thought Kit, there goes Plan A. Although multiple plans were expanding in front of him with such rapidity that he felt uncertain about saying anything. He looked harder at Moth.

'You agree with this?' Kit asked Moth, directing all eyes upon him.

'It's up to Elsa,' Moth said, glancing at her for reassurance before turning back to Isabelle, seeing she had finally looked at him. Moth responded to Kit without breaking his eyes from Isabelle. 'But I talked with Nat about living here or somewhere else. She enjoyed being in Swansea. I think she finds all this,' and he shrugged at the room around him, 'a bit hard to understand. She's not sure where she belongs.'

'But that's surely a matter of time?' Isabelle protested. 'Another change is the last thing she needs.'

'We all need change,' Elsa said. 'And this time Nat will be going through it with us, not on her own. This house has changed beyond recognition since you were all children. It's a business now so much more than a home, and we're so used to it we don't see it. Riverdell can't financially survive without having that business in some way or another. It's a colossal house to maintain. Hester and Natalie, and I, felt so much more relieved in Swansea, so much more relaxed.'

'It was a bloody holiday,' Kate said with exaggerated outrage. 'Of course you felt relaxed, that's no reason to toss the whole baby out with the bath water.'

'It's a pretty cool house,' Moth added. 'In Swansea, I mean. Feels like a normal house. It felt normal to Nat too.' Everyone stared at him, like he'd conspired in the event. 'Kit took me, when I was staying with him.'

Kit grimaced as they all looked at him. 'Work's work, I didn't know it was part of all this!'

'It's not just the house, it's the environment,' Elsa said. 'Nat's used to a different sort of school, to an urban environment, to many things other than what we can provide here. She will be rebuilding her own life with us, not trying to fit into our way of life. There are excellent schools that Moth can consider attending, be nearer to her. I know this is all such a shock, and it will take time to work out the details. But I'm convinced this is the way to go forwards.'

'Well I'm thrilled for you,' Kate said, flicking a hand across her trousers. 'Just thrilled.'

'It's my hope that Hester will come with us,' Elsa said with a wince at her tone. 'At least for a while, to give herself a new focus too.' She looked at Rob with a flustered, timid smile.

'You seem determined to cure everyone's ills bar your own,' Kate told her.

'Have you discussed this with her?' James asked.

'Not explicitly,' Elsa said. 'And I'd appreciate being able to do so myself.'

'I'll bet,' Kit said. James threw him a sour look and he threw his hands up in the air. 'I'll shut up, shall I?'

'That would make a nice change,' James told him, and asked Elsa, 'How long do we have to think this all over?'

'It's not a case of thinking it over,' Rob told him. 'Your mother already signed the documents handing over the Estate.'

'What?' Isabelle wailed.

Kit resisted the urge to take her hand again.

'I know this is sudden,' Elsa said, rubbing her forehead with tiredness. 'I'm sorry it couldn't be done more, more...'

'... humanely?' Kate offered.

'... gently. But it is done. Riverdell House, and the estate, now belong to you, Isabelle, and you will need to think about what you want to do with it all.' Elsa looked at her with a pained expression. A smile trying to be encouraging, harbouring guilt. 'I don't want you to feel for one minute that you are alone in this. I have never been alone in managing Riverdell. You have all been part of this with me, and I, we, are now here for you. Kate, Kit, James, and you too Moth, all of you, we must get over this shock and make decisions about how to proceed, together. Now that it is released from my custodianship there is free choice about what we do, and how. There is an awful lot to think about.'

Silence filled the room. A hesitant clock ticking silence that irritated Kit even more than the morning had. Was nobody but him excited about this? He was twitching to talk about the possibilities. Itching to say how many times he'd offered ideas to Elsa that she'd always turned down. Ways in which assets could be sold, revenue raised, reinvested. I mean, come on! How long did he have to wait to share the fun they were going to have? Kate's eyes bored into his with a salty vengeance, daring him to speak. She was in a spectacular bad mood. Surely, at least she could see the potential unleashed in this room.

'I must go and find Hester.' James walked across the room and behind Elsa's desk, kissing her on the cheek. 'You know I'll do what I can to support you, Mother.'

Kit watched him walk out of the room. Watched Rob follow his retreating back with, what, was that jealousy in his eyes? Well, well. Kit would sooner have faced a biker in a fist-fight than go deal with Hester right now. Moth stood up next.

'I don't think you need me any longer,' he said. Isabelle looked at him, her face scrunched up in blinking discomfort. 'Rather you than me,' he told her with a grimace. 'You'll figure it out.'

Kit watched them. Wondering what they were talking about. Isabelle unable to respond. Close to tears he'd warrant.

'May I tell Nat later?' Moth asked Elsa.

'I'd like you to tell her, that would be wonderful, but I'd like to be there too. Could we do it together when she gets home from school? I'm desperately hoping that Hester might be with us too, if that's alright?'

'Of course,' he said. 'She'll be so excited. I can't wait to tell her. I'll see you later.'

'Thank you, Moth,' Elsa told him. 'You've been a wonderful support.'

Kit looked at Moth with surprised eyes. A wonderful support. Last night he'd looked ready to kill her with her own tea tray. Kit's eyes narrowed. Had he even talked to her about going back to school, or had he kept that plan to himself? Thinking about his own quiet offer to buy the house in Swansea, Kit struggled not to grimace as Moth walked out of the study. It felt like Elsa had brought a crocodile to a show and tell pet session and he was trying to stuff a budgie down his shorts, wondering whether Moth had shoved his own weasel away, or bought it out into the light.

'We have some final paperwork to sign,' George said to Elsa.

'Yes, I understand.' Elsa looked across at Isabelle. 'I think I'd like a moment alone with Isabelle. Would you all mind waiting for us in the sitting room?'

'Of course,' George said, rising and nodding at Rob, offering his hand to Kate, who huffed but rose. She put a hand on Isabelle's shoulder in passing, glaring at Kit who hadn't moved. Kit gave Elsa his million-franc smile. She would have to kick him out, there was no way he was leaving Isabelle. Who knows what she might say or do? This was the beginning of a new start for them, he wanted to be involved in every decision that lay ahead.

At the door Kate stopped, turned back, said 'Kit, get out here now. If I'm being kicked out, the least you can do is keep me company. Not to mention get me a drink, a stiff one.'

'It's not even midday, Kate,' Elsa protested.

'Do I give a damn?' Kate returned. 'After the shock you just laid on us?'

Kit watched Elsa and Kate lock eyes. Sparks could have flown from the sharpened pitchforks that lurked within.

'Perhaps you'd better get the sherry out?' Elsa told Kit. 'Kate might be right, a drink would do us all good.'

'What am I?' Kit asked. 'The domestic servant?'

'But you do it so well,' Kate told him, holding the door open.

Kit capitulated. At least there was some effort at humour in the room. He rose, smoothed his trousers, straightened his jacket, and kissed Isabelle on the cheek. 'I'm coming straight back with the sherry,' he told Elsa.

'Wonderful,' she said.

Kit walked out, feeling the silence resettle behind him. In the hallway he stood for a moment with Kate, watching the doors settle too, closing Elsa and Isabelle into the study, and Rob and George into the sitting room, leaving them alone in the corridor.

'Well, that was exciting,' Kit said.

'Yes,' Kate said. 'Yes, I wasn't expecting that.'

'You didn't have a clue?'

She glanced up at him, looking punched out, her face pinched, her eyes blurred. She held her hand out and he took it, pulling her closer. She leant against him, her head on his shoulder, and shuddered. A ripple of anguish that went all the way through her.

'Hey, you didn't know.'

'No,' she mumbled. 'I had no idea. Poor Isabelle, this is the most awful, awful thing.'

'She just inherited the whole family pile,' Kit told her, trying to keep the glee out of his voice. 'How is this a disaster? You need that sherry. You're not thinking straight.'

Kate pulled away from him, wiped a tear from the inner corner of her eye, and stood up straight.

'I can't help but think of that old saying, "What a tangled web we weave" and wonder...' Her voice cracked, and she attacked another tear threatening to breach her lids.

'You need to sit down,' Kit told her, and he guided her towards the sitting room door, pushing it open and taking her through to where the men were stood by the empty hearth. 'I forget you're not invincible sometimes.'

'Well,' she said, aiming for waspish, 'it's not every day you find out your dearest friend has been keeping secrets from you...' but it ended in a strangled wail choking on a sob and, for no reason that Kit could fathom, she burst into tears.

He had never seen Kate cry. Scream, shout, threaten, abuse, groan, yes, but not cry. It was the most uncomfortable experience. She had no idea of how to weep. Brushing tears away and spluttering with irritation whilst trying to gulp the blasted lump in her throat away.

George pulled the immaculate handkerchief from his pocket with the smug pride of one who is always ready for such occasions. Rob took her arm and led her to the sofa where he pressed her to sit down.

'I'll get the sherry,' Kit said and went to the dining room.

He grabbed as many schooners as he could slot between his fingers, the bottle, and rushed back to Kate. She was spluttering with distress, and the incredible kindness of three men seemed to hasten her irritation, and her tears. George bemused at being unable to stem the flow with his hankie, and Rob battling guilt-riddled tears himself. Kit felt himself stuck on the way to a laugh and realised her distress was going to make him cry too, gulping the lump back down.

'Good heavens,' Kit told her. 'Get a grip, woman, you'll have us all in tears. It's an inheritance without a funeral, why the hell are you crying?'

'Shut up and give me a sherry,' Kate retorted, reaching for the glass he was filling. 'You better go share that round in the study too.'

'I'm not wanted in the study,' Kit told her, trying hard to keep the tetchiness out of his tone, desperate to be with Isabelle and unable to leave Kate in such distress.

'I'll take it,' Rob said.

Kit poured a large glass out for himself, gave him two

empty glasses and the bottle, saying to his retreating back, 'Make sure you bring the bottle back.'

Kate downed her sherry in shaking gulps, adding, 'And don't be tardy either, Rob.'

'That's more like it,' Kit told her as he sat down on the sofa next to her and took her hand. It was shaking, and she didn't snatch it back. Grimacing at him, a hot spot of blush discomfort rising in her cheeks. He laced his fingers through hers and she gripped on, gulping down her sherry.

Rob walked back into the room with the sherry bottle and sighed as Kate and Kit held up their empty glasses in perfect synchronicity. He came across and poured for them, glancing at the empty glasses Kit had put on the table and at George, whose face was a studied perfection of emptiness. Rob put the bottle back on the table.

'How's it going in there?' Kate asked.

'About as well as in here,' Rob said.

'That makes me feel better,' Kate said. 'As long as someone else is having a bad day.'

'Perhaps you ought to take that sherry bottle and find Hester?' Kit suggested.

'Spiteful pig,' Kate told him. 'I would advise against finding Hester, myself,' she said to Rob. 'Your persona non grata is now in extremis.'

'I fear the role of the messenger is never a welcome one, Robert,' George said in a pompous attempt at sympathy. 'You will find it gets a little less onerous with practice.'

Kit and Kate looked at George with matching scowls. Kate held out his soaking handkerchief in irritation. George retreated to the other sofa with the resigned look of a man who was both used to causing tears and to mopping them up whilst being appreciated for neither.

Rob went and stood by the fireplace, silent and polite. Kit reckoned Rob had about another two years before he started wearing a pocket handkerchief himself. In fact, it surprised him that he didn't already. Perhaps there was something to him after all, to have thrown the towel in on the IVF front and walked out on all his worldly possessions, to be resisting the polite manners of his superiors. It proved his rule, you never knew a person, they could always surprise you.

Kate twirled the glass in front of her, watching the thick coating on the inner glass shimmer in the light. 'I never much liked this stuff, but you can see how it comes in useful.'

'Sugar in a glass,' Kit told her. 'You look much better.'

'I feel it,' Kate said. 'I do apologise, most inelegant.'

'Yes,' Kit said, wondering if he could leave her yet. 'You need to practise a little more, weeping is not your strong point.'

'Your concept of sympathy could use a little work too,' she replied but she squeezed his hand tighter, clinging on like she'd heard his thoughts.

Well, that was fine. He'd never let her down yet and maybe today wasn't the day to take sides. There was plenty of time to work it all out. The future was just getting started.

ACKNOWLEDGMENTS

A writer is the spy amongst you. I am indebted to the many families who welcomed me into their homes and lives and inspired so many of my characters. Riverdell would not exist without that experience. I do hope no one is offended.

My deep thanks to the members of Hay Writers' Circle, who challenged and encouraged me to become the writer I wanted to be. Heartfelt thanks to Kerry Hodges and Alan Oberman for their faith and for specific feedback on the project of Riverdell.

I am most grateful to Peter Salmon, my editor, who survived submergence in the first wallowing drafts and helped get them shipshape and to the incredible team at Oriel for bringing this series to my readers. I am thrilled to have found my publishing home.

Beyond that I owe a debt of support to my mother, my brother, my partner, my daughter. All of whom have sustained the process in myriad ways.

Alan and Ella, this one belongs to you.

ALSO BY MARIANNE ROSEN

Coming in April 2021...

Book 2 of the Riverdell Saga

The Halls of Riverdell

Continue the journey with Isabelle, Moth and Kit as they adjust to the huge changes life has thrown upon them. Meet Beth, the quietest member of the four friends as she takes a bold new step in life and love. Watch Riverdell as it adjusts to the changes thrust upon it.

Sign up to Marianne's newsletter at www.mariannerosen.com to keep updated with release details.

RIVERDELL HOUSE

Riverdell House is a fictional house in a real location. It is a love song to all the wonderful houses I was fortunate enough to work in during my wonderful career as an interiors consultant.

When I sat down to write this story, I began not with a sentence but with a line, a stroke drawn on a clean sheet of paper which was the first wall of Riverdell. That line spread, into the two wings of the house and the entrance that nestles in their crook. I expanded upward into the attic bedrooms, downward into the basement and each room was a memory of some other home I had worked or lived in.

I filled in colour charts, selected furniture, chose door shapes, designed window treatments, raised ceilings, widened fireplaces and discarded the trappings of life: clothes, books, cups, sweet wrappings. Only once the house sat before me, a full spread of floor plans and decor schemes, did I let the characters in.

Of course they didn't like what I had done, any more than new owners like what has been left by the former. They tossed out my ideas, presented fresh ones. But Riverdell was strong enough by then to take the new fancies, as many old houses are tolerant of the fads that pass through them. As you can imagine, Kit and I had many arguments long into the night. He won most of them.

Finally, Riverdell and I had to decide where the house belonged. Though we considered options there was only ever really one; the Dinham Green in the magical and quaint rural town of Ludlow. A place reclaimed by the Millennium Trust that was a tired old space of tumbledown cottages and disused tin-roof swimming pool. Now it is a green and glorious space, with a thriving cafe in the old mill buildings and a popular place with both tourists and townsfolk. The cottages are enviable homes. It is also now home to the fictional house of Riverdell and I hope that you get to visit Ludlow and sit on the Dinham lawns and imagine yourself looking out from the windows of the glorious house, as I do whenever I visit. You can walk the weir as Isabelle and Moth did, listen to the town that rises above the river.

Houses are made of empty rooms. Homes are rooms filled with love, memories, souls and secrets. Riverdell is a home. Testament to the love, the commitment, the traumas that many families go through in turning their purchased house into their dream homes. If you think a home is made of colour, fabric, paint or furniture, it is not. A home is as alive as a person, though its walls do not move or talk, yet it can show and speak. Homes have many stories to tell and I am rather addicted to them.

Marianne, Ludlow, 2020.

ABOUT THE PUBLISHER

Oriel Books Ltd is an indie publishing house dedicated to promoting the careers of indie authors.

Combining traditional publishing practice with modern digital vision we work to advance and promote the careers of dedicated, series-based authors at every stage of their journey.

If you have enjoyed this book consider joining us as a beta reader, working to help develop the stories of new authors in your favourite genres, in the Reading Room initiative.

If you are an emerging author with a strong idea for a series of books, consider pitching your novels to us.

Details can be found at www.orielbooks.com